# Delicacy

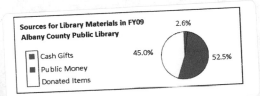

**Previous Books in the Sensations Series**
*Scent*
*Echo*

SENSATIONS BOOK 3

# Delicacy

# C. L. KELLY

**ZONDERVAN®**

**ZONDERVAN**.com/
**AUTHORTRACKER**
follow your favorite authors

*Delicacy*
Copyright © 2008 by Clint Kelly

Requests for information should be addressed to:
Zondervan, Grand Rapids, Michigan 49530

**Library of Congress Cataloging-in-Publication Data**

Kelly, Clint.
    Delicacy / C. L. Kelly.
        p. cm. — (Sensations; bk. 3)
        ISBN: 978-0-310-27309-7 (softcover)
        1. Homeless persons — Services for — Fiction. 2. Cookery — Fiction. 3. Senses and
sensation — Fiction. I. Title.
    PS3561.E3929D43 2008
    813'.54 — dc22

                                2007045569

The poem on page 134 is from *Dining Room and Kitchen* by Mrs. Grace Townsend (Home
Publishing Co., copyright 1901 by W.B. Conkey Co.).

*Interior design by Beth Shagene*

*Printed in the United States of America*

08 09 10 11 12 13 14 • 22 21 20 19 18 17 16 15 14 13 12 11 10 9 8 7 6 5 4 3 2 1

*To Nathan: my pride, joy,
and hot sauce master.*

# Delicacy

# Chapter 1

If things got any worse, Cassie Dixon would drown herself in the Pasta Fagioli.

At the best of times—when there were adequate supplies of everything and at least three-fourths of the staff showed up clean, groomed, and on time—lunch hour at the Taste of Success was a pleasure. The crew meshed, the patrons asked for the recipes, and Chef hummed to himself until Cassie imagined the very exterior of the converted warehouse near Fisherman's Wharf shimmered as appetizingly as a honey-glazed ham.

Today was not the best of times.

For starters, the Fagioli was late. Her tomatoey beef-and-bean soup was an Italian comfort food specialty and a drawing card, especially on San Francisco's abundant fog-shrouded days. It was a menu mainstay. Today, when she had gone in search of garlic, the lean ground beef she had carefully browned suddenly vanished when her back was turned. The twelve ounces of sweet Walla Walla onions she had so expertly chopped not half an hour before had mysteriously eloped with the ground beef. Someone had mislabeled the sage "oregano" and the painfully shy new girl had slipped on Jorge's just-mopped floor. Like blood on new-fallen snow, the forty-eight ounces of fresh hot spaghetti sauce the girl carried in a large, quite breakable earthenware bowl splattered savory gore from one end of Chef's spotless kitchen to the other. Stainless steel refrigerator doors, sparkling glassware, pots and pans hanging high overhead, Chef's immaculate white uniform—it seemed that not an oven mitt was spared.

"*Stupido! Deficiente! Imbecille!*" raged Chef Raoul Maggiano. The pale, cowering girl looked as if she might add her stomach contents to the red ooze flowing under stove and rack.

Sucked of its oxygen for ten terrible seconds, it was as if the room featured motionless garden statuary wearing gargoyle grimaces. No one moved until Jorge broke the spell and reached a sympathetic hand to touch the girl's arm. She shrugged it off and drew back before dashing down the short hall leading from the kitchen to the dining room.

A French-Italian force of nature, Chef Maggiano lunged at the fleeing novice with a giant slotted spoon.

"Trina!" Cassie received but a single answering sob and then the girl was out the door. If they ever found her, Cassie guessed it would take a miracle to get her to come back to the program.

The apoplectic chef tore off his apron, muttered an unintelligible deprecation, and stormed from the kitchen.

"Ya know, I think maybe I saw the second hand on the wall clock over the spice rack stop in midsweep." When he was certain that Chef was nowhere near, Jorge allowed his darkly handsome face to split into a radiant grin. "Maybe I should call the astronomical lab at Palomar. Ya know, in case the sun stood still." That earned him a couple of laughs before he led the shaken crew on an emergency search-and-clean mission. You might joke about Chef out of earshot, but he was one man that, if you valued your culinary certificate of completion, you did not cross.

*God bless Jorge.* Every Italian kitchen needed its joker. And Jorge was an especially hardworking one. For all his lack of seriousness, Cassie liked him. Liking Chef Maggiano, on the other hand, was a little like getting to know a wolverine. All teeth and claws. *Blast that man—why is he so insensitive?*

Every Tuesday was Celebrity Chef Night, and a different chef each week taught the food crew to prepare and serve an expensive three-course meal to the public.

They performed an amazing service. What might cost patrons thirty to fifty dollars a plate at a chef's gourmet restaurant set them back just sixteen at Taste of Success. The chefs donated their time and all proceeds went directly to underwrite those enrolled in the culinary arts program. Many of the special dinners were sellouts as much as a month ahead of the actual event.

Chef Maggiano, for all of his explosive rants, had been with the program from the beginning. Besides personally twisting arms in the Restaurant Association for volunteers, he currently employed eight graduates of the unique food program at his restaurant, Pasta Bella. He had flown them, as he did every member of his large staff, to Italy to study and experience the food, wine, and culture of his native land. Consequently, he tended to keep his employees longer than the industry standard, and for most of the wide-eyed program graduates, it was their first time outside the United States.

"A pound of ground round for your thoughts," said a voice in her ear. "What happened here?"

"Make it two pounds of the round and a sack of onions and you can have my thoughts and the numbskull to go with them." She accepted a brush of Nick's lips on the nape of her neck before waving him away and jamming a stray lock of hair back behind an ear. "That new kid Trina dropped the bowl of spaghetti sauce for the soup and escaped just before Chef would have beat her with a spoon. I knew putting someone that skittish with Maggiano so early in her training was a mistake."

"She take it or she go!" Chef was back, his change of uniform starched whiter than white. His face, round as a fish bowl, had faded from magenta to coral red. "Kitchen tough place. Not for

11

weak ones." He gave a rude chin flick and all but spat. "Maybe she more suited front office work. Pah! Let her, how you say, count-a the beans!"

As if that were the last word on the matter, he shooed Jorge and his busy band of cleaners away from his chief domain, the gas stove where a large pot of his prize dish simmered away. The entree for tonight's Celebrity Chef's repast was Pasta Puttanesca, or, literally, "Harlot's Pasta." Cassie had finally convinced him at press time not to place the English translation on the printed menus, but like so much else where the fiery chef was concerned, it had been a heated exchange.

Nick set a brown grocery bag and a red and white plastic net sack of onions on the counter next to Cassie. "You're welcome. A scant 10 percent fat content in the hamburger like you requested. More oregano, just in case. I'll grab you a couple jars of the commercial sauce out of the pantry." He gave her a suggestive wink. "I must say desperation smells good on you," he whispered. "What's up?"

Cassie bit her lower lip and tried to keep it together. "I just found out that James Waverly is dining with us this evening." The CEO of Waverly Electronics was buddies with several Fortune 500 kingpins, not to mention King Fahd of Saudi Arabia. He was a friend of the Pentagon and whatever U.S. president went with it at the time, held several fistful of military contracts, and powered countless civilian projects from San Diego to Kennebunkport.

"That's great news!" Nick squeezed her arm. "We've wanted to get him back in here for weeks. More funding from him could triple the program overnight!"

Chef Maggiano sliced shiitake mushrooms and artichokes with swift, deft strokes. Cassie grimaced and kept her voice low. "No, not great. Among the celebrity volunteers coming to serve tonight is none other than Philippe Peugeot. You know those two are like oil and water."

Nick's eyes widened and he whistled softly through his teeth. "More like fire and gunpowder. Over the weekend, I saw in the *Chronicle* that Waverly has accused Peugeot in court of bid-rigging on the Port of San Francisco expansion." For years, Peugeot had accused Waverly of running a monopoly with unsavory ties inside the halls of Congress.

Cassie massaged her temples and emitted a moan. "Then let's just burn the place down because nobody's coming out of this alive. What a fund-raising disaster! We'll probably lose them both."

Nick glanced at Chef and waited until he noisily hacked an onion into submission before whispering in Cassie's ear, "*Tu sei una stella … la mia stella.* You are a star … my star. *Come sei bella.* How beautiful you are. We'll get through this, together. Just tell Peugeot we overbooked on volunteers and won't be needing his services this evening."

"You're kidding, right?" Cassie shook her head. "Peugeot's large financial donations come with the understanding that he will serve Taste at his good pleasure and eat at Taste whenever he desires. He adores Chef's Puttanesca."

Nick gave her his best sad this-is-why-I-prefer-the-wilderness-over-politics expression and, without another glance at Chef, she kissed him on the lips. "You've not forgotten your Italian, my handsome gondolier."

He raised an eyebrow. "It's how I lured you, how I captured you, and how I fully intend to keep you, *cara mia*, my darling. And the gondolier thing? Just a cover. I actually play forward on the Italian World Cup Soccer Team. Tell me where you're staying and I'll deliver you an autographed shin guard."

She patted his cheek. "Down, boy. Get me through this night and you can have me lock, stock, and browned in olive oil."

"Deal. Now for something to really cheer you up. Two things, actually. For one, Father B is on tonight's guest list as well."

Cassie smiled in genuine relief. She loved the tidy, garrulous priest of St. John's Episcopal Cathedral. He had been her family's pastor ever since she could remember, and he had helped the Dixons through some exceedingly foul weather. "I've got dibs waiting on his table. You can have the corporate feuders. I wonder if Father Chris will come along."

"And miss *Wheel of Fortune?* Doubt it."

"Too bad we don't have karaoke. Can't you see Father B doing his imitation of Roy Orbison doing *Pretty Woman?* I'm so glad he's coming. Maybe I won't drown myself after all."

"Well, just remember he's doing the Mission bus run for Ace. That might keep him away. But let's hope not."

Chef Maggiano gave a dramatic turn and fixed them both with a disdainful eye. "The food, it makes itself? Talk, talk, talk while day go poof! You take-a the page from Italia's ladies of the night. After day's work, they make-a the frisky sauce, the zesty, full-bodied bits. My sweet Puttanesca ..." The dish originated in Naples, made by the ladies of the night, and was placed in their windows to lure customers to the bordello.

Chef poured crushed basil into the palm of his hand and added it to the pot. Next came oregano, parsley, and red pepper flakes, all first sprinkled into that measuring spoon of a hand. He stirred. Smelled. Tasted. Nodded. "Entice. Is nice."

The doors had opened and Cassie heard the lunch crowd streaming in. Not only was the food excellent and reasonably priced but the genius renovators had taken a drafty corrugated metal box of a building and transformed it into a fine dining experience. Hardwood floors. Walls of deep forest green and burgundy. Heavy oak tables and chairs. Shaded drop lamps and wall sconces in the classical Tiffany style. The Taste had a comfortable elegance reminiscent of early San Francisco.

"Two blackened salmon and a portobello," called the first waitress, a young woman in black sheath dress, auburn hair cut short and stylish by a volunteer hairdresser. Her name was

Frieda, all German sass and a hankering for illicit drugs. The old Frieda, anyway. The new Frieda snapped the order form to an overhead rail and sent it down to the grill where Jorge, hands washed, and tall Germaine, from Georgia, watched over the portobello mushroom steaks and salmon filets for the specialty sandwiches.

"Cobb salad and a side of sweets," called Aaron Joel Rafferty, who preferred AJ, but whom Chef called Alonzo for no apparent reason. Because the sweet potato fries were a house specialty and in constant demand, a stocky young lady named Carmina did nothing else but fill, lower, raise, and scoop out deep-fried baskets of them without stopping. Today she added a light dusting of Italian spices. She had a disposition as sweet as the fries — a little slow, but utterly devoted to her assigned station, and one of Cassie's favorites.

Cassie was relieved — and surprised — to see Trina slink back into the kitchen. She hung back under the industrial ladles and colanders, buttoning and unbuttoning a cow-brown sleeveless sweater that no thrift store would miss. Pale as china, she was a slip of a thing, a kitchen sprite who had long ago lost — or been robbed of — her elfish spirit. Sometimes she seemed as slender and as insubstantial as a spaghetti noodle, but who wouldn't be a mere shadow of a human being given her horrific background.

"Trina, honey, atta girl! Show Chef what you're made of!" The girl, unmoving, blinked and stared straight ahead.

Trina had fled a slave's existence and worse at the hands of three male relatives, possessing only a smoky blue kitten as thin and inconsequential as she. She hid it in her jacket pockets until it became too big and noticeable and the homeless shelters turned her out because they didn't accept pets. That ceased to be a problem after two street thugs grabbed the cat and threw it off a freeway overpass after Trina refused their advances. When asked why she hadn't turned to prostitution to support herself, she said in a barely audible croak that her dear aunt had told her never to sell "the sweet center of me."

After attempting suicide four times, she landed at the Gospel Rescue Mission where she was told point-blank her last hope was Taste of Success.

Cassie motioned to Trina to join her at the stove. The way she cringed her way to Cassie's side, like a kicked dog, was pathetic to watch. Chef's lips pursed, his face unyielding, but he said nothing. Cassie guessed that even a haughty chef was not blind to how little the thin girl had in the way of defenses.

Cassie showed her how to sauté the ground beef in oil in a large ten-quart pot until just brown. She took the girl's birdlike hands, placed them firmly around the wooden stir spoon, and in twenty-fingered tandem worked in the chopped onions, slivered carrots, diced celery and tomatoes, two cups each of red and white kidney beans, eighty-eight ounces of beef stock, oregano, pepper, parsley, Tabasco sauce, spaghetti sauce, and half a pound of dry pasta shell macaroni, all of which Nick metered into the soup one ingredient at a time. The women stirred and simmered as one, much as Cassie and her mother had done long ago. Blue gas flame, bubbling contents, flavors combining in culinary sleight of hand, their shared closeness—a long absent intimacy that smoothed the girl's worry lines, flushed the ghostliness from the sober narrow face, straightened the cowering spine, and made Cassie wonder how many pots of Pasta Fagioli were required to restore eighteen years of loss.

Chef leaned over, gently pried the spoon from their hands, and ladled up a sample of their handiwork. Eyes shut, lips and tongue probing subtleties, he began a slow nod. His eyes popped wide at last and fixed Trina with a light that must have originated in Tuscany.

"Pleasing," he said. He handed the spoon to Cassie and kissed the girl on the top of her head. Because Cassie and astonishment held her firmly upright, Trina shrank only a little from his approbation. "Why?" Chef said. "Why so much a cook as you so skinny?"

The girl looked at him frankly, her fear no longer a tidal force. It was almost as if she had sought and received permission to smile. The pallid skin gave birth to a wan expression, all the more poignant in that only a caring mother could see happiness in it. In a voice scratchy with what Cassie surmised was scant use, she said, "Always had so little food, why get attached?"

Chef nodded and cupped a hand tenderly to her cheek. "You back. Mean Chef no can knock you out. Now Dr. Chef tell-a you, eat three bowls Fagioli and-a one plate Puttanesca. Fat come on you, happy, like big Italian mama!"

Around them was workmanlike rush and bustle, banter and hustle as dish after dish was created and dispatched to the diners beyond. Above them, twin ceiling fans kept the heated air moving and, with a mild rumble, exhaust hoods propelled cooking aromas to the building's exterior. But on that tiny island in the stream of activity, Trina not only broke out a smile any would recognize, she laughed.

*Thank you, God.* Cassie felt truly grateful. No matter what political footballs got tossed around the dining room tonight, the program worked.

"Where's the Fagioli?" demanded Frieda, hands on black-sheathed hips. "People ain't too happy about the delay. I got one table, six guys, all construction types"—she rolled her eyes—"think they're God's gift to the female gender. They said they don't care if the line goes out the door and down the block, they're not giving up their table until they've got their Fagioli. They've shared four baskets of sweet fries and drained half a tank of Coke syrup. They really like your fries, Carmina. Perfect, every time."

Carmina hunched her shoulders and waved Frieda off. Nonetheless, she smartly and equally loaded the next set of empty baskets for delivery to the hungry diners and hummed as she did so. Maybe by the grace of God the day had taken a turn for the better and Cassie's fears were unfounded.

"By the way," Frieda added. "The line? It's out the door and down past Mr. Fiduski's novelty shop. He's happy as a clam. Sold three rubber chickens, a boxing nun windup, and two whoopee cushions, all within the last half hour. What do I tell 'em?"

"You tell them another thirty minutes," Cassie said. "Please convey our regrets and give them a voucher for a free bowl of soup next time they're in. And take a couple of baskets of sweet fries to the folks in line and tell them how much we appreciate their patience. And tell Mr. Fiduski we want a percentage of line sales." She gave the student a wink. "Thank you, Frieda."

Nick caught Cassie's eye. He motioned toward the walk-in freezer and mouthed the words "North Pole," code for "meet me in frozen goods."

"Uh, Trina, this is your Fagioli and you heard how much demand there is for it out there," Cassie said. "Let's turn the gas down a tad and you give the pot a good stir every five minutes or so. Watch it like a hawk. There's a food thief in the area. I'll be back in five myself. Will you be okay?"

Trina took a deep breath. "Yes." Probably unused to being put in charge of anything, she nevertheless looked determined to tend this pot. Her pot. Another reassuring nod from Chef seemed to seal the deal. Against all odds, she was a cook.

In the freezer, Nick removed bricks of cheese from boxes and arranged them on a shelf. Cassie said, "What's up, Luigi? You said you know a second thing that will cheer me up." The frigid air refreshed her after the overheated kitchen.

Nick gathered her into his arms and presented her with an exceptionally friendly greeting. "*Mi manchi, cara mia.* I miss you, my darling."

"Miss me? You've been in here all of three minutes. Okay, Don Juan, give. Why all the smooching? And should we be carrying on in the corporate freezer while everyone else slaves away just beyond the door?"

Nick looked smug. "You will regret your suspicious nature once I tell you that I convinced Cody to sing at tonight's ceremony."

Cassie threw her arms around him. "Oh, Nick! That's wonderful! He knows to come at seven and that he'll get dinner?" The graduation ceremony in which all the diners took part was in honor of two students who had recently completed the food preparation track and one who had completed the hospitality track. Cody Ferguson was a deaf fifteen-year-old and good friend of the Dixons and sweet on their eighteen-year-old daughter, Beth.

"He'll be here, stomach growling. He wouldn't tell me what he's singing, but knowing him, it'll be clever and appropriate. Know what'll cheer me up? A thick slice of Chef's Chocolate Opera Cake smothered in local berries and drizzled with hot caramel sauce."

"I take it you've given no thought to how far you'll have to run to work that off?" She gave him a reproving once-over, then smiled. "Oh, Nick, that is the best news about Cody! This evening will be so special, even if Waverly and Peugeot do challenge one another to a duel. Thank you for suggesting it."

"You're welcome. Now may I please have a second helping of your appreciation?"

She was only too happy to oblige.

Kenny! No one outside the program is allowed in the kitchen without express permission. Please leave." Cassie wondered how long he had been standing there by the stove watching, scratching at the scabs on his chin.

She sounded to her own ears like a recorded scold, the coldly officious female voice that warned patrons they were not allowed to park in the departure zone of the airport drive, but Cassie didn't care. You had to be firm with people who lived on the undisciplined streets. Kenny Burstyn was trouble. Homeless for several of his nineteen years, he'd been kicked off the program's culinary track at eleven weeks for continued drug abuse.

One thing for sure, Cassie guessed she had a prime suspect in the theft of the ground beef and onions earlier in the day.

"Hey, Carmina, 'member when I used to be your fry guy?" Carmina did not look up from cleaning the industrial potato slicer. She was sweet on Kenny until, hurling obscenities, he'd been escorted from the building by two burly policemen.

Kenny waited, and when Carmina said nothing, tossed his uncombed head—more of an involuntary twitch—and edged closer to the simmering pot of Fagioli. It had been reduced by half at lunch, thanks mostly to the six-man wrecking crew from the nearby construction site. Cassie was protecting the remainder for when they reopened for dinner. She was counting on it to mellow Waverly and Peugeot, the battling millionaires of San Francisco.

*God, forgive me, I don't want that walking tempest of bedbugs and BO anywhere near the food.* She was only a fair Samaritan. She needed to work on being a good one.

She forced a Betty Crocker hominess into her voice. "Ken, how 'bout we fix you up a nice bowl of soup in a Styrofoam container and you can take it and a slice of warm buttered bread with you?" It was against policy to act as a soup kitchen, but Cassie sensed danger. She didn't like the way Kenny stared at nothing and jammed hands in jacket pockets to scrabble constantly at the threadbare blue and black wool fabric as if controlled by someone—or something—else. She was gripped by a sudden irrational fear of those hands. Not contained by the jacket pockets, she thought they might snake into the fragrant air and seek out her throat.

"No!" The defiant word came with a wild jerk. Kenny's skinny hip bumped the soup pot, knocked it partway off the burner, and sent the orangey red Fagioli slopping over the rim and onto the gleaming stove surface. With a sputter and sizzle, the liquid made contact with the gas flame and the air smelled of burned Fagioli.

Cassie caught her breath and motioned to Jorge to leave the red lettuce he and Trina were tearing for salad and take Kenny outside. But before Jorge could react, Kenny slid back his right arm, extended the sleeve of the jacket, gathered the extra cloth into his cupped hand, and took hold of one of the pot's hot metal handles. He carefully steadied the pot back over the center of the burner, bent, and took a deep sniff of the contents.

"S'more Tabasco," he slurred. "When you think you've got enough in there, two plops more. So sayeth Cheffy. Hey, where is Raoul the Ghoul anyway?"

"Here, Kenneth." Chef cautiously circled around from behind the pantry shelves, a meat mallet clenched in a hammy fist, a tight sneer on his lips ringed with beads of sweat.

Kenny reared back, spittle forming little foamy beads at the corners of his mouth. "Hey, Chef! Chef!" His words were loud, grating, mocking. "What's the poop of the day?"

Chef, who only a month before had threatened Kenny in his kitchen with a meat cleaver, lost it. "Pasta e Fagioli is ze zoop of ze gods, and stop-a the loud talk or I break-a you neck!" he shouted. "The customer no like-a shouting from kitchen!"

A maniacal wink dismissed him. "And whatcha got cookin' over in that corner, Cheffy boy? That wouldn't be Red Light Ravioli I see?"

Purple veins wormed across Chef's forehead. "Pasta Puttanesca, you son of sea cow!"

Jorge stepped between them and brandished a pair of salad tongs at each of the combatants.

"Chill, both of you, or I call the cops!"

Nick entered the kitchen with Philippe Peugeot. He rushed to Chef, grabbed his wrist, and lowered the mallet. He pointed at the boy. "Ken, you've been warned. Don't you move!" He snatched the phone off the wall hook and punched in 911.

Kenny hesitated only a second before beating it out the back door, tossing over his shoulder an ominous "Watch yourself, Cassie Dixon, and remember this night!"

# Chapter 2

Nick checked outside along the staff parking strip and, seeing neither Kenny nor anything else of a suspicious nature, secured the back door closed. It had a crash bar on the inside for emergency exit, but during much of the day it had been propped open to help cool the kitchen.

"He's gone," Nick reassured a visibly relieved crew. The kitchen quickly returned to its former efficient hum. More of the volunteer evening waitstaff had arrived and were receiving orientation. Members of the San Francisco Giants front office were there along with volunteers from the Heinz Corporation.

Peugeot, the neat, sharp-eyed aristocrat of commercial real estate and property development, possessed a physical carriage and disconcertingly direct gaze that suggested you were being scanned for flaws and found wanting. A short man, he wore an expensive white silk shirt and platinum tie, ruby and gold cuff links, and charcoal gray slacks with a crease at least as sharp as most of the implements in the Taste knife drawer.

"And my motorcar, Nicholas, is unmolested?" Peugeot's voice was glossy as egg custard despite an underlying insistence. When he spoke, he did not want to be gotten back to. As many a subordinate had learned to his regret, when Peugeot asked a question, you gave the answer then and there and hoped to heaven you had done due diligence.

"It rests as you left it, sir, one eye open."

Peugeot drove a Peugeot. Although he was not heir to that auto dynasty, despite his name, he stopped just short of wearing the automaker's rampant lion on a neck chain. He liked for you to ascribe animal characteristics to his moonstone silver 607 Executive Saloon with dark gray velour interior, a motorcar that communicated with itself in many ways without your having to be involved. Brake from sixty miles per hour to a full stop in just 2.7 seconds, and the hazard lights turned themselves on. Resume driving and the hazards turned themselves off. The headlamps talked to the windscreen wipers and in mechanical détente decided when best to turn on, given the current conditions of lighting, weather, and probably barometric pressure. Even the tires warned the driver of any loss in air pressure.

Nick had heard these features described in loving detail, as a man might describe his fiancée. Zero to one hundred miles per hour in 9.9 seconds. Top speed 150 miles per hour. Twelve-speaker sound system. Double-layered side windows. Triple-sealed doors. "Sleek as a feline," always with emphasis on the sibilant "s."

"Excellent." Peugeot barely smiled. "She's lithe, corners like a gazelle, and is fleet as a cheetah on the straightaway. That means the lower the lowlifes, the greater the risk she will be hunted to extinction. That is a large drawback to Taste's philosophic vision, Nicholas. There are so very many impoverished, why scrape about the bottom for the dregs? I mean, you don't recruit for the program from among the African refugee camps, so what's wrong with pulling in a higher class of poor? I want on that board, Nicholas. No one like that glassy-eyed freak show who just fled out the back would ever slip past on my watch."

Before Nick could stop her, Cassie reacted. "They're precisely who this program is for, sir."

One of Peugeot's waxed pencil-thin eyebrows bent in annoyance. "People like *that* are a blight on society. They consume

24

social services like mutant locusts while those with a hope of making it out of the gutter feed on the crumbs."

"There are no throwaway people, Mr. Peugeot!"

Nick imagined the angry flames beginning to lick around Cassie's reddening ears. Her white apron stained with bloody Fagioli, she gripped a large ladle that with one deadly swing could forever shutter the place and bring another Dixon dream to dust.

"Fifteen minutes to show time!" Nick sang the warning. "Places, everyone!" He stopped short of clapping his hands like a stage director signaling everyone to toe their marks and met the blank stares of the kitchen crew, already as in place as they knew how to be.

Cassie and Peugeot glared at one another. Jorge, ever sensitive to scullery politics, grabbed a startled Trina about the waist and waltzed her to the center of the tiled floor. "We're ready to wow 'em!" he said. He released a wide-eyed and moonstruck Trina, extracted three walnuts in the shell from his apron pocket, and started to juggle.

Cassie turned heel, hurried to the freezer, yanked it open, and disappeared inside with a slam of the door.

Shining brown eyes fixed on the flying nuts, amusing patter putting smiles on most of the faces in the audience, Jorge almost missed the advancing chef until Maggiano loomed over him. "Buffoon! *Imbecille!*" The irate maestro took repeated swings with his whisk, Jorge feinting and dodging like a nimble prizefighter eluding a plodding opponent.

And always the walnuts remained airborne.

Just out of whisk range, Jorge snatched one of the nuts out of the air with his right hand while continuing to juggle the other two with his left. "Your eyeball, sir?" He offered the walnut to Chef before plugging it into his own eye and holding it in place with a squint.

"Argh! 'Tis the pirate's life for me!" Jorge hopped on one leg and, walnuts still flying, backpedaled out of the kitchen to much applause. Chef, the beginnings of a grin on his sweaty visage, gave hot pursuit.

Nick shook his head and laughed. "Okay, team, the circus has moved on. Let's assemble the grilled peach and *serrano queso azul*, *mache*, and red wine *vinagreta* on the salted lettuce leaves. Go, go!" Chef had done his job well. The salads rapidly took beautiful shape and would taste exquisite.

Nick clapped an arm around the disapproving Peugeot's shoulders. "You're lead for the volunteers tonight, Philippe. Thanks to you and an army of others, guys like Jorge are given a new lease on life. When he came to us four months ago, he was down, defeated, guilty with the shame he'd brought to his family. Out of work, depressed, he'd turned to petty thievery and even beat up one of the counselors at the Mission. Now look at him. Happy. Well trained. Proud. He graduates tonight. Has a job all lined up at Palermo's, an apartment nearby, and can finally save up enough to help his mother and little brothers get by. He might easily have slipped through the cracks if it weren't for you and all the others who keep us afloat."

Flattery worked on Peugeot. Nick suspected the man needed Taste for a tax write-off and to polish his reputation for ruthless and not always aboveboard business dealings. So what? This was a clear case of the ends justifying the occasional mean opportunist. He'd come around.

Peugeot's disapproval was as showy as his car. "That was hardly what I would call a display of good sense and professionalism, Nicholas. You should have put an immediate stop to it. What does such foolishness say to the other homeless in the program? Disrespect for authority, unsafe practices in the kitchen, impeding the culinary flow—these are what you teach?"

"Joy, Philippe, that is the lesson here." He wasn't going to back down just because Peugeot owned some of the world's most exclusive waterfront. "Joy of accomplishment. Joy in a hope-filled future. Joy of living. That's what we just celebrated here together. Everyone knows what Jorge was like in the beginning. This program brings people back from the dead, my friend, and you just witnessed a resurrection!"

Peugeot huffed. "With you, it is always religion. To survive, Taste must be less a sawdust revival and more a business proposition. You want to start a catering service to help low income and the elderly. Do you know how much that will cost? No one is going to put a dollar into it with this kind of loose supervision. If you truly wish to build that house, Nicholas, then you had better get this one in order."

Peugeot stalked off in the direction of the waiting volunteers in need of instruction. It was ten minutes before the seven o'clock dinner hour and the anticipation of a dozen volunteers, five instructional staff, and the kitchen crew reached a heightened buzz. Celebrity Chef Night was special for everyone, especially when it included a graduation.

A cold hand placed icy fingers in the crook of Nick's arm. "Has that self-important peacock gone to mind his own business?" Cassie looked as if she had remained longer in refrigerated isolation than intended. Gone were the soft golden highlights in her hair, replaced by a stiffness usually sprayed from a can. Her nose was the red of someone too long ice-skating.

"I think we may be spending too much time at the North Pole." Nick gave her a hug. "Brr. You went from fiery hot to wintry chill in a hurry."

"Sorry. That guy always gets under my skin."

"Can you say 'diplomacy'? Remember, it's the Philippe Peugeots and the James Waverlys of the world who keep the lights on around here."

He felt her go rigid. She released a moan into his lapel. "I forgot about Waverly. Can I go home now?"

"Cass, easy does it. You've hobnobbed with the rich and famous before; you came close to being one yourself. You just stroke their egos, put their names on the wall, and cash their checks. Think you can remember that?"

"Yes, captain. I smoke their eggs, pin their hides to the wall, and break their necks."

"Cass ... "

"Don't worry, it won't happen again. I'll tell the runty little ... I'll be sure to apologize to Philippe the Magnificent."

Nick smoothed her hair and kissed a chilly cheek. "That's my pepper girl. He mentioned the catering project tonight, which tells me he's been thinking about it. We mind our manners and he might just bankroll the whole thing."

"Mob money."

"Cass ... "

"Okay, okay. Stoop and grovel. I've got it."

# Chapter 3

CEO James Waverly held command at the center of the room. His attractive wife, a brunette dressed in black taffeta and purple-blue sapphires, joined him at his table, as did three of his favored business associates and their wives, all suitably attired in evening wear calculated to be seen and admired.

Cassie watched Waverly survey the room. His gaze took in the smaller tables around his, tables crowded with other, lesser patrons. Mere shuttle craft to his Enterprise. A haughty countenance, the sure set of broad deal-making shoulders clearly announced that his was the command ship in this galaxy.

Three waitstaff had been assigned to the Waverly table and they hovered nearby. Waverly was known to drop tips big as car payments. Cassie drew close.

"We have those special little *peppercinis* you like so well, Mr. Waverly." Waiter No. 1 beamed.

Waiter No. 2 nodded wisely. "From Calabria."

"At the toe of the Italian peninsula." Waiter No. 3 all but curtsied.

"Enough with the geography lesson." Waverly smacked the table, making the silverware—and the waiters—jump. "Just bring me the blasted *peppercinis*!"

All three scurried away to do his bidding.

Cassie bit her tongue.

In fresh blouse and perfume, apron consigned to the laundry bin, she turned on her heel and went to stand near the cashier's station. She kept one eye on the kitchen, in case Kenny decided on a curtain call, and one eye on the dining room and the small stage where Cody would sing and from which Jorge, George Wilson, and Faye Lackamore would shortly graduate. She waved at Cody. Daughter Beth had driven her friend to the restaurant and then left to finish a research project for world history class. Cody looked nervous, pacing a tight circle in anticipation of his song.

"Psst! Cassie!"

Norma, the head cashier, motioned from behind the register. At her elbow stood Peugeot, looking as darkly troubled as she'd ever seen him. Cassie's stomach clenched.

"Yes, Norma, what can I do for you?" Cassie hadn't planned on giving Peugeot an apology this soon. "Philippe," she said, giving him a slight nod. She received none in return. *The smug, supercilious* douleur. It was French for "pain."

Norma appeared to be doing some intestinal clenching of her own. She was a pleasant, capable woman in her early fifties, retired from thirty years in hospital food service management. It took a lot to ruffle her potatoes. "As I was just explaining to Mr. Peugeot, we have three of our most capable hospitality students attending the Waverlys this evening under the leadership of tonight's graduate, Miss Lackamore. Still"—she gave the impatient Peugeot a sideways glance—"the gentleman insists on serving the Waverly party and asks that we reassign one of the students to another position."

Cassie mustered as warm a smile as was available under the circumstances. "Philippe, let me say first how sorry I am for my behavior in the kitchen. I realize, of course, that you are as concerned with the success of the program as I am." She thought no such thing, but knew that Nick would approve of her tact, however manufactured. "It was rude of me."

She waited for a response. And waited. Peugeot rapped immaculately manicured nails on the glass counter in which were shelves of Taste cookbooks, Taste teas, and Taste souvenir aprons of white linen emblazoned with "Taste of Success" in fancy lettering the hue of concord grapes.

Cassie wanted to see if the graceless French pygmy, cuff links and all, might fit on the lower shelf next to the take-out boxes. Instead, she said, "Really, Philippe, don't you think it wiser to serve a more neutral table?"

"We are grown men." Peugeot's words were filled with offense and resolve. "Nothing is improved by avoidance. Jim Waverly is an admired entrepreneur. I merely wish to mend fences. It is only in Taste's best interests for us to bury our differences."

"Philippe ... " Now she sounded like Nick the scold. Where was he? She wasn't in charge of the dining room. That job fell to Gordon O'Neal, chairman of the Taste board. But tonight he was in San Diego for an administrators' conference. Nick was subbing for him. Then she spotted Nick, patting Cody on the back, no doubt giving him plenty of attaboys ahead of his song. The Dixons held a great deal of affection for the deaf teen who thought Beth was God's gift.

"It would not be in anyone's best interests for you to stand in my way, Cassandra." His eyes practically bored a hole through her.

Cassie caught her breath. *Does he dare threaten me, threaten Taste, because Azure World, my dream company, collapsed? I'm a corporate footnote, so I've lost all respect, and no matter how shady he is he thinks he's my superior? Let the two spiders tangle and may the victor choke on his own web.*

"I wouldn't think of it," Cassie said. "Norma, please reassign one of Faye's associates to another table. Mr. Peugeot, have a lovely evening."

Without another word, she turned, fists clenched, and strode to the nearest table. "Hello, folks. Nigel, right? And don't tell me. Cora ... Hathaway. How's that adorable son of yours ...

Peter? What lung power! Did he stick with the trumpet or slide over to the trombone?... Oh, he's at band camp this week? You two are so faithful. Thank you for joining us again this evening!"

That she said these cheerful things despite a jaw tight as a drumhead seemed to go unnoticed by the convivial Hathaways.

Cassie was shocked to see Trina emerge from the kitchen looking frantic. Mousey as she was, she rarely ventured forth when the dining room was open for business.

"Oh, Cassie, that creepy guy's back. You know the one. You kicked him out earlier today."

"Kenny?" Cassie's hackles rose. Was she the only one on duty around here? "Where? How'd he get in here?"

Trina led her back toward the kitchen. She lowered her voice. "I think he slipped in when the front doors opened for dinner. He's like one of them, you know, ap ... appa ... you know, ghost things."

"Apparitions?"

"Yeah, that's them. All shimmery and see-through. Not there, then there. Kenny looks at me all funny. You know, like he'd like to put me in the soup. That's when I came and got you."

*The soup!* Cassie marched into the kitchen just as Kenny, blearier and slouchier than ever, leaned over the pot of Fagioli and snuffed up a lungful of the mouthwatering aroma.

"Kenny! You back away from there!"

The thin man, hair dull and wild, teeth scummy from inattention, facial scabs bearing recent scratches, jerked up from the pot. A tray of freshly ladled Fagioli sat on the stove top next to the pot. Some had splashed onto the tray and the stove, some had dribbled down the sides of a couple of the bowls. Where was Jorge? Out for a smoke?

On the opposite end of the stove, on low simmer, the spaghetti and its rich savory Puttanesca topping awaited their entrance. Chef could be heard mumbling in the pantry.

Kenny peered at her, fingers working the top of a worn paper sack clutched to his ribs. She got the distinct impression that though his body was present, he was not. What was in the bag?

"Ken." She kept her voice soft. "Let us get you some help."

He jerked back as if she had forced his hand onto the gas burner. "You don't!" He said it around a thick, uncooperative tongue. "You don't tell me! You got me kicked off the program. You kicked me out today. You hate me! You're killing me! I hate you! I hate this place! You'll see, you'll pay!"

Cassie froze at the wild accusations and threats. How much was menace; how much drugged babble? The stick man bent and jerked, limbs and digits involuntarily quivered and spasmed.

It pained Cassie to see this meltdown. "Carmina."

The girl looked up from her sweet potato fries.

"Frieda and the others are busy with a full house tonight and I don't know where Jorge is. AJ and his team have to finish plating the salads. I want you to please take this tray of Fagioli out to the waiters and tell them to come get the rest. Do it now, please." If she couldn't keep Kenny away from the soup, she'd keep the soup away from Kenny.

Carmina looked at her in surprise, eyes wide. She started to say something, then thought better of it. Without a word, she washed her hands at the sink, dried them, smoothed her hairnet, hefted the tray, and made for the dining room. She was not an out-front person, but when duty called, Carmina was among the first to answer.

Nick found her. "Cass, Cody's about to go on. You should—" Kenny swayed, then jerked still. The two males stared at one another. Nick's words were calm, but strained. "Ken, let's make you up a nice bowl of Puttanesca and get you on your way.

Cassie, maybe you and Trina should put the Fagioli on the fast track."

Cassie threw him a grateful look and started to fill bowls. Kenny stayed put, but at least his eyes were hungrily fixed on Nick's every move. She could smell the boy over everything else in the kitchen.

She handed a tray of soup to Trina despite the dubious appearance of her anorexic arms. For her part, Trina looked much relieved to leave Kenny and exit the kitchen. Cassie prayed for tray-carrying angels.

On her way out to the dining room, Cassie passed close to Nick. "See if you can get a glimpse of what's in Ken's sack."

A recorded fanfare burst from the overhead speakers. Cody Ferguson in yellow spandex pants and red-sequined jacket vaulted on stage, a wireless mic clamped in his fist, and slid forward on his knees. To a recorded orchestra, he belted, "Food, glorious food! We're anxious to try it. Three banquets a day—our favorite diet! Just picture a great big steak—fried, roasted, or stewed. Oh, food, wonderful food, marvelous food, glorious food!"

The audience roared and Cassie cheered. Good ole Cody. After getting lost in the mountains two years before—stopping an enraged grizzly bear and nearly falling to his death off a cliff—Cody had emerged more determined than ever to prove a skeptical world wrong. Yes, a deaf kid could make it Big with a capital "B." He'd made a believer out of her.

"Food, glorious food! Eat right through the menu. Just loosen your belt two inches, and then you work up a new appetite. In this interlude—the food, once again, food, fabulous food, glorious food!"

His pitch and volume were pretty much on and his diction—thanks to speech therapy and a love of words—was excellent. His body a tuning fork, he heard plenty of music in his head and wasn't at all shy to let it out.

Bodies moved, toes tapped. Jorge and Chef swayed together like long-lost pals, and two kids at a corner table danced their knives and forks in time to the Broadway tune from *Oliver!*

*Nick wasn't kidding.* Cassie felt lighter and more settled. *It is clever and appropriate. Cody pulled it off.* She was relieved to see the bone white bowls of soup being placed in front of each diner. A couple of tables were already giving enthusiastic nods to the delicious first dish.

It was harder to let go of Kenny's latest outburst. They had to get him the help he needed.

For the big finish, Cody clipped the mic to his jacket, stood on his hands, and walked around the perimeter of the stage upside down, singing, "Why should we be fated to do nothing but brood on food, magical food, wonderful food, marvelous food, fabulous food, beautiful food, glor-i-ous food!"

Cody flipped nimbly onto his feet and the restaurant erupted. He took half a dozen bows and blew as many kisses before, to everyone's delight, Nick thanked him with a ceramic bowl of instant gruel and a silver spoon.

Trina charged the length of the dining room and made straight for Cassie with the hunched purpose of a cross-country skier laboring uphill. *What now?*

Cassie hurried her outside through the front door just before the irate girl blurted, "That pervert patted my tush!"

"What pervert?"

"The fat guy who always tips so big."

"James Waverly?"

"Yeah, that guy."

"Oh, Trina, are you sure it wasn't just an accidental brush of a hand? His wife is sitting right there beside him."

Trina's pinched, angry face reddened, as if slapped by Cassie's words. "You think like I don't know when someone's messin'

35

with me? He like caressed, patted, and tweaked my rear, in that order, the hog!"

Cassie was instantly sorry. "Forgive me, Trina, I never meant to doubt you. I'll speak to him."

"You'd better." Tears of frustration squeezed from the corners of the girl's eyes. "Do I got a sign on my back says, 'Easy Pickings'? Even my father and two brothers think I'm nothing but trash. Used me like I was some human vending machine. Maybe I am if some nasty dog like that with all his millions thinks I am. Why don't God just kill me and be done with it?" She stomped to the curb and slumped down, head in her lap, arms covering her head, and sobbed.

Cassie sat down and placed a hand on Trina's head and the girl collapsed into her arms. The night was cool, but not unpleasant. The air smelled of salt brine and creosote, a reminder of their industrial marine location. Distant car horns blared. A Vespa sputtered past, a gnarled old man in front, a grinning terrier riding shotgun in a wicker basket. A couple, arms tightly entwined, passed on the sidewalk, kissing, oblivious to all life but theirs.

"Trina, you are worth far more than silver or gold to God. People who abuse other people don't know who they're dealing with. The Lord says that vengeance is his and he will repay their evil. Those abusive people have nothing to do with the loving Creator who made you. I know it doesn't seem like it, but Jesus understands how much you hurt, how sick you are of being treated so poorly. Trust in God, Trina, and I will help you every way I can. Starting with James Waverly."

It was all Cassie could do to keep from storming back inside the restaurant, dumping the soup pot over Waverly's bull head, and smashing the side of the pot repeatedly with a meat hammer. But so much rode on the goodwill of even the iniquitous. Should she jeopardize redemption of hundreds in the program for the honor of one?

"Come back inside with me and we'll get Jorge to take you home. Your emotions have been yanked around enough for one day. You like Jorge, don't you?"

Trina looked up and examined Cassie's face, weighing no doubt the degree of trust to be found there. She rubbed the wet from her eyes with a tiny fist and nodded. "Jorge's maybe the sweetest guy I know. He's crazy funny. Some gentleman. I wanna meet the momma who could raise a boy like him. The pictures he shows me of his Lanny and Miquel—so sweet. He calls 'em Pickle and Squirm. Brothers like I wished I had." She wiped her nose on her arm. "He told me he likes me. Can you believe it?"

Cassie pulled Trina to her feet. "Yes, honey, I can believe it. You make a cute couple."

Trina hooted into the night. "Now I know you're lyin', no offense. Jorge's this handsome guy with big muscles and I look like somethin' out of the *Corpse Bride*. He's like one of them perfect sculptures at the museum and I'm this bitty toothpick."

Cassie brushed Trina's hair back from her face with both hands. "You might be surprised how beautiful you are whenever you catch him watching you."

Trina blushed. "Go on. I thought you didn't go down in the wine cellar. That you was a tee-whatchacallit?"

"Teetotaler," Cassie replied. "You go tell Jorge I asked him please to take you home. You both eat first, then go. You won't be penalized for time missed. I'll keep you on the clock and punch you both out at the end of the night. We can manage with the volunteers we have."

"Can't I watch you take that guy apart?"

Cassie shook her head. "No, those things are best done in private. You don't embarrass someone in public, even a pervert. We'll let Nick take the lead."

Trina smiled big. "Good. I like him."

Cassie returned the smile. "Yeah, me too."

As soon as Trina headed for the kitchen, Chef made a bee-line for Cassie, who was still by the front door. He was livid. Even at that distance, it appeared that if he removed his cook's hat, Cassie would see steam rise.

"You feed a *ladro*, a thief! It is a *violazione*, a violation of my person. What you do about?"

He planted himself, legs like pilings, in her way. Chin out-thrust, fists on hips, pink face glowering, he seemed prepared to wait as long as it took.

Cassie held up a hand. "Follow me." She led him out the front door. "Slow down, Chef. You have to remember that Jorge is still a kid. He looks up to you, like a father. You have to be patient with him."

"Jorge? What Jorge? I love-a the Jorge. I kiss him! I talk about the Waverly. He *disturbo*, big-a trouble. He cause-a me *dolore*, much-a pain. He have-a the brains of a *scarafaggio*, a cockroach!"

Cassie sighed. Jim Waverly was a serial alienator. Who was next? Through the glass window, she saw him slop wine into the glasses around him, then lean over and nibble his wife's ear. *How many ears have you claimed, you cad?* It made her sick to think that just minutes before, he had gotten familiar with Trina.

"Tell me, Chef, what did he do?"

Chef looked sad. "He say he steal-a my recipe for the Fagioli, Chef's zesty *minestra*, soup. He going to package and-a sell in *magazzino*, store. *Ladro! Ladro!* Make-a big money with Chef's Fagioli!"

"How, Chef, how is that possible? Your special spices are your secret."

"He say he have-a the contents, how you say, analy-zed in lavatory. They give to him list of what is in. He go make." Chef looked utterly bereft, as if his children had been sold to pay debts.

Cassie had to cheer the man up. "He's bluffing, Chef, trying to impress his friends. Once the wine wears off, he'll forget all about it. He's electronics. Wires, frequencies, circuitry boards. Not soup. Forget he said anything."

Chef shook his head. The sagging skin of his big sad face wobbled. "You no know. *Scarafaggio* no care. Dirty beast take and take-a more. How you say, di-ver-see-fy? Times go bad, electronics go bad, soup left. Always the soup. My sweet little *minestra*, my child." He turned, shoulders limp, and reentered the cheery hubbub. He made straight for the kitchen.

Cassie was almost afraid to go in. Maybe she'd thumb a ride on a passing Vespa, breed terriers, or swim with the sharks around Alcatraz. Something sane like that.

Instead, she took a deep breath and returned to the warm interior of Taste of Success. If trouble really did come in threes, then she had fulfilled her quota: Kenny, Trina and Waverly, Chef and Waverly. All she had to do now was castigate the wealthiest supporter of the culinary-training program, look after Trina, and find help for Kenny. Piece of cake.

She almost backed out of the restaurant. Norma was again giving her the high sign, a heaping helping of consternation deepening every wrinkle the woman owned.

"Yes, Norma, what is it?" Her tone was sharper than she'd intended.

"Hear that?" Norma asked, cocking her head in the direction of the restrooms. Cassie listened. Was that shouting?

"Men's room," Norma said. "Mr. Waverly and Mr. Peugeot. And they're not arguing about who should have won the Super Bowl. Somebody insulted somebody and they nearly came to blows out here before I convinced them to take it elsewhere."

Cassie motioned to Nick, who was setting up the microphones for the brief graduation ceremony. He hurried over.

"I hear them," Nick said. "Those two have been sniping at each other for the past five minutes or more. I didn't catch what set them off, but it's gotten out of hand. Now I finally got Kenny out the door. No time to do more than get him fed, I'm afraid, but he was accepting, if not thankful. Now I'll go see what this scuffle's about. Could you kick off the proceedings?"

"Sure. Jorge's up first. Thanks for dealing with Kenny and putting a lid on those two." Another shout issued from the restrooms and people closest to that end of the house whispered knowingly to one another. Nick left at a run. It troubled her that Kenny still wasn't getting the therapy he needed. Left unattended, his kind of problems only grew worse.

Cody ate his dinner at a nearby table and she gave him a hug. "Thanks, Code-man, you're the number one street urchin in my book! How's the food?"

He watched her lips intently and grinned. "Glorious, of course, and you're welcome, pretty lady. As it so happens, I have a family, but I make more money singing and dancing for all the swells and high-society types. Got a tuppence to spare?"

She cuffed him playfully. "You're eating your tuppence' worth. Now shush."

At the mic, she said, "Ladies and gentlemen, it is our great pleasure to graduate three fine students from the program this evening. The two food-preparation grads each receive a set of gourmet quality kitchen knives that will start them on their careers, and our hospitality graduate receives a gift certificate to the clothing store of her choice to outfit for the job."

The diners applauded with gusto as some servers began removing the soup bowls while other servers brought in the salads. Cassie was gratified to see that most bowls were empty.

From the back of the room, Nick herded the two still-fuming combatants back to their places, Waverly to his seat, Peugeot to the kitchen.

"Don't touch that soup!" Waverly growled. With a clatter, the waiter, about to remove the bowl, dropped it and the plate under it the short distance to the tabletop. "Don't ever touch my soup!" He picked up the bowl and in one long draught, sucked down the remaining contents. "More!" he barked. A second bowl quickly appeared.

Cassie waited a moment for the commotion to die, then filled the awkward silence with a hearty "Join me in congratulating our first graduate this evening, Jorge Ramone!"

To much applause, Jorge, grinning ear-to-ear in his kitchen whites, stepped to the microphone. "Ladies and germs," he deadpanned, "welcome to my bar mitzvah!"

That got a laugh, but soon Jorge's eyes were wet with tears. "I want to thank God—Father, Son, and Holy Spirit—for saving me from myself. I was all set to fail and doing my best to throw everything away that my blessed mother had taught me. My little brothers cried themselves to sleep because I was not there. I loved them, loved them all, but it was like I didn't care. I saw no way up, so I let myself down, deeper and deeper, until I broke a man's jaw because he cared for me more than his own comfort. Emilio"—Jorge pointed into the audience at a man twice his age—"I owe you my life, man! I broke your jaw and in excruciating pain you hugged me back. You could not speak, but your tears spoke for you. You and my mom and my brothers are my angels. You got me into this program because you knew I was meant for better. I won't let you—"

A bloodcurdling scream stopped him cold. Mrs. Waverly, the screamer, shook her husband, whose hands tore at his throat. She screamed again. "James! James! What's wrong? Oh God, what?"

In reply, James Waverly teetered a moment in his chair, breaths coming in irregular, reedy gasps. He groaned and made to rise before splashing facedown into the Pasta Fagioli.

# Chapter 4

Father B braked, double-clutched the ancient bus, rammed the spindly shift stick forward to slow the beast, ground worn gears that could ill afford to be ground, peered through a windshield smeared in dirt and bug grime, and prayed aloud a furious stream of the holy and the profane.

"God love a duck; be thou merciful to turkeys, human and fowl. Get over, you dolt, get over! What, Mack, did Cracker Jack issue your license? Look out, thank you, Jesus, oh no!" Every time he hit the brakes or wrenched the wheel to avoid disaster, springs protested and metal clattered like corrugated tin in a typhoon. With each dip and pothole, his thirteen street-weary passengers sprang off their seats and fell back into place, lolling like bobblehead figures, skulls knocking against windows, thin arms and legs as rattle limbed as Dorothy's scarecrow.

"Never again, Ace Longfield! You don't need a vacation half as much as I need my sanity!" Ace was the gap-toothed ex-addict, ex-transit driver who had reformed, rescued a wheezy decommissioned school bus from the wrecking yard, painted it the colors of a 1960s psychedelic acid trip, emblazoned the sides with "Jesus Rocks!" and daily drove San Francisco's alleys and backstreets in search of winos and the drug-fried to chauffeur to the Gospel Rescue Mission. This was the second time he had roped in Father B to sub for the evening shift while he went to visit his sister in Grand Rapids.

*Never again.*

Ahead, the way wove between a taxi cab and bicycle altercation and a double-parked delivery van. The gap to Father B
looked exactly one bus wide with a margin of error of maybe a
prayer book's width on either side. He hesitated.

To back up and go around was suicide in this traffic. To stop
and attempt to proceed with sensible caution meant entering
the fray and risking further delay, maybe even having to medi-
ate the dispute. Josie didn't hold dinner for anyone. If his passengers missed out, he was obligated to find them sustenance
at Operation Night Light, and that would take another twelve
congested blocks of heart-stopping hunt-and-peck. He'd never
make it in time to administer Communion to the Midnight
Church at St. John's Cathedral, and coming up against a closed
door, some of the most fragile might drift away, never to be
seen again.

As it was, he'd missed tonight's graduation at Taste of Success. He was to have brought the benediction, God's blessing on
new lives, but he'd let the Dixons and the students down. And
now like some aging weekend hippie, he wore an oversized tie-
dyed T-shirt over a brocade vest stitched with the symbols of
ancient Christendom. His pride and joy, that vest, and he'd be
defrocked before he took it off just to satisfy a sixties throwback
like Ace Longfield.

Eyes grim, jaw set, Father B scratched his goatee and made
his decision. He upshifted and stomped the gas. With all the
grace of a wounded hippo, the bus lurched forward, horn blaring, engine snarling, a vehicle possessed.

Cabbie, cyclist, and van operator scattered as the bus, its
driver gesticulating wildly, stormed the gap.

Whether by divine intervention or dumb luck, the bus
cleared the mess undented and squirted out the other side.
A right turn at the next corner, two more blocks east, and it

heaved to a stop at the curb in front of the Mission in an undignified cloud of billowing diesel exhaust.

"Jesus Rocks!" Father B declared, throwing open the door. He pumped a fist in the air like a movie tough guy. "All ashore!" When a person drove as seldom as Father B, sometimes attitude was all the defense he'd have if hauled into traffic court.

He kept his seat, arms sore and tingling. "Takes a sumo wrestler to steer this monster," he muttered, giving the dashboard an "I'm-in-charge" thump with the heel of a hand. He checked the side mirrors for signs of traffic cops and, seeing none, breathed deeply and permitted himself a half smile. Anything more would have been iniquitous.

The homeless men, all but oblivious to their near brush with eternity, filed silently off the bus. All but one.

Father B looked into the furtive eyes of Kenny Burstyn. The thin boy looked away, knees tucked tight beneath his chin, sneakered feet on the seat, a rumpled paper sack clutched to his chest. He looked unwell. Too much time spent on the streets and in the arms of who knew what chemicals.

"Okay, Ken, last stop. Let's go see what Josie's got for us." He kept it light, his expression kind. *I'm here for you, kid. I'll go with you. Let's feed that gaunt haunt's frame of yours before it disappears between the grates of a sidewalk steam vent.*

Kenny's dirty fingers, nails chipped and chewed, scrabbled at the top of the paper sack. His head sagged, scabbed chin touching chest, only to snap back again. The lips were rimmed with a scummy film. Stubble grew from moist sores, flicked raw. In the midst of the ruin, hawk brown eyes with flecks of purest gold peered from bloodshot whites runny with the same upper respiratory trouble that leaked from the boy's nose.

*What's become of the barefoot farm boy who once laughed and played until survival became the only game? To survive to medicate and to medicate to survive.* It wasn't much, but it was what he knew about Kenny, what Kenny had told Father B in a more lucid moment.

One thing was certain, to earn and keep his coveted slot in the culinary program, Ken had to stay clean and sober for two months prior to and all during training. It cost Taste of Success a lot to shelter the trainees and $1,500 each to feed, transport, clothe, and provide medical services until they graduated. It was obvious from his smell and appearance that this rail of a gaunt-cheeked boy/man was not doing well and was blowing his only hope of escape.

"We'll get you some medical treatment once you've eaten, Ken, but you've got to want to break free. Ken?"

Through titanic effort, the boy focused on Father B's left cheek. A tear traveled down the side of a narrow nose, a clean streak in a storm-dirty sky. A small quavering voice said, "I wouldn't be with me if I were you. You don't know what's done this night."

Jabber by Shakespeare. Junkies were always babbling about something. "Nonsense. I want to make certain you get some dinner and a place to sleep. You've not been taking care of yourself and it's catching up to you."

The boy let Father B take his elbow and they moved toward the open door. "I t-told her it wouldn't go well. Why did she have to run me off like that?"

"Who, Ken, who do you mean?" They stepped onto the sidewalk and Kenny started to veer away. Father B took a firmer grip and guided him into the warmth and noise of the Mission.

The junkie's reply hardly registered, faint as it was. "She's the cause. She sent me away." He said more, but it was lost in the welcome of "Preacher man!" that boomed through the open window of the serving line.

They had entered a large room, big as a gymnasium. Folding tables covered the floor in long rows from one end of the room to the other. Green plastic tablecloths covered the secondhand

neglect, and around some of them the last of that night's homeless guests spooned and forked salad, a hot meal, and dessert
into hungry mouths.

Aproned waitstaff, once homeless themselves, cleared tables,
ferried stacked dishes into the dish room, put uneaten food
away, and made the dining hall clean and ready for breakfast the
following day. Hundreds of thousands of meals and many more
thousands of gallons of coffee, tea, and milk were served here
every year. Many of Father B's after-hours parishioners—street
people, colorful teenaged rebels, and those who fit in nowhere
else—would arrive for Midnight Church, bellies filled by sweet
Josie and her crew.

The aroma of a good, serviceable supper hung in the air. It
wasn't the gourmet fare at Taste, but then the Mission was more
concerned with plain stick-to-the-ribs cooking that helped a
man or woman or family consider the claims of the Christian
faith. For haute cuisine, see Taste.

"Preacher man!" Josie boomed again. She was a short, husky,
big-bosomed woman who had crushed more than one guest in
her ample arms. Even the more disruptive clientele suddenly
found their manners when squeezed in Josie's compassionate
embrace. "You cuttin' it mighty fine, Mr. Hellfire and Brim-
stone. You think just 'cause you got God's ear you can waltz in
here any ole time and Miss Josie'll just lay you a spread? Don't
be testin' me now! We don't take no MasterCard here!"

She wagged a plump finger under his nose, which he caught
and kissed. "Josie, dear, this is Kenny Burstyn. As you can see,
nutrition hasn't been Kenny's number one priority. I need you
to fatten him up. Please give him a dining companion who will
ensure he finishes every bite. Then maybe a visit to the infir-
mary. Can do?"

"Leon!" When Josie bellowed the name, a mountain of a man
emerged from the dish room, wiping hands as big as a catcher's
mitt on a damp half apron tied at the waist. He towered above

the other crew members, tightly muscled and sporting a head of imposing dreadlocks.

"You rang, Mother Jo?" Another boomer.

She reached up and patted Leon's cheek. "You know I did. Now this here's Kenny. You dish him up some kitties and puppies, a little of that bread puddin', and a big ole glass a whole milk. None a the 2 percent, y' hear? He needs all the percent he can get. Looks to me like those bones a his're just cryin' for their calcium!"

Father B noticed that during Josie's take-charge instructions to Leon, Kenny's sickly pallor had gone from pasty to chalk white. Now he clamped the precious sack to his chest as if in the hope it might ward off a vampire attack. "K-kitties? P-puppies?" The words came out in a croak.

She didn't laugh, but eyed the boy with kindness. Leon and Father B followed her lead. "You po' boy, it's just a down-home way of sayin' catfish and hush puppies." She patted his shoulder and Kenny cringed only a little. "Glad for you, Miss Josie's from the Big Easy. Southern cookin's her specialty!"

Kenny safely under Leon's wing, Father B gave Josie a hug. "Thanks, Jo. You're a good friend."

She gave him the skeptical once-over. "Before you go butterin' me up, there's someone I want *you* to meet, Preacher Man."

She led him down a short hall to a small side room. It contained a soda vending machine, a cherry red couch, two straight-backed chairs, and a pixie of a girl he guessed to be seven or eight years old. She was sitting on one of the chairs and wearing a lemon yellow top, lime green skirt, and purple plastic sandals. Short red hair, more chopped than cut, framed a merry face with Tinkerbell freckles and two tiny rhinestones in delicate earlobes. The probing dark eyes were far too serious for the made-for-play face.

"Becca, this here's the holy man I told you 'bout. You call him Father B and tell him what you want for Christmas. Your ma's soon done shoppin' them clothes." The good used clothing room was the next door down.

The little girl nodded and Josie left the room mouthing the words "good luck."

"I know a joke," the girl said. She swung her feet under the chair and gripped the sides of the seat with arms rigid.

"Oh, good, I like jokes." Father B published a parish newsletter called *The Sheep Skin: News for Ewes, Rams, and Lambs* that he liberally salted with funny bits and terrible puns. It helped ease the sting of life and kept the religious from terminal self-righteousness.

"There was this lady trying to get ketchup out of the bottle. She tried and tried, but it wouldn't come." Becca told the joke in a strange monotone, not at all like a child eager to make a grown-up laugh. It reminded Father B of a toy windup baby that parroted whatever it had been programmed to say.

"So the phone rings and this lady asks her four-year-old girl to go answer it." Becca swallowed twice before continuing. "The little girl goes, 'It's the minister, Mommy.' Her mommy frowns, so the little girl says into the phone, 'My mama can't come to the phone and talk to you right now. She's hitting the bottle.'"

Instead of laughing or looking at her visitor for his reaction, Becca just sat there, silent and disinterested. The toy baby had switched itself off.

Father B sat down in the other chair and forced a smile. What an odd choice of joke for one so young to tell a stranger upon first meeting. How little she had enjoyed telling it.

"Now I have one for you," he said. "What do you call a sleeping bull?"

He waited, but it didn't look like the girl was giving it a speck of thought. The feet swung, the hands gripped, the dark eyes probed a spot on the far wall.

"Give up?"

"Yeah."

"A bulldozer!"

Again he waited. Again in vain.

"Do you like riddles, Becca?"

"Yeah."

"Can you tell me one?"

"Okay." She stopped and clicked her tongue against the roof of her mouth, a mechanical jukebox searching for the requested record. "What do you call a line of dolls?"

Father B made an exaggerated show of thinking. "Hmm. That's a good one. I don't know. What *do* you call a line of dolls?"

"A barbecue."

He supposed it was a typical kid joke and wouldn't have given it a second thought if the punch line had been accompanied by snickers, wise looks, and maybe a "Get it? A Barbie queue, you know, a line of waiting Barbies?" or some such overkill. But no, just this odd rote telling without feeling, without personal investment of any kind.

"Ha!" He forced the reaction any half-pint comedian wanted, but suddenly he was imagining a naked Barbie doll roasting over an open fire and it didn't seem at all funny. *Snap out of it, Wills. She's just a little girl, not Carol Burnett, for Pete's sake.* Still, he had to be sure.

"Do you know any other jokes, Becca?"

"One, but I don't know if I should tell it."

He didn't know if she should either. But if she was reluctant to tell this one, maybe it was the one that would confirm the sick feeling growing in his gut. "Go ahead. I'll stop you if I think it's not one you should tell."

"Okay. I can prove that Adam and Eve had a perfect marriage."

Father B didn't like where the joke could go, but said nothing.

"You say, 'Go ahead, prove it.' Say that."

Father B swallowed. Twice. "Oh, okay. Go ahead, prove it."

In that familiar monotonous delivery, she said, "Adam didn't have to hear about all the men she could have married and Eve didn't have to hear about how well his mother cooked."

They were silent again. Laughter, even if he could have mustered a chuckle or two, didn't feel any more appropriate right then than the old joke told not by a grown-up, but by a Tinkerbell in yellow, lime green, and purple.

Father B cleared his throat. "Miss Josie said you would tell me what you want for Christmas. My, you do plan ahead." He managed a smile. It was at least two hundred or more shopping days until the blessed holiday.

"What do you mean?"

His hands felt clammy and his neck itched. He needed to get over to St. John's and prepare the elements for Communion. Why had Josie made him talk to this girl? "I mean, Christmas is seven months away and already you know what you want?"

"Yeah. Same thing I've always wanted for Christmas."

He wanted to shake her alive, to snap her out of this infuriating lethargy. He leaned forward, rested arms on thighs, and cupped hands together. Forcing calm into his voice, he said, "So tell me, Becca, what has a good little girl like you been wanting for so many Christmases?" He felt like a department store Santa about to hear all about bikes and games and cell phones with cool built-in cameras.

To his utter shock, she turned her head and looked straight at him. Her eyes brimmed with tears, her chin crinkled, and her mouth trembled with a terrible sadness. "I want a house and a room of my own. I want to quit changing schools every year, sometimes more." A sob tore from her. "I don't ever want bad men to beat my mommy up and steal her gas money again."

She stopped and again that vacant stare, though now wet with tears. When next she spoke, Father B had to lean in close to catch the words. "And I want my mommy to laugh again when I tell her my jokes."

He held out his arms and she crawled up into the safety of his heart. She wet his T-shirt through to the vest beneath and snotted on it and he didn't mind.

When at last her little body stopped heaving and she was quiet again, he smoothed her hair and patted her back.

From against his chest, he heard her say, "Father B, I like your shirt. Are you really a holy man?"

Now he was silent a time before the words would come. She waited.

"No, honey," he said at last, "but I want to be."


Who-whee, you is one scraggly, bony white boy." Leon watched Kenny put away a second plate of "kitties and puppies." He washed it down with a tall glass of whole milk.

With all the intervention going on, the drugs had worn off enough for Kenny's appetite to surface again. Kenny knew it wouldn't be long, though, before the appetite for more heroin superseded all other considerations. Then it would be all about feeding the need. Everything about him, every atom of his physiology, was hostage to the need.

He eyed Leon. The man obviously didn't use, not with a body by Adonis, but he might supply. What'd he have to lose?

He wiped bits of southern fried on a sleeve, looked around to ensure there were no other ears within listening range, and scooted closer to the big man along the bench of the cafeteria table.

Leon recoiled. "Man, you smell like what passes through a catfish. When's the last time you applied soap and water to that saggy butt o' yours?"

It was lost on Kenny. "Man, I need to score me some bull-dog, you know? You probably don't deal out of here, but you tell me when and where, and I can pay you top dollar. Say five full decks?"

Five fifteen-gram bags of heroin. This time Leon recoiled from the stench of Kenny's proposition. "Shut that talk, man. I'm done with Dr. Feelgood and all the stuff that comes with that stuff. You crazy freak, you might as well ram oil-soaked rags down your throat and light 'em on fire. Miss Josie don't allow no users in here. You best take what's left of your puny brain and drown it in the Bay. What's you got in that bag you so hot to protect anyway?"

Kenny shot to his feet and looked frantically around for an exit. While he'd shoveled food with one hand, he'd kept the paper sack clamped securely in the other. He knew he should have thrown it away or burned it, but the heroin whispered something else: "Keep it or they will find you and kill you." Only he could protect the sack.

"Whoa, man, easy does it." Leon's soothing words had the opposite effect. Kenny knew that sound—the sound of them disarming you, strip-searching you, convicting you, strapping you to a gurney, and giving you one last eternal fix. No, he'd done the world a service back there at the restaurant. He didn't deserve these words of soothing deceit. No, Kenny Burstyn deserved a medal, words of acclaim, a presidential commendation. So what if in ridding the world of a worse sinner he had snared a sure supply of euphoria? He just needed a little something to tide him over until the first delivery. Business. That's what drug deals were. Taking care of business.

"Now you just relax there, Kenny, my man." Leon circled the addict warily as if he might get bitten should he fail to take sufficient care. And still he spewed the soothing lies mass-produced by the system that said the Kennys of the world must comply. Kenny would not comply. He would gnaw off his own foot rather than wait in the trap until the Trapper came in for the kill.

At the periphery of his vision, Kenny saw them coming. The Trapper's apprentices. Closing in. Tightening the noose. Miss

Josie was back there. Big woman, bigger shadow. One appren-tice picked up a rolling pin, no doubt thinking he might beat the druggie's brains flat as crepes. And still Leon wouldn't shut up. "Be a hero, Kenny, end this now. We gonna get you the help you need. Miss Josie has lots of connections. Don't be a fool!"

"Ken, what on earth?" Father B, holding the hand of a pale little girl, entered the room. "Kenny! Stop and think. We can help you get clean. We'll get you back into the culinary-training program. You have my word."

Leon words. Josie words. Father B words. Too many words. And louder than them all, Cassie Dixon's words: "Kenny! You back away from there! You're out of the program—don't come back until you're clean!" She'd ruined his one chance to con-quer this thing. Well, he'd fixed her. Fixed her good.

Kenny lunged, grabbed the sixteen-ounce milk glass he'd just emptied, and smashed it against the end of the table. He was left with the weighted bottom of the glass bristling with wicked shards. Kenny brandished the broken glass in slicing arcs and the others jumped back. The limp paper sack was wadded and pinned in the claw of his other hand.

Sickness swept over him and a fever seized his mind and lungs. He glistened with sweat. Withdrawal. Bloody demons raked him with their teeth, embedded his flesh with their relentless fangs.

Sirens. *Approaching fast. Have to go. They can't have my sack. They get my sack, they'll know.*

He whirled, threw the sack hand around Josie's neck, and pressed the blades of glass against her carotid. She let out a whimper. "Back off!" he shouted. "Back off!" Leon and the crew dropped their arms at their sides. The rolling pin hit the floor with a *thunk*.

Shuffling backward, Kenny pulled Josie with him toward the door. "One scream, Miss Jo, and I will spill your blood all over that nice apron of yours." He stuck his head out the door, heard that the police were still several blocks over, and gave Josie a shove that sent her stumbling into Leon.

They gave chase, but powered by remembered heroin and a voracious hunger that knew but one food, Kenny proved surprisingly nimble and fleet of foot. Within seconds, he vanished into the accepting embrace of the streets.

# Chapter 5

*C*assie needed Nick.

Last night, by the time the police had completed their initial interrogation of everyone present at Celebrity Chef Night, the Pasta Fagioli and the wine had been sealed and removed to the CSI lab for analysis, and Taste had been festooned with yellow crime scene tape and locked tight for who knew how long.

Exhausted, she and Nick assembled the Taste board of directors, including Gordon O'Neal, who had caught the next flight back from San Diego. Little had been resolved.

Now Cassie grabbed a cab to El Paraiso where Chef Rita Gonzales allowed the culinary trainees to make and assemble meals for home delivery to low-income elderly and to prepare catered meals for weekend events around the city. In the face of Waverly's death, it was good work for everyone's peace of mind. The shut-ins looked forward to the tasty, nutritious food—and the cheery encouragement of the delivery team—highlights in their lonely existence.

Other celebrity chefs had called to offer their help. It was the only bright spot since Mrs. Waverly screamed, the cable snapped, and Cassie's stomach plummeted forty stories to the basement. The gourmet titans of the Golden Gate, bless their haughty hearts, had wasted no time circling their dessert carts.

Traffic was light this late in the morning. The cabbie whistled a snatch of something inappropriately jaunty. Inappropriate to her mood, that is. It was an otherwise sparkling spring day, much too light and fresh, considering what she knew. It should be a dark virulent day filled with angry thunderheads and evil portents.

She was again on the verge of tears. Why, when they were doing comfortably well as partners with good friend Mags O'Connor in Choice Brand Beautifiers, couldn't she and Nick be content? Why invite trouble volunteering on the tough side of the tracks?

Because they could make a difference. Couldn't they?

She rolled up the window, a shield against the bracing tang of salt air and the ocean shore's cry of gulls that were altogether too independent and unentangled.

Though a copy of that morning's *Chronicle* lay on the seat beside her, she couldn't bear to read of last night's tragedy. Just that quick, Taste had been cast into public relations hell and it would take a miracle to save the program. Nobody wanted to eat where the cuisine was so bad that corporate tycoons keeled over from food poisoning. Thankfully, Mark Butterfield, her ace troubleshooter at Choice Brand, was again on damage control.

Of course, it wasn't a food-borne illness. Not in the toxic, bacterial sense of the term. It took people hours to feel the full effects of a bad menu choice. And where was the vomiting and the diarrhea that preceded salmonella poisoning? No one dropped dead on the spot from bad meat.

Small comfort. For Trina's own self-confidence, Cassie had given her charge over the pot, but no way was Trina taking the fall for this disaster. It was Cassie's soup, her ground round, her tomatoes that Waverly had been eating at the time of his demise. *Why, God? Why am I cursed and a danger to others? First Azure World, now Taste. What do you want from me? To go live in the wastelands like a leper?*

Cassie needed Nick.

Dear funny Nick, who liked to quote Woody Allen's "The lion shall lay down with the lamb—but the lamb won't get any sleep." Strong, loyal Nick, who wouldn't divorce a wife on leprous grounds.

Comforting, practical Nick, who wouldn't recoil from her for thinking what she was thinking, which was too awful and un-Christian to think about.

They needed their Chinese bed-and-breakfast. That's when they ordered in too much moo shu pork, seafood fried rice, and curried prawns from Guandong Harbour and ate in bed. They fed one another with chopsticks and giggled like teenagers over the silly fortune cookie sayings Chef Handsome Fong always included with their order.

Cassie went first. "Man who run behind car get exhausted."

Nick's turn. "Woman who run in front of car get tired."

"Man who keep feet on ground have trouble putting on pants."

"Woman with one chopstick go hungry."

The best Chinese bed-and-breakfast was one where they never got around to the fortune cookies.

Cassie swiped angrily at a tear. She was not a weepy female. But it ate at her and no amount of covering it over with happy pillow talk would change a thing. The awful thought that moved into her mind was not about to be evicted by any other thought.

*I'd like to stick a fork in this taxi driver's whistle. Then we'd see just how jaunty he can be.*

It didn't work. Even another awful thought was not awful enough to supplant the ugly squatter already in residence.

And before she knew it, the first squatter had been joined by an equally ugly second and they were two festering boils sharing the same space.

At least the second was not a new thought; it just hadn't been full-blown until now. But all day yesterday, it had flitted about and pecked away at her conscience, trying like a nagging child to get her to scream its name.

Well, now she could. *Kenny Burstyn killed James Waverly. To make good on his threats to me. He hung around until he spotted his chance and put something in Waverly's soup as revenge for getting kicked out of the program. His mind is so riddled with holes punched by the drugs, he thinks ruining it for everyone will make up for all he's lost.*

She hadn't been that blunt to Lieutenant Lloyd Reynolds from the homicide division of the San Francisco Police Department. The same Lieutenant Reynolds who had investigated the deadly events surrounding the fragrance scandal that put Azure World six feet under. For the first five minutes of the Waverly interrogation, Reynolds couldn't stop looking at Cassie and shaking his head. He probably thought she was a serial killer.

She hadn't been that blunt because she had so far heard no one but the voice in her head use the word *murder*. She had mentioned to the lieutenant the trouble with Kenny, his proximity to the Fagioli more than once during the day, and the strange brown bag he kept so tightly clutched to his person. But not her darker concerns. Let the police make of it what they would. She wanted to rid herself of the societal prejudices that said all homeless people were weak, predatory losers who could easily get off the streets if they chose to. Or that what they chose to do was to mooch off those who had homes and worked hard for their money.

How much of her suspicion was based on these stereotypes? Far more murders were perpetrated by tax-paying, gainfully employed citizens with checkbooks and library cards.

"*Please* stop whistling."

The cabbie looked in the rearview mirror and shrugged. "Suit yourself, ma'am."

The sudden quiet was too quiet. It reminded her of the bargain comedian they'd hired for the grand opening of Taste and the uncomfortable silence that followed his attempted humor. "If it weren't for the foghorns in the bay, I'd have no social life at all." Not many laughs, but oh so affordable. She couldn't even remember the comic's name.

Father B, now there was a warm, funny man. And far too busy for one person. She wished he'd slow down. His no-show for the graduation ceremony hadn't really surprised her. She should have asked Pastor Fitzgerald from Hope Community Chapel.

Any ordained clergyman would have been qualified to bring both benediction and prayer for the dead.

As soon as Father B saw the morning paper, he'd call her cell phone.

And that brought her back to the first ugly squatter in her head. "Wanted: Ordained priest with extensive experience in successful exorcisms to dislodge a giant tick in my brain the size of Texas." All right. She'd say it. See if it just sat there in the front passenger seat sneering at her or, once exposed, threw itself under the taxi's wheels.

"I'm glad James Waverly is dead."

She hadn't meant to say it aloud.

"Pardon, ma'am?"

"No, nothing. Please let me out at the next corner. I've decided to walk from here." The air would do her good.

The cabbie's disembodied eyes viewed her with suspicion from the rearview mirror. Had he heard what she'd said about Waverly? Savvy cabbies were students of human nature. They put two and two together before most people even realized that it was a question of math.

At least she had just a two-hour shift at El Paraiso. Nick would meet her there and after the shift they would lunch at Ensign Baldy's at Fisherman's Wharf. Later in the afternoon, they might go into the office and work on the booth for the International Fragrance Formulators trade show. Nothing too far afield. Lieutenant Reynolds wanted them available for further questioning once the lab results were in.

She paid the fare, sat on a bus bench to collect her thoughts, and watched the Yellow Cab screech around the corner in search of other occupants who didn't talk crazy or mind a cheery whistle.

*How can the death of a man with a wife and children and such grand aspirations make me happy? Especially one who regularly pays—paid—the bills for something as good as Taste?*

A seagull sailed down to the pavement and pecked at the remains of someone's breakfast bagel. Swiftly joined by four more gulls, the first to the trough flew at two of the opportunists in an ill-timed move that left its meal exposed. The two remaining feathered thugs divided the spoils and flapped seaward, beaks full, leaving their victim to squawk forlornly over its loss.

"That's how it is in the naked city." Cassie started walking. "There are the hunters and the hunted."

She couldn't help it. Morose was just the right mood to be in. Jim Waverly was a law unto himself and proof again and again that if you hired enough lawyers you could erect a barrier of litigation to keep you out of prison for life. In your place, jail cells fast filled with the poor and the exploited who couldn't afford to make bail and whose worldly possessions fit in a shopping cart or a brown paper sack. They have Jesus, their advocate and high priest, Father B would remind her. They also had the Jim Waverlys who were not above surrounding themselves with poster children whom they would never stoop to touch.

*I'd better call Father B for a pastoral tune-up, have him remind me again there's power in the blood of Jesus.* She didn't like herself like this.

Her appreciation of Waverly had hit zero when Trina told her how he had harassed her. It was one thing for him to come on to Cassie, which he had done on two occasions, quite another for him to sexually harass a young woman with little or no way to prevent it.

When Cassie had threatened to report him after the first time, Waverly had urged her to try. "Someone with your lack of credibility will be laughed out of town should you be so foolish to come up against me." He had her cornered in the hall to the bathrooms at Taste. Then he leaned over her, breath heavy with garlic and sausage, and said, "Actually, if we took the time right now to get to know each other a little better, I think you'd be amazed at how much we really have in common."

She barely resisted kneeing him in the groin. Instead, she looked him in the eye. "You are pathetic. Your wife works so hard to buff your public image when what she ought to do is expose you for the lech you are." She went home early.

Cassie didn't tell Nick because he might have done something about Waverly that would have gotten him arrested. She didn't tell him the second time either, because it might have caused Taste's funding to dry up and blow away.

After six months of Celebrity Chef Nights, the word was out in the city and the reservations phone consistently rang off the hook. One Thursday night, Chef Blake Patterson of Cormier's was working his magic with steak and portobello mushrooms, and Waverly and his entourage was ensconced at the usual tables. Supposedly at the request of Laura Waverly, Cassie was summoned.

The Waverly party was well into the Napa Valley Merlot and greeted her with jovial *bon ami*. "Cassandra." Laura's voice was a throaty alto. "I can't tell you how pleased I am with everything about Taste. I do so admire you for picking up the pieces and soldiering on. It can't have been easy."

Laura deserved Cassie's pity more than Cassie needed Laura's, but Cassie chose not to put too fine a point on her reply. "We are very fortunate to have Choice Brand doing better than market expectations and to be able to champion a cause as deserving as the students of the Taste program. I'm pleased that you see the good in it. We certainly value your support."

James Waverly, nose red as a navigation beacon, stopped in midconversation with a smartly dressed male consort and spoke too loudly. "Support? Lord love a lizard, little lady, is that what you call what I do for this place? *Support?* I bloody built this dump into a showplace and I can tear it down if I so choose. Not support. No, no, I'm the bloody blood supply!"

Laura tried to shush her husband and redirect his attention, but he roughly cast her aside. He dismissed Cassie toward the kitchen. "Bring me a custard, cutie. In fact, bring me a dozen cuties ... I mean cussers ... oh, my head ... " He slumped against his wife, taking a yard of tablecloth with him. Though she had seen it in the movies, Cassie started when Laura Waverly picked up her water glass and unceremoniously dumped it, ice and all, in the face of her inebriated man. He spluttered and flailed and his wife asked for coffee. One look at Laura's hot, distressed face and Cassie brought two pots and enough cups for the whole lot. She felt sorry for any wife of Jim Waverly—scuttlebutt said he'd had three or four—and the cross she had to bear.

A half hour later, the sheepish tycoon had motioned her over. "The wife informs me that I have behaved badly. For that I apologize. A little token of my regret." He handed her a napkin. Tucked inside was a hundred-dollar bill and a lewd drawing of two grappling stick figures.

The electronics CEO wore an angelic smile, daring her to react. With forced calm, she folded the napkin, money still inside, and stuck the whole wad in his coffee cup, where it soaked up the contents quick as a lamp wick. "No, thank you. Your having come and left is payment enough."

She was halfway to the kitchen before she heard Waverly let out a roar of laughter. "Now there's a gal with spunk!"

She shuddered despite the balmy day. There was a poisoner loose in the city. "You can't drain the swamp of all the bad guys." Nick's caution rang in her ears. "They just live in the muck at the bottom until the rains return."

She couldn't wait to see him, needed his John Wayne imperturbability. Of course, when it came down to it, he could be as volatile as the Duke's movie persona.

Nick had his angry streak. The don't-mess-with-me-or-mine John Wayne. It both endeared and infuriated. Right now, she needed the security of his strong arms.

A cloud crossed the sun and the day dimmed. Cassie dodged a delivery van and ran to the El Paraiso side of the street. She'd hoped he'd be leaning against the restaurant wall, give a mock wolf whistle, and invite her over for a friendly hello. He would roll his eyes suggestively like the big ham he was and greet her with a big hug and warm lips.

A burst of wind gusted from nowhere. Dust and fast-food wrappers swirled across her path. Fur matted with crankcase oil, a smoky gray alley cat slunk from beneath a battered Fairlane parked at the curb. The car was filled to the roofline with clothing, black plastic garbage bags, and newspapers.

Ears flattened to its skull, the cat gave a silent hiss and disappeared into the weeds.

Not a creature stirred outside El Paraiso. Of course not. Nick was at his post rolling enchiladas or assembling quesadillas. Disappointment jabbed, then apprehension. *I'm being silly.*

She was late, that's all. The rest of the crew probably was inside at work, the no-nonsense Rita Gonzales cracking the whip. In a half hour, the lunch crowd would begin to arrive and the kitchen would be busier than "burros and bees," as Rita liked to say.

Cassie glanced into the adjacent alley, but no vehicles approached. *I hope Rita makes her special corn cake with sweet milk and tomato salsa. Smeared with butter, drizzled in honey ...*

Something rattled down the sidewalk behind her. She quickened her pace, heart thudding.

Reptile-quick, an arm encircled her throat. She fought the arm, fought being dragged to the ground. She wanted to scream, but could not, wanted to kick or gouge a hole in the attacker, but could not see him. A backward jerk closed off her airway, rough jacket cloth abrading bare skin. She thudded against a moving body that, like the snaking arm, was all wire and bone.

Nick felt the tire go flat and pulled to the curb. He groaned. Still two miles from the restaurant. He could change the tire as fast as he could jog there.

He had the number of the El Paraiso on speed dial and punched the button. The Taste board members were understandably panicked over the Waverly death, and Chairman Gordon O'Neal wanted to meet with Nick and Cassie later that afternoon. Most of the board were involved in the corporate world and well knew the fragile nature of the public trust. Of course, they would cooperate fully with the police, but they wanted a plan of action to counteract the negative publicity already circulating. What remained unsaid, but was clear from their pointed questions of Nick, was that the Dixons knew more than a little about negative publicity.

On the other end of the cell call, someone picked up, and the loud bang and clatter of a kitchen running at high speed made it hard to hear.

"Hola?"

"Rita?"

"Si, is you, Neek?" Rita had always called him "Neek" from the day they'd met, even though he suspected she could shore up the single syllable if she wanted to. Despite her degrees in the culinary arts and numerous awards for outstanding cuisine, it was sometimes best for business to lay on the Hollywood Spanglish.

"It's me. Sorry to say, I just got a flat tire and will be another twenty, thirty minutes at least. Can I talk to Cass?"

"She no here." Rita sounded harried. "*Bueno*. She need rest. You tell her take life easy. I so sorry how it go last night."

A slight tremor of worry prickled across the top of Nick's scalp, but he suppressed it. *Cass is strong. Lives a full life. Has survived worse than this. A lot worse. She's fine. Running a little behind is all.*

The way Waverly lived, he could have dropped dead at a medical convention. A fluke. Simple as that. The medical examiner would reveal the obvious and they could all get back to business.

"Work's the best thing for her, Rita. Always has been. When you see her, please let her know I'm not far behind."

He closed his cell, debated whether to call road service, decided the wait would be longer than the fix, and went around to the trunk of the KIA Amanti and removed the needed tools along with the spare tire.

The problem was with the left rear tire, fortunately, and he had plenty of room to maneuver.

The Dixon newlyweds had suffered a flat on the way to the airport for the flight to Cabo and their honeymoon more than twenty years before. The day was hot. The limo driver waited for road service while the honeymooners waded in the marshy ditch. They splashed each other, threw muddy things, and laughed at nothing and everything. Back in the limo—smeared, barefoot, and flushed with promise—they became dangerously overheated until Cassie grabbed a bottle of sparkling cider from the minibar, shook it, and sprayed him in the face. He returned the favor and, for the second time that day, they had happily disgraced themselves. They required a complete change out of soggy clothes in the airport restrooms.

Nick grinned and loosened the lug nuts slightly before jacking the wheel higher. *Love makes fools of us all.*

The first, and more monumental disgrace, had occurred at the reception buffet table en route to the Cutting of the Cake.

"You danced like a dervish." Her teasing excited him. "Did you even know I was in the room?"

"*In* the room?" He leered at her. "You *were* the room. No one would pay me any attention unless I distinguished myself."

She blushed at the compliment. The pearl white satin wedding dress with lacy empire waist and French lace sleeves was a work of art. Tiny pearls graced her upswept bouffant and a necklace of pearls accented the fawn brown of a perfect tan. The collective gasp of the witnesses at her grand entrance was for her beauty. Her parents wept openly at first sight of their only child now so obviously and artfully a woman.

And thus ensued the formal, predictable, clichéd wedding-by-the-numbers portrayed in a thousand movies. Her mother had wanted a lovely traditional ceremony and she got an unassailably lovely and undeniably traditional result.

Then a couple of "I do's," a blizzard of photos, and a dozen dances later, the bride paused at the chips and salsa, selected a suitably shaped chip, and scooped it into a deep pool of her mother's extra chunky, extra tomatoey secret recipe. Nick saw something else in his new wife's sparkling nothing-can-stop-us-now expression—a current of madness seizing control, a madness that said, "We are the only two people in the world and I'm about to do something that will set this day apart from all others and you will love me for it."

And she nailed him with the salsa right in the middle of his snow-white tux shirt.

The generous splat of red tomatoes, green chilies, and even greener jalapeno peppers bled ruby red all the way down to the burgundy cummerbund.

Around them, figures moved in slow motion and turned in their direction. From somewhere a cry of warning pierced the band's rowdy rendition of "Ain't Misbehavin'." Someone exited the men's room, then turned back and shouted "Food fight!" to those still inside.

Nick's initial shock quickly caved to the creeping madness. Like jungle fever it entered his bloodstream and commandeered his right arm. With one deft move, his hand grabbed a large chip, dredged up Mexico's finest, and let fly.

The salvo struck Cassie just above the breastbone and drained into the bodice of the wedding gown. She released a loaded chip from each of her exquisitely manicured hands and turned the groom's shirt into a war zone.

The battle was joined.

With shrieks of laughter and disbelief from combatants and spectators alike, salsa rained down on Mr. and Mrs. Nicholas Dixon. The balding wedding photographer, Nick's cousin Louie, risked life and limb to capture the blow-by-blow. By the time Cassie's mother arrived, countenance dark as the Grim Reaper's, the salsa bowl was half empty, the white walls of the corridor connecting sanctuary and fellowship hall required repainting, and the wedding bill ballooned.

Abigail Seton could not take her eyes off the ruin that was her daughter's wedding dress. Though Cassie was sweaty, sticky, and grinning like a court jester, her torso belonged to the miraculous survivor of an inept firing squad. Her father had left the room, having no stomach for either the prank or its aftermath. For certain, any future daughter of Cassie's, on her wedding day, would not be wearing the "something old" pearl white gown, now "something stained" with countless red accents.

Cassie knew that at that moment her mother would have annulled the Dixon marriage in a heartbeat. Hers could be a conditional love. It was partly that knowledge, at least subconsciously, that had compelled Cassie to behave so badly, to risk being shunned. She wanted her parents to love her and Nick "for better or worse" just as the newlyweds had pledged to do for each other.

And she was right. Nick had loved her for it. They kept a special album just of Cousin Louie's food-fight photos and agreed to show it to Beth one day—after she was safely married.

Mop and bucket were found and order restored to the buffet, but Cassie's mother never did forgive either of them for "the incident." Convinced that he had instigated the disgraceful carnage, Mom Seton took nearly two years before again warming up to her son-in-law and making him a home-cooked meal.

Nick laughed out loud and removed the flat tire from its axle. Their actions had been foolish and insensitive and difficult to live down. But at the time . . .

*Ah, there's the culprit.* A large sheet-metal screw, common enough in this industrial section of town, imbedded to the head. He reached for the spare tire and seated it firmly into place.

He smiled again. Sweet Cass. They'd clear up this Waverly mess. She meant everything to him.

She fought for oxygen, to remain upright, lost a shoe, beat, slapped, and tore at the arm with its covering of coarse cloth.

Pepper spray. Left pocket. Reach.

Can't reach. Need air.

No air.

"Earthy Mexican Cuisine. Bold. Unforgettable." Brick. Masonry. Dumpster. Flashes of brown red fading to black.

Arm slackened. Rush of air. Sweet God, air. "Ixtapa-style cuisine. Reservations Required."

Sour stink of unwashed flesh. Raspy grunts.

Reach. *Reach!*

Tight again. Vice tight. No feeling in hands. Lost pocket. Can't swallow. Unconscious. Darker now. No. *No!*

A weed. Growing. Second-story window ledge. Focus on the weed. Clutch to life. A crack. Cling. Dirt. Life.

"You want it so bad, lady, I'm gonna give it to you." Hot, stinking breath. In her ear. In her brain.

That voice.

*Him!*

Arm wrenched behind and up. Pain. Rough. Grating. Cheek against wall. Face to brick. *Behind* her. Pressing. Dominating. *Behind.*

Revenge.

*"No! God, no!"*

Suck air. Scream. Can't ... can't breathe ...

"No? *No?!*" Lips hard in her ear. Rubbery. Wetting her hair. Forcing against her. Urgent. "Not this time, Cass Dixon! You don't order me. You're not the boss. Not now. *Not ever!*"

Burning. Shoulder on fire. Arm breaking? Stop. Stop it!

"Hurts me, Kenny. Please. Stop."

"Shut up! Just shut your face and don't say my name! Don't ever say my name! You're gonna listen to me for once. You think you know so much, but you don't know nothin'! That's why I'm gonna give it to you, lady, and you're gonna take it. You'll see what a man I am to do what I'm gonna do. Hear me? Say anything and you'll be sorry. Just take it and it'll be over."

She stared into the brick. At an ant inches away. Waited for the horror. *Oh, God, Beth, Nick ... love you ...*

As suddenly as it had come, the weight lifted and with it, the pain. Air flooded her lungs. Feeling returned. Wire and bone uncoiled.

"Are you deaf?! Turn around and take it before I lose my nerve!"

Can't be happening. Can't.

Slowly, wincing at a thousand needles jabbing her arm from paralysis, she turned to face her abductor.

Inches from her now, at the end of a lanky arm, a gaunt fist held a crumpled brown paper bag.

She did nothing but breathe. He cursed. "Take it!"

Cassie put out a shaky hand and closed on the bag. Their fingers touched, his icy cold and pale as death.

He twitched. Eyes blinked. Nose ran. Lips jumped. Sweaty. Thin. Pale. So pale that in the right light, she thought it possible to stare right through him.

He was drained as if a vampire had gotten to him first.

He shuddered so violently that in her fear, she thought he might disconnect from all his joints and become a small, insignificant pile of discarded limbs.

For one lucid moment, a shadow sped across his face and sick, watery eyes may have contained tears of regret. "You don't see me, Dixie." The detested nickname he used to ridicule for once contained no contempt. "Not unless I shout at you. Make you pay attention. You think all I am is a hopped-up junkie. Troublemaker. Maybe that's all Ken is, but maybe if you hadn't run me off like you did, I could have shown you. I was gonna give you the bag yesterday. Before the trouble. I was. But all you wanted was me out. So I delivered the stuff. I got me thirty bucks and what was done with the delivery is another's to say."

Her mind crawled slug slow. What is he saying? Is it important or drug babble? "I ... I'm sorry if ... you know, if ... "

He kicked at the ground. She jumped. "Sorry would have been good couple a weeks ago, lady." Kenny chewed the stub of a nail, dirty and ragged. He started to back away. "No good now. You're a prayer woman. I heard you pray grace. Try a prayer for Ken. Tell Nick he should watch you better."

He turned, hesitated as if unsure where he was, and jerked from the alley at a shambling gait.

Someone came out the side door of the El Paraiso and heaved a plastic garbage bag into the Dumpster.

She thought she heard her name.

*Help ...*

Running feet. Strong hands pulled her up. Strong arms carried her into the moist warmth of Old Mexico, a can of unused pepper spray clutched in one hand.

*When ... when did I fall to the ground? Yesterday? Years ago?*
"Nick?"

# Chapter 6

It was late afternoon, and Cody Ferguson stole another glance at the gorgeous girl driving the Miata.

It was his ninth appreciative take on her since Beth Dixon had picked him up in the sporty ride that was her jewel. Even when her parents had suffered their fall from the heights of fashion fragrance, they insisted she keep the car despite the family's sudden move to shakier financial ground. It was paid for and their daughter's one real material splash. After spending three weeks in Honduras caring for orphans, teaching them loud praise songs and building them up as God's children, Beth had returned a changed person. She'd held a yard sale and sold a lot of her possessions. The money went to the Mission. She shopped a lot less.

The Miata and its twenty-four-carat shine remained. It was now less a symbol of wealth and more a bright reflection of Beth's own personality. She wanted to discover God's shine in people and help them see it too. After graduation, she planned to apply to one of those Mercy ships that sailed the world's oceans, spreading compassion and healing in every port.

But for this super sunny day, Cody and his best friend were dressed in tuxedo and gown. All grins and glamour, they were on their way to not one, but two proms. He'd managed without drawing blood to pin her with a midnight blue rose corsage to match her dress. She had returned the favor with a crimson rose boutonniere and made him blush by telling him the hybrid was named Passion Prince. In the outdoor digital photos taken by her dad, Cody's red face and the rose looked as if they'd come fresh from the same florist.

"They're going to be so excited to see us!" Beth glowed. "The looks on their faces ... " She turned in at the familiar address, negotiated the curved driveway, and parked the car at the front entrance.

"Here we are." Cody opened his door. He went around to open hers and bowed low. "Welcome to Cinderella's Castle!"

The sign on the wall beside the automatic sliding double doors read: "Fairview Senior Community."

Beth popped the trunk and piled Cody's arms full of shiny white boxes, each bearing the name of "Fran's Floral" in forest green script.

Beth stepped back to appraise Cody and smiled. "Perfect. Special delivery by a hunk in a tuxedo. Does it get any classier than that?"

Cody's face flushed and he thought again how gorgeous she was. Hair all upswept. Skin golden with California sun. Eyes alive with laughter and promise. The gap was two and a half years between their ages—he would turn sixteen at the end of summer, she had recently celebrated her eighteenth at Disney's Space Mountain, her favorite amusement ride. She had clung to him in the dark and they screamed like lunatics. He loved that she was strong and cared little about the difference in their ages or his deafness. She preferred his company to the males in her own class, whom she found superficial and too concerned with how much more money they could make by going to the right college.

Still, they were a kiss away from their first kiss.

He wondered if they ever would. What they had would never amount to more than just buddies, what with her going off on the high seas and all, but a guy could dream.

"Who-whee! You two fall off a wedding cake?" The wheezy greeting from across the wide atrium came from a razor-thin gentleman in mashed golf hat and tan sweater, a cane in each hand.

"Hey, Charlie, how's your swing?"

Cody saw where Beth was looking and guessed she had delivered a greeting in a voice loud enough to penetrate the old man's impressive array of hearing hardware.

"Let's just say I could tango circles around you, toots."

Cody laughed. He could read lips like a pro, and he liked the man's spirit despite his failing abilities. Given enough time, Charlie Monahan could maybe meet you out front before he forgot where he was going or why. Under no circumstances should he be challenged to a game of chess. Not unless you could spend the night.

"They're in the dayroom, giddy as peahens." Charlie waved a cane at the hall behind that led to one of the community's large and airy gathering places. "A couple of 'em got dates, don't ask me how. The gals gussied up like dance hall tarts, pardon my French. They're wearing enough pancake batter to make a tall stack at Aunt Bea's Diner."

The crotchety talk was just Charlie's way. There was a spark in the man's eye, if not a spring in his shuffling step. This was an occasion. All the seniors had been invited, and though most would decline, at the very least the novel idea had piqued memories of the good old days when they had hair and hormones and future hopes. Short-term memories were fading fast, but oh those long-term recollections.

Heads turned in their direction from a big-screen TV, a game of Chinese checkers, and three or four ornate armchairs that dwarfed the tiny old people sitting in them. Dimming eyes sparked with interest, gray heads nodded, and nurses at the front desk stopped in their rounds to grin and watch.

At the entrance to the dayroom, Beth took Cody's arm and they swept in with exaggerated steps like royalty. At least, as much like royalty as possible with an armload of flower boxes threatening to tumble.

Ten people—eight women, two men—sat in wheelchairs at a large table meant for board games and jigsaw puzzles, dressed in their best. The room reeked of gardenia, rose, and lilac water with a strong after-scent of Old Spice and Aqua Velva. Lipstick in bold colors liberally applied reestablished the lost boundaries of faded lips. Nails were accented to match. Aging figures bloomed again in fashions popular well before the birth of rock 'n' roll—large print florals, lace collars, fur wraps, neckties flopping with hand-painted fish.

Cody set the flower boxes on the table. He held Beth's hand as she gave an abbreviated curtsy. He followed with a deep bow.

"You two look fine!" Alice Platz gave Cody's tux sleeve a tug and winked.

"Hey!" Albert Crenshaw wagged a crooked finger. "You back off there, sonny buck. Ally's *my* date."

"Al, you old fraud, you haven't paid me any attention since the last space shuttle launched and now you own me?" Alice winked again. Her mascara was a little off and one eyebrow was slightly higher than the other, but the nylon stockings and new strappy heels she wore said she was born to dance. Even her wheelchair matched Al's with red plastic streamers flying from the handlebars.

Cody hugged her. Alice and Al and the others were full of great stories and deep regrets. He and Beth had been visiting them at Fairview off and on during the year. Mrs. Dixon had set it up. Some of the old folks had older adult kids lost on the streets of San Francisco; others just enjoyed getting out now and then to Celebrity Chef Night at Taste. When he learned that these ten had never experienced the prom—some unable to afford it at the time, others having dropped out of high school, a couple of them too shy in their youth to say yes to a member of the opposite sex—Cody suggested to Beth that they throw them their own prom. She loved the idea. They scheduled it for afternoon, enough time for Beth and Cody to make their prom at Ocean View High later that evening.

"Welcome to the Fairview Senior Prom. Our theme this year is 'Tropicana Sunset'!" Cody produced a paper party parrot in pineapple and orange feathers from one inside pocket, jumped onto an empty chair, and suspended it from the chandelier. From the other pocket, he drew a paper fuchsia and yellow sun, fanned it full, and placed it in the center of the table.

"Imagine yourselves on a white sand beach in Jamaica." Beth swayed to an imaginary Caribbean rhythm. "Waves lapping, soft breezes blowing, palm trees rustling, the sound of a steel drum playing 'The Girl from Ipanema'—"

"The ka-ching of my hotel bill rising, ever rising." The quip belonged to Tommy Lee, a long-limbed giant in brown high-water slacks and a checked sport coat of butterscotch and white.

"The inability to tell if that pinging noise is the smoke detector in need of a battery change or my pacemaker on the fritz." Al grabbed his heart for dramatic effect. His jowly face was as unchangeable as Huckleberry Hound's.

"Hush, you two!" Edith Bradshaw's entire body scolded. She was a round, big-boned woman and Tommy's date. "I want to hear the steel drum." She waved for quiet and cupped a hand to her wrinkled ear. She wore a chef's salad of a hat, covered in plastic flowers, artificial birds, and a feather-and-reed weaving that, now empty, might once have been a nest.

Al made the international sign for "cuckoo" and Edith back-handed him good-naturedly.

Beth's smile was radiant. She knew how much a night like this meant to people who rarely received visitors and whose childhoods had been scarred by unrelenting hard work and deprivation. With wide gestures she directed their attention to Cody, who had faded back toward the archway to the kitchen. "And now, ladies and gentlemen, live from the Montego Bay

Showroom, give it up for the Sultan of Swoon, your Master of Melody, the incomparable Cody William Ferguson!"

Cody stopped, back to them, and threw his chin onto one shoulder. With a candle for a microphone, voice a cross between Wayne Newton and Willie Nelson on a bad day, he launched into an emotion-wringing rendition of "Red Roses for a Blue Lady."

" ... your best white orchid for her wedding gown!" At the song's conclusion, the seniors erupted in applause, broad smiles, and cries of "Encore!"

"Before the next song and an all-dance number, it's corsage time!" Amidst excited chatter and exclamations of delight, Beth and Cody moved among their friends and helped them add the carnations and rose boutonnieres to their finery.

"I'm too fancified." Al frowned. "I was a dock foreman before I took over at Amalgamated Crane and Gantry. I swore you wouldn't catch me dead in a flower until I *was* dead."

"Put a cork in it, Al," Tommy said, "or you will be. Gangsters wear flowers, so take it from me, you fit right in."

"Speaking of gangsters ..." Cora Scheidemann, hands bird-like and knotted with arthritis, leaned forward in her wheel-chair. At the same time, her twin sister, Dora, leaned forward in her wheelchair. She said little, allowing Cora to do much of the talking for them both. The spinsters, one right-handed, one left-handed, mirrored one another much of the time. "I see in the papers"—Cora fished the front page of the morning *Chronicle* up from the seat of her chair and held it high for everyone to see—"where Jim Bob Waverly died unexpectedly. Wasn't that pirate a friend of yours, Albert?"

Al refused to look at her. He mumbled a reply. "We were passing acquaintances is all. Same neighborhood as kids. Same bus to school. Like that." His face clouded over, made darker by bushy white eyebrows and a head of snow-white hair.

Tommy gave Gwendolyn Parks a knowing look and Gwendolyn passed it on to Barbara Shapiro, who said, "We all know you did business with Weasel Waverly, Al. If there was shame in that, half the city would have to hang their guilty heads."

Alice took her date's bear paw of a hand in hers. "Shush now. The kids worked hard on this." Al took back his hand.

Beth motioned to Cody to get singing. The mood was rapidly turning somber.

Jaw set, eyes filled with smoldering resentment, Al glared. "The business we did is none of your business, Barbie, you old snoop! Waverly got what he deserved after how he treated my father like dirt. Too bad it came thirty-five years too late for the old man to dance on that goon's grave!"

Gamely, Cody belted a spirited version of "My Little Grass Shack," complete with hula. Beth motioned frantically to a woman peeking through the glass window in the swinging door to the kitchen. In swept four servers with a sheet cake and plates, two trays of fruity pink drinks with skewers of fruit chunks and little pastel parasols, and two bowls of assorted nuts.

The writing in icing on the cake read: "Tropicana Sunsat Senior Prom, Memories Are Made of This!" The cake was a tropical rainbow of colors, misspelling and all.

Cody finished to a smattering of applause. Everyone looked angry. Gwendolyn, a tidy woman in a gray suit, tissues stuffed in the sleeves, wanted badly to say something. She was a peacemaker, so Beth urged her to speak up.

"All right then." Gwendolyn's voice was silky calm. "Nuts don't agree with my intestinal tract and they get stuck in Dora's dentures. Or is it Cora's? Can we send them back for some of those little butter mints? They come in pastels."

"Thank you, Gwen, for that practical reminder." Beth gave Cody a panicked sign to punch the boom box on switch.

Instantly, Barry Manilow bounded into the room to croon about the "Copacabana."

With a sigh of relief, Beth watched Tommy and Edith move slowly onto the "dance floor" between tables, followed by three of the single women. Though most could do little more than scoot their chairs a few inches one way, then the other with their feet, the seniors maneuvered as best they could to the music. Alice looped an arm through Al's, but the stormy-faced man refused to dance. She finally coaxed him into sharing a slice of cake.

"Whew!" Cody pulled Beth off to the side. "What has Al in a twist?"

Beth took the glass of fruit drink he offered and enjoyed the cool smoothness on her dry throat. "Apparently there's some history where Al and Mr. Waverly are concerned. I don't know much more than you, and you were there last night when Mr. Waverly collapsed. What happened?"

Cody shook his head. "One minute Jorge's pouring his heart out in gratitude to everyone who made his dream come true, the next thing I know Mr. W. gasps a little, grabs his chest, and smashes face-first into the soup. It was crazy for a good half hour while your mom and the staff tried to keep anyone from leaving. No easy trick when there's a dead guy in the room. Your dad and that arrogant Mr. Peugeot kept up CPR the whole time until the paramedics arrived. It didn't do any good. It was awful. Naturally, everybody's a suspect, including your parents, even the two Smith brats who are barely old enough to tie their own shoes. Even me."

At a metallic clank behind them, they turned in time to see a grim-faced Alice back up, give her platinum wig an adjusting tug, and again ram her chair into Al's.

"You old harpy!" Al leaned away from the collision. "You drive like a screwball. Hit me again and I'll sue for reckless endangerment!"

"I'd like to see you try!" The usual tremor in Alice's limbs was now a full-blown case of the shakes. "You can be a miserable old coot if you choose, but don't think for a minute you're going to drag me down with you!"

Beth cringed. Those two liked each other, but you'd never know it from the way they argued about everything. Al must have put his foot in it yet again.

"Shrew!"

"Ingrate!"

Most of the others looked annoyed. Tommy leaned forward as if eager to have a ringside seat. Only Cora looked genuinely distressed. Dora patted her arm.

"Loon!"

"Jackal!"

The two combatants glared at one another. Tommy rubbed his hands together and made knowing eyes at the other partiers. "I say we have the wedding right now. We've got the dressy duds, the cake, the flowers, the witnesses. Get Frankie in here. He's a retired minister."

"Yeah, Church of the Divine Doohickey." Barbara stiffened her back. "Remember when he gave that sermon on sand? Edith had to be revived and I had to be sedated!"

When it was clear that Alice was backing up for another run at Albert, Cody stepped in front of her. He leaned over and grasped the arms of the wheelchair.

" 'To live is like to love.' " Cody looked deep into Alice's fiery eyes. " 'All reason is against it, and all healthy instinct for it.' "

Beth watched the woman's gray eyes moisten and a dawning recognition replace aggravation. Her age-spotted hands unclenched from the wheels and fluttered at the soft yellow scarf about her neck. "Samuel Butler." She said it in the breathy way of a young woman for whom romance was as yet untried.

Cody smiled. "'Tis better to have loved and lost than never to have lost at all."

The soft violin strains of "Moonlight Sonata" floated over from the boom box. "Alice Platz?" Cody's gaze never left hers. "May I have the honor of this dance?"

She looked both flustered and delighted. Cody began to move.

The chair swung slowly in time with the music. Alice, eyes closed, powdered face emancipated from all former irritation, swayed gently side to side.

Cody tapped Al on the shoulder and cocked his blond head in Alice's direction.

Al shook his head. "I ain't learning no Butler."

Cody chuckled. "No Butler. In fact, the less said, the better." He winked and laid a hand on Alice's. Her eyes fluttered open. "Alice Platz, may I introduce you to Albert Crenshaw, who has requested to cut in?"

Alice waited.

Cody nudged Albert.

Al cleared his throat. "Alice, you probably don't want to, but can we dance?" He said it without making eye contact.

She looked irritable, but gave a slight nod. "Why, yes, Albert, we can."

Following the couple's lead, the others joined the dance through "Tennessee Waltz" and a jazzy sax rendition of "Moon River." Beth cut in on Edith at one point and Tommy blew her what he assured her was a "fatherly" kiss.

The song ended and Tommy snapped his fingers. "I wanna shake what God gave me! This slow stuff's for old fogies. My kingdom for some jitterbug!" Beth gave him Elvis's "Blue Suede Shoes," and the others cleared the floor for the whirling wheelchair and flying legs and arms of their gangly friend. Despite his wild enthusiasm, Beth could see that Tommy had once possessed the moves.

It wasn't Fred Astaire, but for Tommy and his adoring fans, it was a lot of fun.

Beth twirled the tiny paper parasol in her drink and watched their friends eat cake. The room, so tense earlier, now echoed with laughter and friendly chatter.

Cody watched Beth. She was the eighth wonder of the world. "Tommy's a scarecrow on steroids."

She turned to him with eyes aglow. "And you, sir, are a prince! This was really a sweet idea and look what a hit it's turned into. And you went through with it even after what happened at Taste last night. You promised this and you delivered. I can't believe how you disarmed the argument with poetry and got everyone having a good time again. You're amazing!"

Cody's cheeks warmed and he looked down at his shoes. "Not really. Alice told me she likes Butler, which we happened to study in English lit last fall. I didn't want her to end up in jail is all, and from the look in her eyes, I think she was ready to do twenty to life on Al."

"You are a rare guy and a special person, Cody William."

He looked up and Beth—beautiful, beautiful Beth—was right there, leaning in, lips about to dock with his.

When they did, a bolt of electricity nailed him to the floor.

And then it was over. One tick of the atomic clock. An undetectable twitch in geologic time. But before he doubted that it ever happened, he experienced a "Let there be light" moment and it was good.

"You ever thought about being a diplomat?"

He knew she'd spoken and in a flash communicated the meaning of life.

His vision cleared in an instant and she was back to twirling her parasol and watching the seniors of Fairview eat cake.

His lips had lost all feeling. "Sorry, could you repeat that? I have trouble hearing sometimes." Deaf joke. Ha, ha.

What, he wondered more times than he could count, was a lovesick person's way of explaining away why in a million years he didn't stand a ghost of a chance of becoming more than her good buddy?

"I asked if you've ever thought of becoming a diplomat."

He stalled, like he always stalled. "A laundromat? No thanks, all that spinning makes me dizzy."

She looked at him funny, not because he was funny, but because he was suddenly dizzy, pale as a sailor in a hurricane. He thumped hard onto a chair.

Nearby seniors turned in his direction. Their lips moved, but he forgot how to make words out of lips, tongues, and facial expressions.

Beth handed him her drink. She was close again. Fanning him. Rubbing his neck.

He inhaled the scent of her perfume and took a big swallow of pineapple, mango, and orange fizz. Not too big a swallow, of course, lest he revive and she stop rubbing his neck.

# Chapter 7

Father B walked arm in arm with Cassie down the sloping lawn behind the Dixon Tudor brick home on Twin Peaks with its panoramic view of San Francisco Bay.

He said nothing and she loved him for it. She didn't care for clergy who felt it was their God-ordained duty to fill every silence with some homiletical nugget as if because they had mortgaged all to pay for seminary, they were going to dispense wisdom if it killed them.

They listened to the birds and their own hearts until Cassie decided it was time. "Largest deepwater harbor in the world. Isn't it breathtaking?"

Father B patted her arm. "Mesmerizing. I can't get enough of it. And with a city built on forty-six hills, you, my dear, are fortunate enough to live on one of them."

She hugged him close. "I saw a red-tailed hawk right out there last week and three Mission Blue Butterflies in the garden. Such a gorgeous iridescent lavender. They're making a comeback, you know."

"Glad to hear it. They used to be relatively widespread, but now are rare as perfect church attendance. The Twin Peaks colony has everyone's hopes up. I'm fine with discussing the order *Lepidoptera*, but just so you know, we've about exhausted my knowledge on the subject."

The twinkle in the tidy priest's eye was the same one found there whenever he told choir jokes, or Moses jokes, or jokes about changing a lightbulb. He'd told so many in the Cathedral newsletter that the unamused church secretary had put him on a joke fast for three issues.

"Tell me, Cassie, why couldn't the butterfly come to the dance?"

She waited until she sensed from his fidgeting that he was about to burst. She liked to torment him with delayed punch line gratification, given the many groaners he had inflicted upon her. "I don't know, Father B, why couldn't the butterfly come to the dance?"

The priest turned and faced her, holding both her cool pale hands in his warm brown ones. "Because, my dear, it was a moth ball!"

She laughed, more at Byron Wills's droll expression than at anything the silly joke had to offer. "Hope, Father. That's why I'm so taken with the Mission Blue. Almost extinct, it's fighting its way back."

"Just like you and Nick."

Gretchen the Great Dane whined from the kennel next to the tree line. Without a word, Cassie signed for the dog to lie down. It immediately complied, big head resting on big paws, chocolate brown eyes taking them in.

Cassie shook her head. "I feel like such a pariah. Like you've taken a huge risk just coming here to talk to me."

The priest sat down on the lawn and rested arms on knees. "It's natural for you to feel that way. Rest assured, Satan has all of my pertinent information and knows how to find me without your help."

She sat beside him, legs outstretched, staring at neglected toes in need of a paint job. "I'm a lightning rod for the most uncharitable thoughts about others."

"That bad?"

"Worse than any hanging judge who ever lived. Like I have no faults. Who do I think I am? No one's ever mistaken me for Mother Teresa."

Father B gave her leg a swat. "In your shoes, I would have slapped St. Francis himself. Don't forget that Jesus got a might peeved at more than a few people for their errant ways."

Cassie sighed. "I can't take much comfort in a militant Jesus right now, no matter how deserving of correction the Pharisees in this or any town. What I need is 'precious Lord, take my hand, lead me on, let me stand ...' Got any of that in that fancy vest of yours?" She said it with affection.

He smiled, reached into a vest pocket, and withdrew two wrapped toothpicks. "Cinnamon," he said, offering her one. "Best thing on the menu at that little Creole dive over on Divisadero. Dinner starts with a glass of water laced with bleach and goes downhill from there. But the toothpicks! Exquisite!"

She was curiously comforted by the sweet tingle of the cinnamon, the smooth contours of the wooden pick.

Father B hummed the chorus of "Precious Lord" in a honey-rich baritone, then sang the words "I am tired, I am weak, I am worn ..."

"Amen." Cassie closed her eyes and slowly rocked side to side in the warm sun.

"Best part's comin'. 'Through the storm, through the night, lead me on to the light.' "

Cassie added her passable soprano. "Take my hand, precious Lord, lead me home."

They sat for minutes in the day's stillness that admitted only the light buzz of a wandering honeybee and the soft snuffle of a napping dog.

"Will the storm never end?"

"Some nor'easters go on five days or more, ferocious as can be, but they always end. That's what rainbows are for."

Cassie hugged her legs. "Can't we just cut to the rainbow?"

"Tried that once in seminary." Father B plucked a blade of grass and wrapped it around his toothpick. "We were assigned the mother of all papers on 'The Congruities and Inconsistencies of Calvinist Thought Found in the Writings of the A-Team.'"

"The A-team?"

"Augustine, Anselm, and Aquinas. I'd pulled three all-nighters in a row and had nothing left for a fourth. So I cut to the rainbow by all but plagiarizing an examination of the A-team's views by Anglican theologian Francis J. Hall. My laziness almost cost me my degree. Worse, as I was informed, it robbed me of experiencing the nor'easter of Hall's richly complex examination of man's free will and God's sovereignty. Thankfully, the dean was a man of mercy who took fiendish delight in personally ensuring a second chance in which I suffered my own personal nor'easter, complete with hurricane, blizzard, and torrential downpour. But I can tell you in minute and grisly detail the nuances of foreknowledge, predestination, and what are often referred to as the 'ungraspables' of the divine mysteries."

Cassie lay back on the grass, hands behind her head. "So you're saying that we flourish in adversity? Seems like every clergyman must take an oath to say that when he doesn't know what else to say."

Father B chuckled. "Only at weddings and funerals. Listen, my dear, the apostle Paul told the Corinthians that troubles and struggles are necessary evils, yet are quite small and don't last very long in the big scheme of things. A little distress, a *lot* of blessing. You can't shortcut the process any more than I could shortcut the seminary research."

"Great. I come to you for solace and all I get is six more weeks of bad weather."

The priest's warm brown eyes glowed with compassionate mirth and a timeless assurance. His arm encircled her and the hug it became covered a calendar of stormy nights. "Spring will be all the more glorious, dear Cass. You recall that it wasn't until after a terrible earthquake that our Redeemer rose and sealed our pardon."

Cassie nodded. "You're right, it wasn't. God willing, we'll make our comeback just like the Mission Blues."

"That's my girl."

"I'd still like to give St. Francis a good slap."

"I'm sure even he deserved one from time to time, as do we all."

"You mean it?"

"I do."

"I like you."

"I know."

# Chapter 8

The Golden Gate Bridge glowed in the distance, a javelin of yellow-orange spanning the opening into San Francisco Bay from the Pacific Ocean. Kenny Burstyn stared at the bridge and considered the options.

He could jump from the famed suspension bridge and smack the cement-hard surface of the water below at God-knew-what velocity. He might throw himself in front of an RV driven by a retired Midwest tax accountant en route with wife and grandkids to Disneyland. Then there was the sometimes popular method of grab a passing female jogger, hold a knife to her throat, threaten to do a duet off the side, and dare the SWAT team sniper to end your life but not the jogger's. Suicide by cop.

Or he could do nothing and continue his miserable existence as Kenny B., the loser from Truckee.

Technically he was from Sacramento, but born in the backseat of a Ford Falcon parked alongside the Truckee River a couple of miles from where it flowed out of Lake Tahoe. "Pull over, Jimmy, I gotta puke."

To hear his father tell it, pregnant women were always puking. But no sooner had nineteen-year-old James Burstyn pulled off the highway and turned to look at his nauseous wife of less than six months than he saw the crown of his son's head and it dawned most vivid that life as he knew it was over.

Jimbo cut the cord with a nail file and wrapped his boy in a clean white T-shirt. Because it was raining and Faith Burstyn really had to puke, his dad placed baby Burstyn in an empty potato-chip bag and the family went out into the night to do its business.

They say it is the rare individual who has memories from before two or three years of age, yet the rushing of the Truckee River on Day One was inside Kenny's brain still.

Everything else between the birthing and the suffocation was spotty remembrance at best.

He looked away from the Golden Gate. No way he had the adrenaline to do the bridge today. Everything had gone into getting Cassie Dixon to pay attention and take the bag.

So why all the dark thoughts? He hated that he'd scared her, but something in him rose up and he wanted to have that power, that terror over her. It felt good for the moment but was hardly the stuff of long-term pride.

A police cruiser peered around a Dumpster in the alley across the street from the vacant lot he was in. Kenny dropped to the ground behind a pile of steel rebar and waited until the cruiser crept past.

*Nobody here but us rats.*

Now he tried not to think how scared she was, him up against her all warning and threat. He tried not to think how scared he was when Theodore Braithwaite crushed the snot out of him.

Kenny was five, his friend Teddy six and forty pounds heavier if he was an ounce. Teddy had a weird habit of always sitting or falling on top of skinny Kenny. "It's like sittin' on nuthin'." He was a handsome, husky kid, even at six, but always with that stupid, chocolaty grin of his. Chocolate was Ted's candy of choice and the only flavor his grin usually came in.

The suffocation happened when they went to the state fair with Ken's dad, "just the guys." They zipped on the Zipper, flipped on the Fling Machine, and yelled themselves hoarse on the Dipper of Doom. They mimicked the hogs in the livestock barn and laughed like hyenas when a hypnotist made people strut and crow like roosters. They watched chain-saw wood-carvers turn logs into sea captains and cheered lumberjacks competing at ax-throwing and tree-climbing.

It was the best time. When they were hungry, they mowed their way through cotton candy, elephant ears, and mile-high bison burgers, washed down with about a gallon of fresh-squeezed lemonade from a refreshing plastic fountain in the shape of a giant lemon. Hand-dipped chocolate-coated ice-cream bars rolled in nuts put a stupid brown grin on Teddy's face where it naturally belonged.

That was when they saw it. They were strolling past the Bucking Bronco ride, slapping their bloated bellies like irreverent Buddhas, when a carnival barker halted them in their tracks.

"Step right up, dudes and dudettes, for the Great Money Scramble. That's right, for just one dollar, a mere one hundred pennies, twenty measly nickels, or ten thin dimes, you have a chance at fabulous riches beyond imagining. Buried somewhere in that pile of sawdust is a check for a hundred dollars—you guessed it, an amazing ten thousand pennies, two thousand nickels, or one thousand thin dimes. All yours *if* you can find it before our official time clock takes one turn around the dial. Think of it, kids, all that stands between you and that bike, that boom box, that trick skateboard is time and sawdust. Find that check in one minute and I will use this pen"—he held one aloft—"to write your name on the 'pay to' line of that check. Hand me your dollar, kids, and I will hand you loads o' fun and a chance at a fortune!"

Kids appeared from all directions and dollar bills bombarded the barker like autumn leaves in a windstorm. Ken and Tom looked wide-eyed at one another, then at Ken's dad.

"What am I, made a money?"

"Please, Dad, we'll pay ya back! We will!"

Kenny thought his friend's head might fly off its neck he was nodding so hard.

"Ah, a loan is it? If you don't find that check, you rake leaves tomorrow, got it?"

More hard nodding.

With Ken right behind him in unison step, Teddy plowed a path up to the barker, who wore red-and-white-checked pants, matching jacket, white shoes, and a green bowler hat. He snatched their money and swept them aside to join the other excited kids at the starting line.

The cap pistol fired and they were off like army ants on the attack. Ken figured the check was deep inside the pile. Like a mole, he dove low and tunneled deep inside the huge mound of fragrant wood chips to be the first. A bigger, stronger Tommy shoved him forward from behind.

Everything went dark. Wood dust and chips flew up his nostrils and down his throat. He inhaled at the wrong time and chunks of fiber clogged his airway and coated his tongue with the sour taste of green wood. He choked and coughed and there was no air.

Only wood.

Teddy's weight bore down on him from behind, pressed him flat, drove the last of the oxygen from his lungs. He struggled, legs and arms heavy and useless.

He wanted to scream but couldn't—pinned, unable to breathe, unable to move.

Red sparks flew around the inside of his eyelids. The cries of the other children faded. No light. No air. All went black.

Suffocation.

When the weight lifted and light again flooded the world, Kenny wasn't sure what world it was. Was it heaven? Surely hell didn't have blue sky and a man in checked pants and green bowler hat bent over, shouting, "Son? You okay, son?"

Ken wanted his dad and as soon as he saw that was who held him, he burst into tears and another coughing fit. Paramedics came, he rode to the hospital in an ambulance with the siren on, and his mother met them there and covered what she could reach of him in a million kisses.

Teddy stood on the other side of the bed looking white as a ghost—except for the dried chocolate ring around his mouth.

Last Ken knew, Ted Braithwaite was an accountant for Starbucks Coffee in Seattle. They hadn't spoken in years.

James and Faith Burstyn operated a poultry business outside Sacramento and waited for their only son to come to his drug-fried senses. Parents and child hadn't spoken in too long.

When did people drive off the interstate of their lives and down a one-lane road to oblivion? When did they go barricade themselves inside a shack in the woods and refuse to answer their mail? And when, oh when, did they arrive at such opposite conclusions to life's imponderables that they could no longer share the same space?

One minute you're leaving your mother's body, the next you're leaving her values system. What happens in between? Somehow, he knew, it came down to suffocation and how much of it a person could tolerate.

He rested forehead against rough rebar, mashed the raised metal cross-hatching hard against skin. The suffocation theory was crap and he knew it.

He pulled away from the steel and ran a dirty finger over the industrial brand now impressed into his forehead. African tribal families didn't separate over generational suffocation. They planned for the parting of the ways, the emancipation of children, celebrated such things with parties and dances and intimate coming-of-age rituals. Only sophisticated Western man permitted himself the luxury of sweating the small stuff, of bartering love of family for being "right." Instead of swallowing pride, asking forgiveness, one turned to a supermarket of justification with aisle upon aisle of sex, substances, and other sops for delaying the inevitable.

Before long, you were as old as your dad the day he became a father—your father—and you wished you were dead.

Kenny knew he shouldn't remain exposed like this. They were looking for him by now.

He hoped Mrs. Dixon would pray for him. That his mother would. He was never lucid long enough to pray for himself.

*I'm lucid now.*

The smell of fried chicken wafted over from Virgil's Southern Comfort. It was a greasy spoon that backed onto the vacant lot. Judging by the quality of his Dumpster, as informally rated by the toughest street critics, Virgil generated some of the tastiest grease this side of Memphis.

Kenny eyed the surrounding streets, then did a careful scan of the alley in both directions from Virgil's back door. No more police and no winos in sight.

He raised the lid on the Dumpster, stomach responding with rare interest in the contents, and held the lid until it hung down free and quiet. He climbed up, looked in, spied a promising patch of last night's discards, saw that it was fly-free, swung a leg over, and catlike dropped down beside it.

A half-eaten drumstick and a thigh, untouched. They disappeared inside a coat pocket along with a half dozen jo-jos and a small Styrofoam container of slaw into a second pocket. *Someone forgot her doggie bag.*

A door opened with a "Yeah, yeah, hold yer fire. Who 'n the devil left the lid offen the dumper?"

Ken crouched in the darkness beneath the unopened half of the garbage receptacle and took a tossed black bag heavy with waste off his shoulder. The lid slammed down before he could cover his ears.

He waited an extra few beats after the door to the restaurant banged shut and the ringing in his ears subsided before he lifted the lid a crack and looked out. All clear.

He took his meal on the ground, cross-legged, in the shelter of a shuttered parking attendant's shack up against a weed-infested chain-link fence. No smell of urine and empty wine bottles kicked to the side, it made a comfortable enough place in the sun. The lot had gone automated a year before and he wasn't likely to be spotted by authorities or bothered by other wanderers until he saw them first.

The lunch withstood further scrutiny. No cigarette ash. No mingling with liquids. No fly eggs. Sun not yet hot enough to spoil. Nor was it overly greasy. As Dumpster meals went, it bordered on four stars.

The chicken leg rose halfway to his mouth before he stopped and lowered it back to his lap. He stared into the far distance and thought again of Teddy, his parents, and the sound of the Truckee River.

Ken bowed his head and wondered if the words would come. For the longest time, they didn't. A bell rang in the distance. A boat horn sounded. A seagull chuckled and a companion got the joke.

He again brought the chicken near, liked the feel of it in his fingers. He singled out the herbs and spices, pictured the platters of farm-fresh roasted chicken served three times a week at home. He could breathe. Hear. See. Smell. Taste. He could remember.

He lowered the chicken a second time without eating. This time, lips moving, the words did come.

# Chapter 9

Lieutenant Reynolds whisked Kenny Burstyn's lunch sack to the crime lab. He called back in an hour and the board meeting was postponed until later that evening. Given the deceased was James Waverly, one of the wealthiest men on the West Coast, the ME's report had been fast-tracked and the autopsy completed overnight. Those results, coupled with the analysis of the sack's contents, had revealed cause of death as sure as a compass needle testified to true north.

The lieutenant would meet them at Taste at four o'clock.

Nick would not let Cassie out of his sight. They had a long lunch at Ensign Baldy's, but despite the excellent food and convivial surroundings, they ate little and soon even the garrulous bon vivant Baldwin "Baldy" Beeson retreated to his sour cream cod and cherry-basted sole.

"I still think you should go to the ER and get checked out. You could have been killed! Thank God your guardian angel was on duty."

The incident in the El Paraiso alley was still a frightening haze to Cassie. "I'll be fine. No doctors, no paperwork. I don't want the *Chronicle* to get wind of this. And, by definition, a guardian angel is *always* on duty." She wasn't trying to be pedantic, but to focus on thoughts that comforted.

"I'm so glad I married a theologian." Nick picked at his mango cheesecake, compliments of the house. "Kenny has become highly unstable and needs to be taken off the streets."

"Taken where? I'm the first to admit I think he's guilty, but has he gotten a fair shake?"

Nick let his spoon clatter to the table. "A fair shake? He's roughing up women—*my* woman—and nearly scared you to death. He throws threats around like candy from a busted piñata and now we're supposed to show him sympathy? Drugs make monsters out of choir boys, Cass, you know that. He could strangle you, dump your body in the Bay, and wake up the next day more worried about where his next fix is coming from."

"I don't think so—"

"Really, Dr. Dixon, and what degree did you get in psychology school?"

"Don't get testy. I'm just saying that after all this, he decides to voluntarily turn over this bag of his and confess to ... to something. That's not the act of a psycho killer."

"Nor is it grounds for a Nobel Prize. Look, Cass, don't lose sight of Ken's part in whatever happened to Waverly. He's connected to a man's death somehow. He was paid $30 for the part he played. Thirty pieces of silver, if you ask me. Our little Ken is part of a conspiracy to remove Waverly or discredit Taste, or both. He's got to be stopped before someone else dies."

Cassie looked sadly at the slumping dessert. "Exactly. Kenny is somebody's puppet. I think there's a spark of life left in him, and I feel so responsible for getting him kicked out of the culinary program. He really went downhill after that. I wish there were some way to start over with him."

Nick took her hand in his and kissed it. "There is. Let the police find the guy and get him into some kind of rehab. Father B might have some connections there. Once he's dried out and served time for whatever crime he's guilty of, maybe try him in the program again. It's a long shot, but this time it's certain we took him into our trust too soon. He wasn't free of his demons yet."

He peered at her, into her.

"What?"

"You're amazing. How many people would be worried about the future of a man who just attacked them?"

"He's not right, Nick. Clean and sober, Ken wouldn't do that. He wants help."

Nick shook his head. "Amazing."

*Nor am I free of my demons.* Cassie had been troubled ever since Nick's telling statement at Baldy's. *Demons of doubt are stains on the human soul. It's so hard to surrender the past. It's one thing to be acquitted by the world, even by God, and quite another to declare yourself "free to go."*

Lieutenant Reynolds looked old and threadbare, like a favorite bath towel still in service long after its intended usefulness had vanished. As long as it held together, no way would you discard it.

His stout six-foot frame was bent like that of a man continually stooping for doorways. A discount brown suit hung tightly from rounded shoulders, lumpy like a straw-stuffed effigy. A wide necktie from the Depression sported gold diamond shapes against a field of mustard yellow. He had that hangdog look and the heels of his shoes had long since been worn to the outside so that now he actually walked on the leather where the paper-thin soles still clung to the uppers. Cassie guessed they hadn't seen polish in more than a year, if ever.

His speech was clipped and clinical. "What we're dealing with here is the introduction of tropane alkaloids directly into the soup, most specifically Mr. Waverly's soup, as no one else present, including members of his immediate family and his extended entourage, appears to have been adversely affected.

"The alkaloids represent a very diverse group of compounds that include the opiates and the belladonnas. Toxic symptoms typically do not occur before thirty to sixty minutes after ingestion, but in cases where cardiovascular weakness is present, a heart attack may be triggered by the sudden introduction of this poison. Mr. Waverly was under a doctor's care for serious heart problems and when jolted by the alkaloid, suffered coronary failure. The poisoner had to have known that."

Throughout the restaurant, Reynolds's plastic-gloved investigators dusted surfaces, lifted fingerprints, and generally poked about. With a sinking heart, Cassie watched them. Were they looking for poisons in the spice rack?

Lieutenant Reynolds watched Nick and her carefully. Was he gauging reaction? "What they found in the brown bag was *Datura stramonium. Datura* from the ancient Hindu for the word *plant*, and *stramonium*, New Latin derived originally from the Greek—*strychnos* or nightshade, *manikos* or mad. We know it by its more common names, Jimsonweed or locoweed. Quite commonly found on pastureland, it would drive the chickens and the cows quite mad."

In his study of flora for their work among perfume-bearing plants, Nick had covered poisons. "Yes, Lieutenant, and mandrake, deadly nightshade, henbane—all these alkaloids have long histories of hallucinogenic use dating to centuries before Christ. They were often used in alcoholic beverages to increase intoxication. The Yaqui women of Mexico still take Jimsonweed to lessen the pain of childbirth. Think how many died before they got the dosage right."

The lieutenant nodded. "Right you are, Mr. Dixon. Didn't realize you were that well-versed in nature's pharmacology."

Cassie started, tried to recover. She shot Nick a warning glance.

"Don't worry, Mrs. Dixon." Lieutenant Reynolds was tough to read and not at all comforting. "I would have been more suspicious if your husband had played dumb, given the nature of the fragrance industry. Of course you folks would have a ... ah ... specialized understanding of the plant world. But what would your motivation be for stopping the gentleman's heart? He was the chief patron for Taste of Success. Kill your sugar daddy? I don't think so."

"Would anyone care for a fruit juice?" Cassie felt a sudden need to get up. Was the investigator fishing for guilt? Was he employing a reverse psychology to get them to think they had been eliminated from the list of viable killers when all the while he considered them the prime suspects?

"You just relax." The lieutenant's tone was meant to soothe. "Fowler! Please bring the lady a ..."

He looked at her and she was forced to say, "Raspberry sparkling water." The thought of a crime scene investigator rifling through the refrigerator ...

"... raspberry sparkler." Reynolds looked at Nick, thick caterpillar eyebrows raised.

"Bottled water." Nick's exasperation showed.

"And two bottled waters. Thank you, Fowler. Now, Mr. Dixon. To pick up where you left off. It's true that people through the years have made innovative use of the alkaloids. In their ignorance at Jamestown in the seventeenth century—Jimson is a compressed form of the word *Jamestown*, as I'm sure you know—the soldiers boiled the leaves for salad. For eleven days after, many of them went berserk, running around naked, acting like monkeys, and had to be confined so as not to further damage themselves. But in concentrated form, highest being in the roots and seeds, as little as a half a teaspoon of Jimsonweed seeds has been known to cause death from cardiopulmonary arrest. The bag you got from Kenny Burstyn still contained more than two teaspoons of seeds and there was probably plenty more to start with."

"Where would he find Jimsonweed around here?" Cassie wished Fowler would hurry up with the drinks.

"Pocket farms in the area, vacant lots. It's a hardy species and more common than you'd think."

"How would a guy as fried as Burstyn know about Waverly's heart condition?"

"Precisely." The policeman gave Cassie an assessing look. "You were in charge of last night's soup, were you not?"

*He thinks I poisoned Waverly!* "Surely you're not implying—"

He held up a long-fingered hand. "The implications take care of themselves, Mrs. Dixon. All I'm doing is sorting through the raw data."

"Then you need to sort the fact that Philippe Peugeot insisted on personally serving the Waverly table. He wasn't needed and was told that. Still he insisted." Cassie felt uneasy implicating the commercial developer, but she wanted the police to spend their time on possible leads, not chasing false ones.

"Wasn't needed and wasn't appreciated, I take it?"

She did not like the tone of the question. He probably questioned his wife the same way he did his suspects. "Did you at any time allow the pork chops out of your sight? Is that sauce bottled or of your own making? Do you know for a fact that the rice originated in Southeast Asia?"

They accepted their drinks from Fowler, who went back to checking for clues. Cassie twisted the cap from her bottle and was revived by the mild sting of the drink's carbonation. *Why does Reynolds keep staring at me?*

"Mrs. Dixon, just how strong was your dislike for the deceased?"

Cassie choked on her drink. Nick patted her back until the coughing subsided. "My apologies." She knew she looked flustered and guilty as sin. *You can't convict someone for not liking a person. So why do I feel so convicted?*

Reynolds smiled a professional smile. "Sorry. Old investigative trick. Lead the discussion in one direction, then throw a question from left field to see how a person reacts. Your startled response tells me it's unlikely you poisoned Mr. Waverly. A typical poisoner is more calculating, smoother, if you will, ready with an answer. No, you're more likely to shoot a person than poison them. Or hire it done."

*Does he want me to think he's eliminated me when he really hasn't?*

Nick glowered. "Really, Lieutenant, aren't you supposed to be searching for solid clues, not reaching premature conclusions? Cassie cares deeply about this community and you have no right to suggest otherwise. She's a wife and mother and can't even step on a spider without feeling remorse. Hardly the profile of someone out to do harm."

Reynolds folded his long arms like a praying mantis and half sat on one of the dining tables. "No accusations. All we're doing here is exploring the dimensions of this crime. Laura Waverly says there was no love lost between her husband and Mrs. Dixon. She freely admitted that he could be a lush and make inappropriate remarks when in his cups, but the way you responded to him, Mrs. Dixon, was with what could only be described as animosity and open hostility."

"He made passes at the help ..." Cassie fumbled. She tried to avoid Nick's eyes. "He thought nothing of sexually harassing me, little Trina Fisk, maybe the customers, for all I know. He thought his patronage of the homeless training program bought him the right to chase skirts—"

"Waverly bothered you? And you didn't tell me?" Nick looked ready to juice carrots with his bare hands. "You should have said something, Cass! No one can buy enough privilege to do that! I would have shown him where to get off—"

"Shown him how, Mr. Dixon?" Reynolds's eyes narrowed, head swiveled like a mantis in preattack mode. "By sickening him in a way that would give him a strong taste of his own medicine?"

Nick looked angry and miserable. "I don't murder people, even lowlifes like Waverly. Vengeance is the Lord's."

"Mmm. Indeed." Reynolds's bottled water remained untouched. "But how much Jimson is too much Jimson? Were you even aware of Waverly's heart condition?"

Nick shook his head. "We don't take lives, sir. We're about helping others live life, about spreading hope where it's in short supply. You ask anybody. My style is to confront, head-on. Had I known of his lechery, I would have gone to him and told him in no uncertain terms to lay off or face unwanted publicity. I think I know what makes a guy like that tick and most of it has to do with not losing a penny of corporate profit."

"Mmm. Perhaps. But you see some of the threads I must follow."

"I just hope you're hunting for Kenny Burstyn. Not only is he a danger to himself and others, he all but confessed to the poisoning."

"Ah, yes. So your wife says. Of course we'll pick Kenny up. My guess is he's someone's pawn. But to be honest, Mr. Dixon, there is no shortage of persons of interest in this case. Chef Maggiano. Trina Fisk. Jorge Ramone ..."

"... defending Trina's honor."

Cassie looked ill.

"Laura Waverly ..."

"... putting an end to the philandering."

Nick put an arm around Cassie.

"Or a business associate fed up with being a footman to a tyrant king. You see what we're up against, folks. Before this is done, I'll have offended everyone connected to this place. Sorry it had to happen to such a nice effort just when the place was gaining a fine reputation for its homeless program and all. But you do understand that I have to do my job and that the place must remain closed during the active investigation."

"We understand, Lieutenant." Cassie's head began to pound. "And you understand that we have to fight to save this place. We're not letting go of the new lives and the new hope that come from Taste of Success. This is God's work and God's going to save it!"

Reynolds looked thoughtful. "Glad to hear that, Mrs. Dixon, because it will take divine intervention before this is over."

Nick stiffened. "How's that?"

The chief investigator looked around the room and gathered his suit coat tighter about him as if taking a sudden chill. "Well, I was just thinking. As you well know, Mr. Dixon, rural people sometimes use another common name for Jimsonweed, one with otherworldly implications."

Cassie's eyes flicked to Nick's.

He did not avoid them, his expression equally troubled. "Yeah, I do. They call it the Devil's Trumpet."

# Chapter 10

By six o'clock that evening, the television media were all over the poisoning at Taste of Success.

"In breaking news, KRON-TV has just learned that corporate CEO James Waverly died of cardiac arrest linked to poisoned soup while dining last night at Taste of Success. The shocking incident occurred in front of a packed house gathered for Celebrity Chef Night at the popular restaurant dedicated to training the homeless in the culinary arts."

"In an exclusive interview only on KNTV-11, the wife of murdered electronics giant James Waverly says her husband had more than a few enemies. The City on the Bay was shocked to learn late this afternoon that at least one of those enemies may have received help from the innovative food service program heavily underwritten with Waverly funds."

"Speculation runs high, sources close to the Waverly family told KPIX-TV, that yesterday's death of San Francisco megamillionaire James Waverly was a revenge killing that may have been masterminded from the inside. It is alleged that criminal background checks of the once-homeless restaurant personnel at Taste of Success where Waverly died are not sufficiently thorough."

The Dixons had their home and business phones forwarded to an answering service which, inside two hours, had fielded more than a hundred calls from media outlets around the globe. They responded to none of them. There was one phone call, however, that Cassie personally had to return.

"Newsroom. Rory Brainard speaking."

Cassie knew if she could expect fair treatment from any newshound out there, it would come from investigative reporter Rory Brainard of the *Chronicle*. He was smart, educated, and decent.

"Rory? Cass Dixon. Our number one concern is protecting the reputation of Taste of Success. A hatchet job will sink the program. What can we do?"

"You shoulda called me soon as Waverly hit the table, Cass. I think the genie's out of the bottle. Next edition's headline's already set: 'Waverly Poisoned at Dinner.' I tried to get it softened, keep the food angle peripheral, but there's some in this business who don't care who goes down as long as it sells papers. I've already heard from Fletcher's crowd and they demand blood."

Margo Fletcher led the anti-homeless faction that wanted San Francisco free of street people. She was a rabid member of high society who believed that lost commerce, lower property values, and unsanitary health conditions could all be laid at the ragged feet of the homeless. She had the ear of the mayor and seized upon any excuse to ban "the crafty beggars and shifty-eyed opportunists" from the city. She wanted them rounded up and dumped far from the Golden Gate.

A good day for Margo Fletcher would be the day Taste of Success closed for good. "A misguided program like Taste attracts riffraff that eventually drain the city's resources dry." It mattered little that Cassie had solid statistics showing that the city's homeless population had declined since Taste opened and that Taste's graduates made their own way. They were upstanding citizens, a drain on no one.

"Rory! Don't do this to me. You could do a series of think pieces on what it takes to turn the homeless around. Show people that Taste is one of the most effective intervention programs going. What about that Adopt-a-Homey idea we were kicking around? Sponsor a person in the culinary arts program and get a nice charitable tax deduction."

The pause at the other end of the line was telling. Rory, an ex-coanchor for KSFE, hated dead air. At last he said, "Cass, we've given your program quite a lot of ink already and you don't even know if tomorrow you'll have a program. Readers want to know who killed James Waverly, so until all this clears up, there's no space for do-good stories on the homeless. From a quick read of my mail, take it from a friend: You and your homeless need to lay low. Way low." She knew the regret in his voice was genuine.

*Your homeless.* On the verge of tears, Cassie held onto the phone long after Rory broke the connection. He was right. Taste made its debut five years too late. By then, San Francisco was spending $200 million a year on one of the worst homeless problems in the country. As many as five thousand people spent virtually all their lives on the street.

Numbers weren't the issue. They had to try to transform a few. Each life was precious. Cassie rubbed her temples. *Lord, what do we do? Please don't let this destroy everything we've built. We can't let AJ and Frieda and Germaine and Carmina down. They need this program; they need this success.*

And she knew deep down that she needed it too.

Cassie listened to the mantle clock strike ten and knew that Nick would soon return from his jog. Beth was at the library studying for finals with a friend, but should be home any minute. She wished one of them was around to brainstorm with her. Not babysit her. She'd only stop replaying the creepy encounter with Kenny Burstyn when she faced those demons on her own. But just to talk and sort things out ...

A cold shiver trickled down her back. When she'd thought it was a sexual attack, it was the worst fear she'd ever experienced; when she knew it wasn't, she felt the most amazing grace.

Now she felt at loose ends, alone and unsettled. She called the Taste students to tell them they should stay home and not talk to any reporters until things could be sorted out. Trina burst into tears. She shared a loft in the Mission District with three young girlfriends, all four trying to make it in a city ruled by fat cats. Cassie had done the math and kept coming up short with the amount the trio would need to cover the monthly rent, but she didn't want to question their attempt at independence. Give them credit for trying. For sure they all needed whatever modest wages they earned to supplement their subsidized rent allotment and keep the lights on.

"Have faith." Cassie's words to Taste's students were reassurance to herself. "We'll keep you on payroll for the time being. Nobody's losing anything."

One step forward and two steps back.

She went to the kitchen, poured herself a diet cola, and sat down to read the restaurant review by the most feared of all West Coast food critics, the legendary McTavish.

"The sauce was clumpy, the salmon fatty as Santa's rump. Could the cold, bland vegetables really have been the scrapings from other patrons' plates? That's how they tasted. The potatoes were grainy, and what on earth are 'fresh, pan-seared mushrooms'? I so had my heart set on the cold, stale ones. And save your 'cave-aged fromage' for those who wouldn't know Gruyère from Cheese Whiz. We both know it's just an excuse to jack up the price of dinner by twenty bucks. And you call yourselves The Wild Walrus. How precious. However, judging from my dining experience, you are, at best, The Wounded

Walrus. Keep trying. Better yet, stop trying and open a used
bookstore. Let us hope that your taste in reading is more refined
than your ragout."

*Ouch.*

She winced for the owners of The Wild Walrus. The scath-
ing column by the one-word terror, carried twice weekly in
the *Chronicle*, was syndicated in papers across the nation and
in several international periodicals. A rare four-star "McTavish" had established a handful of fine restaurants around the
city. The more common negative reviews had dashed many a
budding restaurateur's hope of culinary stardom. The column,
filled with caustic comments, witty scolds, and an occasional
dollop of cooking wisdom, also sold papers—lots and lots of
papers.

McTavish bestowed tasty stardom on Christy Jo's, a hole-in-
the-wall with six tables that served a deep-dish apple pie that
now shipped worldwide. McTavish posted a $50,000 bounty
to anyone who could duplicate the recipe because the crusty
senior citizen who ran Christy Jo's would not part with her
ancestral ingredients no matter the price. No one had as yet
claimed the bounty. The mail-order pies made Christy Jo Fanning a wealthy woman.

But McTavish torpedoed the $25 million investment for
Del Ray on the Bay. It had it all—panoramic 180-degree water
view, seating for five hundred, a massive three-story aquarium,
a world-class chef—everything but the one thing it, in the end,
required: the approval of McTavish. "DRB is a colossal waste
of space." Those seven words were the kiss of death. McTavish
cautioned readers to enjoy the aquarium, but beware the food,
"the quality of which can be found for a fraction of the price
and none of the pretension at any good steak-and-salad chain."

When sued or otherwise attacked for a particularly vicious
review, McTavish gave a stock answer: "Does anyone ever thank

me for saving this great city from the mediocre and the mundane? Mine is but the opinion of one person."

Exclusive. Reclusive. Mysterious. Cassie had not found anyone who might disclose anything personal about McTavish or admitted to ever having met the person. Rory refused to discuss it. McTavish was a conundrum, probably the imaginary brainchild of a collection of writers in the *Chronicle* marketing department.

And yet, Cassie couldn't help herself. Reading McTavish was a guilty pleasure she shared with thousands in the Bay Area, although she did think it sometimes went too far. Yet she was grateful that the two mentions of Taste of Success that made it into the column were of the more neutral wait-and-see variety. She scanned the rest of the column with only one eye open, praying the scandal wasn't in it. It wasn't.

The column ended with a wicked list of complaints waiters have for customers:

"Calling female servers Honey, Sweetie, Toots, or Susie and male servers Buddy or Champ. (Have you ever had scalding hot coffee dumped in your lap? Accidents happen.)

"Asking if you can order from the children's menu. (You can't.)

"Going to a trendy restaurant and asking for ranch dressing on your baby greens salad. (Don't.)

"Taking your vegan friend to a classy surf-and-turf establishment and griping about the lack of menu choices. (Stop it.)

"Putting your used plates and glasses on the clean table next to yours. (Remind me to put my feet on your table.)

"Asking for a culinary art masterpiece with sauce on the side or that it be sautéed in regular oil instead of olive oil. (You want it your way, go to Burger King.)"

Cassie indulged in a much-needed chuckle. Say what you would, McTavish believed in seizing the bull by the horns.

She stopped and looked at her hands. Each was curled in midair as if grasping a horn. What was she doing cowering behind the castle walls awaiting her fate? The victors were the ones who took the battle to the enemy. Stared them down. Called their bluff.

To get it her way, she would demand an audience with the great one. Love or hate the acerbic critic, everyone listened to McTavish. Either she would lose her head or, if God allowed, receive the golden scepter. Simple as that.

Without thinking, Cassie felt her neck and chin and was glad for the time being to find them right where they belonged.

Rory tried to dissuade her from a fool's errand, but Cassie was undeterred. That, and her offer to send over an entire box of baklava by Chef Stamos Athenokis worked their magic.

"Then there are a few things you need to know." Rory sighed and Cassie loved him for it. "McTavish doesn't keep an office with us grunts at the *Chronicle* building. McTavish writes out of the Rayon Building on Lamoureaux. The whole third floor. Test kitchen, the works. The dragon-at-arms is Clarice Young. Young's favorite flowers are tiger lilies. Her sweet tooth favors mint patties from Sees Candies. Don't go before two. McTavish never arrives before two, preferring to skewer another eatery on the way in. Good for the adjectives, follow?"

"I follow. Thanks, Rory, I owe you one. You didn't tell me the McTavish weaknesses."

"There aren't any."

"None?"

"None."

"Then—"

"Then, nothing. You're at the mercy of the fates. It'll take a miracle to even see McTavish. If you do get an audience, it'll be for the sole purpose of removing your impertinent head from your impudent shoulders."

*At least we're all agreed on that.*

"Don't mention my name. In fact, don't go at all, Cass. Why invite trouble?"

It was Cassie's turn to sigh. "We both know it's only a matter of time before McTavish weighs in on Waverly's death. I've got to take the initiative, Ror, you know I do."

She listened to her friend slowly exhale. "I'm no good Catholic boy, Cass, but I'm stopping by Holy Ascension this afternoon to light a candle for you. Remember how to dial 9-1-1?"

"Funny, Rory. You can emcee my roast. Seriously, I'll be fine."

She didn't feel so confident that afternoon when the taxi deposited her at the Rayon Building, Sixth and Lamoureaux. The concrete-and-glass edifice rose twenty stories toward a boil of dirty, threatening clouds. Somewhere beyond those, astronauts were buckling together an entire space station. How complicated was a brief chat with a food columnist?

She kept her spirits light right up to the moment she grasped the brass handle on the heavy glass door marked "McTavish Enterprises" and stared through to the rigid-jawed Clarice Young seated at a huge oak console. The cabbie had agreed to walk her inside and he reached for the door.

"No! I mean, not just yet, please." *What am I doing here? I don't have a clue what to say to McTavish. I didn't even ask Rory the man's first name. Nick was against my coming, but I'll not become a trembling neurotic because of Kenny.*

She didn't realize how long she stood without moving until the trim woman at the console motioned through the glass for her to enter. Cassie nodded, managed a slight smile, and felt the ridiculous weight of the ridiculous bouquet of tiger lilies and the ridiculous box of Sees mint patties wrapped in gold foil. *Could I be anymore transparent?*

She nodded, the cabbie opened the door, and she entered. The driver did not follow.

Without ceremony, the receptionist immediately relieved her of the items she brought. "Well, you've obviously been apprised of who I am. Who are you?" Not ungraciously, she added Cassie's flowers and candy to two other flower-candy sets on a crowded credenza at her back. Those flowers looked nothing like tiger lilies.

"Cassandra Dixon." She reached out and took the woman's cool hand. "I represent Taste of Success and would appreciate just a few minutes of Mr. McTavish's time on a matter of mutual interest."

The woman's amused little smile—more of a smirk, really—irritated Cassie. Her pale skin and short jet black hair complimented an austere black skirt, black blouse, and black half jacket. "I'm Clarice Young, as you've surmised." She nodded without a hint of self-consciousness in the direction of the bribes, then consulted a date book open on the desk. "You don't have an appointment."

"If that's a problem, may I schedule one?"

"McTavish doesn't take appointments."

Cassie felt her blood pressure rise. *Why does everyone perpetuate this pretentious last name business?* "What?" was the only thing she could think to say.

"I'm sure you can appreciate that were McTavish to keep an open office, every Tom, Dick, and"—she paused to give Cassie the once-over—"Mary would want time, and how would the work get done? Will there be anything else?"

Cassie frantically searched her mind for anything to say. "Yes."

The woman's left eyebrow arched. "And what would that be?"

Cassie bit the inside of her cheek. "Mc-Ta-vish ... "

Clarice leaned closer as if encouraging Cassie to cough up the rest.

Cassie folded her arms and blurted, "... needs my list of customer rebuttals to the complaining waiters list of ... of complaints." It was a lame finish, but it was all she had.

An amused, if calculating interest shone from the receptionist's carbon black eyes. She punched in a number on the phone, covered the mouthpiece, and waited. "You tell Rory he can pick me up here at nine Friday night with his dancin' shoes *on!*"

Startled, Cassie could only nod. The receptionist must have been tipped off by the tiger lilies. Next Cassie heard a single barked word—whether from the phone or a nearby office, she wasn't sure.

"Cassandra Dixon to see you. Taste of Success. Says the customers strike back on the waiter bit in yesterday's column. No, a Rory Brainard referral. Uh-hum. I see. Will do."

She replaced the phone in its cradle. "McTavish says this is a bad time. You can try again in a week or two."

Cassie stared at the woman in disbelief. "Please, I—"

"I'm really quite busy, Mrs. Dixon. If you'll excuse me."

Cassie looked at the massive oak desk, its deep-shine surface devoid of anything but the date book and the phone. She looked at Clarice Young's pale face devoid of any sympathy. "Thank you, Ms. Young." Cassie turned to go.

"You won't forget my message to Rory, will you?"

Without looking back, Cassie reached for the brass door handle. "Oh, I'll tell him all right."

She yanked on the door just as the phone gave a two-note ring.

"A moment, Mrs. Dixon. McTavish asks if you know anything about tender roasted pumpkin ginger and coconut soup."

Cassie spoke to the door. "Roasted pumpkin method or soup base method?"

Clarice relayed the question, listened a moment longer, then replaced the phone. "McTavish will see you now."

# Chapter 11

Nick threw an arm around Jorge Ramone's neck and pretended to give him a punch to the head. He liked the kid, liked how he carried himself, his physical strength, and his strong love for his family.

Jorge, once a high school wrestler with a promising future, twisted free of the embrace and, in a blur, brought Nick to the floor. The boy's smile was as broad as an Aztec sun. "I've still got the moves, old man. Still got the moves!"

Taste of Success remained a cordoned-off crime scene, but the police allowed Nick and Jorge to remove dairy products, eggs, three pots of prepared soups, and other items with a short shelf life out through the back loading bay. They were taking them to Miss Josie's Mission kitchen where they'd be put to good use.

"You keep workin' out?" Nick hoisted one end of a wooden pallet of forty-eight dozen eggs, Jorge the other. Grunting, they jockeyed it carefully into the back of a delivery van with "Taste of Success" emblazoned across the sides in letters the color of purple grapes. They cracked only one egg and Nick set it on the loading dock clear of their path.

"You know it. Now that I ain't comin' to the program, maybe I can get in six, eight hours of running, conditioning, weights, flex training, even a little tai chi." Muscular as he was, the young man learned a lot about grace and balance from the ancient Chinese art of tai chi therapy.

"Phew! Makes me tired just hearing you say it. You going for some bodybuilding competitions?"

"Nawh. I don't want to put that much into it. Plus those entry fees kill. This is more for my own security and personal satisfaction. 'Sides, chicks really dig guys who ripple, know what I mean?"

Nick grinned. "You bet. I'm fighting 'em off all the time. Mrs. Dixon says I need to stay in condition so I can fix the rain gutters, mow the lawn, weed the flower beds—"

"Can you say 'domestication'?" Jorge shook his head. "No tyin' me down, man. I'm free, free at last! No drugs, no jails, and no little sweet things orderin' me around. 'Cept my mama. She'll be givin' orders in heaven and ole Saint Peter better hop to or he's gettin' thumped on the skull just like me!"

"I thought your mama was four foot eight."

"Yeah, so, what's your point? That bony finger o' hers has no trouble findin' the target!"

Nick carried four gallons of milk to the van. "What about Trina? She sure thinks you're something."

Jorge plunked two crates of four gallons each alongside Nick's one. "I don't know. I tried callin' that new apartment she's got with those other three chicks, but it just rings and rings. Sometimes she's real warm to me, other times not so much. It's like she's afraid of gettin' too close. I want to. I feel all protective of her, know what I mean? I called her my little Trina Belle and she liked it."

He looked embarrassed by the emotion in his own words.

Nick pretended to take no notice. "Yeah." He wrote down the milk count. "Women can be unpredictable, no doubt, but I'd say Trina's got you in her sights."

Jorge's smile was as shy as his words. "Pff! She's had a hard go. To trust guys again, I don't know. 'Specially not a Latin volcano like me."

"Don't put yourself down, Jorge." Nick winked and gave him a fatherly slap on the back. "You're strong, good-looking, and smart. Yeah, you're rough around the edges, but not too rough. You can go as far as you want. You said some neat stuff at the graduation. I was real proud of you."

They sat on the van's tailgate and rested. Jorge's face clouded with the subject they'd both been avoiding. His shoulders slumped and he stared into his hands. "I can't shake the thought of that guy in a fancy suit layin' facedown in his soup bowl, deader than dead. Gave me nightmares."

"Yeah, me too." Nick wasn't getting much sleep. Poor Waverly. Even a ruthless negotiator and womanizer like that didn't deserve to end up that way, killed in front of the people he so much wanted to impress. Nick's neck hairs vibrated and a creeping coldness made him shudder. *Dear God, help them find Kenny before anyone else gets hurt.*

Cass promised to call at three. It was two-thirty. She'd insisted on seeing McTavish alone, stubborn like her mother, but promised to have the cabbie escort her inside the Rayon Building. Nick had insisted on picking her up from there. Fried on drugs, Kenny could not in any way be trusted. "You sure you don't remember seeing anything from up there on the stage? Anything suspicious, somebody a little too interested in the soup course? Anything at all?"

"Nope. I was too busy rememberin' everybody to thank. The police asked me the same thing when they took my fingerprints. I been rackin' my brains, but so far nothin'. Sorry."

"Don't sweat it."

"Do you think he went to heaven?"

"Waverly? Can't say. He made a lot of enemies; a lot of his business dealings were questionable. God will know what to do with him and we know we can trust God."

"He musta had some good in him. Look how he supported Taste."

Nick didn't want to pop Jorge's view of things. So what if Waverly used Taste to polish his own image. What was meant for evil, God could turn to good, and Jorge, for Nick's money, was as good as it got. "God can use the just and the unjust to accomplish his will. We all struggle, that's for sure."

"You're a good guy, Nick. I hope I don't ever let you down."

"So you think that shining me up like this is going to keep me from beating your rear in air hockey?" An air hockey table in surprisingly good condition was a recent donation to the Mission.

"Listen, Methuselah, I'm three goals up on ya 'fore you can find the on switch."

"You're all talk, muscleman. No crying to your mama when I mop the floor with you. Boo hoo!"

He almost dodged the broken egg on the loading dock.

They started to pull away from Taste when a sharp rap on the driver's side window made them both jump and Nick hit the brakes.

Philippe Peugeot, immaculate in Callaway tans and wrap-around rose-tinted Roberto Cavalli sunglasses, motioned to Nick to roll down the window.

"Nicholas." He didn't bother to acknowledge Jorge. "A word, please." As he disappeared to the rear of the van, it was clear that the word he wanted was private.

"Hang on, buddy." Nick gave Jorge's leg a slap. "I'll make it quick."

Peugeot waited, hands on hips, by the pristine front bumper of the moonstone silver 607. Car and driver formed an island of creamy smooth prestige and achievement in a restless back-alley sea of weeds, potholes, and industrial hodgepodge.

"Philippe." Nick searched his brain for a suitable animal analogy, but came up empty. "Have you managed to get some sleep? You know, since the incident?"

"Sss-leep? I was fortunate to change socks before a mega-millions breakfast meeting at six the next morning. Rest assured, I have lodged a formal complaint with Lieutenant Reynolds's superiors. I am partners with the developer who built the building that houses his homicide unit, for the love of heaven! I will not be lumped in with the usual suspects and subjected to all manner of indignities. Had anyone come at me to extract my DNA, I was prepared to give him or her a nasty bite not soon to be forgotten!"

Nick stifled a grin at the thought of Peugeot spending the night at the animal shelter while under observation for rabies. "They think Waverly's soup was poisoned. That and a weakened heart ... he didn't stand a chance."

The property developer looked as if his milk-and-honey world had soured. "That is not all about the man that was weak. His judgment was weak. His ownership portfolio was weak. His bottom line was weak. He drove a Hummer, like some pathetic weekend commando." Peugeot delivered the ignominious list of Waverly's shortcomings with teeth-sucking disdain. "James Waverly had all the aptitude and savoir faire of a bacteria-infested sloth."

"Philippe, please. The man is dead, murdered, and his killer is still on the loose. It all points to Kenny Burstyn, that drugged-out kid who got booted from the program."

Peugeot registered zero surprise. "I warned you about him. Not everyone is grateful for small favors. Drugs make monsters of men."

"And victims of us all. Taste has been closed indefinitely until the authorities sort this out. That hardly matters, though. The bad publicity alone will probably sink us."

Peugeot leaned back against the sleek motorcar, crossed his feet at bare ankles, and smoothed an expensive fawn-colored cashmere pullover. "Tut. Nicholas, you surprise me. Did you not tell me that a man of faith is, by definition, an optimist? When a door closes, a window opens, et cetera?"

"Yeah, well, I suppose—"

"No supposing. This is a pivotal moment in the history of your program. An opportunity to make Taste of Success more palatable to the earnest investor who is more than happy to associate with the downtrodden, provided the face of the poor is given sufficient appeal."

Nick didn't like where this was going. "It's not *my* program. It's the community's. What are you getting at?"

Peugeot removed the sunglasses, eyes penetrating, adjusting to the brightness. "It is not like you to disassociate. It's when times appear the worst that we must embrace the cause to which we are devoted."

He was twisting Nick's words, a sports car in overdrive.

"My meaning is clear. Instead of hard-luck heroin addicts like Kenny or the panhandling bum that everyone knows is running a scam, you make your poster child the boy in that van over there—handsome, virile, ethnic without being too ethnic. Instead of the tattooed sideshow woman—"

"Frieda. Her name is Frieda."

"It may as well be Frieka. You certainly knew who I meant. Why would you want her around your customers? Have you so soon forgotten basic marketing? Beauty sells cooking schools as well as perfume. You put the striking Guest Chef Felicity Fairchild on your advertising in nothing but an apron and I guarantee the public will move on from the dearly departed Jimbo Waverly."

Nick took a deep breath. "It's not about the guest chefs, Philippe. And Jorge's physical condition is not typical of our students. They come in all sizes, shapes, and colors and most of them haven't been taking care of themselves. We hope to get them there one day, but it takes time. The most important thing is that they see themselves as precious in God's sight and able to change into productive members of society."

Nick could see that Peugeot's tolerance for the discussion was wearing thin.

"How noble, Nicholas. How sweetly altruistic. The reality is that you run your little social experiment out of a converted warehouse that sits on a mountain of gold. The property under our feet, this entire waterside block, will soon be rezoned for commercial high-rise. A major player could buy this block, put up a thirty-story all-weather office and retail mall and under-write a dozen do-good efforts like yours. Or put you out of business altogether."

Peugeot's chuckle contained little mirth. "You think too small and small thinking means you will never rise above a soup kitchen mentality. I have seen it before. You are at the mercy of the wind. Experiments like yours get bounced from one insecure charitable facility to another, just like the people you serve. My model ensures permanence. It would not be long before you had television specials and direct-mail saturation and more development money than you could ever spend."

Peugeot's eyes flashed his vision as brightly as the jewel-studded rings on his fingers reflected daylight.

"Is that all, Philippe? If you'll excuse us, we've got perish-ables to deliver."

"Yes, Nicholas, that is all for now. Are you familiar with the fennec fox?"

Nick counted to five. "No, can't say as I am."

"Inhabits the desert lands of Egypt. It can dig so fast in pur-suit of prey that it looks as if it is sinking into the ground before your very eyes. You wouldn't want that to happen to Taste of Success."

Nick waited, sensing there was more.

"You should be hearing from the Taste board of directors sometime today or tomorrow." Peugeot replaced the sunglasses and slid like a raindrop from the gleaming finish of the 607. "You listen to them, Nicholas."

Nick watched the sleek motorcar purr past. He didn't doubt he was in for an earful.

# Chapter 12

It was weird how at each cubicle Cassie came to with raised eyebrows, the occupant urgently pointed her onward, ever deeper into the bowels of McTavish Enterprises.

She imagined coming eventually to a giant office with real walls and a door and acres of plaid carpeting. At its center, like Oz behind the curtain, would sit a wizened little Magoo of a man at a rolltop desk, the enfant terrible of food critics. If she shouted "Boo!" he would run for his life.

The image was her equivalent of the dinner speaker imagining the audience naked. And it helped some until a throaty roar from a wide-open doorway ahead made short work of her nerves.

"Where are my oven mitts? Who in the name of Pope Benedict would move a person's oven mitts? Clarice? Where is that woman who knows my soup? If she's in the powder room, you tell her to do her business on her own time! *Clarice!*"

From across the vast terrain of cubicles, one head poked up, one set of arms motioned frantically for Cassie to get on with it. *Clarice. She has to be standing on the credenza behind her desk!*

Cassie held her breath and darted through the doorway at the back of the building from which the roaring came.

She stood in a high-ceilinged room tight with ceramic white kitchen appliances, stainless steel sinks, and a phalanx of mahogany cabinetry down two sides.

The air was redolent of melted butter and pumpkin spice.

At first she saw no one—until an oven door slammed and a perspiring red moon of a face with piercing button eyes rose above a wide commercial stove. Parked atop the moon, like a flattened lunar lander, was a red tartan beret and thin wisps of rust red hair. Below the moon was a generous mouth outlined in wide coral red and, below that, a snow-white long-sleeved blouse covering broad rounded shoulders and an ample bosom. The blouse was caught at the throat by a red rhinestone broach big as a baseball. In wide, thick hands the color of flour and protected by a cloth towel was clamped a square glass baking dish with steaming orange contents.

Large damp sweat stains marred the blouse below the meaty arms, but were far less revealing than the truth of who this must be.

She minced no words. "Muira McTavish. Muira means 'from the moor,' not 'off the turnip truck.' So if you'd be so kind as to stop standing there with mouth agape and come tell me what's missing from this dish, I can have my dinner."

Cassie rushed forward and was met by a voluminous tartan skirt and red patent leather pumps with cloth tartan bows. She spied a clean spoon in a dish drainer at the sink and scooped out a small bite of the roasted pumpkin along with a bit of the sauce. She blew to cool the sample, then placed it in her mouth.

Salted butter. Check.

Minced ginger. Check.

Ground cloves. Check.

"Where did you get fresh pumpkin this time of year?" Cassie surmised there was nothing Muira wanted that Muira couldn't get.

"Somewhere in Asia. Sugar Pie Pumpkin is the devil to import out of season." The McTavish growl was a collaboration between deep voice and gruff disposition. "More inspectors and customs agents to sweet-talk than God has apples. Clarice, whom you met, knows what songs they like to be sung. So what's missing?"

"Cardamom."

"I'll be rubbed in sea salt! Of course cardamom! I'm pushing sixty, give or take ten years, and some days I couldn't come up with Arnold Schwarzenegger's initials, let alone an herbal cousin in the ginger family. Off the record, of course. You're not wearing a wire, are you?"

"I should say not."

"Then say it."

"I'm not wearing a wire."

McTavish looked Cassie up and down, eyes aglitter. "Who sent you, really? Is it that little dung beetle at the *L.A. Times*? You tell that pip-squeak he's persona non grata until full-length bathing suits come back in style. He's got the discriminating palate of a turkey vulture. What'd he pay you?"

Cassie mustered her best smile. "No one paid me anything, honestly. I'm not with any media. I'm with Taste of Success. You probably heard about the terrible incident at Celebrity Chef Night. We're in trouble and I thought, uh, that maybe you could ... I don't know what."

"Sure you do. You want to use me." McTavish watched her blush and allowed her to flounder a moment or two longer. "No shame in that. Happens all the time in American journalism. You get me in at such-and-so syndication firm and I write nice things about your fund drive to save the South African dust mite.

"So, tell me, do you use the optional cider vinegar in the soup base?"

Cassie nodded. "Absolutely. Nothing optional about it. It's as important as the pan drippings. The drippings lend a richness and depth to the flavor while the vinegar provides the bite. Actually, more like a light nip. But just a smidge—no more than a teaspoon."

"What's your garnish?"

"Finely chopped chives and a pinch of ground clove."

McTavish stirred a simmering pot on the stove top with one hand and inserted a knife into the orange flesh of the pumpkin with the other. "Smashing! We'll let that cool a tad, then skin the pulp and blend the works. Add the vinegar and bon appétit! Join me?"

Cassie breathed deeply the invigorating scent of diced onion, garlic, ginger, lime leaves, crushed red peppers, and coconut milk rising from a steaming soup pot to mingle with the aroma of spicy pumpkin. Her answer belied her hunger. "Thank you, no. My husband will pick me up soon. As you might imagine, there are a lot of fires to attend."

McTavish, eyes shut, sipped loudly from a wooden spoonful dipped from the pot. "Mmm, smashing! Here, have a sip." She replenished the spoon and handed it to Cassie.

Cassie blew and savored. "Ah, yes! That's hearty. Love the rough-chop ginger. Never give balcony seating to that which deserves main floor, front row center."

McTavish's tiny eyes tangoed with enjoyment. "Bravo! You should have your own column!"

Cassie didn't remind the critic that she herself had used the balcony line in a previous column dismembering a Brazilian bistro named Rio Chic for being "all brass and no rhythm."

"You won't neglect a sprinkling of kosher salt just before the addition of the vinegar?"

"Never!" McTavish motioned to a white laminate counter flanked by six tartan-upholstered bar stools. She removed a tiny tape recorder from a skirt pocket, set it on the counter, and switched it on. "Now give me your customers' strike-back list."

Cassie perched on one of the stools, laid her hands, palms down, on the cool countertop, and mentally sifted through all the service gripes she knew:

"Calling for a reservation and being placed on hold to the Top Ten Disco Hits of the Eighties. Then, in parentheses, 'America doesn't torture, remember?'

"Arriving on time for a reservation only to be told to wait while they 'get the table ready.' (What, the varnish isn't quite dry?)

"Being asked, 'Do you know how the menu works?' (Sure, I pick things out, you write them down, and I wait while you go get them for me. Questions?)

"Watching the order get cold while the waiter finishes a conversation with a coworker. (No, your gall bladder operation isn't more important than my poached salmon served hot.)

"Hearing, 'Is everything all right?' or worse, 'How you guys doin'?' (The truth? The crab cakes aren't fully thawed, the lipstick on that glass should have stayed in the dish room, and the carpeting needed replacing *before* Carter left office.)"

McTavish beamed and applauded. "Smashing!" She snapped off the recorder. "Any more?"

"At least a dozen."

"Have them faxed to my office. Clarice will give you the number on the way out."

Cassie fought the sinking feeling that she was leaving empty-handed. "Have I been dismissed?"

"Do you have what you came for?"

"No."

"Then I wouldn't let some Scottish hussy throw me out, would you? What do you need?"

Cassie studied the backs of her hands. "Help. Someone committed murder last night and used Taste of Success to do it. It's all over the news. James Waverly won't be the only casualty. Hundreds, thousands of homeless people who might have other-wise been trained to be productive citizens again, to believe in themselves and be given back their self-esteem, will lose it all because of this one stupid act.

"These are good people, Muira. Underneath the grime and the stale clothes, it could be you or me. A couple of bad choices, some family estrangement, a run of bad luck, and boom, we're on the streets. I can't stand to see these folks thrown away or the volunteers and cooking coaches at Taste made the villains because somebody had a grudge against me or anyone else. Am I making sense?"

McTavish said nothing, but went to the only cupboard with a combination lock. She stepped up on a small stool, punched in the code, opened the cupboard door, and extracted an old thick book.

She brought it to the counter, spread it open, and read aloud:

"We may live without poetry, music and art;
  We may live without conscience, and live without heart;
  We may live without friends; we may live without books;
  But civilized man cannot live without cooks.
  He may live without books — what is knowledge but
    grieving?
  He may live without hope — what is hope but deceiving?
  He may live without love — what is passion but pining?
  But where is the man that can live without dining?"

It was as if McTavish forgot that Cassie was in the room. Her voice dropped, took on an uncharacteristic softness, and she was lost in another world. "My grandmother wrote that a century ago. My mother read it to me every night at bedtime, just before prayers. My father was a chef of some international fame and gone a lot of the time. He cooked for Greta Garbo, FDR, and the king of England back in the day when tongue, head cheese, and mutton soup brought comfort to the table. Squirrel pot pie, boiled rabbit in liver sauce, sauerkraut-stuffed goose—smashing! But I digress. Every night that he was gone my mother read me a recipe from this book and I prayed for Daddy and 'cooks everywhere.' He died of malaria halfway round the world."

Suddenly, the critic's head snapped up, eyes narrowed, and she fixed Cassie with a warning glare. "Not a word of this to anyone. I make my way by being blunt. Blunt sells. No room for sentimentality. But we might be sisters when it comes to the kitchen. Anyone who would use food as a weapon against an unsuspecting victim is lower than slime. What are you thinking?"

Though she would hate to be on her bad side, Cassie couldn't help but like the flamboyant Muira McTavish. "We need good press to combat the bad. Not just think pieces on the philosophy behind Taste, although those are needed, but something really flashy that will command the whole attention of the Bay Area. Celebrity endorsements, maybe. A Bite of San Francisco? I don't know. But I do know that you have everyone's ear from Santa Rosa to Salinas and beyond."

McTavish straightened, countenance shining with native intelligence. It was as if Cassie could see straight inside the McTavish brain. Lights blazed, gears turned, pistons fired, and whatever came off the assembly line of her creativity was destined to be a doozy.

"You wait. Let me get back to you. If what I'm thinking can gain any traction at all—and if it can't, I'm not the great-great-great-great-great-granddaughter of Archibald McTavish, Laird of Glencairn—then Taste of Success will soon be on everyone's radar screen." She sprang to her feet. "My soup!"

Cassie was halfway out of the room when she stopped, turned, and watched McTavish with swift moves assemble her pumpkin delicacy. "One last question?"

"Shoot."

"Why haven't you ever visited Taste of Success and reviewed it?"

"I have and I will."

"You have?"

"Of course. You don't think I dress like this all the time, do you? Like Sherlock Holmes, I have my disguises. One of my favorites is the washed-out, street-weary, dishpan look. Straight hair, no makeup, flak jacket, jeans, ratty sneakers ... Clarice looks even more convincing in her weekend tattoos and fake nose ring. We've been to a couple of Guest Chefs and one regular lunch hour. The waiters always seem surprised we have money."

"And?"

"And nothing. You wait for the column to appear and pay for the paper like everyone else. With what you've told me today, you won't have long to wait. Now can a lady eat her soup in peace?"

Cassie smiled. "I don't know how to thank you. We're having a benefit and demonstration lunch at Guandong Harbour on Monday. Will you come?"

McTavish gave a dismissive wave. "I'll be there, if you swear to keep all this to yourself. Now would you go? All this tender talk could put a girl off her feed."

$\mathcal{S}$hove over, pigeon waste. I ain't here to cuddle with nothin' that smells like you."

Disoriented, Kenny Burstyn pretended the voice filled with mockery and disdain was classic movie dialogue.

"A hard dame like you should talk." It wasn't his best Bogart, but it would do. "Whatta ya doin' in this gin joint if you don't like gin?"

Not enough sarcasm.

The drugs dulled the sarcasm.

But this was no gin joint and he was no Bogart. This was St. John's Cathedral and the offended woman in the pew was not drugged out. She was a stranger. Incredibly tall like the World's Tallest Woman he saw on the Discovery channel. Tall with a rubbery head that sometimes split into two heads when he stared too long.

"Look, whack job, 'less you want to get maced, maybe you should find somewheres else to sit."

He went to the floor of Midnight Church, the stone floor in front of the altar. He prostrated himself, one cheek flat against the cool slab, its ageless geology absorbing the heat of heroin fever.

The top of his head pressed against the bottom step leading up to the altar rail. He pushed harder until the immovable stone ground his hair down through his skull and into his brain where it grew like moss and sucked up all the juice and moist bits that kept a brain wet. He backed off, remembering from somewhere that a dry brain wasn't good for you.

Father Somebody would soon enter from a side room and get the show started. Kenny thought the priest's name was just a single letter of the alphabet, but he couldn't come up with it. Not when the two girls on his right and a shirtless, hairless guy on his left swayed on their knees, arms outthrust, palms up, eyes closed, voices rising and falling in a foreign language. They looked happy enough, but heroin could plaster something like it on your face, something that turned out to be more jeer than joy.

Beware strangers bearing glassy grins.

He was nose to toe with the Biggest Pair of Shoes in the World. He looked up at the Tallest Priest in the World, sixteen feet if he was an inch. Of African persuasion, judging from the hands poking out of the vestments. Perhaps he was Father A for "Africa." But his head was so far away that it disappeared into the darkness above the altar and was unrecognizable.

"G. K. Chesterton said, 'The riddles of God are more satisfying than the solutions of man.'" The words came from the Tall Priest who was already at the homily. What happened to the "Our Father" and the Creed? "And one of the greatest of all riddles is the riddle of living water. Once you drink this water, you will never thirst again."

From somewhere low and deep in Kenny's belly came a thirst, but not of a kind that was quenched with a beer or an orange juice. This was a craving, a longing older than the stone beneath. Kenny knew that if he could just reach the top step of the altar, he would find the eternal spring.

He climbed, using elbows and forearms, legs as numb and useless as the paralytic's. Two steps. Three. At the fourth and top step, sweet water gushed from beneath the altar rail. It splashed over his chest and back, healed the sores and cough, the dementia and dark dread. There was Jesus, motioning him closer, wanting him to bathe in the everlasting waters of his love.

He would take some of the healing waters to the man who paid him, who still found him useful. Then he could drink and together they could bring the body of the dead to the fountain for resurrection.

*I forgot to hide.*

With a cry of exaltation, Kenny splashed in the torrent, washed his face in it, rubbed his body clean with it. Agate clean, rolled smooth against refining sand.

He gave a mighty shout. "I believe! Let my cry come unto thee!"

He didn't have to hide. Evil hates the light, but Kenny welcomed it. He couldn't be evil if he loved the light.

And then he looked into the face bent close to his, calling his name. It had come down sixteen feet from the darkness overhead and he knew the letter of the alphabet was "B." He felt a gentle hand on his head.

"Father B?"

"Kenneth. Let me help you, son, help you get straight."

That's what the police said. "You need to get off that stuff, son. Clean up your act. Go straight. And be our guest in lockup until you do."

Kenny shoved the priest, leapt to his feet, and could not remember how to get out of there. He turned in a circle and the room shifted, a spinning vortex of organ pipes, marble columns, candelabra, leering faces, and grabbing hands.

He jumped pew to pew, kicked and spat at his pursuers, and at last burst from the tomb into the garden. He almost went back for some more of that sweet water, but two big guys wanted to tackle him. When at last he dashed into traffic and ran down the center line to a cacophony of screeching brakes and blaring horns, they tired of the chase.

Kenny made for the curb and collided with a metal and cement trash barrel. *Why does the man still pay me? Why am I still useful?*

He coughed so hard that by the time he turned into the alley, he was bent chest to knees and groping for a place to lean.

Had he hurt that lady? He couldn't think of her name. Trixie something? Why did she take his bag away?

The rattle beneath his breastbone produced a thick gray-yellow phlegm. He spent the next couple of minutes clinging to a Dumpster for dear life and spewing chunky wads of viscid mucus onto the pavement at his feet.

When at last the coughing subsided, he was pretty sure he owned a couple of cracked ribs. All he needed was a punctured lung to finish him off. Or a zealous priest bent on exorcising him of the one thing left that gave him any relief.

A door opened, a stab of light, and the hard-edged laughter of people serious about their drinking flushed from the interior of The Three Sicilians. Kenny faded into the shadows and flattened himself against the back wall of the antique store. Frigo, the night cook, didn't like druggies hanging around his Dumpster. The risk could be worth it. Kenny once scored a pile of spaghetti in clam sauce, only slightly scorched, delicately seasoned with cigarette ash.

He froze. A hundred feet down the damp alley, like Lucifer in silhouette, the man stood by the open driver's door of his car. It was how he always waited for Kenny: Both feet on the pavement, chin resting on arms crossed on top of the door frame of the expensive, low-slung foreign make, staring at Kenny's approach through the driver's side window.

No smokes. No drinks. No curses. Quiet. A watching reptile.

He gave Kenny the creeps. Those were the Grim Reaper's wheels. That was the Grim Reaper's wheelman.

He doubted now that the man was interested in the healing waters.

Knew he was not.

He should have been there first. The man didn't like to be kept waiting. Especially by a walking stick like Kenny. A walking stick of heroin.

Kenny stumbled toward the car and driver. His legs felt all funny, like the bones were melted and the flesh replaced by two sacks of spiders. He wobbled onward, becoming increasingly crippled the nearer he came to the silhouette.

Fifteen feet from the car, he could stand no longer. He sank to all fours and crawled, ignoring the sharp gravel washed to the center of the alleyway and the greasy slickness that met his hands.

He was at the man's feet when one of them sliced through the darkness and kicked Kenny's arms from under him. Unable to catch himself, his forehead banged against the open car door and his nose, upper lip, and one side of his face ground into the muck and gravel-littered pavement. Stars exploded across his vision. The racking cough returned.

The man shrieked, examined the door, and stomped Kenny's head with hard shoes. He kicked the thin rib cage and this time Kenny heard bones crack.

Just before blacking out, it snowed one-dollar bills. If he came to in time, there would be thirty of them.

The next morning, twenty-six people sat at tables in the dining room at Taste of Success sipping coffee or bottled water. They were the trustees of the culinary-training program and its principal staff and volunteers. Cassie hoped this gathering was more productive than the last board meeting at which a lot of hands were wrung and no answers were reached.

It should be. Lieutenant Lloyd Reynolds, his investigation of the physical premises now complete, had called the meeting.

"I assure you, Lieutenant, as spiritual adviser and chaplain for Taste of Success, there is nothing but honor and the best intentions in everyone associated with the program. I'm confident that what you're investigating is an outside vendetta that unfortunately played itself out at Celebrity Chef Night. It could have come to a head anywhere."

Cassie could have kissed her priest then and there. He, and the church behind him, brought credibility and a sanctified concern to Taste's mission.

Reynolds paced the center of the room and looked at Father Wills without expression. "And what makes you so sure?"

The Anglican priest looked especially trim and dapper—and believable—in gray suit and blue silk tie. "The victim was James Waverly, a man with many rivals and adversaries. His several questionable business dealings are well documented, and he possessed a penchant for confrontation and high-handedness. Pardon my saying so, but it is not unthinkable that more than one person danced a jig at the lifting of Waverly's thumb, however shocking the way in which it was done."

"Yes, and a number of them were present here that night." Lieutenant Reynolds surveyed the gathered faces. "This stays in this room, but much of it's a matter of public record. Chef Maggiano was convinced that Waverly would steal his soup recipe and mass produce it. It's no secret that Philippe Peugeot hated losing three prime development projects to the Waverly machine. Trina Fisk was distraught over Waverly's unwelcome advances. Jorge Ramone could have played the macho avenger of Trina's honor."

He gave Cassie a meaningful glance before continuing. "Even Heinz CFO Barry Silvan, who was here volunteering with a number of his key officers, was once in line to take over as COO of Waverly Electronics. He had the seniority, the education, the special skill set, but Waverly passed him over for a junior partner. Within six months, Silvan was out at Waverly and forced to answer false accusations of financial improprieties leaked to the press."

Nick scoffed. "Forgive me, Lieutenant, but you can cross Jorge off that list. Trina too, for that matter. These are just hard-luck kids trying to start over. Believe me, Jorge's choice of weapon would not be poison. He would confront Waverly man-to-man and tell him to back off. One look at the boy's biceps and you'd know that."

"Then you admit that Jorge might have had it in for Waverly?" Reynolds stopped in front of Nick's chair and waited.

"Well, no ... I mean, it's possible, but Jorge's a good kid."

"A known thief good enough to break the jaw of a relief mission counselor? How do you counsel with your mouth wired shut, Mr. Dixon?"

"That's the old Jorge!" Nick shot forward to the edge of his chair and glared at the investigator.

Cassie put a hand on his back to calm him. "Jorge's doing real well, Lieutenant, one of our best graduates. He starts a new job at Palermo's next week, and his apartment is clean and neat. He's helping his family. Please don't jeopardize his chances."

Reynolds scratched his neck. "I'm more concerned with him jeopardizing his own chances. Did you know he's seeing a prostitute?"

Cassie felt she'd been clubbed with a ball bat. "What? He's not like that. He treats women with respect and I know he's sweet on Trina."

"She's the prostitute I mean. We've got him under surveillance and right now he's at Trina Fisk's shared apartment. Went there after he helped you, Mr. Dixon. You didn't know they've been turning tricks in that house?"

Cassie was stunned. "Trina? A prostitute? No way! She escaped from an abusive home and hated Waverly for his unwanted advances. She told me two guys once tried to get her to sell herself, but she wouldn't do it even though they killed her cat. She thinks Jorge is sweet, a real gentleman. Go easy, Lieutenant. Trina's been suicidal."

He gave Cassie a look midway between sympathy and pity. "So she tells you, Mrs. Dixon. You have to know that street kids like Trina say what they think they have to say to get what they want. They play on your concerns and, in the end, they do what they've got to do to survive."

Nick's anger spilled over. "And so what? They can never earn their way out from under suspicion? Once a filthy street rat, always a filthy street rat? When do they get their second chance? When can they once and for all shed the stigma? When, sir? When?"

"I guess when those of you not yet worn down by the sick crap I see every day break through and convince them that they can live decent lives. I'm glad Taste of Success is here, Mr. and Mrs. Dixon, don't get me wrong. But I'm here to catch the bad guys, and if that means that good efforts like this get caught in the cross fire and have to close shop, you have my regrets."

"I'll bet we do." Nick turned his chair around and straddled it backwards. "What about Kenny Burstyn? Find him and this puzzle starts to fall into place."

"Maybe." Reynolds removed a credit card from his wallet and used a corner of it to dislodge a bit of stubborn breakfast from his teeth. "But any one of the people I've named could have put Kenny up to it. Not too many heroin addicts I know who could pull off a poisoning on their own. Too much thinking required."

"Feed him, slip him a few bucks, and I hear a heroin addict will dance like a marionette." The declaration belonged to Gordon O'Neal, Taste dining room manager and chair of the Taste board of directors. Nick filled in while he attended a business conference in San Diego the night of the murder. Resembling the actor Robert Wagner, he darkened his hair professionally and liked to frequent tanning beds until he was the color of a Cuban cigar. "Childless and tan" was Cassie's unflattering portrait of the twice-divorced O'Neal. Whatever else he was, he was a silent partner in Guandong Harbour and helped turn the Asian hot spot into one of San Francisco's elite eateries and its chef, Handsome Fong, into restaurant royalty.

"Handsome sends his highest regards to all. If there is anything he can do, anything, his services and goodwill are at our disposal."

It was the kind of grand gesture typical of the city's gourmet chefs. They numbered 140 gourmands—the showy, the eccentric, and the bombastic—and came from the city's best restaurants to make Taste of Success everything its name implied. It was the "teach a man to fish and feed him for life" principle in glorious action.

Sometimes the chefs' rhetoric resembled the balloon that got away—highly inflated and impossible to bring back to earth. Cassie wanted to compile a cookbook of their favorite recipes to raise funds for Taste until the negotiations bogged down around priority placement in the book, which food photographer to use, who owned the copyright, and, if unable to include them all, which chefs would be left out and why. The project was on the shelf until a Houdini stepped forward who could help her escape the snarl.

More questioning. More disbelief. Long faces made longer. "And no one leaves town for any reason until I give the word." Reynolds scanned the room, making eye contact with each person. "Sorry, folks, I can guess what this place means to you. We're working hard to solve this crime sooner than later. You're taking a big risk feeding the public. Make street people the cooks as you have and your risk goes ballistic. I hope this turns out good for you, but you might want to rethink the business you're in. Maybe put the homeless in distinctive uniforms and have them clean up the city. Pick up trash. Paint over graffiti. Wash the sidewalks. Call it the Pride Patrol. I'd support something like that. A lot of the mess is theirs to begin with."

Cassie had heard enough. "That's fine, Officer Reynolds. But this is no chain gang, community service approach. We take good people and make them better. We give them a future, a skill with which they can feed themselves and others, one they can take pride in, one that offers them enough to live on and to one day raise a family on."

Nick tipped his chair forward. "That's right. Keisha White came to us from the shelter thinking this must be a program for men only. She knuckled down, used her southern cooking flair to best advantage, and followed up on every housing and employment lead we gave her. She's now day lead at Alligator Soul and has her own apartment, where she feels safe for the first time in years. She got the courage to call home and plans to spend Christmas in Baton Rouge with her mom and four sisters. Not bad for someone who a year ago had no permanent address."

There were nods and murmurs of agreement around the room. A large woman in coppery braids and dark green caftan thrust her arms at the lieutenant. "Listen to him, honey. He's talking life change. I'm Bessie and I work with Keisha at Soul. That girl sings almost her entire shift and makes the meanest, baddest jambalaya on the West Coast. You come see. It'll make music in your mouth!"

As if in church, the woman next to her let loose a hallelujah. "Bless me, Jesus! Funky blues with a kick!"

To a chorus of laughter and excited assent, Reynolds held up a hand. "Okay, okay. I can see I'm outnumbered. But James Waverly's future is over. My job is to find justice for him."

"His kind of privilege don't buy justice." The large woman's face was sad but determined. "Mr. Waverly received the wages of his labors."

This time the buzz in the room was more subdued and punctuated with angry mutterings.

"And where did you say that Kenny boy's got to?" The big woman stared the lieutenant down and the mutterings increased.

Lieutenant Reynolds motioned to the two detectives with him. "I know you're upset, folks, but addicts who don't want to be found can be tough to apprehend. We're working on it. But whatever you think of Waverly, know this. He had a family and a right to life. He's been denied that life and we will do everything within our power to find his murderer. I suggest you do the same."

The officers were gone, leaving behind the merry tinkle of the bell above the door. Cassie looked at the colorful collection of those remaining and the somber, bewildered looks on many of their faces. Every one of them was a friend and she ached seeing the somber expressions that overtook them. *Heavy hearts, like heavy clouds in the sky, are best relieved by the letting of a little water.*

"Cass, Nick, a word, please."

They looked at Gordon O'Neal motioning to them from the hall leading to the kitchen. Nick nodded. "Let's take five, gang, then meet back in here."

O'Neal smoothed black sideburns and folded his arms. "Now I can predict what you two are going to say, but please hear me out. We received an offer this morning of a million three. Several board members think we should take it."

It took a moment for his meaning to register. "For what, you mean the whole restaurant?" Nick stared unbelieving.

Cassie exploded. "A million *three?* For the building, maybe. The property is worth ten times that."

"Not when it's under a house of murder."

"Thank you, Bela Lugosi."

Nick absentmindedly rubbed the smooth corner of the stainless steel prep sink. "Philippe Peugeot told me just this morning that this whole block is soon to be rezoned commercial highrise. He said we're sitting on a mountain of gold."

O'Neal couldn't meet Nick's eye. "It was Philippe who made the offer."

"What!" Nick slapped his hand against the sink and the resulting bang made them all jump. "You can't be serious!"

Cassie fought down the anger. "That man should be fighting to get us every dime he can find, not exploit our situation and kick us while we're down!"

O'Neal nodded. "Okay, but he thinks he's doing us a favor by offering us what he calls a sweet spot in his building over on Harrison. Twice the room with space for classrooms, a lecture hall, storage, *and* a huge catering prep area so we can service seniors and shut-ins like you're always going on about."

"And half the visibility, half the parking, and him as landlord. Not to mention the nine million he'll gyp us out of." Nick made no attempt to hide his bitterness.

O'Neal sighed. "Unfortunately, it's not your decision or mine. The board will discuss the offer and the board will decide. Are you so sure this is the best use of these resources?"

Cassie gave him a funny expression. While she didn't know the details, she did know Gordon came from a rough background. Maybe it included getting the fight knocked out of him. "You think we should take the deal. . . . Gordon, you sound awfully close to surrender."

O'Neal wouldn't look at her. "I just know from experience that worse things can happen."

Cassie removed a long-handled spatula from the overhead rack and sliced the air to make her point. "I've handled every utensil in this place. Helped paint the walls, pick out the car-

pet, choose the china. Over there's where I sliced my finger to
the bone and Chef Marty Costello wrapped it in a clean linen
napkin and applied pressure until the cab came to take me to
the emergency room. He left Jorge with instructions on how to
finish his specialty Pepper Pomegranate and Walnut Dip and
away we went, the world-renowned seafood expert applying
pressure the whole way."

"Cassie, you know I—"

"Let me finish. Chef Rita Gonzales of El Paraiso, with the
Julia Child laugh. Chef Robert Teller of Oceans Away, whose
amateur table magic keeps the patrons guessing. Chef Handsome Fong of Guandong Harbour, the Asian tour de force who
is everyone's friend. Some we love; some we fear; nearly all have
earned our respect. It is a giant omelet of cooking talent. They
believe in our students and in this place right here."

She turned and pointed the spatula at O'Neal. "A whole
army of the good, the caring, and the famous brought this
building and this dream to pass. We don't barter in people's
lives. This is the place that God blessed and this is the place
where we'll rise again!"

O'Neal looked at Nick, who put an arm around Cassie and
squeezed. "You heard the lady, Gordo. Gird your loins and let's
go talk some sense into the rest of the board."

# Chapter 14

Cassie knocked louder a second time. "Trina? Trina, open the door. It's Cass Dixon from Taste. Trina!"

She heard voices followed by a thud from inside the unventilated attic walk-up on the city's west side. Accessed from the outside of a run-down three-story, the tiny apartment's faded yellow door opened onto the elements. The spidery wooden steps offered a dizzying view of a garage roof twenty-five feet below.

Cassie was about to start kicking the door when someone inside slid back a dead bolt and opened a gap as far as the chain would allow. A single wide and heavily made-up eye blinked against the bright light of day.

"Let me in, please. I'm a friend of Trina's."

"She ain't here."

"Is this where she lives?"

"Usually."

"So where is she now?"

"Beats me."

"Then I'll wait."

"Go way, lady. You bad for business."

"And what business might that be?"

"What you think? We bake the Girl Scout Cookies and sell 'em door-to-door."

Cassie stuck her foot between the door and the jamb. "So how much for the little mint ones?"

"Lady, you takes your foot back or I'm gonna—"

"Mrs. Dixie, that you?" It was Jorge's affectionate name for her and it was Jorge's voice. She turned and saw the broad-shouldered, trim-waisted life of Taste taking the steps two at a time with a breathless Trina in tow.

Behind them, a short male in gray sweats and an orange knit stocking cap backed down the steps and hurried away.

The chain rattled, the door flung open, and an Asian woman in boots to her knees and a tight skirt that stopped well short of them shoved past Cassie and looked over the landing rail at the fleeing man.

"Dang, lady, you owe me $30." The woman wore enormous hoop earrings and a sleeveless blouse two sizes too small for the demands made upon it.

She turned and glared at Cassie, who said, "We can always settle up when the police get here."

The woman managed a tight smile. "No need to get all legal on me."

"And where have you two been?" Cassie took a step down to allow the smirking woman to reenter the apartment.

Jorge and Trina arrived at the landing below. "Out walkin'." Jorge, face set hard, caught the Asian woman's eye. "Every time they bring a man in, we go for a walk. We been out a dozen times today."

The Asian woman stopped, wet her lips, and bent at the waist to give Jorge a thorough look.

A pale, thin man came out of the apartment blinking and buttoning his shirt. Jorge blocked his path and jabbed the man's skinny chest with a substantial finger. "Listen, John, you spread the word that 102½ Eckles Street is no longer a brothel." Two hundred pounds of loathing, he towered over the frightened, sweaty man. "I'm goin' to be camped on this doorstep, and any guy who thinks he can step over me will get a one-way ticket over the side."

The man nodded and practically flew down the steps.

"Oh, Trina, how could you live here?" Cassie took the frail girl in her arms. "This is no place for a decent girl to stay."

"Whatever." The Asian woman stomped inside and slammed the door.

Trina started to sob. "Rents are more'n two grand a month most places and here I got me a couch for $190. I wash in the kitchen sink and use the toilet downstairs. Ain't much, but even with the, um, traffic, it sure beats the shelter."

Jorge stroked Trina's hair. "Only a curtain separates her couch from what's happening on the other side. Four girls share this hole and two of 'em are trickin'. Smells bad in there."

Trina buried her face against Cassie. "If Taste shuts down long, I'll be back on the streets."

Cassie winced. The girl had about as much flesh on her bones as a small poodle. "No you won't. I know some people who can help. You're done with the streets."

"She can come to my mama's tonight and for as long as she needs." Jorge squeezed the girl's shoulders and Trina turned a tear-streaked cheek in his direction. He kissed it, then looked over their heads at the walk-up. "You're right, Mrs. Dixie. This is no place for her."

The girl wiped her nose and hid her face against Cassie.

"Trina, I want you to go back in that house and get your things. Go on. Just grab and go. Call out if you need us."

The girl nodded, wiped her eyes, squared her shoulders, and went inside.

"You sure that's smart?" Jorge looked worried.

"She needs to grow some backbone. She'll be fine."

Trina quickly joined them again on the landing. She clutched a plastic garbage bag of her few belongings and Cassie ached when she saw how small the bulge was. "They said I was a fool, but I'm pretty sure they meant themselves."

"Good girl." Cassie smiled. "I have a surprise for you two and I need your help. Tomorrow is a benefit lunch for Taste at Guandong Harbour. Handsome Fong himself is officiating and AJ earns his wings. He'll showcase a special dish of his own creation that I can promise you will rock the house!"

Jorge laughed. "Cassie Dixon, talkin' the talk! Ole AJ, huh? This I gotta see. Who'll be there?"

They started down the stairs. "Influencers. We've invited the crew from the *Chronicle* food section and all of the city council members. Of course the mayor was too busy, always is. I think he's avoiding us."

"Any moneybags?"

"Jorge!"

"Sorry. Any people of extreme wealth who want to adopt a Hispanic kid who can juggle, tell jokes, and boil water?"

Trina giggled.

"Maybe. But I did invite one person who I think likes us and has the ear of a few hundred thousand people with stomachs. I want her to meet you and hear how your lives have changed. I don't want to say who just yet, but if this person comes, you'll be shocked and amazed."

Jorge hugged the two women at his side. "I'm always shocked and amazed by you, Mrs. Dixie. Always!"

The next day, the gleaming kitchen at Guandong Harbour was controlled pandemonium. A full house awaited the debut of Chef of the Day Aaron Joel Rafferty's showcase special—crab and avocado omelet with French Brie, caramelized baked onion blooms, and seven-grain toast with orange-clover honey.

Cassie worried a knot in her apron string. She prayed that AJ would make a huge splash. He was being considered by the

San Francisco Convention Center for a sous chef position in food service. He had two little sisters and a mom and was the survivor of two drive-bys for refusing to join the gangs. High stress didn't seem to bother him. If he got the job, he and his team would eventually serve up fifteen hundred to five thousand meals at a time. The director of convention food service would be at lunch today scouting the talent.

Two days ago, under the tutelage of Taste chef instructor Clarence Teel, AJ pulled an all-nighter planning and rejecting menu after menu. He thought he was set to go with spinach salad, goat cheese flan, and macerated strawberries followed by herb-crusted roast chicken in a light tomato sauce and savory house-made gnocchi when at four a.m. that plan was derailed by a unique omelet solution that involved nine of his favorite flavors and textures.

"Spinach and chicken is what is expected. Crab and honey, now there's a twist." Cassie was delighted with AJ's natural ease around ingredients and their combinations. "Delighting the senses, that's the call I must answer."

She fought the knot without success. *Why am I so apprehensive?* But of course there could be but one reason. This was Taste's first restaurant meal after the tragic Waverly dinner. What if Kenny came back with more poison and—

No, she couldn't dwell on such things. Why couldn't she be light and spontaneous like Beth? Ever since her missions trip to Honduras, Beth appreciated things so much more. Cared more for others. Again this afternoon she and Cody were going to visit the residents at Fairview Senior Community to help them decorate for their Spring Arts Festival and Soiree. The two teens seemed to be growing in their affection for one another.

Cassie forced a smile.

They didn't know about the incident in the alley with Kenny Burstyn and she wasn't about to tell them.

The beautiful room with its oriental silks, black-lacquered furnishings, low lighting, and bubbling stream filled with golden koi was full, and most were committed fans of the culinary-training program. Several people came to her before lunch was even served to express their regrets over what happened. To a person they pledged their ongoing devotion to the students and the program. And thank God, without too much arm twisting, the board majority had voted down any ridiculous attempt to buy the program's chief material asset at a fire sale price. Most agreed any such offer was an insult.

Everything would be fine.

Cassie nodded at Jorge and Trina, seated next to the kitchen entrance. It was a comfort to have them near.

*Where is McTavish?* Lunch was about to be served and the woman was nowhere to be seen. Her sinking feeling said that her act of bravado the day before was blown off for the pathetic little effort it was. A shudder went through her. *What if she writes up my visit in caustic McTavish style? I'll be the butt of the joke and Taste will bear the scars.*

No, everything will be fine.


He finished writing the message on a single sheet of standard bond copier paper.

6:57 a.m.

He read over the message. "You will be paid $6.5 million in full for the building and property now occupied by Taste of Success. No objections. No negotiation. No police. You have until three o'clock today to say yes. Post that one word—YES—on both sides of the marquee at Guandong Harbour. If by three I hear from you, you hear from me. If I don't hear from you, you hear from Grim Reaper. P.S. Too bad Beth's cell phone's gone missing. NO POLICE!"

Plastic-gloved fingers folded the sheet of paper and slid it inside an equally plain white envelope. He printed on the outside before taking a wet sponge to the gummed flap and sealing the paper inside.

There was no smile, no sense of satisfaction. This was business. If anyone could sway the board of the food-training program, the Dixons could. And now he'd made sure that the Dixons would.

Mickey boy! Quit yer nose pickin' and come 'ere." The stout, jowly bicycle messenger dispatcher waved a thin white envelope. "We been busier 'n fleas on a mongrel. Almost forgot this one. Found it unner the door this mornin' inside a second envelope wit' plenty a money and instructions like. No name, address, nuttin'. Now we gotta express it to Gu-an-dong Harbour, dat fancy schmancy food joint in Chinatown. Gotta be there by 12:30 p.m. You get it there in twenty, there's an extra ten in it for ya."

Mickey, a wiry string bean of a kid in second-skin black tights, yellow and black racing shirt, and battered metallic blue bike helmet, grabbed at the envelope Smitty held just out of arm's reach.

"Twenty, Mick, ya read? Twenty-one gets ya zip. Maybe I should wait and give it to Wilder. That guy once went from Eighth and Market to Embarcadero without ever touchin' down!"

"Yah, yah, and the punk was raised by wolves and fed magic syrup by the holy angels. I heard it all, Smit. Just gimme the stupid message."

Mickey jumped at him.

Smit faked left and danced right. "Jealous?"

"Of what? A guy who's drunk by ten and drops architect blueprints at a fertility clinic? I should be jealous of Adolph bloody Hitler!"

Smitty eyed the clock. 12:12 p.m. "Eighteen minutes and countin'."

Mickey darted behind his dispatcher, snatched the envelope from between pudgy fingers, and leapt astride the saddle of a taped and wired bicycle bearing the scrapes and scars of long service.

Across the outside of the envelope in large, neat block letters were the words "Urgent. Personal Delivery. Cassandra Dixon. Guandong Harbour. Before three p.m."

Lightweight gray shoes like ballet slippers became one with the pedals and Mickey flew around three gentlemen in suits and briefcases and into traffic.

Legs pumping, eyes darting, he attacked street, sidewalk, and alley with military precision. Red lights, aggressive taxis, lane-hogging buses, and fist-shaking pedestrians were no match for the Prince of Stealth.

A veteran and winner of many an Alley Cat—a harrowing race down side streets by competing bicycle messengers—Mickey's drug of choice was speed. The velocity kind, not methamphetamines. Race obstacles included elevators, stairs, and oversized packing crates—the wilder, the better.

Uphill and down he raced through the clots and congestion of San Francisco commerce, ducking, feinting, dodging, correcting, legs a piston blur. Car horns and trolley clangs, low-rider cars and thumping bass, jackhammers and snorting garbage trucks were his blood-stirring symphony; exhaust fumes, hot steam, damp asphalt, and marine brine his intoxicating perfume.

With five minutes to spare—the wind in his face, freedom in his veins, and this close to a spare ten-spot in his pocket—Mickey darted into the narrow service lane at the rear of a Chinatown apothecary. It was a one-block sprint to the delivery entrance at Guandong Harbour.

Behind, a piercing screech and the loud bang of metal on metal. Mickey turned to look.

Ahead, a truck loaded with commercial windowpanes backed into and blocked the alley.

At 12:25 p.m., bike and rider slammed full force against the side of the truck, shattering both Mickey and the truck's load of window glass.

Shortly after one o'clock, Cassie hushed the crowd and introduced the hesitant AJ, in white coat and floppy chef's hat, to a room full of adoring fans. The standing ovation went on for most of two minutes.

"Take a bow!" Cassie held his arm and noted with affection the sweaty sheen adorning the young man's sparse blond mustache.

"Another!" Again, AJ dipped awkwardly from the waist and acknowledged the generous applause. Under his breath, she heard, "My onions are scorching!" She knew his kitchen staff would mind the onions.

Finally, Cassie quieted the patrons and they resumed their seats. "Ladies and gentlemen, won't you agree, the proof is in the omelet?" An appreciative murmur rippled across the room and heads nodded, but before applause could again break out, Cassie continued. "Taste of Success takes the latent talent found inside friends like our Chef Rafferty and brings it out into the sun where it can flourish and produce a harvest of benefits to both the community and to the developing chef. And now I give you the man whose generosity provided this beautiful setting for our benefit today, the inestimable Handsome Fong!"

A short, tidy, and meticulously dressed man, two large gold rings on each hand, stepped from the shadows to a thunderous ovation. Cassie only hoped the diners were as enthusiastic with their donations as they were with their approbation.

Fong spoke in a clear, cultivated manner, giving the history and philosophy of the program. "In conclusion, as I am sure most of you know, we wish to broaden Taste's reach and begin catering nutritious meals to the city's shelters, senior centers, and other care facilities serving the lower-income populations. Your generous gifts today will help fund the additional equipment needs required to launch this large undertaking."

Fong took a breath, as if carefully weighing his words. "Of course you are aware also of the tragic events that unfolded earlier this week. Someone, in a misguided quest to settle an old score with James Waverly, has with the same murderous stroke placed Taste of Success in a precarious light. I ask you, please, to write letters to the editors of all the media outlets, the mayor and his council, to anyone you can think of with influence. Tell them how important this program is to our city, that it must not fail, and that it is more important than ever in helping San Francisco shed its title as the homelessness capital of America!"

He looked from guest to guest, made eye contact, and with the merest of nods massaged the philanthropic urges at each table. "Please take the gift envelopes at the center of your tables, fill them out, and carefully consider what you can do to boost the program, provide the skills, and take the 'less' out of 'homeless.' Then double it and place that amount in your envelopes—cash, check, or credit card. Fill out the privacy flap of your envelope, seal it, and present it to one of my lovely assistants as they stroll the room. And thank you, thank you, from the bottom of our hearts."

It was 1:40 p.m. and board president Gordon O'Neal, framed in the doorway to the kitchen, signaled the band leader. A live jazz combo began a soft rendition of "Shanghai Serenade." Cassie watched AJ make a swift escape and Fong glide from table to table in the dining room, no doubt maximizing everyone's charitable spirit. If only McTavish had been there to witness the love.

"Psst!"

In the candlelit shadows, two people by the wall motioned to Cassie from richly upholstered, high-backed chairs flanked by pots of living bamboo. As she neared their table, she made out two modestly dressed women, one large and one slender. As soon as she made out the tam-o'-shanter perched on the larger one's head, she was sure.

"McTavish! Clarice! I'm so glad you came."

Clarice gave a furtive look around and nodded.

"Keep it down, toots." McTavish waited for the young woman at the adjoining table to leave for the powder room before snagging the vacated chair with a white sneaker and dragging it over. Her male companion started to rise in protest when McTavish growled, "Keep your britches snapped, champ. We'll be just a sec."

The man upon hearing the mannish admonition, sank back to his seat and took a long drink of his wine.

Cassie swallowed. "I feared perhaps you couldn't make it. There's a young couple from the program I'd like you to meet."

"Sure, after I digest. We slipped in the back way. Good thing we brought our ID or they'd a had us out parking cars. I'll say this, there's enough pearls and Gucci bags in this room to feed a small Caribbean nation." The food critic forked an ample bite of omelet into her mouth. "Mmm. That lad knows his crab. Sweet. Moist. Tender. The honey and the caramelized onions in perfect balance, the Brie and the clover making peace with the smooth, perfectly ripened avocado. And four-star toast, for the love of the Mackenzies and the MacBrides! Not some namby-pamby cloth-bound bread basket, oh no! Rather brawny earthen squares of oven bread, all hot and full of grainy impudence! Seconds, garçon, seconds!"

A wide-eyed waitress did the critic's bidding while Clarice scribbled furiously on a steno pad.

"I've a plan." McTavish chomped half a slice of toast in half and chewed, eyes closed. "You came to me for a plan and I have one. Come to my office at five and I'll lay it out for you. Now, as you were. Go, go! Based on this meal, I believe you must relieve this room of a great deal more riches. Tell Fong no one gets out of here for less than a grand.

"And another thing. Fetch me that Rafferty kid. I hear the bidding war's begun for his services. I can get him twice any other offer or my name isn't Muira McTavish!"

# Chapter 15

The 2:52 p.m. San Francisco Muni bus stopped in front of Geraldine Lassiter Preparatory School. Beth Dixon, in red Converse low-tops, new stone-washed jeans, and blue short-sleeved blouse, slipped off her book bag and boarded the crowded vehicle headed for downtown. Her mom had the Miata for the day. The senior community was only four stops away.

*I hope Mom doesn't try calling me.* She was always forgetting her cell phone in her locker at school and today was no exception. At least she hoped so. Come to think of it, she didn't remember seeing it after third period. Too much on her mind this year, what with advanced placement classes and volunteering at Fairview. Too much to remember.

*You'd think I was in love.*

She quickly dismissed the idea and threaded past standing passengers toward the rear, careful not to step on toes or jostle several avid book readers. When she got to where Cody Ferguson was sitting—neatly dressed in brown loafers, khakis, and a long-sleeved Denver Broncos football jersey—his face brightened apologetically. In the seat next to him, the seat she knew he attempted to save for her, sat a footsore, graying Hispanic woman with an oversized purse, two shopping bags, and a weary face that wished for day's end.

Beth smiled. Cody stood and she sat.

"Thank you, kind sir. May all your crops be bumper ones."

He gave her a puzzled look. "You want to try that again? Your book bag was in my line of sight. I could be wrong, but I'm guessing you want to skip the seniors and ride bumper cars."

She knew he was kidding around and her mock annoyance said so.

"Much homework?"

She grimaced. "Just a killer paper for A.P. English. 'Ten Reasons for Shakespeare's Continued Popularity.' Ten! I think Miss Crunk won't be happy until half the class is dead from brain strain. You?"

Cody made smug. "Well, m'dear, as strange as it may seem, I use study hall to study, therefore my homework load is reduced to deciding whether this year's class gift should be new shoulder pads for the Ocean View High Sea Wolves or a step-on steel drinking fountain to replace the old ceramic one with the twist handle."

"Gosh, when did you stop drinking from bucket and dipper?"

"Very funny. You know, I think this is the day."

"For what?"

"The day I beat Al at checkers if it's the last thing I do."

Beth shook her head. "A noble goal, but I'd say you're about fifty-five years too late. I think he was taught by Attila the Hun."

"Then I'm going for Alice's sympathy. First I play the deaf card, then the innocent boy just trying to help out the old folks card, and for the coup de grâce, hmm, the 'if you're not nicer to him, Al, you'll ruin it for all of us' card. That should do it."

"Just sing her 'Let Me Call You Sweetheart' and Alice will wring the guy's neck for you."

"Ah, Al's not so bad. He's had a hard life and what's he got to show for it? His kids never come see him and in that wheelchair, his roamin' days are done. I know how he's gotta feel. I sure want to die with my boots on. You know, I bet he and the others can help you with your paper. Some of them had to be alive in Shakespeare's day."

He peered out the window at the familiar landmarks and pulled the bell.

Beth stood and smiled at the woman with the shopping bags. "*Dios te Bendiga!* God bless you!"

Twenty years vanished in the woman's return smile. "Ah, *gracias. Buenos dias!*"

No sooner had the bus moved off without them than Cody caught sight of the lunch wagon parked on the dead-end side street between the senior community and Von's Grocery. "That reminds me." He smacked his lips. "How long has it been since I had that PB and J with banana and pickles for lunch?"

"Ugh."

"We're not getting picked up 'til six."

A man waved to them from beneath the awning that provided shelter for walk-up customers. "I'm packing up, kids. Made a little too much ahead, so tacos and dogs are half price. Sloppy Joes, two bucks. For the lady, a Sloppy Jane with tofu meatballs, red sauce, nonfat cheese. I'll toss in a bag of chips and soda for another fifty cents. Deal?"

From the look in his eyes, Cody clearly fought, and lost, a nasty case of the hungries. She grinned. "Got any money?"

He dug in his pockets and handed her a five.

"You go inside and proceed to get clobbered by Al. You know he's had those checkers warmed up for an hour and gets upset if we're late. I'll go grab us something decent from the gut truck." She heard herself and laughed. "Boy, there's an oxymoron!"

"Can you manage?"

"I got it. Go!"

With a reminder he liked everything "extra sloppy," Cody took her book bag and ran for the front doors of Fairview.

The white step van sparkled in the sun. It looked new and everything she could see gleamed, from the soda cooler and cold meat storage compartment to the stainless steel coffee urn and frankfurter steam table. She looked for a name—The Magic Hat or Freddy's Food on the Run—but there was nothing painted on either the cab doors or the sides of the wagon. Even the menu was generic and unbranded. "You sure keep your wagon looking nice. I don't think I've seen you around here before."

The burly middle-aged man in unspotted white pants, blue shirt, and white paper food-handler's hat looked better suited for construction or heavy lifting. "Nice of you to say. Haven't had it long; my first time in the area. But my rig's got all drop-shelving, antisplash edging, and a nice double sink with full-sized basins. Listen to me. What do you care? But I do hope to add hoagies and maybe some gyros by summer. My fresh fruit selection could use some work. What do you think? Apples? Oranges? What?"

"Peaches and pears. Oh, and bananas. Those are my favorites."

"That so? What can I get you, little lady?"

A small digital clock on the counter read 3:20 p.m.

She gave him their order and sat down at the little portable steel folding picnic table to wait. She heard him rattling around inside, the opening and closing of metal doors. What a perfect setup for her Uncle Ruggers once he ever tired of the far reaches of the earth. He could keep moving and park a lunch wagon anywhere. It was his love for jungle medicine and helping sick kids that inspired her to think about serving on a hospital ship one day.

"Sir, can I ask what you think of Shakespeare?"

Without warning, the awning overhead collapsed, enveloping Beth in the raw industrial smell of new plastic. She tried to stand but was thrown to the ground, the weight of someone on top of her, the smell of car oil and aftershave in her nostrils.

The shock of a needle punched through plastic and into her arm was second only to the realization that there were no food smells coming from the wagon. And wasn't a dead-end street an odd out-of-the-way place to set up for business?

And that she'd forgotten to scream.


Fleet Feet Bicycle Messengers called Guandong at 4:09 p.m. and asked for Cassandra Dixon.

The last of the lunch guests were gone and the restaurant was being readied for the regular Thursday supper crowd. In gifts and pledges, Taste of Success had raised in excess of $100,000.

Cassie gave Nick a victory kiss and went to the phone, filled with confidence. If this was the degree of public goodwill they could count on, Taste would rebound and then some. Ordinary San Franciscans loved this underdog and she had yet to hear the McTavish plan.

"This is Cass Dixon. May I help you?"

"Yeah, Mrs. Dixon, we're, uh, holdin' an envelope for you that was marked for express delivery by 12:30 this afternoon. My apologies, ma'am, but the messenger was on his way to you when he was in a bad accident." It sounded as if the man choked, than recovered. "Da police didn't find no envelope 'til we was told of the incident and they looked the scene over a second time. So much glass and blood ... sorry, ma'am, you don't need to know all that. They found your envelope, pretty wet and beat up, but still sealed in one piece, ya know? If yer still there—course yer there, I'm talkin' at ya—we'll send it over by cab. The sender went to some trouble to make sure you get it. Can ya wait?"

Cassie gripped the phone. "Who is the sender, please?"

There was hemming and hawing at the other end, then, "Sorry, can't say. It came to us all anonamoose-like but with da bill paid. Says urgent on it."

Unnamed anxiety rippled over her arms and hands. "I see. And you are?"

"Smitty Jordison, ma'am. Day supervisor for Fleet Feet Bicycle Messengers. We been in bizness bunch a years. Don't lose many, messages, that is. Maybe two in my time. Mickey's a good kid, like one of my own. Better 'n my own, the ungrateful sods. He's hangin' in barely. He turned his head last minute or he'd be dead as dirt right now. He got a sister in Boseman, but her phone's all disconnected."

"I see. Thank you, Mr. Jordison, for following through on that message. I'll wait here until it arrives. Please let me know if we can be of any help where Mickey's concerned."

"I'll do dat, Mrs. Dixon. Very kind a ya. And know we be sorry if dat late message is a problem like."

"I'm sure it'll be fine. Good day, Mr. Jordison, and thank you."

She gripped the receiver until an insistent beeping on the line reminded her to hang up.

Excuse me, Al. Can ya wait and go for the kill when I get back? I think Beth could use a hand. Just be a minute."

The path to Cody's demise was clear. Al's thick fingers twitched to grab up his lone red checker and end the suffering. His saggy jowls lifted in a slight smile. "Make it quick, sonny. The jump-meister has another village to pillage!"

Cody patted his opponent's shoulder and headed for the door of the dayroom. "That's what I like about you, Albert. You really know how to encourage the young people. Let's get those streamers up when I get back."

Alice, in pale green slacks, pink smock, and a silver neck scarf patterned in white gardenias, cut him off in her wheelchair and looked into his eyes. "You shouldn't eat that fast-food slop. We'll ask the gals in the kitchen to heat you up some of last night's hot potpie."

Al wheeled his chair alongside hers and set the brake. "It was not hot and never saw a pot. Had microwave stamped all over it and enough preservatives to embalm King Tut and six of his buddies. Leave the boy be, Allie. A little tube steak swimmin' in chili never hurt a guy." He smacked his lips.

He earned a disgusted look and a cold shoulder before Alice rolled over to a table to resume cutting smiling daisies from yellow construction paper.

Cody grinned at the elderly soap opera and made for the exit doors. How long did it take to dump some sauce on a bun—or tofu meatballs, for that matter? Beth was stalling.

*I'm going to tell her. Enough beating around the bush. You like someone, you tell 'em. Be direct. "Beth, I want you to be my girl-friend. Officially. I want you to wear my picture in a locket around your neck. When should we get married? How about next Sat-urday?" Whoa. Too much information. Keep it friendly, but not that friendly. Something between "I want to carry your books" and "How many kids do you want?" Maybe "Beth, I can smell you from here and you smell great" or "Your smile haunts my dreams more than a two-headed zombie!"*

Nerves made him goofy. Or was it love?

He laughed and waved at the aged twins, Cora and Dora, leaving the women's restroom in the lobby waiting area. "Hi ya, ladies, we're starting to decorate. Did you see Beth in there by any chance?"

"No, sorry, dear." They spoke the words as one.

An unnamed misgiving tapped his spine. Where ...

He exited through the automatic doors and halted.

No Beth. Only the lunch wagon making a hasty U-turn in the middle of the dead-end street.

The front tires of the wagon bounced up onto the curb, nar-rowly missing a hydrant.

Cody started running.

The wagon lurched to a halt, paused, rammed backward, jumped the opposite curb, and struck the chain-link fence bordering the grocery store property.

*No one drives a lunch wagon that way. No one who's legit.*

Cody's legs and arms blurred, driving him across Fairview's driveway and the long, neat lawn that he sometimes mowed for free.

The wagon suddenly shot forward at a tight turn and leaned precariously sideways before righting itself and speeding to the corner.

The man at the wheel looked lethal, pleasant smiles gone, not at all the sort of man who would drive a lunch wagon.

Cody caught the vehicle as it fishtailed right onto the four-lane thoroughfare without stopping. In a final burst of speed, he leapt for the rear bumper and grabbed hold of the handles on the rear double doors just as the truck accelerated.

Someone pulled even in the curb lane, motioned wildly to him, and reached for a cell phone. The lunch wagon sped up. Pavement rushed past at what had to be fifty miles per hour. Cody, frozen in fear, looked through a back window into the lunch wagon.

Beth, sunlit body motionless, lay on the floor mere inches from where he stood. Every time the driver swerved around a car, Beth's head flopped like a rag doll's and banged against the side of the stainless steel grill unit. He had to get her out of there.

*Is she dead?* His chest constricted. How long could he hang on?

Without warning, the lunch wagon cut off a cement truck, shot off the main thoroughfare, and swerved onto a rutted track paralleling a set of railroad tracks.

*God, oh God, help ...*

The wagon bounced, bottomed out, careened across rutted, weed-strewn terrain. Cody's feet slipped, shins collided with the metal bumper, arms stretched to the breaking point. Ignoring the pain, he fought for footing, teeth gritted. Like a charioteer straining to halt runaway horses, he tried to flex his knees and let them act as pistons against the shock of the uneven roadbed.

*Don't let the doors be locked ... please ...* He wrenched the right-hand door open just when the wagon hit a particularly deep pothole. The door flew wide, nearly dragging Cody from the bumper. He stayed with it and, on the next rut, the door started to swing closed. Before it did, Cody forced his body into the gap and clawed his way inside. The door slammed shut behind him, the wagon jerked to the left, and he was knocked sprawling on top of Beth.

*She's still breathing! Thanks, God! I've got to get us out of here ... how? Jump? Beth's unconscious. She'd never make it ...*

Another five minutes of jarring passed before the truck slowed, stopped, and quickly reversed. The sun abruptly disappeared from the window. They must be inside or under something. Cody tried to stand.

The sudden stop threw him off balance. Cody rammed headfirst into the grill unit. He fell backward against the rear doors and moaned, sure that not a single square inch of him had gone unbruised.

When a few seconds later the doors opened, he twisted around and stared into the barrel of a snub-nosed revolver.

Cassie didn't know why, but the dirty, water-stained envelope was a viper in her hands. The boy meant to deliver it now fought for his life.

Her hands shook. The word "urgent" made her want to never open it. And what would it mean that she had not received it before the requested three p.m.?

Why not a phone call, an email, a telegram? The envelope had arrived by cab like a statement a mafia godfather would make. The horse's head in the bed.

Breathe. Believe. Trust.

Having prayed for calm, Cassie stilled her hands and slit open the envelope.

# Chapter 16

The man holding the gun wore a black ski mask, black athletic sweats, and black sneakers. His lips showed through the slit in the mask. They were wet, too large, and carved into a sinister grin like a jack-o'-lantern's.

Beth stirred and sat up, movements groggy.

"Shut your eyes! Don't look at me! Sit down! Turn around!"

When Cody took too long to comply, the man grabbed his jersey, yanked him to the floor of the truck, and smacked him across the head with his free hand. The gun menaced inches from Cody's eye. *If he hits Beth . . .*

Cody helped Beth turn away, their backs to the gunman. Suddenly all went black, Cody's head inside what felt and smelled like a nylon sack. A rough hand cinched the covering at his neck and tied it off.

Cody panicked. *Too hot. Too tight. No!* He reached to untie the shroud and was punched hard in the rib cage. He gasped, but managed to speak. "You hurt her and so help me I'll—" He was silenced by a hard punch to a kidney and lay gasping on the cold metal floor.

Gloved hands pinned his wrists together behind him and bound them tight with what felt like leather strips. The man's body stretched heavy against his as he leaned over, his mouth and chin against Cody's neck. He knew the guy was speaking some threat because he felt the resonance vibration and the hot air expelled against his ear. The smell was of stale breath and a hint of anchovies.

*He doesn't know I'm deaf.* The man moved to Beth next, probably tying her up in the same way, and Cody could only imagine what the thug whispered in her ear. He felt sick. If he could have gotten hold of the gun ...

Cody blocked out the dark thoughts and concentrated on catching his breath. His side and lower back hurt bad. He was glad he'd gone out for wrestling and bulked up or something important might have gotten busted.

A rear door banged against his buttocks and in seconds he felt the engine start and the truck back up. *Where to now?*

Beth moved, her fingers touching his head. *Easy, Beth. I'm still here. I ... I'm sorry.* Tears stung his eyes. He thought of his mom and dad. *Dear God, let me see them again.*

"Beth?" He didn't know if he could be understood through the fabric around his head. "Beth?" He said it louder. "Beth, if you can hear me, tap my head three times."

He waited for what seemed an ice age before he felt her fingers tap against his skull. *One ... two ...* The pause went on too long ... *three!*

"Beth, you okay?"

Three more taps, faster this time.

"I l-love you, Beth." His voice caught. "I have, uh, you know, since forever."

When three more taps came, Cody smiled. Beth shifted her weight and scooted around until her head came to rest against his.

And still the truck drove on.

N*o negotiation.* As soon as Beth's phone went to voice mail, Cassie frantically punched in the number for Fairview Senior Community.

"No, Mrs. Dixon, they're not here. It was the strangest thing. We saw Cody for maybe fifteen minutes and then he left. Never did see Beth."

Cassie fought for control. *God, please* ... "Can you remember anything he said or did, anything at all that might explain why this visit was any different?"

"Now that you mention it, on his way back out Cody asked the Webster sisters if they had seen Beth in the bathroom. They said no, he gave me a little wave, and was gone. I don't recall her ever coming into the building today. Is something wrong with the kids?"

"No ... maybe. What time was that?"

"Couldn't have been much later than 3:30 or so."

When she hung up, Nick pulled her close. "What, Cass? Talk to me."

Her chin trembled. "They're gone, Nick." It wasn't much above a whisper. "They've disappeared."

Nick reached for the phone. "We've got to involve the police. Somebody wants that waterfront property and they've already killed to get it. We'll talk to the authorities now, together, get Lieutenant Reynolds down here, show him the note, every rotten word this maniac wrote. We've got to find Beth and Cody before—" He smacked the receiver against the countertop, face red. "I swear, if anyone hurts so much as a hair on their heads—" One-handed, he put it on speaker phone and punched in 9-1-1.

Shaking, praying, they held onto each other. The waitstaff looked at them curiously, but continued to reset the tables.

Cassie feared she would be swept out to sea. *Dear Jesus, dear Jesus* ... The roar of desperation in her head beat against the rock of "In God we trust."

Cassie grabbed the phone and broke the connection.

"Cass! What the Sam Hill are you doing?"

Cassie pulled him into a secluded booth. "We can't, Nick." She said it in a fierce whisper. "Just listen. They think we ignored the warning. As far as they know, we received the message they sent and our silence is our answer. We've got to get word to them somehow, beg them to release the kids without involving the authorities. We've got to get the 'yes' up on the marquee in case they're still watching. Go tell Handsome he's got to let us do this. We could put a coded message out on the TV and radio stations to let them know we didn't ignore them, that we would not risk our babies this way, our precious, precious—"

The fear tore from her in a sob. Nick squeezed her hand, face pale with worry. He walked her back to the counter. "Sweetheart, no, this is far bigger than what we can do alone. We have to call the police and then I'll call Cody's folks."

She heard little else, barely registered the rings, the click of the phone, until, through the storm of her emotions, she heard the 911 dispatcher's words with frightening clarity: "What is your emergency?"


He stood at the pier railing watching a tugboat churn slowly against the waves, fighting for every foot against the prevailing winds.

He wanted to kick the wooden railings apart, smash them to kindling. Who did they think they were dealing with, some amateur? That they could just brush aside his threats?

True, he never meant for Waverly to bite it, just get real sick, sick enough to walk away from Taste and never look back. Stop his financial support. Create a little bad press. Get everyone's shorts in a bind, force Taste into a depressed sale, and do them a favor by offering a decent fraction of what it was worth.

Business.

If it weren't for the Dixons. Without them, the others would cave in a heartbeat. At least a third of the board were nervous Nellies who would cross the street rather than have to deal with a homeless person. They were there because it looked good on a résumé. You were only as good as a résumé larded with community service. You put in an occasional appearance, cast the odd meaningless vote, and kept your name on the letterhead. But push come to shove, no one wanted to be associated with a cursed project. Before he got done with it, Taste would be as cursed as Dracula's castle.

The devil was in the Dixons. Were there two people more likely to draw fire from the gods? Yet here they were, doggedly persisting. Thumbing their noses at him. And who on the board would vote against them? Ever since those two came along, the sheep were only too happy to follow.

The Dixons were fools who should have gotten the hint when their perfume went south. Christians! They were like crabgrass the way they defied any attempt to get them to leave. The more you attacked them, the more they spread. *Give me a good atheist any day.*

He thought the kidnapping would make it as personal as it could possibly get. Apparently not.

"So be it." He had an ace up each sleeve and woe betide the Dixons that they had forced him to play them.

He flipped open a cell phone, poked the number on speed dial, and waited. The tough little tug had won half its length in headway when a voice answered. "Yeah?"

"Get rid of them." He snapped the phone shut, slapped the top of the rail, and smirked. Two hundred Maricopa Square was as good as built.

The van lurched to a sudden stop, the rear doors flew open, and Cody was thrown onto a pile of something that flattened like cardboard under his weight.

Beth followed, her back landing against his legs.

The coverings were yanked loose and ripped from their heads.

Two sights immediately registered. One, they were lying in a downtown service yard amidst an untidy pile of discarded cardboard packing boxes and smelly black garbage bags. Two, the gun at the end of the masked man's arm was pointing right at them.

"You tell your mommies they need to keep a closer watch on you!"

Cody froze, eyes shut.

The gun fired twice.

The man jumped into the food wagon and sped off.

Cody let out his breath. The guy had shot to miss. *Thank you, thank you, God!*

"Beth? You okay?"

Cheeks streaked with tears, she opened her eyes and slowly nodded.

"Untie me. I tried an old trick I saw in a movie. I kept my wrists bent and my muscles tensed so now the bindings shouldn't be tight at all. Don't cry. Here, I'll back up to you like this and you see if you can untie 'em."

At first, it was as if Beth's fingers wouldn't work at all. She fumbled at the leather. But the more she worked, the more she succeeded.

"That's it! Beautiful, Beth. I feel them coming loose! Keep it up!" His side felt like he'd been rammed headfirst by a bull.

In another minute, he was free and working on the leather strips that bound her hands much tighter. When at last they came away, he winced at the ugly red marks encircling swollen wrists. "That's it, Beth, we're free!"

She looked at his hopeful grin, rubbed her wrists, and started to cry again. She lay her head against his thigh and let him pat her back. He did it self-consciously, amazed and awkward at her warmth and proximity. "It'll be all right, Beth. Those s-shots were meant to s-scare us. Worked for me. How 'bout you?"

She said nothing, but pulled her knees to her chin, shoulders shaking.

"You know, I can think of a million places nicer than this to hang out. I was too scared to think of it before—and you were too doped up—but do you have your cell on ya?"

She shook her head no.

"Good, I don't have to feel quite so stupid. Whatta ya say we go ask to borrow a phone and call our parents? Before you know it, we'll be home safe." Though he said it with all the courage he could muster, he questioned using the word "safe."

The cell phone announced itself with the opening bars of "Brahms' Lullaby." Cassie snatched it up. "Beth? Beth! Thank God! Where are you? Are you okay? How's Cody? Oh, Beth, honey, thank the Lord! Nick! Nick! They're okay! They're not hurt! Oh, Beth, sweetie, don't cry ... we're coming, Beth, we're coming ..."

Cassie, Nick, and Cody's parents, Sheila and Andy Ferguson, converged on the downtown police precinct led by the flashing lights of Reynolds's unmarked cruiser.

Beth and Cody came running and the next ten minutes were a chaos of tears, smiles, hugs, and six different conversations at once.

Lieutenant Reynolds waved his arms. "All right, folks, let's settle down please. We've got some questions for you now about the kidnappers. We'll take each of the kids into a separate room where the respective parents are welcome to attend, but we do the questioning right now, got it? Time is of the essence. Cody and Mom and Dad, go with my associate Laurie Mercer. Beth, you and your folks join me in this room."

Cassie couldn't take her eyes off Beth or stop holding her hand. They sat close together, Nick holding Beth's other hand, while the lieutenant conducted the questioning.

"Can you describe the vehicle in which you were held?"

Beth looked bewildered. "Cody was so brave."

Reynolds coughed. "That's nice, miss, but the truck? What make and model?"

She looked at him as if he had asked her what planet she considered home. "I-I'm not sure. You know, one of those white lunch trucks."

"Did you catch any part of the license number?"

"No ... no. I was buying us some lunch, not thinking about getting kidnapped."

"The detective knows that, Beth." Nick looked ready to punch something. Cassie knew he didn't like what he would consider the inaction of the moment. "Think hard, honey. Any part of it at all. A letter, a number, in state or out—"

The lieutenant looked sad as a bassett. "Mr. Dixon, please, I'll do the asking."

Nick shrugged as if to say, "Be my guest."

"Now, miss, was the man who waited on you the same man in the ski mask?"

Beth appeared confused. "Don't think so. He was heavier, meaner."

"Who was?"

"The gunman with the mask."

"Meaner how?"

"His voice had some threat in it. I think the nice man drove while the mean man rode in the passenger seat."

"Describe both men. Everything you can recall about each of them, no matter how insignificant it might seem."

For twenty minutes, Beth haltingly pulled every detail she could from her memory. In the end, it wasn't much. "Sorry. I was in shock and the first guy gave me a needle with something in it that slowed me down and fogged my mind. I think I might have passed out for a while."

Reynolds nodded. "I understand. Did you hear anyone use a person's name at any time?"

Beth sighed and shook her head.

"How about the gun? If I showed you a book of weapons, could you tell us which one looks most like it?" At the end of three grueling hours, the incident was only slightly less sketchy than when they'd started.

"He told us not to look at him, but I could hear him breathing like ... like some kind of a-animal." She stopped, the tears welling over and dripping onto the table.

Nick slapped both hands on the table. "Does she have to talk about that now, Lieutenant? She's been through enough without reminding her of the filth some sleazebag said."

Reynolds gave Nick an exasperated scowl. "Do you need a break, Mr. Dixon? Considering this guy said little, what he did say could provide us with important clues as to nationality, vocal abnormalities, who knows."

Nick looked at Cassie, who dabbed at Beth's face with a tissue. She squeezed her hand. "It'll be over soon, Beth. Go ahead and say what you remember."

Beth spoke to the top of the table. "He said he liked me and maybe I might want to date him sometime. He said he'd look me up later. Then he laughed a dirt ... dirty laugh ..." Beth burst into tears and Cassie held her.

Nick stood up and shoved his chair back. "That jerk! I'll break his neck!"

"No, Daddy!" Beth wailed. "Don't. It sounds too much like him ..."

Nick wilted like a diseased dandelion. He slumped in his chair and Beth wrapped her arms around his neck and wept.

Reynolds cleared his throat. "Let's change the topic a moment. We picked up some partial tire impressions on the lawn bordering the senior community where the truck made its hasty escape. It's pretty hard to hide a lunch truck, and those impressions may help us make a positive ID."

Two uniformed police officers—one man, one woman—entered the interrogation room. Reynolds nodded at them. "Now I need for Beth and Cody to go with these two officers to separate dressing rooms where you will be asked to remove your outer clothes and place them in the provided bags for analysis of any dirt or threads you may have picked up while inside the truck. We'll provide you with coveralls and sandals to get you home."

Beth and Cody reluctantly complied. As they left the room, Cassie choked. *I don't want them out of my sight even five minutes.* She started to rise until the weight of Nick's hand made her stop.

I need you to find someone for me, Francis. Someone who doesn't want to be found." Father B smiled up at the towering giant, half expecting to be patted on the head.

Francis Welch was living proof that if the fire's hot enough, anything will burn. Six-foot-three, two hundred eighty pounds packed solid, he was what Father B called "my enforcer." A former member of the Lords of Lucifer motorcycle gang, he grew weary of the lack of discipline and leadership. And the name.

"I don't want to be an officer of Satan. What's the Messiah like?" The biker who questioned Father B was dressed in leathers, hair down to his waist, tongue surgically "forked" like a snake's, and scarred forehead tattooed with twenty-eight hatch marks for the twenty-eight noses broken against it. The night that Francis forsook the Prince of Darkness and pledged himself to the Prince of Peace, seventy-six others ran to the altar at St. John's to get eternally cleansed. It was the biggest single batch of conversions in the cathedral's history.

While many of the priests at St. John's and within the diocese frowned on Father B's unorthodox network of "sanctified undesirables," he thought of them as his Baker Street Irregulars, the street urchins that Sherlock Holmes employed to run surveillance and glean information.

Against charges that the practice was byzantine, Father B was uncowed.

"His name is Kenny Burstyn and he loves his heroin. Don't hurt him. I need you to bring him to me."

The biker's eyes glowed with purpose. "How much persuasion can I use?"

"Francis, do we need to go back over this ground?"

The biker, who could crack walnuts in the crook of his arm, had trouble meeting the priest's eyes. "You mean that whole mercy/grace thing?"

"Look at me, Francis. Never forget that you and I are *in peccatis natus es totus*, sinners from birth. Because we've been forgiven much, we must forgive much. This is a lost sheep we're talking about. Find that sheep. Bring him in. Take good care of him in transit, yes?"

Francis lifted his head with its impressive mane. "Yes, Father Wills. You can trust me."

Father B regarded him and smiled. "Yes, Francis, I believe I can."

# Chapter 17

Jorge Ramone looked into the woman's eyes and saw only pain.

No matter the seductive body language, the provocative dress, or the shocking language on the pouty lips, the eyes did not lie.

"The last ten to my name." He waved the bill in the air and saw the pain turn to business. She was hungry. Likely she hadn't eaten since yesterday, a noose of need cinched tight around her pretty slender neck by the man who employed her. Not so tight as to kill; not so loose that she'd soon forget who it was that punched her meal ticket.

"Ten bucks, you tell me where Trina's workin'."

The heavy makeup lifted into a wolfish smile. The prostitute tugged at the tight gold lamé jacket hugging her minimal Midwest attributes. Serpent-quick, she snatched the money from his hand and deposited it deep in the gap between girlish breasts. "Just caught her act over at the BART station, Sixteenth and Mission. Pathetic. You best hurry, Latin lover boy. Last I see, she be knockin' her head against one a them paper boxes, the *USA Today* kind."

Jorge ran, fists pumping, heart banging out dread with every beat.

*Don't, Trina. Don't do it. Don't you die.*

The note said she didn't want to mess up his life like she'd messed up hers. "You're going someplace and have a family who loves you. I won't drag you down. I'm going back to what I used to do. Thank you for letting me dream a little. Love, T."

On he ran, past cars and buildings, past signs and lighted shop windows, past winos in doorways, past outstretched hands of transients, hands that jabbed in and out of his vision as if disembodied from the faded beings that scraped for existence from concrete and asphalt.

He knew now what she meant to him. At first, he'd just wanted to protect her, but that had turned to something stronger. She brought out the best in him and he wanted to bring out the best in her.

In the heat of his racing mind rose one terrible vision: Trina, kitten soft, pushed from the overpass, falling into the maelstrom of freeway traffic below, battered and crushed again and again by heedless motorists.

*My Trina, my Trina . . .*

At first, he didn't see her in the evening bustle and glare. A herd of people exiting the BART rail station stampeded past.

Then he did see her and felt ill.

She lay in the overflow trash from a stuffed garbage receptacle provided to keep the city tidy. Skirt hiked midway on pitifully thin thighs, one arm draped lazily over the chain securing a *USA Today* newspaper dispenser, she looked asleep. Except for the blood.

Blood smeared her forehead, darkened the roots of her hair, streaked down one cheek, accumulated at the point where ear and neck joined. The pixie earlobe with its tiny twinkling rhinestone stud was crusted in blood.

"Oh, no. My sweet Trina, no!"

He half fell to the curb and gently lifted her head and torso into the cradle of his lap.

Horns blared. A siren tore past on the way to other misery. People, chattering into cell phones and arm in arm with one another, hurried past. Few turned or even broke stride.

His cheek, wet with tears, scrubbed softly at the drying blood.

Her breath, terrifyingly light, brushed against the dampness of his skin.

*Alive.*

A black sedan with out-of-state plates pulled to the curb five feet away. A woman in puffy strawberry bouffant, white knee-high patent leather boots, matching hot pants, and leopard-spotted halter top strode closer and watched the passenger window disappear into the door before leaning in with a loud, "Hello, sugar. What's on yo mind tonight?"

The car door opened.

Jorge jumped to his feet. Trina pressed to his chest, he bumped aside the working prostitute and collapsed into the front seat of the sedan beside a startled middle-aged man in three-piece suit.

"Get us to the hospital and I'll give you a hundred bucks. Now! Go! Drive!"

Wide-eyed, the balding man hit the gas. With a crank of the wheel and a screech of tires, he cut off an SUV and ran a red light. The last words Jorge heard from the prostitute were, "Hey, ya freak! Are you nuts?"

He rocked Trina and kissed her eyes. *Why won't she wake up?* The driver said nothing. Jorge looked at him. "Thanks, *amigo.* You're sent from God, ya know? *Watch it!*"

They brushed a jaywalker and in a hail of curses hurtled on. *Father, Son, and Holy Spirit, help us not die gettin' there. Bless this guy and forgive him. Forgive me. Help my sweet Trina pull through. Let me take care of her and leave our old lives behind.*

He crossed himself and then remembered to add, *and please let Father B have an extra hundred lying around the manse.*

Bishop Harold Steiling gave Father Byron Wills a long, apprais-
ing stare. "I only hope you have a better idea for this year's
diocese fund-raiser than last year's pathetic variety show. What
was Downey thinking?"

Father B shifted uncomfortably against the hard seat, one
of six matching chairs that furnished the visitors' half of the
bishop's dark-paneled office. It was Father B's considered opinion that the chairs were carefully chosen to exact the highest
degree of distress, this from a man who had little interest in
being visited, but took maximum relish in reminding his call-
ers who was boss. "What the Reverend Dale Downey lacks in
creativity, he more than makes up for in generosity." Father B
smiled pleasantly. "But yes, I do believe I have a suggestion that
will not only do well for us this year but erase any lingering
doubts about the past."

Something little short of a royal edict went out from the
bishop's office each year reminding every good Episcopalian in
the diocese that as regarded the fund-raiser, it was his "bounden
duty" to SUSO — Father B's wry acronym for "show up, shell
out." Detrimental to the bishop's already dyspeptic disposition
were the steadily declining amounts raised by the event. Last
year's collection of laughable magic acts and karaoke singing
talent hadn't netted enough to restripe the cathedral's parking
lot, let alone replace its leaky roof.

Every year the chairmanship of the fund-raiser changed
hands. More than one priest had transferred out of the diocese
after a failed sausagefest or kiddie carnival catastrophe. Father
B's fellow priests dreaded the assignment and privately referred
to it as Steiling's "rocky shoals of the damned."

"Then it is you who are the magician, Byron. What have you
in mind?"

Never would the bishop lean forward and show any eager-
ness for a priest's ideas. Instead, he leaned back in his expen-

sive burgundy-leather-upholstered office chair as if daring to be convinced.

Father B took a deep breath without giving away how deep. "I propose an olive oil tasting."

He allowed the idea to twist in the air between them, resisting the urge to give explanation, forcing the bishop to inquire further.

Steiling, dressed in dark "business ecclesiastical," pursed thin lips, dark hair against dark chair, and gave no ground. "Spoken like a reformed alcoholic."

"Reformed and reforming, as so many are." Father B said it cheerily, open with all about his ongoing battle against strong drink. "This gives us the cachet of a wine tasting without any of the nasty side effects."

A stately mantle clock ticked off the silence until the bishop at last spoke. "And what do *you* mean by an olive oil tasting?" Implied was that everyone else, most certainly the legislative and judicial head of the diocese, knew the regular meaning of the term.

In the interests of time, Father B forfeited the advantage. "I propose a grand tasting event in a tony hotel ballroom. Sometime in the fall ahead of the gift-giving season. Media. Celebrity guests. The cream of California olive growers with international guest growers. Just $250 a plate, the menu replete with olives and fine olive oils, followed by a tasting competition in which our experts evaluate competing oils and crown winners in several categories."

Steiling's eyes lit with interest while the rest of him remained detached. "Novel. Sophisticated. Appeals to the upper crust. Everything is donated, of course." The words underscored what experience confirmed to be true. Few could match the bishop's mathematical acuity when it came to toting up the take for any given event.

Father B smiled. "But of course. With entry fees, corporate endorsements, and admission price, I would not be surprised to raise in excess of $150,000. There's your roof."

"There's *your* roof, Byron." He waited while his assistant poured them coffee in white china cups bearing the compass-like emblem of the worldwide Anglican Communion. At its center was the cross of Christ.

They sat a few moments in the sensory thrall of the dark liquid that had traveled to them from another hemisphere.

"Byron."

The word came with sharp edges. Father B looked up and met the piercing glare of eyes the color of gunmetal.

"Yes, Harold?"

The two shared seminary roots, but little else. Whereas Father B had been content to attain the priesthood for the purpose of working on hearts from the inside, Steiling had hopped aboard the political fast track and aspired to administrative leadership. Where Father B resisted promotion or anything that would distance him from the people in the pews, Steiling treated every assignment between him and the bishop's chair like a hurdle to be cleared on the way up. Though a good portion of the job description was to be a shepherd to the shepherds, they both knew this bishop preferred to lead men by hooking them along with the crook of his staff. He studiously avoided—or delegated to others—those situations wherein he might be required to carry a man to safety in the shelter of his arms.

The bishop took another sip of coffee that did not seem to sit well. "I am told that some of the regular almsgiving, building-maintenance-pledging members of St. John's have raised an eyebrow at your so-called Midnight Church. They are rightly suspicious of a rough and highly unorthodox subculture operating in their church after hours without official sanction or oversight."

"I have received no specific complaints."

"Perhaps none that you have chosen to recognize as such. A Carl Farnsworthy, for example, says that he has overheard you call these ruffians your underground army."

"An affectionate term, I assure you."

"Is it also a term of endearment to call one Francis Welch your 'enforcer'?"

Father B shifted painfully and wondered if the chair in which he sat had been obtained from the estate of Vlad the Impaler. "It is."

The bishop shook his head. "Really, Byron. Have more respect for me than that. Francis Welch is one of the Lords of Lucifer, a dangerous, deadly, and highly unlawful motorcycle gang. Do you know the crimes he's committed?"

*Blast this chair.* "No more than I know or care about the exact nature of the crimes committed by the thief on the cross. Of such is paradise populated. And for the record? He's an *ex*-member of the gang."

Steiling snapped upright in his chair. "Don't play pious with me, Reverend Wills. I'll not have the people of my diocese threatened"—he held up a warning hand when Father B made to protest—"*implied* or otherwise, threatened nonetheless. The man approached Leona Carney on the church steps last Sunday night, and she thinks he was after her purse. He has a surgically forked tongue that very nearly caused the old woman a heart attack. You need to take better care of the people on your church rolls, Byron, or you won't have any people—or a church either!"

Given the back of the bishop's chair while its occupant stared out the office window at the lights of an adjacent high-rise apartment building, Father B spoke quietly. "Have more respect for me, Harold, than to hold over my head unfounded accusations from informants of questionable motivation. Pardon me if I again appeal to Scripture, but the well do not need a physician. If Christ did not come for the Lords of Lucifer, then he came for no one and I am in the wrong line of work."

The bishop swiveled back to face Father B. This time he did lean forward. "Of course Christ came for the least, including those whose tongues are forked. But that is why we have the Gospel Mission and other Christian works specifically equipped and trained to serve that population."

"We're an inner-city church, Harold. You can't pick and choose an inner-city congregation. And Francis wasn't interested in Mrs. Carney's purse. He was trying to help her up the stairs." He thought a moment, then swallowed hard. "Why don't you come to Midnight Church, meet Francis, see that while the after-hours folks are colorful, they're also sincere."

The bishop shuffled papers on his desk that didn't require shuffling. "My hands are quite full with the eight-to-five church, thank you. As yours should be."

"Are you telling me to quit the homeless, give up on the Lords of Lucifer?"

"Is it on your own time?"

"Always."

"And can you really raise more than a hundred thousand for us this year?"

"I can and, Lord willing, I shall."

"An olive oil tasting?"

"An olive oil tasting."

"Then watch yourself, Byron. When complaints land here, I have to take them seriously."

"Of course."

The bishop saw him to the office door.

Father B slipped into his coat and turned to face his superior. "Did you know, Harold, that there are seventy-two official descriptors for the complex look, feel, flavors, and fragrances of the olive?"

"I did not."

"Some are bitter, briny, peppery, or fruity, while others are nutty, earthy, prickly, or buttery. Some look glossy, some have a cooling mouth feel, others smell and taste grassy."

"Spare me, Byron. I leave it in your hands, but so help me if this idea busts as badly as the yodeling ventriloquist and her twin dummies, I will have your head on a platter."

"If you did, I'd have to slap you with another olive oil classification."

The bishop sighed. "And that would be?"

"Harshy."

Father B barely made it across the threshold before the door shut on his sore backside with resounding finality.

Francis Welch sniffed the air. He could fork his tongue like a snake's, but too bad he couldn't use it to detect aroma like one.

Still, he was closing in on the quarry. The homeless and the street kids pointed him on like they were all part of some giant human tracking device. The addicts who were using when he found them weren't reliable. People who wanted to bum smokes or score in some other way were flaky too. Subtract those out and you were left with a good number of clear-thinking listening posts who were only too happy to help if he'd do that flicker thing with his tongue.

Some even sat still while he laid Jesus on them.

"He's your Savior, brother, and lawyer, all in one. You think he wants you slummin' on the streets, a string of broken relationships trailing you like toilet paper stuck to your shoe? No way. He wants to deal with your sin, fix the broken stuff, get you back with your tribe. Mercy and grace; grace and mercy. Pray with me."

Those that protested or shrugged it off quickly found their knees when Francis flexed twenty-inch biceps or brandished the forehead against which more than two dozen noses had snapped. "Saint Peter said get 'em into the kingdom with fire if need be. Don't make me set you on fire!"

Once he had his repentants lined up, heads bowed, he prayed, "Good God Almighty, you saved this hellion with a forked tongue, so I know you can save me. Say that."

When all had dutifully repeated the line, he went on. "You can better believe I'm sorry for what I done. Sorry for the people I've hurt. Sorry for the waste I've made of me and my life. Say that."

Some forgot, some mumbled, all made a stab at it.

"Take me, Lord Jesus, and clean me out, fill me up, make me new! Cover me in your shed blood and forgive me for what I was and make me what I can be. Say that."

They tried.

"Make me new. Watch over me. Give me courage to go make things right. Help me live for you now and forever. I believe! Say that."

A chorus of "I believe."

"Louder!"

"I believe!"

*"Louder!"*

*"I believe!"*

"Now, as I was saying before you got religion, there's this dude who worships Big H right now, but God says find him. Before it's too late. You get to be a part of that and, best of all, when you tell me what I need to know, I get out of your face. So here's who I'm after ... "

Now Francis stood at the edge of a park, closed for the night. The smell of fresh-mown grass filled his nostrils. It took him back fifteen springs before to a bare-chested boy sword-fighting with two other bare-chested boys. All three wielded wooden sticks, two on one, leaping and dancing from rock to rock to tree to bush, now gaining the advantage, now losing it, "dying," leaping back to life, free as birds.

Free.

Tears streamed down his face, tears of a lost youth, tears of a lost innocence, tears for those two friends who died in a gang shooting when one of them was mistaken for the intended target, which was—Francis.

How could he ever go back and fix that brokenness?

Tears also for this boy wanted by Father B, wanted by God, but yet a while in the clutches of Satan and drugs. Another brother of Jesus lost in the inky black of sin.

*Can't go back; must go forward.* The voice of Father B echoed in the night. "Find someone for me, Francis. Find that sheep. Bring him in."

Trina awoke, a man holding each of her hands, an IV drip attached to one arm, a gauze bandage across her forehead.

"*Hola*, baby girl!" Jorge brushed the hair out of her eyes and leaned up to kiss her nose. "Welcome back."

She couldn't take the intensity of his adoring eyes and turned to meet the kind gaze of Father B. "Dear Trina, you are safe."

The compassion in the priest's look was only slightly less stressful than the devotion in Jorge's.

She looked up at the ceiling and closed her eyes.

"What, Trina. What is it?" Jorge stroked her fingers.

She licked her lips. Father B held a straw in a glass of ice water to her mouth. She drank thirstily.

Jorge brushed the back of his hand against her cheek. "Why, babe, why'd you take off like that?"

"Note." She said the word without opening her eyes.

"Yeah, I read it. You don't want to mess me up or drag me down. That's crazy talk, baby girl, crazy talk. I thought we got past all that garbage."

Father B started to rise. "I'll leave you two to talk while I go in search of a toasted cardboard sandwich in the cafeteria."

"No!"

He and Jorge exchanged concerned looks. Trina's eyes blazed. "I ... I want you to stay. I don't think Jorge wants to believe any of my past and he's gotta see that I'm no good for him. I thought it could work, but then I remembered all I've done, all the mistakes—"

"Stop!" Jorge trembled at her side. "I don't want to hear that, okay? People were mean to you. They used you and beat you down. God's forgiven all that and ... and I'm no bargain either."

Trina sniffed. "You mean the anger, the acting out? Forget it, Jorge, you're a better person than me and always will be. Forget it!"

Jorge struggled to speak, tears flowing once again. "No, I ... you don't understand, Trina."

"*You* don't understand. I think I love you so much and that's not good for you. That's why you have to save yourself for a girl deserving of someone like—"

"NO!" It was more the cry of a wounded animal than a word. Father B came around the bed and encircled Jorge in his arms.

"What, Jorge? Say it, son. Nothing is too much for God."

Jorge gulped, breathing hard. "I never told no one before, but once when I was fifteen some of the guys I ran with dared me to ... to ... " He stopped and hung his head.

"Go on, son. Once you've said it, it loses its power over you."

Trina held Jorge's big hand in both her tiny ones. She kissed it and held it against her cheek. "What, Jorge, what is it?"

All at once, he stopped shaking, his voice drained of emotion. "They dared me to torch a deli near my house. We was always shopliftin' stuff from there, and the owner finally told us never to come in there again or he'd call the cops. They wanted me to teach him a lesson. So I started a fire late at night, never thinking that the owner and his family, even a new baby, lived above the deli. Neighbors got 'em out in time, but they coulda died in there. They knocked the charge down 'cause I was a minor, but I spent most of a year in juvie. Those were good people, Trina, they didn't deserve a low-down arsonist like me setting their home and their livelihood on fire. I'm so sorry!"

"Oh, Jorge, don't, don't, shhhh ... " He lay his head against her shoulder and let her pet him.

Father B placed a hand on both of them. "Father in heaven, behold your children Trina and Jorge. Lift the Devil's hold on them and, in the power of Christ's blood, rid them of all loathing and assure them they are new again, clean again, untouched by the sins of the past. Lift the darkness from them, Lord, and set them free in body, mind, and spirit now and forevermore!"

Jorge kissed her. "Thank you, Jesus!"

Trina felt a lightness in her heart and it was good.

# Chapter 18

Part 1 of the McTavish Plan to Save Taste of Success was a private banquet for California Governor Mitch von Bruegger and his honored guest Yoshiro Tamaguchi, Japan's minister of trade. Get this right and it could save the culinary program's bacon and mean hundreds of millions to the state's economy. The esteemed minister was interested not only in fresh citrus but boatloads of specialized medical technology. This included highly sensitive diagnostic and monitoring equipment developed but not yet available in most U.S. hospitals. That this new technology had escaped the attention of Japan's tech wizards made the day especially rich with promise.

Cassie breathed in the succulent aromas of old Italy and gave an approving nod. Now that Beth and Cody were safe with Nick's folks and under twenty-four-hour state police guard at their secluded lake cabin, she could more fully appreciate the magnitude of all that the Scottish force of nature had pulled off in forty-eight hours.

And this despite the press starting to put two and two together. The headline in today's local section of the *Oakland Tribune* didn't help: "Success Flops? Homeless Rehab Program Takes a Hit." It wouldn't be long before the national media took up the drumbeat. Cassie bet it was only when a certain tenacious food critic threatened to quit that the *Chronicle* gave one to the cross-Bay competition and spiked the story—for now. Even the McTavish clout couldn't muzzle the newshounds for long.

The effusive mustachioed and tuxedoed von Bruegger, his equally hearty wife Jillian in a voluminous black Mario Garve original, the state director of trade Blaine Waterstone, Gordon O'Neal, Cassie, Nick, McTavish in smart red and black Scottish twill, and the ever-volatile Chef Raoul Maggiano in starched white formed a receiving line for the official Japanese entourage. The expansive entryway to the dining room of Pasta Bella Ristorante was lined with lavish bouquets of fresh long-stemmed roses in reds and yellows. Beyond them, much of the Pasta Bella waitstaff glowed in spotless white serving jackets. All were coached in the finer art of bowing and in doing nothing whatsoever to cause an international incident.

The kitchen staff, keeping clatter to a minimum beyond the swinging doors, were all senior Taste success stories. Jorge with his jokes. AJ back for a command performance. Cece Craven, the little Haitian gal with the giant appetite and a flair for desserts. This was their meal, their chance to shine and show the world they were worthy to feed kings and kingpins.

And it was their chance to cover over the poisoning and the kidnapping with something positive and life affirming. Lieutenant Reynolds said the clumsy child abduction was a warning shot, and because it came after the poisoning and the kids suffered no lasting harm, the Waverly death was likely a botched attempt to frighten. It now seemed likely that the killer had been unaware of the tycoon's heart condition.

It was no secret the governor was one of the program's biggest fans. He had been there to help cut the ribbon at Taste's restaurant opening and declare it "both a model of mercy and of business savvy." He had invited Taste to cater the annual black tie "Governor's Heroes Awards" dinner at the capitol, where the administrators and trainers of Taste were surprised with first-place honors as they were preparing dessert to be served.

Today's state security detail included a taste tester who sampled every dish as it was prepared throughout the morning and again before serving. He so far showed no signs of succumbing.

Cassie watched the white stretch limo ease to the curb at the awning-covered entrance to Pasta Bella. Burly men in dark suits and even darker glasses surrounded the vehicle from which emerged a tidy Asian man impeccably dressed in soft gray.

*Thank God for Governor Mitch.* The popular governor was in a second term and known for sticking by people he believed in, however unpopular the stand might be. This state luncheon gave them his high-visibility trust, and she and Nick were grateful. Watching the big man meet the direct and assessing gaze of the trade minister with cool-eyed savoir faire, it was all she could do to keep from kissing him on both cheeks.

"Welcome, your excellency," von Bruegger boomed. "May your palate be graced by some of the finest food in North America. Chef Maggiano and the team from Taste are among our state treasures!"

From the corner of an eye, Cassie caught Chef wriggling with pleasure. *The big puppy* ... For all his explosive rants, the gourmand had been with the program from the beginning. Taste had imposed upon him more than any other chef in town and always he had risen to the occasion. He was the source of much drama, but no one had given more to the cause.

Tamaguchi's head cocked to one side and his face lit with a smile of jocular delight. "After today, my esteemed governor, you may find that I will have imported more than just those things for which you have bargained."

Von Bruegger and Maggiano beamed as if they'd swallowed a canary apiece. The media had made much ado ahead of Tamaguchi's state visit about his craving for Italian food. "For a snack, sushi; for a meal, pasta!" he told reporters with what one amused observer called "Roman gusto" and a sour opposition of Japanese nationalists back home dubbed "displeasurable diplomacy."

Cassie suspected good old Mitch would personally gift wrap Chef Raoul and send him by diplomatic pouch if it meant securing the trade deal.

She took the trade minister's cool hand in her own. It was delicate and parchment smooth, disarmingly familiar. "Your excellence." She dipped her head, bent slightly at the waist, then straightened, surprised to find him looking her in the eye.

He murmured so that it stayed between them. "Mrs. Dixon, I have been told of your unfortunate troubles, still more of your admirable resiliency. What you do for the less fortunate requires utmost courage. I commend you and insisted you remain on our culinary staff. Do not forget that the most serene garden is shaped by years of wind and rain."

He was gone before she managed a weak "thank-you."

Nick hooked one of her fingers with one of his. "You okay?"

She nodded and swallowed. Would heaven send her a sign all the way from Tokyo?

McTavish passed over a hankie and whispered, "Here, toots, you've sprung a leak." She patted the matching tweed tam on her head. "The guy's a regular samurai of smooth talk, I'll give him that."

Cassie managed a crooked smile. She whispered, "So are you. How'd you pull this off?"

McTavish pursed a cherry-rimmed mouth and looked inscrutable. "Would you ask Houdini how he escaped the Water Torture Chamber? No, ma'am. Let's just say it took a pinch of this and a smidgen of that. You ain't seen nothin' yet. Wait 'til round two."

Von Bruegger lifted his goblet high. "I propose a toast to the friendship between us, between our people, and between our two economies. There is strength in trade. Long live Sony and Toshiba! Long live Sunkist and Philips! To a bright future on all sides of the Pacific Rim!"

Raised glasses on both sides of the long banquet table met in the middle with the sweet ring of crystal.

The menu, printed on elegant place cards at each setting, promised starters of fresh-steamed mussels and the house-cured salmon with mustard crème fraîche. Ahead of the spinach salad with creamy goat cheese flan and macerated strawberries, a tureen of chicken soup Italian style—tender bits of young chicken in a savory broth of chicken stock, rosemary, sage, garlic, and a judicious dash of Chef's secret spice blend. The main act was signature fried oyster *panino* and the *scrigno di Venere*, a beggar's purse of delicate pasta fattened with spinach *taglionini*, pepper ham, mushrooms, onions, and baby peas. For dessert, Cece's specialty tiramisu cannoli soaked in rich espresso.

A feast fit for foreign dignitaries. Cassie was honored that she and Nick were seated beside McTavish and O'Neal, across from the von Brueggers and their esteemed Japanese guest.

Around a mouthful of succulent salmon, Tamaguchi, eyes closed, face wreathed in rapture, nodded vigorously. "Exquisite! World class! Tell me, Governor, how much money have you received from tribal gaming interests?"

Von Bruegger thirstily drained his water glass, missing the slight opening of the visitor's eyes which contained the merest glint of mischief.

The governor blustered a moment, smoothed the sleeve of his wife's dress, then gave up all pretense of control with a loud if discomfited laugh. "My dear minister, what has that to do with the price of tea in Tokyo?"

Tamaguchi responded in kind and the glint changed to a merry twinkle. "What do they say in Hollywood? 'Gotcha!'"

Everyone laughed, even the vigilant bodyguards. Cassie predicted that the sprightly and shrewd emissary from the Japanese ministry would strike a handsome trade agreement, one with terms most favorable to Nipponese interests. Mitch had met his match.

Jillian von Bruegger, a large big-boned woman, less tolerant of male jesting, locked eyes with Tamaguchi. "If you are that well-informed, sir, then you know that both Republican and Democratic coffers have prospered from Indian largesse. Cassie, these mussels are melt-in-your-mouth divine!"

Tamaguchi nodded and polished off the salmon. He was offered more by the attentive female server, Felicity Breem, who was one of the two or more people a month who attempted suicide off the Golden Gate Bridge. She was stopped by an alert off-duty patrolman who caught her by the waist just as she leaned out to jump. She got sober, entered the culinary-training program, and was one of Father B's most committed catechists.

Nick gave Felicity a quick thumbs-up and received a shy grin in return. "Vice should never be state-sanctioned," he said. "Governor Gray Davis opened that Pandora's box when he called for the tribes to donate $1.5 billion from their casino profits to help erase the state budget deficit. After all, so the argument goes, they don't pay sales tax for purchases on reservation land, and they ought to cough up when the state's in trouble. I say the gambling age should never be lowered to eighteen, that's for sure."

The servers removed the starter dishes and replaced them with stout cobalt-blue soup bowls with handles.

"Nick expressed much of my position." Von Bruegger's expression was considerably more poker-faced now than when the question was first asked. "If the tribes wish their sovereignty, then they must act socially responsible. Tell me, Yoshiro, do you always throw lighted firecrackers into a crowded room?"

Tamaguchi raised his hands in mock protest. "My friend, do not fault me. It was my chief of security who paid me $50 to ask the question!"

The table roared with laughter, glasses were refilled, and an air of *bon ami* prevailed.

Cassie relaxed. The good old boys were playing nice and the food was superb.


Philippe Peugeot shook Gordon O'Neal's hand. "Gordon, I must place credit where it is due. You and the board of Taste have come right back and said to this community, 'Do not misjudge us. We poisoned no one. We are an asset to San Francisco. Instead of moaning about a problem, we solve it.'"

"Well, I—"

"No! No false modesty, please. You have two of the world's most powerful men out there in the dining room forging what could be a beautiful agreement for all of us. The art of the deal, Gordon, you know it well."

"Philippe, I don't think—"

"Nonsense, Gordon! You didn't like my offer and it was rejected. Happens all the time. What we must do, like reasonable men, is take another run at it. A meeting of the minds. Taste, with a few minor adjustments, can set the standard wherever it's housed. Why tie up prime waterfront real estate with a social welfare program? Adjustments, that's all, like my finely engineered motorcar. Some minor calibration, a bit more torque, and we're skimming over the savannah lean as a hungry cheetah."

The two men stood among shelves of large tins containing tomato base and whole sweet tomatoes imported from Italy. The kitchen staff was a study in contained efficiency baking, sautéing, stirring, chopping, blending, and tasting the array of delights called for in the menu. Chef was a pink-faced cyclone of activity ordering, correcting, cajoling, berating, commending, and driving his staff to new heights of gustatory excellence.

"Not-a too hot with the soup!" Chef ordered. "I want-a they taste nice spice, not eat-a the heat!"

"Hey, AJ!" Jorge shouted from the gas stove, where he ladled the chicken soup into a large ornate silver tureen. Across the floor at the grill, AJ fried oysters. "How does an Italian get into an honest business?" He carried the tureen to a screened cooling table near the rear door.

AJ expertly flipped the oysters with one swipe of a spatula. He grinned. "Do tell, Ramone, do tell."

"Usually through the skylight!"

With a roar, Chef chased Jorge from the kitchen. "*Imbecille!* You like-a me tell the Mexican jokes? You like-a me tell the one about the Mexican peasant and the chimpanzee? Huh? *Stupido!*"

Peugeot stopped him and clapped an arm around his shoulders and another around those of O'Neal. "Gentlemen, please, everything is under beautiful command here. Let us go meet our guests and wish them bon appétit. Chef? Lead the way. This feast, and the credit for it, belong to you and your team!"

On the way past, he nodded to the state's taste tester, a balding, humorless man in a blue suit who spooned chicken soup into a shallow bowl. The man raised the bowl to his lips and drew its contents into his mouth. Eyes closed, he paused, swished the liquid around his palate, then swallowed. A few seconds passed before he daubed his lips with a paper napkin, the only residue a small spark of acceptance in the eyes.

When Peugeot glanced back, the man stood at the grill and gazed upon the steaming mollusks with undisguised desire.

The back door to Pasta Bella Ristorante, propped open for ventilation, admitted the salt tang from off the Bay and a nondescript figure, white-coated like the others, but unnoticed. A face lay shrouded beneath a cascade of unruly brown hair and the bill of a baseball cap. The heavy lid of the soup tureen rose. It remained suspended for fifteen seconds, followed by a soft splash, then was gently replaced. The little soup that spilled was quickly absorbed with paper towel.

Through the back door slipped both figure and paper towel. The lid on the Dumpster rose and fell.

Moments later, Felicity and Cece, one on each side, lifted the tureen and carried it to the governor.

"Cassie, would you do the honors?"

She loved her generous friend and favorite politician. How like him to share the spotlight. She placed a hand on the lid of the silver tureen.

"Wait!" Von Bruegger stood, glass raised. "I invite you all to stand and join me in a toast to Taste of Success, for all its tireless and committed volunteers who continue to believe when others have lost hope. For all the lives they have redeemed from despair, and for all those yet to hear the good news that life is worth living to the fullest."

All of the kitchen and waitstaff were herded into the dining room by Chef Maggiano. The governor turned to them. "And for these fine men and women who have proven beyond doubt that a life inspired is never wasted—all it takes is someone to come alongside and say, 'God loves you, you can do it!' They've done it and we shall have the waistlines to prove it! *Saludo!*"

With a chorus of *saludo*s, everyone drank, then applauded. They resumed their seats. Cassie stood facing the officials, raised hands clasped in victory in acknowledgement of the cooks and servers. "Chef Maggiano? We could not begin to do any of it without you, nor without your fellow cooking geniuses of San Francisco, the other gourmet chefs who selflessly volunteer their time. Your talent comes from above! Thank you!"

Chef blew her a two-handed kiss.

With dramatic flair, Cassie grasped the silver lid in both hands and said, "In the immortal words of French satirist François Rabelais, 'The appetite grows with eating!'"

She lifted the lid—thought it oddly weighted—and watched the faces before her turn from delight to horror.

She peered under the lid at a thick black viper uncoiling like the sinewy finger of Satan.

The lid fell with a clatter, scattering floral arrangements and breaking china. The snake, glistening with chicken soup, oozed from the tureen and slithered among plates and bowls and silverware and goblets.

Guests lurched back from the table. Chairs collided.

"Look out! Look out!"

Kitchen and waitstaff panicked and knocked one another to the floor.

Bodyguards fell on Governor, First Lady, and honored guest.

Nick lunged for Cassie, shielded her with his body, and brandished a knife and fork.

O'Neal chased the serpent, cutting it off from the kitchen doors.

McTavish stamped the floor. "Grab it, you fool! Knock its brains out!"

Chef cornered the intruder against the wall and chopped it in two with one blow of a meat cleaver.

When they had ceased their writhing, Maggiano held up the two halves of the five-foot snake, sweat trickling from his brow.

"Rat snake." Nick frowned. He motioned Maggiano closer. "Nonpoisonous. Found in New England and the southern states, not around here. No way he got into that tureen on his own." He glared at the silver serving dish. "They're excellent swimmers."

Blaine Waterstone, the state's trade director, made a retching sound and bolted for the bathroom.

"No one else moves, no one leaves," Nick said. "Chef, secure the rear door, please. Jorge, go with security and assist that man in the restroom. The police will be here in short order." Nick laid down his weapons, kept one arm around Cassie, and punched a number into his cell. "This is getting tiresome."

Jillian von Bruegger yelled something muffled about her dignity. The bodyguards helped her, her husband, and the Japanese minister to their feet.

Yamaguchi's tie was askew and the top button of his suit coat was missing. He looked invigorated. "I once found a rat in my suitcase."

A grim-faced O'Neal looked around the room. "Anyone seen Peugeot?"

# Chapter 19

The next morning, Margo Fletcher and a stout female assistant marched past Clarice without breaking stride.

McTavish watched them come, imperious expressions letting it be known that they were privy to startling inside information that, made public, would forever change the political landscape.

She waved off a frantic Clarice. *So at last the supercilious old tart risks the lion's den. Bring it on.*

McTavish blocked the way into her office, forcing Fletcher and her bodyguard/witness/protégé to wait for permission to enter.

"Margo." McTavish said the name with the inflection and facial composition usually reserved for words like "bloated." She assessed the director of PCF—Productive Citizens First—much as she would a disappointing new restaurant.

The woman's hair, the color of smoggy haze, was bobbed in the latest "I'm way too committed and right to care" pretension of social activists everywhere. Tall and slender to the point of anorexic, she wore copper bracelets on both wrists that all but clanked against bone. The gray pearl necklace caught in the clefts and ridges of the pronounced clavicles like unfortunate tide pool specimens. The designer dress she wore bespoke an expensive righteousness. No sackcloth for this prophetess of doom.

McTavish braced. *To quote the perceptive granny in the old fast-food ads, "Where's the beef?"*

"Muira." Fletcher's narrow sparrow mouth had soured on the word by the end of the first syllable. "Are you going to invite us in or are we to stand here and air this discussion in front of God and country?"

McTavish sucked her teeth. "Have you an appointment?"

Fletcher drew to her full height. "We both know the answer to that. You have been unavailable my last dozen attempts. I thought perhaps I could catch you between humiliations."

McTavish patted her tam. "I do not humiliate, dear woman, I evaluate. Why don't you open a restaurant and experience firsthand what I do?" She felt pleasure at the thought.

"No, thank you, Muira. I'd rather have my fingernails removed with a pair of pliers. We ... Tara here is a student intern working with our organization ... won't be long. Soon you'll be back at your busy schedule of sacking and burning."

The other half of "we" was a plain-brown-wrapper kind of coed, no doubt a Berkeley type whose sole function thus far had been to nod at Fletcher's verbal digs and scowl at McTavish's. Her long, straight hair was much too black and her round, bloodless features much too pale. She held a pen and a pad of very blank paper at the ready.

"You have five minutes, Margo. What you came to spout shouldn't take half that."

She motioned them to chairs while she sat behind her tank of a desk. "The meter's running; what's on your mind?"

"You're losing what little objectivity you have." Fletcher talked, Tara scribbled. "You champion the homeless as if the tax-paying citizens of this city somehow owe them a life and a lifestyle that they themselves are too lazy or addicted to make on their own. You're dangerous, Muira, and so is your crusade for Taste of Success."

McTavish felt her hackles rise to new heights. "While I appreciate the compliment, I don't care for your criminalization of good people that society has left behind. Aren't you at all concerned that two hundred people are dying of homelessness in this city every year?"

"I'm concerned about the five thousand people living on the streets sucking up resources, defecating in doorways, sleeping in parks, and sticking their hands in people's faces looking for a handout."

Tara flipped pages in her notebook, chewed a lip, and wrote in a fury, her pencil scratching like a dog at the door.

McTavish locked eyes with Fletcher, smiled thinly, and nodded. "Ah, yes, tourism. Eject the homeless, doze their dwellings, hose down the streets, and let the paying customers in to sunny San Francisco, land of liberality, high-priced souvenirs, and no soul."

"And you would bankrupt the economy with freeloaders and ne'er-do-wells?"

McTavish wanted to slap the notebook from Tara's hands and use it to smack her mentor across her sanctimonious head. Couldn't the coed see what an automaton she had become? "Have you ever talked to a homeless person, Ms. Fletcher? The former merchant marine captain forever doomed for accidentally killing a man on the job? The mother of three who sustained a spine injury in a car accident six years ago and can find relief from the pain only in a bottle of hooch? The young kid whose alcoholic father said to get out and never come back?"

"Most want nothing to do with rehabilitation."

"Really? Do you know there's now a four-month waiting list to get into the culinary-training program at Taste of Success?"

"Stop feeding them and they will leave."

"Starve them out and you can sleep at night?"

"Clean up the city. That's good citizenship."

"And how do you make your money, Margo?"

The activist frowned. "I don't see what that has to do—"

"Oh, it has everything to do with it." McTavish stood, snatched the notebook from a startled Tara's hands, flipped to a clean page, and drew a rude church steeple next to a boxy high-rise.

She used the pen as a pointer. "This, madam landlord, is your building, The Carlson Apartments. This is the Fifth Street Baptist Church next door, which, in the interest of full disclosure, has been at that location fifty-four years longer than The Carlson. Every Tuesday and Thursday, starting eighteen years before The Carlson was built, the church provides a hot lunch at noon free to anyone in need. When the homeless line up for food, the line sometimes extends past the front door of The Carlson. God forbid any of your tenants should ever have to engage a hungry person in conversation, and yet that is the sole purpose for the church's existence."

Tara looked lost without her notebook. Fletcher fiddled with her pearls. "Depressed property values are not good for this city, and I did not invest in the city's economy only to be ruined by the indigent."

"Is your neighborhood zoned multiuse?"

"It is, but—"

"Do you believe in the urban landscape at the expense of urban public space?"

"I am entitled to unobstructed access to my own building and my tenants are entitled to come and go without harassment."

"What if you were to offer subsidized housing—say the first two floors of The Carlton—to anyone who successfully completes the Taste culinary training and becomes employed as a result. That way you have a direct hand in rehabilitating lives, your tenants get to know their neighbors as neighbors, and I might even sing your praises in my column. That way, you go from nasty to nice overnight!" Her smile contained genuine traces of warmth as she handed Tara back her pen and pad.

"And in your world that would make me part of the solution rather than part of the problem?"

"Precisely."

"How tidy." A vein in Fletcher's thin neck throbbed visibly. "But we did not come here to embrace your skid row thinking or to look the other way at clear violations of city ordinances prohibiting sleeping on streets, sidewalks, or other public ways. You should see these people, how they defy the law, throw up their shanty towns wherever they feel the urge, and refuse to move or accept public-housing vouchers."

"Then why, Margo, why come and waste my valuable time?" The two visitors reminded McTavish of one of her least favorite dishes—Angels on Horseback. Fletcher was the thin slice of bacon wrapped around Tara, the plump little oyster. The bacon overpowered and neutralized the poor oyster every time.

McTavish watched the smugness creep over the gaunt features like the return of the tide. "I came to warn you to cease and desist." Fletcher's eyes sparked for the first time since her arrival. "The mayor is not pleased with the use of your considerable media license as a bully pulpit for those who would drain our coffers dry by their lack of contribution to the common good. I would remind you that the mayor has friends at the *Chronicle* and at the newspaper syndicate that disseminates your sarcasm nationwide. We wouldn't want McTavish Enterprises to come tumbling down, now would we?"

What McTavish wouldn't have given for a death ray with which to incinerate the boney elitist. She used the next best thing. "Get out. Both of you. And tell Mr. Mayor the next time he wants to send me a message to remember to entrust it to someone with more class, clout, and credibility than a hate-monger like you. And Tara?"

*Delicacy*

By now skittish at the sound of her name, the coed glanced up from her scratchings, but did not make eye contact.

"If you want to intern with a real woman, call my office. I'll pay you double what you're getting now and show you how to fight for something worth the fight. Okay?"

Tara, poor girl, didn't dare nod, nor was she any longer taking notes. When Fletcher abruptly stood, Tara joined her, but not with the alacrity of before.

At the office door, Fletcher turned. "One final note. It's not just me against the homeless. Los Angeles County reports 84,000 homeless and growing. Something has to be done about them. Even you may have to make some choices you won't like."

McTavish balled her hands into fists. "I have an idea, Margo. How about concentration camps? We put them on a train and tell them they're going to a spa for a day. How about that?"

Fletcher's bracelets clanked as she stormed off, Tara in her wake. The intern gave the barest of waves. McTavish nodded and winked.

The McTavish First Rule of Criticism was never to write a column when angry. But since she was more often than not in a righteous froth, she knew she'd never get anything done if she waited for equanimity before hitting the keyboard.

Within ten minutes of the Fletcher visit, Clarice had Buck Jergens on the line. The unflappable publisher of the *San Francisco Chronicle* listened while one of his top three columnists railed against Margo Fletcher "and her cronies at City Hall."

"Don't you dare let those lunatics dictate the content of your paper, Bucky, or I will personally kick your keister and remove you from my will!"

"Take it easy, McT, I never coveted Aunt Sadie's doily collection anyway, and you know it." He was the only person she let get away with calling her "McT." "Look, you sell more papers for me than Superman on his best day. You even get one or two restaurants right, to the everlasting gratitude of my taste buds. So don't get in a lather over this. But never forget, too, that protest and dissent are the American way. Margo speaks for a lot of folks, but she doesn't give me my marching orders any more than the geniuses at City Hall. Keep your tam on, got it?"

"Got it, Buck. Now get off the line so I can get my column done or you will fire me. And thanks."

"Thanks? After all the antacids I've had to take because of you, I think it's time you rustled me up some of that braised lamb in pomegranate sauce. Now that's what I call thanks!"

"Yeah, I might do that and a chocolate nut loaf for the long-suffering Mrs. Jergens."

"She worships at your shrine every day."

"Tell her I just love her soap."

They spoke maybe three times a year and when they did, they always ended with the same lighthearted banter. Though she didn't always, this time she would make certain he received the lamb dish. She jotted a note to Clarice.

McTavish was still hot, but thanks to Bucky, the fire had been knocked back from a dangerous inferno to a controlled burn.

The unfortunate victim of today's wrath was the retro diner Crazy Slim's in the Mission District. She'd been there twice in the past two weeks, including once with Clarice. The chrome and stainless steel Americana architecture, the tabletop jukeboxes, the white-aproned waiters, the cute curbside waitresses on roller skates — too, too precious. Too bad they'd forgotten to give that same attention to the menu.

"The burgers are bland, the salad's limp as a hairdresser's wrist, and the Kickin' Crab Chowder crawled home the loser in that fight. Don't get me started on the Chocolate Velvet Pie. It was about as tasteful as a velvet painting of Elvis. A 'drizzle' of white and dark chocolate hints that something got wet in the process. But what I was served was Sahara-dry and gritty as a sandbox."

She was just warming up.

"The Steak Philly is a mess of scorched leather slathered in cover-up mayo, honey-pepper relish, and slimy grilled onions on a toasted Philly roll that was so stiff it had to have been toasted in 1857 and left on a rock to cool. And the Turkey Meat Loaf? That bird died in vain, honey, thanks to a boatload of accoutrements that included sautéed mushrooms the consistency of rubber bands, gritty gravy (can turkey gravy and chocolate pie filling come from the same bowl?), and a gelatinous cranberry -orange ginger sauce in which the ingredients sat at separate tables and never spoke to one another all night—kind of like my family reunions.

"Conclusion? Cut the menu in half and focus on making eight dishes the best they can be. And what's with charging almost five bucks for a milk shake? Let's see. One dollar for 'hand-dipped.' One dollar for 'oversized.' One dollar for 'deluxe.' And one dollar sixty-nine cents for 'chunky' this and 'tropical' that. Can't a body get a plain vanilla shake for two bucks anymore? And what's with the 97 percent fat-free health shakes? You take away 97 percent of my shake and I expect to pay you just 13 percent of full price. Real shakes are born fat. Get over it!"

The next order of business for the column was a wimpy rebuttal by the wounded owner of Chuckles Bistro, a comedy supper club in North Beach. McTavish had been as blunt as always. "You spend 90 percent of your time ensuring the chicken is humanely slaughtered, the salad ingredients are grown without a hint of pesticide, and the coffee beans come from contented farmers whose pickers work safe and receive fair pay. Then you expose all that clean, guilt-free food to potty-mouth comedians and graceless, body-pierced servers who act as if I owe them a living. Fire them all!"

In reply, the owner wrote a letter castigating McTavish for her "garish comments" and "sweeping generalities." He suggested that if she took offense at adult comedy and free-thinking waitstaff, she might feel more comfortable at a McDonald's playground.

"Oh, and McTavish, not that this seemed at all important to you, but how was the food?"

Her reply was short and sweet. "If your point is I spent too much time on the peripherals, then let me say it plain. The food was adequate, some dishes perhaps a cut above. The food is not what is at issue here. If you ask me to shell out more than $50 for a meal, do not then place me in a hostile atmosphere where I would be uncomfortable eating whatever choice bits they're having at Buckingham Palace. Treat the diner with respect or go sell shoes."

She knew the comparison would draw the wrath of footwear retailers, which would then make for another lively column in the future.

She was done grousing. The column would close with a commendation.

"AJ Rafferty has distinguished himself as one of this city's up-and-coming gastronomists. His recent performance at Guandong Harbour in support of the Taste of Success culinary arts program was a remarkable debut. His crab and avocado omelet with French Brie, caramelized onions, and rough grain toast, while deceptively simple in the sum of its parts, resulted in a striking and greater whole.

"And most remarkable of all? Six months ago, Aaron Joel Rafferty laid his curly head under an I-80 overpass. A cast-off sleeping bag his bed, a cracked and discarded auto mirror his looking glass, and a rain-blurred photo of his mother and two sisters the only link to home. His mailing address? The Gospel Rescue Mission. His emergency contact? Josie Brown, the Mission's director.

"How could this be? Aaron comes from a loving single-mom family. He has committed no crime other than the crime of attention deficit disorder and resisting the gangs. No crime other than dropping out of school at age sixteen utterly frustrated with feelings of personal inadequacy and a lack of educational resources to help him make up for lost time. He blames no one, does not play the victim, but hit the road so as not to be a bad influence on his sisters who each day that he stayed with them might be tempted to think that academic failure was an option.

"He came to San Francisco as so many do because it was one of the warmest and prettiest options in a sea of mean alternatives. And he waited, waited for Providence to provide. And Providence did provide—in the form of Taste of Success.

"And now AJ is a graduate of a new hope program with a success rate second to none. If this city ever gets behind anything of value, it ought to be 110 percent behind Taste. In its young life, Taste has already emptied our streets of hundreds of homeless individuals who have become successful, contributing citizens because someone recognized their potential and gave them a place in the sun to prove themselves.

"AJ Rafferty makes his professional debut in two weeks at the San Francisco Convention Center. Urge every employer with a convention in its corporate milieu to hold the convention at the SFCC, then go and cheer on this young man and savor his talent. Celebrate his amazing ability to blend the goodness of the earth into dishes of extraordinary taste, color, and presentation. Please tell him that McTavish sent you and was delighted to do so. One more thing. AJ said to tell his mom and his sisters that he loves them very much.

"Oh, and a quick P.S. to Margo Fletcher. Are you certain your building is earthquake safe?"

# Chapter 20

He didn't know where else to turn.

Face swollen, ribs cracked, he was barely able to remember his name, let alone if he'd eaten. One thing he did know, he needed an injection of Big H and he needed it yesterday. He came to in a stairwell, arms streaked raw and bloody, unable to tell if rats had done it or he had.

Twice before when the worms erupted under the skin, he'd taken after them with the edge of a sharp rock. Scraping, scraping, scraping to make a hole for them to exit. Unable to stand their flopping and turning, crawling from wrist to elbow to armpit and back, using his limbs for their wormy racetrack.

Kenny Burstyn balled hands into fists and was surprised that one of them contained a chunk of concrete. The ragged edges were sticky red.

Blood.

*My blood.*

He smashed the concrete against his forehead. Or his arm did. Was he any longer in control of anything?

His head spun, the pain intense. He ground the hard, gritty lump against the thin skin until it bled. He knew the arm would not stop the grinding until the skull lay exposed.

The arm drew back ...

He grabbed the right wrist with his left hand and watched them oppose one another. Tendons stretched, veins bulged, the blood still inside retreated like sea from the shore.

*I'm arm wrestling myself.*

He dropped the concrete lump and burst into tears. He was so far from what his mother and father wanted. Had he followed the Burstyn Family Plan, he would be in his second year of a full-ride banking scholarship. He'd tested for it, won, turned it down. Flat. No discussion. What Kenny wanted was to see the world, starting with San Francisco, only that was as much of the world as he would ever see. When Big H came knockin', Kenny turned over the keys.

*He'll take me in ... the World's Tallest Priest ... touched me ... that warm black hand touched my dirty black heart ...*

Eyes lifted, he tried to focus fuzzy vision long enough to take in the scenic wonders of the stairwell. He was too fuzzed. Crying too hard. Instead he smelled the urine. Heard the wail of distant sirens. Felt the graveyard chill in head and bones. Tasted snot and tears.

*He touched me.*

"Guaranteed bank management position when you graduate." His dad's face swarmed with disbelief. "You'll have the money to travel. Five-star treatment the whole way. Don't do this, Ken."

They didn't understand. He didn't want snooty doormen, foie gras appetizers, and chocolates on his pillow. He wanted to rub shoulders with the people, move about on his own two feet, bed down wherever his sleeping bag landed.

One morning he walked away from his sleeping bag and by evening forgot where he'd left it.

*Don't do this, Ken.*

He gathered knees to chest and met little resistance from flesh. A sack of used parts. He thought he remembered that the deceased could be identified by dental records. Why hadn't he flossed more?

"Come, Kenny boy, come pet the kitty." The stray kitten was taken in by the lop-eared rabbit they called Susie Q. When it triggered the maternal instinct, Susie pulled cottony fur from her chest to line the kitten's nursery. The two were fast friends until the rabbit died without ever birthing a litter. The cat died soon after.

"Everything dies eventually, Ken. It's the way of things. Eat your corn."

Weren't they even curious what he'd become?

He bit his lip and covered his head with bloody arms. *I've become nothing.* "Jesus ... Jesus ... "

The horror overtook him. A fate worse than dying alone in a putrid stairwell ...

*Him.*

What time was it? There was one more job he wanted out of Kenny Burstyn. He told him not to go far; he didn't want to have to look for him. He said that if he had to look for him that he would tie Kenny to the bumper of his car and drag him slowly over ten miles of bad road until there was nothing left.

What time, Jesus, what time ... *What time?*

A shadow fell across the stairwell. Kenny's head jerked up. He tried to rise, but could not. He tried to scream, but found no air. He thought to kill himself, but knew not how.

Through tears and withdrawal shimmered the silhouette of a giant. Backlit by an alley security light, wild hair etched in fire, it towered like the Colossus of Rhodes.

It descended, coming for him, the stairwell quaking with each titanic step.

Kenny thought his heart would stop, wished it would. Wished the hard, unyielding wall at his back would suck him through into the next dimension.

It came for him and as it came, it grew and grew, while he shrank and shrank.

He cowered, arms clamped to head, chin buried against chest, eyes squeezed shut. Hard.

Suddenly the quaking stopped. The thing stood over him. He listened to the crumple and smell of leather and made narrow slits of his eyelids.

The giant knelt before him. A great mane of red hair fell to its shoulders but did not obscure the broad forehead adorned with strange scars, the great flat nose, the fierce assessing eyes. From deep within the massive chest rumbled the words, "Kenny Burstyn? I've come to take you."

Still, Kenny might have remained conscious had it not been for the forked tongue.


Read it again."

Cassie had trouble believing that the "snake dinner" had not driven the last nail into their coffin.

*Jesus saves.*

Nick drained his coffee cup and picked up the elegant white card embossed with the official seal of the Japanese embassy.

"Dear Mr. and Mrs. Dixon, I wish to express my personal thanks for the most interesting and thrilling trade mission I have ever had the good fortune to undertake. In the excitement of what remains an impressive and entertaining banquet, I have not lost sight of the exceptional talent and creativity of your team. The food was delicious and artfully prepared, beautifully presented, and the service outstanding. Please accept this small token of my esteem to be used in your worthy enterprise, and know that I shall extol your good work wherever in the world I travel."

Nick waved an international money order in the amount of ten thousand U.S. dollars and continued: "Your excellent governor and I were able to strike a most lucrative agreement for both parties that should benefit our respective societies for many years to come. Again, my thanks and wishes for a pleasant resolution to that which opposes you. As Japanese tea master Sen-No-Rikyu said of the sublime ongoing, 'Though I sweep and sweep, everywhere my garden path, though invisible on the slim pine needles still specks of dirt may yet be found.' Sincerely, Yoshiro Tamaguchi, Ministry of International Trade and Industry."

Nick pulled Cassie onto his lap. They were at home, the house and grounds once again watched over by security personnel. She could tell he was thinking how much better off they would be if they chucked it all and disappeared to some little pineapple plantation halfway round the world.

"I'm not thinking that."

"Thinking what?"

"Thinking what you think I'm thinking."

"And what do you think I think you're thinking?"

Nick kissed her cheek. "That if we had sailed off to Borneo when I first suggested it, we wouldn't be in the pickle we're in."

She snuggled against his neck. "Go ahead and think it. I'm starting to believe we're not meant for civilization. So what *are* you thinking?"

"How tired I am of this cat-and-mouse game. Of living like we're in the witness-protection program. Of being suspicious of everyone. Mostly of how angry I am that someone would use the kids and our homeless friends as pawns to get what they're after."

Cassie got up, glanced at the clock, and refilled his cup.

Nick sipped his coffee, deep in thought, then whirled toward Cassie. "You don't think it's—"

The doorbell rang.

"Maybe we're about to find out."

Cassie led Lieutenant Reynolds, looking more rumpled than usual, into the kitchen and offered him coffee. "Make it a double, Mrs. Dixon. Black, thanks."

"Hard day at the office?" Nick motioned him to a seat on the couch.

"Hard doesn't half cover it." The lieutenant took the mug from Cassie, siphoned a long, noisy sip, and settled his gangly framework onto the couch. "Ah, medicine, thy name is Costa Rican blend."

Cassie set the pot on the end table warming coil. "Anything new?"

"Everything and nothing. The more I interrogate, the farther away the answer seems. I'll tell you one thing. You people are blessed."

Nick gave a brittle laugh. "Come again?"

Reynolds drained half his cup. "Well, you've not been sued. We've seen no suspicious activity anywhere near the cabin. You have friends in the highest office in the state who, no matter how bad it gets, support you a hundred percent. McTavish has made this her personal crusade. And instead of ruining a huge trade deal, your enemies hand you a sweet deal where all the good guys win."

"What of that poor boy who was trying to deliver the ultimatum from the kidnappers? He's still in bad shape."

"The bike messenger? Yes, ma'am, but that was a fluke. Those crazy kids are always tempting the fates and have a high percentage of workplace injuries. He's doing some better. Tough as nails. He'll be out of the hospital in a week, wiser maybe, but not by much."

"And so where's the downside in your scenario, Lieutenant? There's always a downside." These days, Nick kept a dubious distance when it came to silver linings.

When Cassie waved the coffeepot, Reynolds leaned forward and offered his cup. "Sad to say, plenty of downside, Mr.

Dixon. Everyone has an alibi. So far, we've been unable to find that Kenny Burstyn or trace down the sender of that kidnapping note. Located the lunch truck, yes, but I'm beginning to think everyone and his mother wears head coverings and plastic gloves anymore. You'd think from the TV crime shows that DNA is everywhere, but you wouldn't know it from our lack of evidence. Even the rat snake's not talking." He flashed a sour smile, but no one joined him.

"Didn't anyone see somebody tamper with the soup tureen?" Cassie kept thinking of a wasted Kenny leaning over the pot of Fagioli, a worn bag of poison seeds clutched in his hands. It was like some Grimm's nightmare.

"Near as we can determine, someone had to have entered by the back door of the restaurant and placed the snake in the tureen in the few moments that it sat on the cooling table just after the governor's food taster gave the soup his blessing. Most of the kitchen staff were distracted by an altercation between Jorge Ramone and Chef Maggiano and not paying close attention to much else. And the security detail was off investigating a cat fight two Dumpsters down. A diversionary ruse, no doubt."

"It must be someone familiar with the personalities around here and the patterns we follow. Someone good at covering up, someone above suspicion. Have you interrogated Peugeot?"

"Twice. He wasn't there when the snake made its appearance because he received a last-minute cell call. A fire at one of his residential properties over in Mill Valley. Only minor damage, thankfully."

"Yes, thankfully." Nick stared at his coffee cup.

"I know of your dislike for Peugeot ... "

"I dislike anyone who thinks the homeless are beneath our contempt and not entitled to our compassion." Nick swirled the last of his coffee, then banged the mug to a hard landing on the coffee table. "Anyone who treats his vehicle with more deference than the people we serve. Anyone who ranks our clients by their capacity to raise or lower what he thinks our public face should look like. Bottom line, he wants on the board to enhance his own community standing and then to shape what we offer around his own image. Sorry, but that's how I see it."

Cassie held out a plate of lemon cookies and Reynolds helped himself. "I get it, folks, but insensitivity and poor taste are every American's right. While neither Waverly nor Peugeot would get a medal for square dealing, they've kept most everything that shows aboveboard and legal.

"What about Gordon O'Neal?"

"Oh, Nick, no!" Cassie shook her head. "Gordon's done so much for Taste."

"Why him in particular?" Reynolds sipped noisily.

"No reason. Just looking for any information, really."

Reynolds nodded. "Seems clean. Helpful. Gave us all the background checks on each student in the program. Certainly speaks well of you two. And his San Diego alibi for the night of the poisoning is ironclad. Not to say he couldn't have left instructions for another, but honestly? He doesn't think criminally. You two are much better at that."

Nick and the lieutenant peered at one another over the rims of their coffee cups, one assessing the comment, the other the reaction to it.

Reynolds flashed the briefest of smiles. "The real purpose for my visit is to convince you two to start keeping a lower profile."

"Us?" Nick frowned. "We're fighting for the survival of Taste of Success and you want us to just roll over and play dead?"

Reynolds sighed. "Interesting choice of words. Until we figure out who's masterminding this whole thing, I'm concerned for you and yours. Let McTavish or another spokesperson be the lightning rod for a while. And how long do you think before some eager-beaver reporter ties this misfortune to the Azure

World perfume scandal? You're liable to lose all credibility, and then where will Taste be? Now if you folks will excuse me, I have to get back."

The Dixons saw him to the door. Out on the stoop, he turned. "Oh, there is one other thing, folks. You know it's not beyond the realm of possibility that someone in the commercial district brought a rat snake back from their visit to Aunt Tildy in Florida. You know, to take care of the rodent problem in the storeroom. It comes over to Pasta Bella to visit, climbs up on the counter, gets curious, and ..."

"Lieutenant, do you honestly think that's what happened?" Nick made no attempt to hide his skepticism.

"No, of course not." The detective nodded to Cassie and turned to go. "I think you should join your daughter at the lake cabin. Take the Ferguson parents with you and enjoy a mini-getaway. That's lovely country this time of year."

"Just turn tail and leave?" Nick leaned against the doorjamb, arms folded.

Without looking back, the gangly policeman called over his shoulder, "Sometimes retreat is the most effective strategy. Knowing when, that's the rub."

They watched him go. Nick sighed. "Remind me again what normal feels like."


With one hand, Philippe Peugeot flipped up the collar of the Italian suede jacket against the night chill. With the other, he caressed the diamond finish on the hood of the silver 607 Executive. Warm and glassy to the touch. He imagined the motorcar liked to be stroked. That it purred beneath his gentle fingertips.

Why didn't women respond to his touch that way? Eager, feisty ...

That they did not told him they had been improperly engineered. Give him a luxury motorcar any day, expertly machined to do his bidding. A lithe extension of himself, cunning, stunning, quick, rippling with muscle, bristling with the instinct to survive by preying on all others.

It was the only way to do business. He only wished he had more to show for it.

He slid the sterling silver lighter from a jacket pocket and flipped it open and closed with a satisfying metallic *chink*. He bought it, not because he smoked, but because of the *chink*. Each flip produced a tall, slender flame, yellow white, as neat and precise as his body, as the instrument he drove.

A patrol car entered the alley and slowed to a stop two car lengths away. A spotlight illuminated Peugeot and his vehicle. He turned and looked into the light, a hand shading his eyes, and waved.

The patrol car drew abreast of his position and the driver's side window slid down. "Ah, Mr. Peugeot, it's you. Sorry to blind you."

"Not at all, officer. You're doing your job. I'm just watching over the investment."

"The good people behind Taste of Success are a devoted lot, I'll say that for 'em."

"Thank you, officer, kind of you to say. We do appreciate your vigilance on our behalf. It's reassuring to this citizen that the upholders of the law are keeping watch with us."

"We do what we can. We'll find whoever's doing this, Mr. Peugeot, and put a stop to it. You have my word. That is a sweet car you drive. Don't suppose you're any relation to the Peugeot carmakers? Now wouldn't that be something!"

"Wouldn't it be. No, no, I'm just someone fortunate to share the name of so fine a machine. 'Car' hardly covers it."

The patrolman's bland expression said he missed the vehemence with which the last sentence was spoken. "Right, right.

Well, we'll be back through in a half hour. You should get your-self some sleep."

"I might do that, officer. Thank you for putting my mind at ease."

"Strange goings on with this Taste case. Must weigh on you. And sorry about that fire at your apartment complex this after-noon." The patrolman shook his head. "Deliberately set. Nutso world, ain't it?"

"Definitely nutso."

"The lieutenant wants to talk with you about the incident at Pasta Bella. He's in the area. I'll radio in and he should be here in five. Please wait here and have a nice evening."

"No problem, officer, none at all."

Peugeot watched the taillights of the patrol car move slowly down the alley and finally turn onto the side street and disappear. He suspected that if he were to leave, he would not get far.

He held the spearhead of flame close to his face and breathed in the fog-moist air. He imagined the days when these water-front docks rang lusty with the lingo of Italian immigrant fish-ermen earning their three bucks a week tending cauldrons of boiling crab. Lovers, clutching paper cups of crabmeat cocktails purchased for pennies, gathering their coats against the night chill, and holding tight to one another for warmth.

The slender flame pierced the dark and cast its precision light on the rear door of the Taste of Success.

A restaurant's carefully considered business plan included contingencies. Storm damage. Water damage. Food spoilage. On-the-job injury. Customer accident. Kitchen fire.

Arson.

He flipped the lighter closed and waited in the dark for the police.

# Chapter 21

Cassie had decided that what her nerves needed was to be hauled a couple of stories into the air to teeter on a thin carpeted platform with no walls and little to hold on to.

She missed Mags, her flying partner and doyenne of modern perfume. Because of terrible injuries she suffered when attacked by the Dixons' Great Dane Gretchen, those high-flying days were over for the spunky Mags. Thank God, despite three cosmetic surgeries and the use of a cane, she hadn't lost a bit of the fire that made her a legend in the cosmetics world. "All I need is an eye patch and a parrot, sweet cakes, and we got us an amusement park ride!"

Cassie chuckled under her breath. She hadn't been to trapeze class at the San Francisco School of Circus Arts in too long. This was where she faced her fears. In leotard and T-shirt, legs shaking, she dipped trembling hands into a bucket of chalk and wished she dared slap some of the drying agent under her arms.

The fine print of the death-and-dismemberment waiver swam before her eyes: ... *Do recognize the inherent dangers in acquiring aerial skills ... risk of broken bones or resulting paralysis ... surrender all right to hold liable or prosecute in a court of law ... will hold blameless ... except in a legally established case of willful negligence on the part of management ... do hereby accept full responsibility for said risk ...*

Waiting for her on the platform was the hard-packed instructor, dark haired and swarthy, the spitting image of a fatherly Flying Wallenda. He nodded and unclipped the two safety lines from her belt that ensured a safe arrival from the ladder and clipped on the lines that the instructor on the ground pulled to help her through the flight. She tried to think of something else.

A poisoning not meant to kill.

An assault not meant to abuse.

A kidnapping not meant to harm.

A snake not meant to bite.

Every attempt to discredit Taste of Success had been as clumsy as it was sinister. What looked like the work of an amateur was no laughing matter. The awkwardness of the threats was as comforting as a car full of deranged clowns.

"Your mind is where?"

Cassie shook her head and blinked her eyes. Tomas, the instructor, gave her a look that said she was the reason they had students sign waivers. "Focus, Miss Cass. Without it, you are a rag doll in a cyclone."

Properly chastened, Cassie stepped to the edge of the platform and concentrated on leaning into space from her hips and grabbing the trapeze bar hanging before her eyes. Tomas held onto the back of the rigging belt for good measure.

Just before she grabbed the bar, she felt stomach-plunging uncertainty. *Volleyball. Reasonable people sign up for volleyball to let off steam.*

Her hands closed on the cold bar.

*What if someone has loosened the bolts?*

"One. Two. Hep!" Romas, twin to Tomas, shouted the instructions from below.

She took a short hop and dropped.

For one terrifying second, she was in free fall.

The next instant she soared down and up in a graceful arc and flew across the length of the arena, toes pointed down, hands "glued" to the bar by grip tape.

At the top of the arc, exhilaration was immediately followed by anticipation of the next command.

"Hep!"

Though everything within her screamed "hang on," she let go.

Legs together, arms in front, eyes straight ahead, she fell backward in a sitting position, hoping to heaven the net was not at the dry cleaners.

She dropped into the arms of nylon netting, heart thundering, blood surging adrenaline unleashed.

Gloriously, wondrously alive!

One bounce. Two. Three. On her feet, stumble-lurching over to the edge, flipping over the side, hanging by her arms, lowered to the mat in the strong arms of Romas.

"Again!"

She would have signed a thousand waivers. To experience the terror. Feel the ecstasy. Poke a finger in the Devil's eye.

Nick came to pick her up. "Hang by your hair, Cass. You can do it!"

She stuck out her tongue and he laughed.

Four more times she flew. Four more times she fell. Four more times she showed him, showed herself, that they were in God's good hands.

Alive. Defiant. Shaken, but secure.


He drove the Coast Highway grand-prix-style. The twists and turns at Big Sur. The bends and tight cliff-hugging curves. Leaning and correcting, upshifting, downshifting, braking, cornering like a NASCAR maniac.

Eyes fixed and smoldering, face rigid with malice, hands tight-clawed to steering wheel and gearshift, body hunched like a gravedigger at rest.

The automobile responded as he knew it would. Took all he had to dish out. Gave back all and then some. Was an extension of who he was. Of who he wanted to be.

He didn't like to be refused or thwarted—or worse, ignored. Tonight he was all of those things.

When at last he was spent, he pulled off the highway and rolled to a stop at an ocean overlook. He shut off the engine, opened the car door, and admitted the distant sea.

On this night, it seemed especially indifferent to his frustration. There was a seething sting in the sound of the breaking waves, a villainous hiss to the battered sands. He should have acted alone and knew that going in. Never should have hired a sleepwalker like Burstyn. The training program had too many success stories to think one bad egg could spoil the entire carton. He'd badly misjudged public sentiment, and nothing had gone right from then on. From the reaction of the governor's little lunch party, you'd think the snake was part of dinner and a show.

He didn't like to be laughed at. Dismissed. Ridiculed.

*Oh, Pops. Why did you have that first fling with the goods? Why did you have to keep going back? They told you the heroin would be your Judas. It got you, just like they said it would. How could you choose it over us? You, homeless, just to be closer to the streets, closer to the supply. So desperate you became a cotton shooter. How could you ... inject residue from the cotton you filtered your filthy stuff with? Good thing you died when you did or I would have shot you myself.*

The tears fell; they always did. Certain that salt water was not kind to luxury interiors, he slid from the vehicle. Caught between a Cyclops moon and a phosphorous sea, he felt dizzy and disoriented. It was difficult to distinguish between the bluff above and the beach below.

He teetered on the edge, too uncertain of what lay beyond to jump.

Why not jump? No way to ascertain the exact manner of death. Man exits car to answer call of nature, slips on loose stones, plunges to death. At least as plausible as man commits suicide. As plausible, that is, until they identified his body and accidental death was the only death people would want to accept.

But would God recognize him? That was the bigger question.

He swayed at cliff's edge, toes of expensive Italian loafers hanging over the crumbling drop-off.

Ironic. Only by his verified suicide might Taste of Success go under from scandal—and a thousand deadbeat fathers with it. But given his luck lately, his death would be ruled accidental and a swell of public sympathy would secure the program's place in San Francisco history. And a thousand deadbeat fathers would receive unmerited favor and a better life for having abandoned their responsibilities.

Like cold water in the face, the colliding thoughts steadied him. He turned and, against his better judgment, delivered the left front tire a savage kick. The fates had spoken. He would do something drastic that could be interpreted only one way.

Father B closed the door to the manse and looked to see if anyone was home inside Kenny Burstyn. From the steady breathing and wary alertness, he guessed it had been some hours since Kenny's last score. He was anemic, malnourished, and injured in multiple ways, but by the grace of God and street-smart resilience, very much alive.

It would be morning before they could count on him to begin withdrawal. In two to four days of hell, the boy would suffer excruciating nausea, anxiety, diarrhea, abdominal pain, and insomnia, accompanied by a smorgasbord of chills, sweating, sniffing, sneezing, weakness, and irritability.

Right now, Kenny was preoccupied with trying not to make eye contact with Francis Welch, Father B's towering enforcer.

"Tell him I swear not to go anywhere. Tell him to just stop staring at me. Please!"

"Tell him yourself." Father B said it kindly, but he knew if they were ever to get the truth out of Kenny, it would take a firm hand. Most users dropped out of detox or rejected the idea altogether. A close watch was the only sure path to victory.

"I can't talk to him, n-not with that snake tongue of his."

Francis looked at Father B and flickered his tongue.

"Well, son, if each of us ruled out the folks who don't measure up to code, every one of us would be denied," Father B said. "I could become drunker than drunk in the twinkling of an eye, while you are on the fast track for collapsed veins, several hepatitis strains, AIDS, infected heart valves, and any number of suppurating abscesses. And that's just for openers."

Kenny groaned.

"Diapers!" Father Chris scraped the bottom of a frozen-dinner tray, put what he found there in his small birdlike mouth, and shook the spoon at Father B. "We'll need a supply of Depends for the boy. Judging from the amount of chocolate laxatives he just ate, the constipation will be the first to go."

"Aye. Make a list and we'll have the grocery deliver." Father B pulled a kitchen chair to the couch where Kenny lay curled, dressed only in a clean and very loose pair of briefs and one of Father B's robes. The robe was too short and the boy kept tugging it down in back to block the draft. His bare feet and legs were scratched and scabbed, with the worst of the sores covered over in healing salve and Band-Aids freshly applied since his arrival. Father B insisted he wear a pair of woolen mittens to prevent further scratching and picking.

"Now, Kenny, you need to listen."

When the boy started to protest, Francis reared up, puffed out his chest, and clenched fists the size of small hams. Kenny went limp and Father B continued. "We need to know who you work for. Who hired you to poison the soup and accost Mrs. Dixon?"

The dull, matted hair shook before disappearing beneath a couch cushion.

"Kenny, a man has died. Two kids were kidnapped. People are being threatened left and right. Something else awful will happen if we don't put an end to it. You can do that, Ken. You do, and the police will go easier on you. You don't, and someone else dies, it's all going to come crashing in on you."

Francis cracked his knuckles and neck bones. "You want I should show him some persuasion?"

Father B heard an evil laugh, though none was uttered. "Mercy, Mr. Welch, are you the Redeemed or the Terminator? Let's pray for a little guidance here."

Francis went to his knees, big hands folded at his chin like a child's. He prayed where he knelt, back straight as a door.

Kenny peeked from behind the cushion. Father Chris bowed his head.

"*Sanctus, Sanctus, Sanctus, Dominus Deus Sabaoth.* Holy, Holy, Holy, Lord God of Hosts. *Pleni sun coeli et terra gloria tua. Osana in excelsis.* Heaven and earth are full of your glory. Hosanna in the highest. *Benedictus qui venit in nomine Domini. Osana in excelsis.* Blessed is he who comes in the name of the Lord. Hosanna in the highest. Dear Father in heaven, help Kenny get the monkey off his back. Heal him inside and out and for all eternity. Help him surrender the name of the person responsible for our troubles before anything else happens. Help him survive the misery to come."

"What misery?" Kenny sat up, hyperventilating, eyes darting about like fireflies.

"Detox." Father B looked at Francis and both shook their heads. "Withdrawal. People have been known to swallow their tongues. Gouge out their eyes. Gnaw their fingers and toes off. If they're not stopped. We could stop you"—he looked sorrowfully at Francis who looked mournfully back—"if we were here."

"Why? Where're you going?" Kenny's panic filled the room.

"We have much to do, you know, for those who want the help. If you can manage on your own, we've got plenty of other places to be."

Kenny didn't say anything. Just sat and stared at a bare knee, as if noticing for the first time he had one.

Father B motioned to Francis and they got to their feet. Father B put a hand on the doorknob.

Kenny looked at him, eyes wet with regret. "Aren't you going to call the police? Turn me in?"

"Capital idea. Except they don't have time to get to know you, Ken. Jesus said, don't be quick to anger or to rush to judgment. I know you're more than a heroin addict. You are, aren't you, Ken?"

The boy nodded, tears streaming down. In a barely audible voice, he said, "Yes, I am."

Francis gathered him up, held him across his lap, and rocked him. "You gonna suffer the super flu, little friend, but Francis will stick by you. The Big H is tough, but the Big G is tougher."

"B-Big G?" Emaciated, wearing the black robe, and clamped against the ex-biker's hairy chest, Kenny resembled a weird baby ape protected by an even weirder adult mountain gorilla.

"Yeah, you know, the Big Guy God. Leave him and where would you go? Leave him and it's all desert. He's the Source, the blessed wellspring, little man. Now I say we go check out the cupboards and see what these monks eat."

Father B watched them pour cereal and spread peanut butter on crackers. He looked at Father Chris, who lowered his voice to a rasp. "Gnaw their toes off? Byron, really!"

Uncowed, Father B shrugged. "I'm permitted the occasional literary license when needed. Look at those two pack it away. What's that you're always telling me about the grace of a full stomach?"

Father Chris wrinkled his brow and wiped clean the bottom of the frozen-dinner tray with the remains of a whole wheat roll. "A properly fed man is already half saved."

Father B smiled and nodded.

# Chapter 22

They slow-danced across the kitchen deck to Tom Jones singing "Vaults of Heaven." She clutched him, cheek hard against his chest. Nick liked the way the setting spring sun lit her hair in orange and yellow. She smelled like peaches and cream, but there was nothing soft about the rigid set of her shoulders.

"Relax, darling. Anybody tries to cut in, they'll be facedown on the deck getting frisked by a two-hundred-pound graduate of the San Francisco Police Academy."

"Oh, great. Is he watching us right now?"

"He'd be a fool not to. It's not every day you get to observe Fred and Ginger at work."

Cassie gave an exaggerated cough. He felt some of the tension drain from her.

"Sorry." She kissed his neck. "I was just thinking how great it would be to kiss the kids good-night. Do you think they're moping around the cabin?"

Nick laughed and planted a peck on her nose. "I think they're talking a mile a minute and driving my folks to distraction. Knowing Mom, she's whipped up brownies and popcorn for an all-night *Lord of the Rings* movie marathon. Pops has just delivered a tasty batch of treats to the police surveillance team, is checking the locks for the twelfth time, and is about to launch into his usual Saturday night diatribe against government excess.

Mom will soon banish him to his Civil War history books and he'll fall asleep on the couch. All is well."

Cassie snuggled closer. "Sounds nice."

"So does swaying to the music with you."

"Mmmm. Am I swaying okay?"

"More of a crooked lean. You got any extra hip action in you?"

She swatted his arm. "I can't help it. I hate being so exposed. I hate being someone's target and not knowing whose. I hate waiting for evil to make its next move."

Nick rubbed her back. "I know, sweetheart. I've asked God to end it now so we can cut out the cancer and get on with our lives. These scare tactics stink and I'm not going to let them get away with it!"

They were silent awhile, letting the music work its way inside.

"Did you ever get through to Peugeot?"

Nick nodded. "I did and I told him I wanted to see him first thing tomorrow, *mano a mano*."

Again they were silent until Jones launched into "Love Me Tonight."

"What would you think of a skin firmer with a top note of plum nectar?"

Nick waited for more.

"Mags and I have been toying with an Ester-C concentrate that penetrates deep into the layers of the skin to boost collagen production and smooth wrinkle zones. We want to take it out of the health food stores and into general retail."

"Sounds expensive."

"That's the beauty of plums. Colorful, plentiful, secure supply. Vitamin C, likewise common and readily available, has both good press and fruit-healthy association. Ester-C, of course, bumps it up from common to top-shelf status. But not so much as to upset the profit margin. It costs out nicely."

"Sounds like you've thought it through. Is it meant to be an a.m. or p.m. application?"

"Another beautiful thing. It works through the night and under makeup during the day."

Nick gave her an exaggerated dip. He held her there and bent close to her ear, voice rich with husky innuendo. "Is it edible?"

She scowled. "You wish. But no, it's not for the libido. Choice Brand Beautifiers cannot jeopardize its active, clean lifestyle image."

"Pity. For a minute there, I thought we had us a surefire aphrodisiac."

"Sorry, Lothario. Now either let me up or schedule an appointment with my chiropractor."

He sat on the grass, her head in his lap.

"What?" Nick probed the sparkle in her eyes. "I know that look. You want to haul me up on that trapeze until I confess every sin since kindergarten. No can do, missy. The very thought makes my nose bleed. How about we order in some Chinese and let the fortune cookies work their magic."

Her lips curled in skepticism. "No need to arch your eyebrows, Confucius. The dumbest flea in the circus couldn't miss your meaning. No, let's do something we haven't done in quite a while."

"Skinny-dip in the museum fountain?"

"I've never skinny-dipped in the museum fountain."

"Oh, sorry, that was, uh … never mind."

She pinched him.

"Ow! I was only kidding!"

He pulled her to him and their kiss was filled with longing and urgency for this to be over, to live again a life of normalcy.

"So what were you thinking?" Nick squeezed her tight and wished for answers. "That I'm a world-renowned kisser?"

"That I want to go down to the waterfront and clear my head. Listen to the water and the boats, watch the lights cross the bridge, fill our lungs with salt air. Walk the docks like we used to."

"That was a cheap date."

She grinned. "Remember the Thermos of chicken soup we always took with us?"

"We've still got the Thermos. You think we can find chicken soup on a Saturday night?'

"Handsome Fong's chicken rice special."

"How do we get past the gendarmes?"

"We leave the lights on in the house, I hide under a blanket in the backseat, and you say you're going to get milk. We do need milk, by the way."

"Why you devious little minx. So it's Chinese take-out after all."

"Ah so!"

They had second thoughts about sneaking out and asked the officer on duty to escort them to the pier by following in his police cruiser.

As soon as they pulled out of the drive in the Amanti, the SFPD black-and-white pulled in behind them.

Nick looked back. "We have a tail."

Cassie made a face. "Charming."


Through a pair of Bushnell binoculars, he watched them walk arm in arm to the end of the dock, pour something steaming from a Thermos bottle, and share the contents.

They'd been strolling the docks for more than an hour while a police officer leaned against a black-and-white and observed them from a discreet distance.

They hugged and kissed and murmured in each other's ears, periodically pointing across the brooding waters to the near lights of Alcatraz and the distant lights of Oakland. There were more than a thousand square miles of bay to point to, much of it dark estuaries, wetlands, and marsh. Many more square miles had been filled in with the dredged mud and gravel from the hydraulic mining operations of a hundred years before. Millions of birds fed in the exposed mud flats on dense populations of brine shrimp.

But of far more consequence to him was what was happening on dry land. Resident occupancy in San Francisco was 98 percent and rents were rising nearly 9 percent a quarter. Already average rents in the city were well past two grand a month and climbing, the highest of any U.S. metropolitan center outside New York City.

Which made worse one of the worst homeless problems in the country. Though the city fathers spent $200 million a year on the problem, eleven emergency shelters provided a scant fourteen hundred beds. Estimates of the homeless population put it at ten thousand or more singles, more than five thousand of them permanent. Add another thousand homeless families and you had a recipe for social disaster.

The glass wasn't half empty. It was bone dry and about to shatter.

Take the other day at the I-80 off-ramp to Fifth. Scruffy bearded guy, young, standing there with a well-fed German shepherd and a sign that read, "Starvin Like Marvin." Whose fault was that? He had dropped his window and yelled at the fool, "So why don't you eat the stupid dog?" The guy flashed him a rude gesture, and that made him feel like coming back around and running the moron down.

He would have if he'd been in a rental.

The smelly creeps ruined their own lives in a thousand ways and then stood there staring at you with a look like, "So, cheapskate, why don't you do something to make my life better?" It was like he owed them his success. That if they didn't *have*, then he couldn't *have*. Communists!

And then these two come along, and a host of do-gooders like them, devising plans to reward the drunks and shysters and loonies by making gourmet stars out of them. No shortage of fat cats to fawn over them and tell them what fabulous people they were for "giving a hand up, not a handout." What slop! What about the twisted train wreck of kids and wives and families destroyed by the spineless choices these idiots made? They needed to pay, not get free manicures and other perks on the backs of honest, hardworking citizens.

He paced the edge of the rooftop and spit the vile taste in his mouth off the side. No way he could sit still. No way he could reconcile the hell his father chose to put them through and the Taste model that dressed vermin like Daddy dearest in starched white and paraded them around as suddenly model citizens. No, the homeless lowlifes needed to pay their debt to society, their debt to sons who drew the short straw and got junkies for fathers.

Their laughter, audible from where he stood, galled him. The Dixons should be cowering in darkness, prisoners in their own home, desperately wanting to come to terms. That is, they should, given recent events. Events for which he was responsible. Instead, they sent the children into hiding while they acted like what they faced was no more dangerous than a paper tiger.

They were wrong. This tiger has teeth. While he hadn't wanted to physically harm these misguided souls—just scare them away—it hadn't worked. Be nice to the Starvin' Marvins and you got flipped off. Be nice to the do-gooders who were nice to the Starvin' Marvins and you got laughed at.

They left him no choice.

He signaled to two men on the street below. Dressed in black hoods, black boots, and black wet suits equipped with two miniature oxygen tanks good for fifteen minutes underwater, the broad-shouldered duo crossed the street and kept to the shadows. Harbor Patrol dive team rejects with chips on their shoulders big as conch shells. Five thousand apiece for quick jobs. It paid to have soldiers already on the payroll when the time came.

The glasses provided a front-row seat. He watched the biggest of the hirelings slink out of the shadows, bent over, low to the ground, lightning quick. He came around the opposite side of the cruiser and was on the watching officer from behind before he could react, covering his mouth and nose in a chloroform-soaked cloth. Quickly, efficiently, he took the man down in the bushes bordering the industrial park, there to gag and hog-tie him securely.

The glasses swung back to the cuddling couple, so full of their foolishness that they completely missed the action at the rear of the lot.

Slowly, deliberately, without a sound, the men resumed their travels along the dock, past nets, coiled rope, mounds of covered canvas, and a short-box semitrailer, every step closing the distance to the Dixons.

He spit again, wondering if he would ever rid his mouth of that foul taste.

The men in black would do it for him. Fifteen minutes of air should be more than plenty.


I think our first summer Celebrity Chef Night should feature Chef Bob of Oceans Away and his amazing Cioppino Feast."

"I love it when you talk like that. Give me the juicy details." Nick poured her the last of the soup, then opened his mouth and upended the Thermos so that the slow bits of rice and chicken that clung to the insulated wall dropped into his mouth.

"Mmm ... attractive." She watched him dredge out one final chicken chunk with an index finger and suck the finger clean with a look of pure delight.

"Can't help it. I think Chef Fong spikes it with some secret ancient herb unknown to modern man. You were saying?"

Cassie leaned on the dock railing and hunched her shoulders in the gathering chill. She loved the feel of Nick's strong arms encircling her from behind. "Chef Bob does this special-occasion cioppino loaded with shrimp, scallops, halibut, salmon, crab, clams, mussels, and monkfish beautifully seasoned with bay, basil, thyme, oregano, parsley, garlic, and onion. He pairs it with warm sourdough bread. The salad is baby greens in a fresh lemon vinaigrette and dessert is lavender crème brûlée made with a teaspoon of dried lavender flowers. It's actually a variety of Mediterranean mint."

Nick made a face. "Too much of that stuff and it's like eating perfume."

She nodded. "You're right, overdoing makes the dish bitter. But Bob knows the perfect amount. It's a recipe that's been passed down in his family for generations. Besides, with all the heavy cream, egg yolks, and sugar he uses, you have nothing to worry about."

"Sounds scrumptious, madame." Nick's accent was thick and as fake as a three-dollar bill. "I am impossible to wait for the edible foofaraw!"

Cassie giggled at his antics, knowing her lightness of heart was temporary. "Oh, Nick, I can't wait until we get past this and have the catering business up and running. We should have a special dinner in honor of Beth and Cody's friends at the senior community. It was really their idea."

"Couldn't agree more. Tea and Malt-O-Meal for everyone!"

"You're wicked."

"Just thinking of the denture crowd, dear. Don't want anything to interfere with Al's checkers game. You ready to head back? We should stop by Chef Bob's for a little fish-and-chips. You can tell him what you're scheming."

She stuck out her hand. "First, help me up. I want to sit on the railing like we used to do and breathe it all in."

"But we were crazy back then."

"Nick."

"At your service."

When at last they were seated, legs dangling ten feet above the bay, nothing between them and Alcatraz but one-and-a-half miles of open water, they filled their lungs with the tangy freshness. Cassie closed her eyes, head filled with the raw good health of wind and waves, and practiced breathing out the tension and uncertainty of recent days.

Nick hummed a few bars of "Michael, Row Your Boat Ashore." "Remember how we dared each other to lean out as far as possible without losing our balance and falling in?"

"Oh, yeah. We came close a couple of times."

"Remember when you dropped your prize hair thing in the drink and you wanted me to dive in and find it?"

"It was tortoise shell and you said that if the tortoise hadn't missed it by then, he wasn't about to. Why did I marry a smart aleck like you anyway?"

Nick scratched his head. "I think you thought you could change me."

"Have I?"

"Maybe not my smart mouth, but I have learned to put my socks away and not drink straight from the milk carton."

"Nick."

"What? Most of the time I don't.... Usually."

She giggled again and shook her head.

They held hands and watched the moonlight shimmer on the bay.

They jumped when Cassie's cell phone rang.

"Mom? How are you and Dad doing? We just got done with the first *Rings* movie, and after we make some s'mores, it's on to the second. Are you guys okay?"

"Just a minute." Cassie lowered the phone. "Beth wants to know if we're okay."

Nick made a show of thinking about it. He stared out at the beautiful setting, took another deep breath, and turned his head to look at her. His adoring eyes said she was breathtaking with the moon above, her radiant hair reflecting city lights, and the golden shafts of lighted skyscrapers a surreal backdrop to her charm. At least that's what she guessed they said. "Do you love me?" He said it with all the callowness of a lost youth.

"Without question. Do you love me?"

"Beyond words. Tell her we have to get back to our kissing."

Cassie raised the phone to her mouth. "Beth, sweetie, we did some checking and I'm happy to report we're just fantastic! Daddy wants to know how's everything where you are?"

Nick made a fish face.

"Great! Being in witness protection has its perks. Grams and Gramps have bent to our every whim. Love you, Grandma! Was that a buoy bell I just heard clang?"

"It was. Daddy and I are taking a breather ourselves, only we brought protective custody with us." She looked back to make sure the patrol car was still there. It was. "We're down at Pier 60 reliving our misspent youth."

"Shame on you. Lieutenant Reynolds will pitch a fit."

"Yep, shame on us. But really, we brought the law with us."

"I worry about you, Mom."

"Nothing to worry about, sweetie. Your dad and I are enjoying a wonder—" Cassie was rammed from behind by what felt like a one-ton linebacker.

She hurled forward.

The phone flew from her hand.

She plummeted. Flailed. Hit the water. Shocking cold. Dark, disorienting depths. Senses scrambled. In millisecond flashes, questions pinged across terrified consciousness.

Nick?
Who?
Why?
Die?
God?

Panic. Reason. Panic. Kick for the surface. Rise. *Rise!* Too slow. *Can't.*

In a few precious seconds, she burst through into sweet, sweet air. Gasped. Drank her fill.

*Can.*

Thoughts fired past.

Sodden clothes.

Encrusted pilings.

Strong odor of creosote.

No Nick.

No ladder.

No escape.

She whipped her head around, tried to see the assailant in inky water. Tried to float on her back.

A shadow crossed the moon.

A cruel deadweight pressed her down.

Drove the air from her lungs.

Forced her under.

No air.

No light.

Dark.

*Nothing.*

# Chapter 23

Father B wrestled the beast past Fisherman's Wharf and sent it snorting along the Embarcadero.

A red compact four-door cut in front. Father B hit the brakes, downshifted in a banshee wail of gears, and laid on the horn. "Use your head, you blind beggar, what do you think you're doing? Stick your life out there and I'll give you a lesson in the hereafter you won't soon forget!"

The endangered driver must have caught sight of the snarling grillwork in the rearview mirror, judging by the way the four-door suddenly sped up and shot off the Embarcadero at the next available corner.

"That's what divine intervention looks like, you inconsiderate flake! You just about rang down the curtain and joined the Choir Invisible, hot rod!"

The beast roared and shuddered, threatened to bite the foot that fed it gas, then smoothed out as the odometer again crept upward.

The agitated priest pumped his fist and crooned, "Jesus, Jesus, pre-e-e-cious Jesus, how I've proved him o'er and o'er …" He glanced in the rearview mirror at his passengers.

"Hallelujah!" Francis shouted from the backseat where a decidedly nauseous Kenny Burstyn lay curled and shaking between the mountainous biker and an equally sizable male in long blue hair, brown Fu Manchu mustache, blue jeans, and white cowboy boots. Whereas Francis was all muscle and fire, Blue Hair was all Twinkies and french fries. Francis, in all his masculine glory, had discouraged many a brawl before it ever got from concept to execution—except those he started.

"How's them diapers fit, Ken?" Francis hooked the kid's thrift store waistband with a beefy finger and tugged, peering in at his handiwork. "I asked for the smallest Depends they had. God forget to give you hips or what?"

Kenny looked like a man in search of a place to die. There was a periodic gurgling from somewhere south of his belt. Each time that happened, a pained look of regret spread across watery eyes like spilled paint. Pale, sweaty cheeks puffed out, followed by a horrified look, like that of a pregnant woman in one of those low-budget science fiction films who wishes not to give birth to the alien within but is powerless to stop it.

Beth's frantic voice echoed in the priest's head. "We were talking along just fine, then she sort of gasped, like the wind was knocked out of her. Then nothing, like the phone was ripped out of her hands. I'm screaming, 'Mom! Mom! What's wrong?' Then a *sploosh* sound and it's all dead. Then a dial tone. She said a policeman was with them. Oh, God, Father B, what if ... what if—"

"Don't! Beth, think! Call 9-1-1. Tell them what happened and to get Lieutenant Reynolds down to that pier. Do it!"

He had stormed into the bedroom where Kenny and his guardians were squaring off with heroin and its hellions. "Francis! You and Tiny grab Ken, that barf bucket, and some towels. We're wanted at the docks!"

The church was a scant half mile from the waterfront. They had piled into the bus left idling in the St. John's parking lot. Ace Longfield, that Michigan hippie, had again sweet-talked Father B into subbing. He'd been about to leave on sandwich rounds when the call came.

Two giant boxes of baloney and cheese sandwiches rested on the front seats of the bus. They might be the only food the winos, camped out in doorways and under bridges, would see for twenty-four hours.

The air in the bus was thick with the smell of mayonnaise, reconstituted pig organs, and government commodity cheddar.

With a mighty retch, Kenny emptied the contents of his stomach into a white plastic detergent bucket.

"Atta boy, Ken! Out with the old Ken Burstyn and in with the—"

Another heave and a smell that made Father B clamp his mouth shut and throw wide the slanted side window to admit fresh air. "Lower all the windows, boys, and step lively!"

The sign for Pier 60 came at him. He downshifted. In the distance, red flashing lights. The sound of sirens. Police backup.

With barely a touch to the brakes, Father B cranked the wheel left, hand over hand like a long hauler behind schedule, downshifted, and to a chorus of angry car horns, shot onto the pier and made straight for the far end.

"Okay, boys! In the water! In the water!"

Francis and Tiny stormed to the front of the bus, kicked off their boots, and, long before the bus had rattled to a stop, were out the door.

Father B watched them hesitate but a moment before launching themselves off the end of the pier.


Francis was the first to reach a black-suited frogman struggling with a body that was struggling back.

He grabbed the frogman in a headlock and ripped off his mask. "Who are you?"

The man cursed and tried to bite Francis. The enforcer jammed two meaty fingers into the man's eye sockets and finished him off with an audible head butt.

The other man, now free, whipped his head around, frantically searching. "My wife! One of them has my wife!"

Francis heard a woman's cry among the pilings holding up the pier and power-stroked toward them.

"Get back! I swear, you come any closer and I snap her neck! Back off!"

It was impossible to see beneath the pilings or to pinpoint where the snarled words originated.

Tiny, at the pilings, was another matter. He was so pale, the skin of his face, arms, and hands glowed with the phosphorescence of a jellyfish. Despite his size, he worked quietly from one piling to the next, gaze fixed upon something in the deep dark.

The sirens intensified. Vehicles topped with rotating red and blue lights screeched to a halt at the pier's edge. The storage buildings and stacked materials glowed in apocalyptic crimson.

Vehicle doors flew open. Two handheld spotlights trained on the choppy bay at the foot of the pier. Francis shielded his eyes.

"You, in the water! Stay where you are!"

Then Father B's voice. "Don't shoot! He's a good guy, officers, a good guy!"

Francis, treading water, watched Tiny glide from piling to piling, taking advantage of the sirens to cover any sound. *Easy, big guy. Easy.*

From out in the bay, a light grew brighter, the sound of a powerboat approaching louder. *The water police.* Truth be told, Francis and police and guns and patrol boats had never been a good mix.

He would have fled but for one thing. *He's a good guy, officers, a good guy.*

Nick forced his breathing to slow, distractions everywhere. The large figure of a man moved among the pilings. From the pier above rained shouts, commands, and, thank God, the glorious, comforting voice of Father B.

Lungs protesting, Nick took a deep breath and dove.

*God give me strength.*

With strong kicks, he knifed through the water, heart banging to the rhythm of *Cassie needs me, Cassie needs me ...*

Crazily, he still held onto the Thermos bottle. Did he not want to lose the symbol of those happy days early in their marriage? Why else did he still have it? It made a poor weapon, but it was all he had.

Pure adrenaline propelled him beneath the pier. His shoulder brushed something hard. He slowed, put out a hand, and felt a barnacle-encrusted piling.

Lungs about to burst, he nevertheless performed a slow, deliberate ascent. His head rose from the water silent as a seal's and, face muffled between arm and piling, he sipped air soundlessly.

Eyes adjusting to the darkness, he studied the shadows, sifted them for those that did not belong. The air trapped between the salt water and the decking above was dank with sea slime and foam.

A chill gripped him.

Something moved. Nick, chin submerged, studied the dark until it moved again. Two somethings. *Cassie and the lowlife who attacked her!*

A cry of animal ferocity caught in his throat. He wanted to charge the man who had done this to her and rip his head off. *Dear God, is my Cass still breathing?*

Fingers, stiff and strong, dug into his elbow. A whisper in his ear. "Harbor Patrol's coming. I'll attract his attention. You come up behind."

It was the other giant who had dove off the pier. The man swam into the open, caught in the shine from the approaching powerboat. "You're surrounded, friend. Let her go. Ain't no point now. That's the law in that boat, and the pier above is swarmin' with 'em. Come on, man. Let's end it right here."

Nick submerged once again. Slowly, carefully, he felt his way among the pilings. He counted five between him and the man—and Cassie.

With the surface of the water lit by the patrol boat's searchlight, he could see their feet and legs—the man's thick wet-suited ones and Cassie's, slender in tan slacks and bare feet. *Jesus, let her live . . .*

He circled around behind them, now within ten feet. Another couple of strokes and—

He jerked to a stop, foot tangled in a twist of corroded wire cable.

The last of his breath escaped him.

If he thrashed, he'd alert the attacker.

If he didn't, he'd die.

He fought like a madman, twisting and writhing to break free of the trap before his chest exploded. Jaws locked against the instinct to open them, consciousness faded out and in. Movements slowed. The ridiculous Thermos floated away.

The attacker was on him, tearing at his throat, weighing him down. Nick meant to fight back, but did so with limbs that were those of another, sluggish and clumsy.

He rolled down a long empty corridor, head banging against wall and floor. Thirsty, so thirsty. He came to a water cooler, poured himself a paper cupful, and drowned.

Next he knew, he was lifted by the hair and pulled out of the bay and lay flopping on the deck of a metal-hulled vessel. People yelled and worked on him. Coughing, hacking up water. Sucking down great draughts of sweet oxygen. Smothered in Cassie's kisses.

*Alive.*


On the rooftop across the street, he lowered the binoculars and swore. How in the name of Zeus . . .

Everything had gone south in front of his eyes. If those two geniuses talked, he was cooked. Five thousand apiece didn't buy a whole lot of loyalty.

They *would* talk. They needed an attorney—his attorney. *Now.*

He knew that bus. All painted in mellow yellows and tangerines. It brought peace, joy, love to the scumbags and street trash that soiled the city with their drugged-up lives. That's right. Reward the bloodsuckers who scared off the tourists and drained social services dry. He'd like to reward them with one-way tickets to North Korea.

What was "Jesus Rocks!" doing there? Who were those two Neanderthals who got off the bus and blew his little extermination party to smithereens? Who was that driving the thing?

He sighed. He was no good at this, but what did that matter now? *Nothing works but Pop's curse.*

Fortunately, the Dixons would be far too traumatized to continue.

And there was one more statement yet to make if need be.

Cassie bit her lip. That would go down as one of the dumbest chances they ever took. Irresponsible beyond belief. Did they think they were invincible? She'd dreamed about that terrible weight pushing her under, wanting her dead.

*Thank you, God, for sparing the empty-headed.*

"I'm sorry, Cass. I wasn't there for you."

Without opening her eyes, she pounded the bed with both fists. "We're idiots!"

It was twenty minutes before the anger eased and she could speak again.

She did open her eyes then. She couldn't help but smile at the man in the next hospital bed. He was attempting to eat cubes of red Jell-O with dignity, only partially covered by a powder blue smock that stopped well north of two knobby knees.

He glanced at her. "Hello."

"The nurse admires your hairy legs." She sounded funny to her own ears. Congested. Weary.

"Well, the nurse needs to get a life. I heard you tell the doctor with the dimpled chin about your personal business."

"Excuse me?"

"He asked if you were experiencing any discomfort in your lungs and you said, 'Only when I get excited, doctor.'"

Cassie scoffed at his high-pitched imitation. "I said anxious, only when I'm anxious. Good thing you missed the bedpan discussion."

Nick gave up on the Jell-O. "I still think it would have been nicer of them to give us a double bed. When do we get out of here?"

"We're lucky they don't handcuff us to the bed rail."

Nick turned toward her, held the smock closed behind him, and leaned on one elbow. "Cass, I'm so sorry for not taking better care of you. Thank God they didn't finish what they started."

She looked at him through tears. "It was my fault, Nick. I came up with the stupid idea. Lieutenant Reynolds is furious and that poor officer is this close to suspension. For that matter, Beth came this close to losing us." She sniffed and swiped at a streak of moisture on her left cheek. "We are keeping God busy."

His pained expression said it all. "You okay, hon? I was so scared for you."

She grabbed tissues from the box by the bed. "I guess so. One minute I'm afraid and watching the door for bad guys, the next I'm so mad I could spit. When I pray for confidence, I get a little, but it's usually not long before I feel defeated. What about you?"

She watched Nick shift and wince at the muscle pull in his back suffered while trying to free himself from the tangle of cable in the bay. "Other than a strained back and a bruised ego from being next to worthless when you needed me, I'm experiencing a slow burn. Whoever's behind this has upped the stakes. No more scare tactics. They want us out of the way."

Cassie bit her lower lip. "I wish those two thugs would say who hired them."

"They're too busy cutting themselves a deal before they talk. You can bet they lawyered up before their hair was dry. Meantime, their sugar daddy is still on the loose. It's driving me nuts."

"Those are lovely flowers Mags sent."

Nick spied the enormous bouquet of stargazer lilies that took up one corner of the room and filled the air with exotic scent. They had awakened to the heady fragrance. "She tipped the florist fifty bucks to have them here when we opened our eyes this morning after . . . everything. She keeps Choice Brand humming for us, bless her. No worries there."

Cassie nodded. "Either I imagined it or the nurse said the Fergusons are coming by in a couple of hours. And Father B's supposed to be here this evening to bless the room."

"Wish he'd done it before the meat loaf we just had."

"Jorge called while you were napping to say he and Trina have a giant card signed by everyone that they plan to bring over after seasoning class. Bless Chef Rita for taking them in."

Nick took a sip of ice water. "Aren't we the popular ones. I just hope the kids learn the subtleties of spice heat, not just the upper extremes. You know Jorge. That boy was born in a jalapeño patch. Your show's about to come on. Are you up to it?"

Her show was Part II of the McTavish Plan. The food critic had pulled strings to get her a slot on short notice. "San Francisco Treats" was a popular TV cooking show that featured prominent locals demonstrating how to make tasty dishes using only the ingredients found in the well-stocked kitchen at KSF-TV.

It meant thinking quickly and originally on one's feet.

Cassie had taped the show the evening of the governor's infamous trade banquet. Still shaken by the serpent in the soup, had she strung together two coherent sentences? Not that she remembered.

It happened so fast, could it possibly have a positive impact on the future of Taste? The taping had gotten off to a disastrous start. Had she been able to recover in a convincing manner? Would Waverly's murderer and their attempted murderer be watching the show?

She shifted positions and settled back onto the bed pillows, not at all certain she could bear to watch, but praying it would be good enough to buy some much-needed public support. Bad news was piling up faster than parking tickets on an abandoned car.

# Chapter 24

"What time is it? It's time to eat! What do we love to eat? San Francisco treats!"

The music—a cross between Nickelodeon bounce and game show frenzy—swelled to aerial shots of the city interspersed with platters of mouthwatering delights. The camera finally zoomed in on an aproned Cassie standing at a stove while the show's manic voice intro declared, "Today's signature treat: Cranberry Dijon Chicken! And that signature dish belongs to none other than fragrance designer and promoter of gourmet food-training programs for the homeless, Cas-s-s-s-andra Dixon!"

The live audience, egged on by large applause signs held by hyper sign holders, went ballistic.

And Cassie went blank.

An hour before the taping, she had diligently reviewed the ingredients of the studio cupboards and refrigerators and determined that she could pull off a yummy sweet-tart chicken dish that could go from start to first bite in under forty-five minutes.

But that was before the audience was seated, before the makeup was applied, before the red light on each of three cameras indicated she was "on."

Thousands of Bay Area residents, some of them with pencils poised, others at their computer keyboards, would be expecting to take down the recipe that would make them mealtime heroes.

*They could, if I only had a brain.*

Frantically, she searched her mental recipe box and each time came up empty. The chicken recipe, so familiar she could have made it in her sleep, was nowhere to be found.

*Think quickly and originally on your feet.*

"Treats? You want to talk treats?" What was coming out of her mouth? "Lately it's been more like trick or treat at Taste of Success. You may know that our highly successful training program, that to date has enabled 642 people to leave the streets, find housing, and make their own way in the world, has suffered some setbacks.

"So yes, I was planning to demonstrate another quick dish with everybody's favorite meat. But let's save that for when things are normal, for one of those *Leave It to Beaver* days when everything is smooth as glass and you gals feel like wearing a dress under your apron. Yeah, right!"

Smattering of supportive laughter.

She crooked a finger at the camera and invited everyone closer for some "just us friends" talk.

"But you know how things are. This morning the toast burned, the kids overslept, Fido lost control of his bladder, and you pulled out of the driveway with your favorite coffee mug still sitting on the roof of the van. Things went from bad to worse until the afternoon mail delivery when you personally chased the letter carrier and bit him on the ankle."

Louder laughter rippled through the studio audience, many heads nodding in agreement.

"By the end of a day like that, you don't want foo-foo for dinner. What you want is quick comfort food with a capital C.

What you desperately need, my friend, are grilled cheese sandwiches!"

The hoots that greeted that announcement sounded evenly divided between "You can say that again, sister!" and "You've got to be kidding me, toots! I waited in line for this?"

"We're not talking just any old standard greasy grillie with white bread and American cheese singles. Oh no. We're talking grilled cheese with a twist. We're talking grilled cheese with sass. This ain't your mama's grilled cheese, girlfriend! No, no. This one's packin' heat!"

Cassie's patter continued as she gathered the necessary ingredients, including whole grain bread, sliced Swiss cheese, fresh mango, red bell pepper, a red onion, and a lime.

"Melted or toasted cheese sandwiches, once known as 'cheese dreams,' got their start during the Great Depression as a delicious way to feed families and entertain on a tight budget. Every year, we Americans grill up 2.2 billion cheese sandwiches at home. Now I'm going to show you how to put some kick into an old favorite."

Why could she recall trivial factoids about fried bread and cheese, but was as blank as a sheep about one of her tastiest standby poultry dishes?

*Focus.*

She knew by the way the audience members leaned forward in their seats that she had them. Only a small number of people ever deviated from the familiar melted cheese on toast. She promised them an exotic twist that they could rush right home and make today.

She sent up a silent prayer of thanks.

"Slice and dice the whole mango, half the red pepper, and a quarter of the onion in a bowl, add a couple tablespoons of fresh lime juice, a couple pinches of sugar, a double dash of salt, and some ground black pepper to taste. Now mix it up and set it over here so everybody in the bowl can get acquainted.

Meantime, mix softened butter and curry powder, about three to one, and spread it on the outside of your bread slices. Spread some honey mustard on the flip sides, smear about two table-spoons of the mango mix on top of that, then add the cheese slices, like so. Assemble and grill to a golden brown. I call them my Jamaican Cheese Breezes." She made the name up on the spot.

After five minutes of toasting, punctuated by more inane chatter, she spatulaed six sandwiches from the large griddle, quickly cut them in bite-size sections, and arranged them on plates for two stagehands to whisk out to the audience. Oohs and aahs of delight accompanied camera close-ups of nodding heads and enthused finger licking.

Cassie put six more sandwiches on to toast, waving the spat-ula like a conductor's baton. "Don't be afraid to experiment. Try using sourdough bread . . . it goes great with apple, ham, and cheddar. Croissants, filled with spinach and goat cheese, grill up nicely. One of my joys is salami and mozzarella cheese on Italian olive bread brushed with olive oil. Bacon, mushrooms, smoked salmon—the variations are as endless as they are delicious."

She cut batch two into squares and popped a hot Cheese Breeze square into her mouth and chewed contentedly, eyes shut tight. "Mmm. Heaven! Now when you consume your aver-age eight point four grilled cheese sandwiches over the next year, there will be nothing 'average' about them! With just a little more effort, you can change the ordinary into something really special.

"This is Cass Dixon saying if you liked today's easy gour-met way to spice up the dinner table, then please write a letter to City Hall in support of the Taste of Success program that, through food, forever frees people from a life of homelessness. Copy me your letter at the email address on the bottom of your screen. Include your snail mail address. I promise to send you my recipe for Cranberry Dijon Chicken and at last you will know why the proverbial chicken never made it across the road. Good chow for now!"

Another burst of laughs and wild applause. As the boom camera swept over the audience, the announcer repeated the contact instructions. Music out. Fade to commercial. Done.

Lights up. Shouted instructions from the studio manager. The crowd exited, filled with excited chatter. From the wings came the sound of one pair of hands clapping.

From out of the shadows stepped McTavish, a vision in green tartan. "Clever girl! I won't ask if it was planned or not. It worked. You connected with Joe and Janet Blow. Mr. Mayor had better get off the slopes. He's about to get crushed under an avalanche of citizen mail!"

Cassie's legs went wobbly as pasta noodles. "I could use a chairlift myself. How do those TV chefs do it day in and day out?"

"Tea and schnapps." McTavish rubbed dainty hands together vigorously. "Pull it together, sweet cakes. We're riding a wave and it's time to execute the third and final phase of the plan. My tour de force. See tomorrow's column and get ready for the biggest spectacle since Ben Hur took the chariot out for a spin!"

The following morning, Kenny Burstyn awoke to two opposing and equally powerful sensations.

He embraced life.

He welcomed death.

Life, because the hand holding his was large and strong, brown as a Brazilian angel's.

Death, because there was a monster in his belly, all knives, carving up his guts.

Death asserted itself. "I gotta puke. My heart is beating all haywire. Kill me. Kill me now!"

The walls and ceiling expanded and contracted. He looked around the inside of his head and saw the brains coming uncoiled and hanging in putrid strips the color of ash.

The hand, warm and reassuringly firm, squeezed. Life reasserted itself. "Hush that talk. Hush it now." A meaty thumb stroked the back of his hand while the sweet tips of the fingers beneath massaged the palm.

He brought the hand up and pressed it to his lips. "Are you from beyond?"

A laugh substantive as heavy crystal brought music to his hell.

"What is your celestial name?" It sounded like his voice, but from a great distance.

More crystal. "Shoosh. Just you rest now."

Panic. Would she leave him? "Don't go. God, don't go."

Wonder. His hand pressed to her lips. "God isn't going anywhere, but I am. I gots to use me the powder room."

She was away an eternity in which he writhed and gasped and plotted to kill himself. For the life of him—strange term—he couldn't think of a thing to end it with.

Something—someone?—hulked in the corner of hell, watching. Something enormous with hair and a forehead of scars. He spat in its direction.

She returned. He soared. She sang. Mehalia Jackson deep. Something about babies and mockingbirds and diamond rings.

And then he caught a whiff of himself, a seeping sour sweatiness that humiliated him. It was a stench unfit for her nose. He sobbed. She would leave him because he sickened her.

She kissed his tears. Pressed celestial lips against the lids of his eyes. Got his sourness on her skin. Wiped his brow with a washrag dipped in cool water. Gave him a drink. Sang a song of God's love for red and yellow children. *Do kids come in yellow?* He couldn't remember kids, yellow or otherwise. He thought it might be nice if kids came in chartreuse.

"Thank you, Fleurglimmersy."

"Shoosh."

A knife sliced from groin to neck, filleting him, spearing organs like shish kebab, serrated blade sliding in and out of his throat, severing the jugular, shredding the voice box, sundering the neck in two.

"Kill me!" Back arched, he stiffened in that position, veins bulging, teeth bared, face purpling with blood.

The brown angel hand stroked his arm, wanded the rictus from his face, extracted the paralysis from his spine, sponged the hot blood from his head and back down into shoulders and chest.

With a jerk, he understood he was naked except for a diaper and grabbed up the sheet to hide his shame.

"Shoosh," she cooed. "Shoosh, Kenny boy."

He caught her hand and pressed it to his cheek. He thought he heard Jesus. Unsure, he smiled and heard crystal.

Cockroaches were more reliable.

*Where is that loser?*

He was supposed to check in every night. In case he was needed. Now it looked as if he would miss for a second night in a row.

That was the one good quality the homeless had. They could be bribed. With food, booze, cigarettes, drugs, and, in the case of this loser, $30 a night. Sure it went straight into the idiot's veins, he knew that, but so what? Give a loser money instead of drugs and that kept the blame for any bad choices one step further removed. In his own way, he was giving the guy the benefit of the doubt. The choice was his to do with the money as he saw fit. Sprinkle it with hollandaise sauce and eat it, for all he cared.

But no. Like all the wasted half-wits on the street, he used it to buy poison. Probably killed himself. Overdose.

Idiot. Somebody had to clean his stinking oil slick off the street. Guess who? The decent citizens of San Francisco would be stuck with the bill to bury this guy.

But then, that's how his luck went lately. Every genius he'd hired had failed him.

He looked at the spot where he had stomped the loser into the dirt a few nights before. *Should have finished him off then.*

He crouched down and studied the driver's side door. Pristine. That genius could easily have damaged the finish, falling against it like that.

Good riddance. Even if by some miracle he still lived, the fool's brain was so fried he'd never be capable of stringing together two cohesive sentences. Write him off.

At least the do-gooders were finished. No one would carry on after all they'd been through. In the end, they would cut their losses, write the restaurant and food program off as a failed social experiment, and go back to tending their beauty products company where they belonged. Worst case scenario, they'd move out to unincorporated county land and run what would amount to no more than a glorified food bank. He'd make a preemptive offer on the waterfront property, resurrect Two Hundred Maricopa Square, drop the names of a few potential tenants with rich and well-connected pedigrees, and send diamond earrings to grace a few of the more desirable female ears about town.

He'd have to act fast and give each of his goons in jail a small cut to buy their lasting silence. Operating expense was all that was. Like having his attorney free them on a technicality so they could be his muscle during upcoming delicate business negotiations. Nothing complex about busting bones.

He sat behind the wheel, shut the door, turned the key. The purr of luxury.

*Sweet, sweet luxury.*

He drove slowly from the alley, only slightly aware of a trickle of uncertainty at the nape of his neck. Not until in bed later that night was he able to identify it for what it was.

It was a loose end, loose enough to keep him awake until dawn.

In every break room, boardroom, and boutique on both sides of the Bay, the McTavish column in the next morning's *Chronicle* was topic number one:

"In a city where every other downtown doorway is draped by a homeless person, who will champion the one rehab program that works almost every time?

"In a city where complaining about the homeless problem has become the resident pastime, who will embrace a solution that is so successful, one hundred applicants were turned away last month because there weren't enough resources to fund them all?

"In a city where the only thing more common than fog is corruption, who does not know that more than 80 percent of Taste of Success graduates trained in food prep, quality control, customer service, and project completion go on to sustainable living wage jobs in the food service industry? Who does not know that those good people leave those downtown doorways for good and step over the threshold of a new life to sleep in their own beds under their own roofs?

"In a city where corporate greed is as plain as egg on the emperor's face, who does not recognize a blatant attempt by big-money interests to discredit and destroy a program that works?

"In a city as fair and invigorating as this one, a city so possessed of charm and mystique that it draws people from the far-flung reaches of the earth, who will stand against this evil destroyer? Who will demand that hizzoner the mayor and the city fathers and mothers link arms around this golden program and protect it from whoever would do it harm?

"For my part, dear readers, I challenge City Hall to a good old-fashioned food fight at the corner of Market and Van Ness at noon on Saturday, May 12. Sixteen of the largest corporate retailers in town have agreed to underwrite the "battle royal," and twenty of the state's most prominent movers and shakers have each donated $50,000 for the privilege of entering the fray. All proceeds will go to support Taste of Success.

"The weapons of choice will be overly ripened examples of our state's bountiful agricultural output. Onerous onions. Mucky melons. Squishy squash. Leaky lettuce. Rotten ruta-bagas. Sounds like me mother's recipe for Scotch Broth Stew. Only kidding, Mum.

"Among the dignitaries behaving in a most undignified manner will be James Leonard, vice president of operations for the deBrieze department store empire, and Marsha Osborn, chair of the San Francisco Restaurant Association. Governor Mitch von Bruegger will be there in hip waders challenging all comers. In a twist on the old dunk tank game, anyone who pledges $500 or more can pitch three rotten tomatoes at his familiar face. He says the odds of your hitting him are quite good. Quote, 'As recent political debates in Sacramento show, I make a very large target indeed.' Unquote.

"And, dear reader, if you can knock the tam from my head that day, I will give Taste a check for $100,000 and give you two weeks at a Paris cooking school complete with deluxe five-star accommodations.

"Frankly, dear citizens of this fair city, this is the only cause that could have jolted me from my privacy. Food critics should keep a low profile unless something is so wrong that to remain hidden is the greater crime. I hope every one of you comes down to watch the fun and tie up the town for a day. Maybe then more of us in a position to do something about it will realize just how tasty a treasure Taste of Success really is!

"And by the way, should anyone worry that the police will shut us down, we have obtained all necessary permits. Let's just say we have friends at the SFPD.

"In a city where we want people to come alive and thrive, who can afford to miss the Great Downtown Food Fight? Who can afford to let Taste of Success fail? Not me. Not you. So let's come together and make a mess. In the process, we just might save the farm and some good people who are just a soufflé away from turning their lives around."

Cassie flung the newspaper across the room and ran screaming out the kitchen door into the driveway. "Nick! *Nick!*"

The security detail pulled their weapons.

"Cass, what in the world—"

She leapt into his arms and smothered him in kisses. She laughed like she hadn't laughed in weeks.

Nick peered around Cassie's storm of affection at the officers approaching cautiously. "She's happy. It's okay, she's happy."

He was unhappy. Head-splittingly, gut-churningly, forever-cursedly unhappy.

" ... let's come together and make a mess."

He tore the paper into shreds, hurled them to the bedroom floor, and jumped up and down on them in bare feet.

Every time he made a move, the Dixons countered.

So be it. While they were making their mess, he would make one of his own. Only he wouldn't be using putrid tomatoes. No, the mess he planned to make wasn't the kind you could hose away.

Wasn't the kind where you walked away and had a good laugh.

No more loose ends. He was not inept. Those do-gooders and their little project were damned.

# Chapter 25

Nick watched Philippe Peugeot, accompanied by a uniformed officer, stride along the driveway and cross the lawn past Gretchen's kennel. The fluid ease with which he walked, hands in pockets, the costly soft tan slacks and cashmere sweater the color of coffee and cream, the way every detail of his manner and approach telegraphed self-assurance, precision ...

Nick checked his watch. Philippe, to his slim credit, was punctual and bore none of the telltale signs of a man in fear of confrontation.

Nick called across the yard, "Thank you, Officer Lane. Please don't go far."

The policeman nodded and withdrew a short distance. He stood, solidly planted, and watched through amber-tinted glasses.

Still fifty feet from where Nick sat at a redwood patio table sipping a diet ginger ale, Peugeot lengthened his stride, closed the gap, and sank to a crouch beside the redwood bench.

"Nicholas." Peugeot, suddenly intense and animated, grasped Nick's big muscular hand in his soft, manicured one. "What have they done to you? How is it possible in a civilized society? Attempted drowning? How is Cassandra?"

He was a wolf that talked. He held your gaze, stroked your hand, and signaled to the pack unseen behind you to come forward and take their fill.

Nick removed his hand from the aristocrat's warm grasp and wrapped it around a tall glass frosty with condensation. He nodded at the bench opposite. With reluctance, Peugeot stood, made to place a hand on Nick's shoulder, thought better of it, and sat.

"Cassie is fine." Nick studied his guest. What did he expect to see? Evil smoke billowing from the man's ears?

"Why, Nicholas? Why do they hound you?"

Nick extracted a small ice cube from his glass and pinned it against the back of his throat with his tongue. The ensuing numbness distracted from the hot bile that threatened. "Who are *they*, Philippe? Who wants us out of the way?" He indicated a metal tray on the tabletop and a second frosted glass. The guest chose a can of light lemon tea over diet ginger ale.

"Your tone, Nicholas ... surely you do not think that I—"

"Cut the drama, Philippe. I want answers!"

"And I would know this, how?" Peugeot poured the tea, swirled the contents of the glass, drew in a long sip.

Nick observed the man's pencil-thin eyebrows and felt a powerful urge to connect them with a black permanent marker. "After the Waverly poisoning, you made a lowball offer to the board of $1.3 million. We turned you down and you've not seen fit to come back with a serious offer." In his mind, Nick saw the extortion note, the "second offer" emblazoned there. Did Philippe know about the kidnapping? Did he order it? "Some might score your silence as that of a man who is biding his time until circumstances are such that there is no way out but to sell. Does $6.5 million mean anything to you?"

"Should it? You really think I am a man who engineers circumstances to squeeze cooperation from the uncooperative? Is that it?" Peugeot's expression was more resignation than offense. "Really, Nicholas, is that sentiment worthy of our friendship?"

"Can't say as what we have very much resembles friendship, Philippe. I'd call it professional courtesy, maybe, mutual forbearance, most likely. We've never seen eye to eye on the clients served by the Taste of Success model. Why a man of your interests and cunning even bothers with mercy ministry is beyond me. Might it be that you are more interested in the land than the people who occupy it? I think you're hanging around to gather intelligence that you can use to mine the most gold for the least amount of dollars invested. We could be manufacturing widgets in that building, for all you care."

The speed with which Peugeot's eyes narrowed reminded Nick of a cobra on the defensive. The cobra licked its lips and spoke. "At least widgets imply a return. I have been exceedingly generous to your cause, yet the class of people you serve per dollar expended is commercially unacceptable, however you spin it. You could do what you do on any piece of distressed real estate in the land. Instead, you cater to a bunch of impoverished squatters on prime commercial property and drag down the surrounding real estate values. From a purely common sense perspective, it is wasteful and unconscionable."

Nick clicked the side of the glass against his bottom teeth. "Then make us a decent offer. No, let's go one better than that. You show us your heart's in the right place and make Taste a better than decent offer so that we can thrive in a new location."

Peugeot drank, his head weaving back and forth—the cobra hypnotizing its prey.

Nick waited, then gave a sad smile. "No, you won't do that. You have nothing in common with the old wealthy couple who donated that property to Taste. They knew it would appreciate in value and they wanted us to have a prime location for increased visibility and ease of access to the people who need it most. And you know what, Philippe? Call what that couple did lavish foolishness, but they wanted to give something excellent to God's work. And wouldn't you know, they're still wealthy. And they have the satisfaction of knowing that because of their generosity, there are many hundreds fewer homeless people going nowhere in San Francisco."

Peugeot set down the glass, tented his hands, and lightly tapped fingertips together. "Bravo! Pretty speech! But however much our two approaches to the subject differ, my friend—and I do count you my friend whatever your opinion of me—you have zero proof that I'm behind any of your troubles. I could sue you for defamation of character, but I won't. Lieutenant Reynolds came after me implying all sorts of unpleasantness as well. He found my alibis unshakable. As I told him, you may be assured that if I'd wanted Waverly frightened off—or worse still, dead—I wouldn't have staged such a ghastly exhibition in front of a roomful of guests. If you know anything about me, you know I insist on a certain fashionable elegance about everything I do. Anything less is insulting. I'd not risk my standing for the likes of the ruthless James Waverly."

"I'm supposed to find comfort in that?"

"Find comfort in this, my second offer, $8.5 million and you walk away from what has become, in light of recent events, a haunted house. A more than decent offer, considering the property was a gift."

Nick snorted. "You don't get it, do you? You'll bulldoze the building, put up a commercial high-rise, entice all sorts of foreign investors and tenants, and the only thing haunted will be the visionaries whom you cheated. Those people saw that Taste could work, and by their blood, sweat, and tears made it work."

"Then why can't they take that cesspool of a downtown mission and turn it into something other than a holding tank for drug addicts and thieves? The woman who runs that thing is den mother to the dregs of society!" Peugeot's lips formed a sour curl.

"Josie does an admirable job of meeting the immediate needs of the lost and the hurting, no questions asked. Not everyone drives a *motorcar.*"

"That was snide—"

"You *threatened* us, Philippe. All that talk about how we're like fennec foxes that rapidly dig themselves into a hole. I've got news for you. We're the eagles who rise up and go where none has gone before!"

Gretchen the Great Dane awoke from a snooze in the sun, rose on giant paws, and stretched out the kinks. In the process, she gazed at the two men on the patio, at first waving a tentative tail, then growling.

"Hush, Gretch, Mr. Peugeot is about to leave." Nick turned back to the enigma that was Philippe Peugeot. "Don't you read the papers? The Great Downtown Food Fight is on. Before it was announced, it had raised close to a million dollars for the food-training program. And millions more in publicity and goodwill. The city will have no choice but to embrace us. That's God's doing. I think we can afford to hold tight to what we have."

Peugeot stood, stiff and no longer as smoothly contained. The muscles of his jaw twitched. He gave Nick a doleful look. "If you think that a few politicians making spectacles of themselves in the public street will stop progress on the waterfront, you are more of a fool than I thought." His hands were clenched at his sides, fingers white at the knuckles, less in anger, Nick guessed, as desperate to wrap themselves once again around the steering wheel of a nonjudgmental 607 Executive Saloon four-door of moonstone silver exterior and velour interior.

Philippe waited, and when Nick said nothing more, he took an uncertain step. Gretchen's growl became a snarl. He stopped. "I'm leaving."

"I see."

"Is it safe?"

"The dog's behind a fence. I can't speak for the men with guns."

Nick did nothing to silence the Great Dane's display of dislike, but watched, along with police eyes, until Peugeot passed from sight, gait now drained of all certainty. He was just another self-centered, lonely investor having a bad day. Nick was no longer convinced the tidy wheeler-dealer in the expensive clothes was the one out to ruin them.

A new suspicion gnawed at him, one he liked even less.

No way he done it. I mean, he did, but he like didn't know it, which is like not doing it, ain't it?"

Josie was making zero sense and had been making zero sense from before Kenny's fever broke and he fell into a deep, exhausted sleep. It was the third day and the heroin withdrawal had run its course. The horror was over. He had survived what in street jargon was "the super flu."

Jorge patted her big brown arm. "Whoa, there, mama. Take a breath and speak to us in a known earth language."

Trina gave Josie a hug. "Kenny thought you was a angel."

"Lawd have mercy!" Josie laughed, rocking and jiggling, all of her in on the joke. "Angel, girl? Ain't no wings made can lift Josie 'cause she ain't 'fraid to eat her own cookin'! No, I was sent here to shoosh the boy and give him sumpin' to wake to 'sides Francis's scary mug."

Francis glowered, scars falling into the ditch between bushy eyebrows. "Now, Mother Jo, you know I'm takin' beauty treatments for that."

She laughed the throaty rumble that was music to the down-and-out.

Father B assessed the sleeping boy's condition. "His ribs are wrapped, his surface wounds washed, treated, and bandaged.

Someone has been pulling the strings and making Ken dance. Unless I miss my guess, it's the same person who ordered Kenny to lace the soup. And from the looks of our wasted friend, either he's fallen down a lot of stairs lately or this someone has been ensuring his obedience with beatings."

He grabbed a Bible off an old Philco cabinet radio and squeezed it in both hands, eyes afire. "Sons of perdition!"

Struggling for calm, Father B laid a hand on top of the boy's head. "Sweet Jesus, hear us! Thank you, Savior of all mankind, for returning Ken Burstyn to us. Help him down the rough road ahead. Give him the gumption to enter rehab and beat this addiction. Make him well. Restore his life, his relationships, his will to live. And bring the rotten coward to justice who made a puppet of this boy and made him dance to the Devil's beat! *Vade retro me, Satana!* Get thee behind me, Satan! Protect the Dixons and Taste of Success and all poor souls who wait for the chance to turn themselves around. Give them that chance, Lord, by your *vis medicatrix*, your healing power. Amen!"

Josie, Jorge, Francis, and—waking just then from sleep slumped on a stool in the corner of the room—Blue Hair added their hardy, if disjointed, amens.

Father B took them all in at a glance. "I think what you were trying to say, Jo, is the very thing I've been thinking all along. Kenny may have placed the poison seeds into Jim Waverly's soup, but not because he knew what he was doing."

On the couch, Kenny stirred. "No. *No!*"

Father B stroked the boy's hair until he settled back and began to snore, a sound not unlike a squeaky door hinge. "The Devil's associate was using him, keeping him doped and dependent, and ordered him to do it. Somebody hooked on heroin is only thinking about where the next fix is coming from and when. Who would use another person to do their wickedness? Demons of darkness!"

Again his eyes sparked fire.

Francis, face set in a deadly scowl, cracked huge knuckles. He reminded Father B of a human wrecking ball. *Pity the jaw that meets those pile drivers. Must lose the rage.*

He watched Kenny's chest rise and fall and took a deep breath. "I would remind us that ours is not to harm." He waited until Francis lowered his hands. "Ken should be back in his right mind by now. Ours is to find out as soon as he awakens the name of whoever pulled his strings. And then we go to the authorities with that information and let them do their job. No more commando raids, am I being clear? It will be a miracle if I'm not defrocked over the other night's business at the pier."

The regional council of bishops—The Inquisitors, he called them—were considering disciplinary action. One of them had the effrontery to call him a "rogue priest." In his heart, he knew the Dixons would be dead if he and his irregulars hadn't intervened when they did. Still, his future ministry was in jeopardy if the Midnight Church got a reputation for vigilantism.

Bishop Steiling was his one ace in the hole. Could the newly appointed coordinator of the annual parish fund-raiser count on the bishop to mollify the regional council?

He looked at Francis and wondered if the Lord's disciples ever knocked a few heads. Saint Peter hadn't been above lopping off an ear here and there. He hadn't always been a saint. "Francis? Fire up the bus. We've got rounds."

Father Byron shut his eyes and banished the unruly thoughts. *Forgive me, Father, for trying to buy sacred power.*

But why was someone trying to destroy everything the Dixons and their colleagues were doing to solve the city's homeless problem? Why were the Dixons, who spent so much of their time trying to give people a second chance, the targets of an unnamed evil?

*Fides quaerens intellectum.*

"Yes, Father God, faith before understanding."

Mags, we're back in life's hot seat."

The husky laugh that met that statement soothed like cool water on a bad sunburn. Cassie smiled at the yellow daffodils with orange centers in the planter box outside her kitchen window. She still felt tightness in her chest from her brush with drowning and exhaled slowly. She held the phone tight, willing the mirth to never stop. When it finally did, she said, "And just what's got you by the funny bone?"

"*I've* got the hottest seat in the business, dear girl. Wouldn't know what a cold seat felt like. Now you tell sister Maggie all about it. No more than three hours, though, I've got a roast in the oven."

Cassie smiled and silently thanked God for the woman who had put sophisticated fragrance on the map of post-WWII America. They were fast friends and she had no reservations about spilling her thoughts, misgivings and all, to her dear friend.

"I'll not be a prisoner in my own home, Mags. Shaken as I am by what's happened, I'm not going to hide out or cower in fear. God said that perfect love casts out fear. If I've learned anything in recent years, it's that when all around me the things I trust are shaken to the core, you trust God all the more."

"Put it on a billboard, honey, you said a mouthful!" Through Cassie's entire download of information, Mags clucked helpfully and said "Oh my!" in all the right places.

"Am I crazy, Mags?"

Her friend let a soft whistle out through her teeth. "Every one of us is a little off her nut, kid. If it isn't life wearing us down, it's pollution and fluoride messing with our cells. But you've got to be careful and not take unnecessary chances, especially with this loony on the loose. A poisoning, the attack in the alley, the kidnapping, the snake, the attack at the pier—it's just weird. And why the focus on you two and those precious children? Taste takes a village, right? The police don't have a clue?"

Cassie gave a bitter chuckle. "Clues are all they have, and a hundred suspects, but it's like some clumsy amateur terrorist learning on the job. It has to be someone with access. At first I thought it was Kenny seeking revenge, but all this other stuff takes thought and means. A heroin addict has precious little of either. I think Nick and I are the lightning rods because we're outspoken and were in the news so much, you know … before."

She faltered because of all that Mags had suffered when attacked by Gretchen, who was at the time under the influence of the deadly perfume that nearly destroyed them all and kept the Dixons on the cover of the tabloids for weeks.

"Maybe. But my personal pick from the O'Connor collection of free opinions is that this person or persons figured that because of your previous trials, with one good poisoning you and Nick would fold like a cheap tent and take the whole camp with you. When you didn't, he or she was forced into Plan B, then C, and has been working through the alphabet ever since. Little does this creep know that you and I are graduates of the School of What Doesn't Kill You Makes You Stronger. I may look like five miles of bad road, but I also know how to spit gravel in the eye of adversity. You're from the same mold!"

Cassie rubbed her temples. "I wish. In the darkest moments, I think everyone would be better off if they didn't know me. Oh, Maggie, where would we be without you? You've kept us afloat and not a word of complaint."

"*Nonsense!*" Mags said it with such force that Cassie had to yank the phone away or suffer a blown eardrum. "It's my job and I do my job. Now you listen to me. You get that lover boy of yours to get you a quart of good French vanilla ice cream, a bottle of fudge syrup, a jar of maraschino cherries, and a can of whipped cream. You have him put on a little Harry Connick

Jr. and massage your feet with our Citrus Therapy Balm while you shovel sundae fast as you can. When everything's gone but about a third of the whipped cream, you open wide and shoot straight for the gullet. Do you need me to go over that again?"

"No, ma'am. I've got it. Ice cream. Fudge. Cherries. Whipped cream. Repeat."

"Good. Next time I'll give you my recipe for low-cal Five Cheese Mac and Cheese. You're making a huge difference to a lot of people, Cass. Don't let anything discourage you. Just be careful and listen to the police."

"You're one to talk. What about when you used to race cars?"

"They were jalopies, honey, with a top speed of thirty miles an hour. And we didn't race, we crashed. Into one another. Demolition style. Weekends only."

Cassie wanted to reach through the phone and hug the daylights out of this woman who always made her feel better. "My mistake. Here I thought danger was involved."

"Once I broke a nail adjusting the rearview mirror."

"Still, the potential was there."

"You should talk, Trixie Trapeze."

"Yeah, but we don't crash into each other halfway across."

"Semantics. Do they still have those cute spotters working there?"

"Yes. You should come down on Thursdays and flirt."

"Is that any way to speak to your mother?"

"I thought you were my sister."

They laughed until the tears flowed. Before they were done, Cassie vowed to add Merry Mags Ice Cream Delight to the Taste menu.


After some persuasion, Nick agreed to take Cassie to the Taste restaurant. "I know it sounds silly, but I want to do some cleaning, start getting it ready for the reopening. It'll help me believe it myself." She swallowed hard. *If you have a mustard seed of faith . . .*

Nick looked unsure. "Really? I've got to check on that shipment of cold cream jars. We were shorted."

"You don't have to come in, not with Sid providing security. His gun has real bullets. I saw them. I'll be fine. Go check the jars and pick up the plum cream scent strips from Crowley's. Oh, and grab the microwave from the repair shop. The timer's been fixed and it's been sitting there since Tuesday. You might keep your eyes peeled for rubber rain gear. No way are we going to miss out on the food fight with the guv. Swing by Von's too, if you wouldn't mind. We need milk, a loaf of that good multigrain we like, and a quart of French vanilla ice cream and a jar of maraschino cherries. We're good on fudge topping and whipped cream. Then zip back around and get me and we can go to Theodore's for surf 'n' turf."

He looked at her in amazement. She was flushed that shade of pink he adored and the light of hope danced in her eyes.

"Is Officer Lane going to want to tail me to all these places?"

"Get him some donuts at Von's."

After all that had happened, his courageous little Cassie was game and her appetite was back. "And just what's in it for me?"

She planted an index finger under his chin and drew him close. Her next words came slow and sultry. "I have this new dessert recipe that you, sir, are going to love." She only hoped she wasn't whistling in the dark.


He stared at the label on the bottle of expensive red wine and managed a sickly grin. Though he never drank the stuff, he admired the world of wine making. All that chemistry, all that aging, all that sniffing and sipping, all the beautiful artistry that went into creating the perfect wine label.

A cluster of plum purple grapes embossed with gold leaves against gently rolling hills bathed in amber sunlight. Cabernet Sauvignon, Vintage Farms Private Label, Napa Valley. Ripe tannins, medium-bodied, silky texture, a satisfying finish of cassis and blackberry.

All of which swirled down the sink drain at Taste of Success—$120 of liquid money—a full-bodied gurgle that scented the kitchen with a decidedly voluminous bouquet. They didn't sell much of the stuff, but it had been a Waverly favorite, thus necessary to stock. Who would drink it now?

What did it matter that nearly twelve liters of the once-exclusive wine now mingled with common raw sewage beneath the city? Wine lovers were far too sentimental for their own good.

He swirled the new contents of the bottle and noted how all liquid looked the same through smoky tinted glass, be it the juice of fine grapes or regular unleaded from the pump at the Quickie Mart.

Sad to say, the aroma of gasoline trumped the fragrance of fermented fruit and the kitchen now smelled like a fueling station. How long before the buildup of fumes ignited from the pilot light on the gas stove? Nothing ventured ...

Lined up on the prep table were five wine bottles, in addition to the one in his hand, each with a gasoline-soaked rag stuffed down its neck, each emptied of wine and refilled from a jerry can of gasoline he'd driven to the restaurant under a blanket on the backseat of the luxury BMW. He hoped that after the dust settled no one bought "the bomber's car" at auction, then resold it on eBay.

It had been easy enough to get past the security guard patrolling the restaurant. He waved, was recognized, said he had important paperwork to review, and with the guard directing, had backed the car inside the loading bay at the rear of the building.

He hefted the Molotov cocktail. It was considered a destructive incendiary device and regulated by the Bureau of Alcohol, Tobacco, Firearms, and Explosives. Illegal to manufacture or possess. Long-honored weapon of civil unrest. The poor man's hand grenade.

Feeling both restless and uncivil, he wondered how a man was reduced to this. But the more he thought about it, the more obvious the answer.

The more trouble he caused, the more popular Taste and the Dixons became. All the bleeding hearts cared about was saving the poor homeless person, the underdog, even though those like his father deliberately chose to abandon their families and feed their addictions with the baby food money. Where were those bleeding hearts when the lights and heat were shut off? When the eviction notice came? When your mother wept and tore hair from her head? When the roof over your head had a dome light and belonged to a '76 Ford Fairlane? When your bathroom was a Folger's coffee can?

Why should drug-wasted fathers be rewarded? Why should millions be diverted from sick kids or cancer research to save the sorry hides of bums and deadbeats?

Yeah, he'd done okay in business. He owned some lucrative properties. But it was driven always by the desire to stick it in his father's face. He took no pleasure in any of it. He'd rather be painting seascapes around Monterey. But over his head hung the Damocles sword of insecurity. Of desertion. Of being "trailer trash" and the son of an addict. It was time to make a statement. Maybe in death he could salvage something from a sorry life. Shut the do-gooders up. Anything.

He heard the front door open, the bell ring. "Gordon? Sid said you came by. Gordon, are you here?"

*Cass Dixon? Here? Now? Curse her!* He cursed himself. Cursed God. She would see. Know. Tell.

"In here, Cass. Can you give me a hand?"

He grabbed a butcher knife and slipped behind the spice cabinet.

# Chapter 26

Kenny opened one eye and looked around. The others were outside in the sun, leaving him to sleep off the exhausting battle with withdrawal. Only he hadn't been asleep. The snoring, the muttering—all fake, at least the last forty minutes' worth. He'd heard everything.

The drugs were gone and clarity was back.

He remembered the beatings of which the priest had spoken. The pain. The contempt. The shoes.

For a minute, all he could remember of the man's appearance were the shoes. When you couldn't look a monster in the eye, you formed a relationship with its shoes. He'd spent so much time groveling at the man's feet, they'd become the part of his anatomy with which Kenny was most acquainted. The shoes kicked and stomped Kenny, and the subservient Kenny admired their quality workmanship. Italian leather. Expensive.

Efficient.

After a couple minutes more, Kenny was clearheaded and his heart started to race. Reckless excitement. Mind groping for the externals. First, the vague outline of the man's stocky head backlit by a streetlamp. No, an alley security light. The short hair, frizzy in the corona of light, sideburns dark and long. A look of intense loathing snapped suddenly into focus and Kenny physically shrank from it.

The name. The name. The man's name?

A swarm of hateful, conflicting thoughts rose thick as ravenous insects. Drugged and needy, he had been one man's punching bag, the locus of one man's hatred. Even now, detoxed, psychological cravings gnawed the interior of his skull like wolves on caribou. He needed long-term treatment or he'd relapse, no question.

But once again possessed of rational thought, with clear vision and in control of his limbs, he understood that there was one need more powerful than finding more heroin upon which to feed: the need to crush the monster in the Italian leather loafers before the monster crushed another human being.

How? You went to the monster; he didn't come to you. One thing sure, he wasn't turning what he knew over to the cops until he'd first looked the monster in the eye—and spit in it.

He needed air. Space. Time to think.

The bus in the manse courtyard roared to life, then fell back into a labored arrhythmia. He heard the priest shout.

"Francis! Keep this beast from stalling while I dash into the church and tell Father Chris he's got evening prayers."

Kenny crouched below the bay window and watched the tidy priest—who he now understood to be the Tallest Priest in the World from his heroin hallucinations—hurry across the courtyard and enter a side door of the looming edifice that pointed to the celestial kingdom.

He looked around the spare apartment, then up at the ceiling, and smiled.

Kenny yanked on the holey sweatshirt and raggedy jeans—now washed—that he'd arrived in, jammed bare feet into torn sneakers, and bolted for the kitchen. Banging open drawers until he found one containing miscellaneous items, he rummaged about until his hand closed on a box of wooden matches. He snatched the sports page off the dining table, dragged a chair into the hallway, twisted the newspaper into a makeshift torch, and set it on fire.

After it burned brightly a few seconds, he blew out the flame, jumped onto the chair, and fanned the smoldering end a few inches from the smoke detector—and prayed that priests changed their batteries religiously.

A blaring shriek pierced the air, driving an audible ice pick straight into Kenny's brain. Ignoring the pain, he counted to ten, leapt to the floor, threw the newspaper into an empty metal waste can, positioned the waste can on the chair beneath the alarm, and raced out the back kitchen entry.

Crouched behind the shrubs, he watched the others dash for the front door of the apartment. The giant they called Francis throttled the bus to a sustainable idle before flying out of the bus after them.

Kenny flew into the bus, took the driver's seat, shut the door, revved the engine, stomped the clutch, and rammed the bus into the first gear he could find.

The bus whined and lurched across the parking lot with all the speed of a sedated snail. The priest emerged from the church and stood staring gape-mouthed at the passing bus. Kenny, grim-faced, stared straight ahead.

Casting a glance at the rearview mirror, he saw more people emerge from the manse, point, and give chase. Without slowing, the bus sideswiped a wooden carving of the angel Gabriel and whaled into honking traffic.

*The name. What's the monster's name?*

Kenny gave the bus all the gas it would take. Emblazoned with "Jesus Rocks!" and looking like a survivor of an explosion in a tie-dye factory, the school bus was the most recognizable vehicle in San Francisco. If he was lucky, he had ten minutes before he was surrounded, arrested, and taken into custody.

*No, sir. Not before he looked the monster in the eye.*

*Okay, Kenneth, you've got one shot at this to make your daddy proud. Where's the creature hiding?*

Like a compass needle pointing to true north, the nose of the bus turned southeast, toward the Bay, the waterfront.

The Taste of Success.

Pedestrians, cabbies, cable cars, and bicycle messengers parted before the tie-dyed whale. Kenny ground gears, slammed brakes, and fought the steering wheel with skinny arms taut with tension. The closer he came, the more he believed.

*He's there.*

*He's the one.*

And he knew something else. It wasn't the culinary program or Cassie Dixon that was to blame for his defeat. It was a tan man with shoe-polish hair, an alien invader who snatched him from training where he was off to a good start, got him hooked on heroin, and turned him into the chairman's lackey. The man had a malformed soul and, whatever his game, figured that a piece of homeless garbage like Kenny the kid was so far removed from lofty circles of leadership and trust that no one would ever tie the two together.

The monster hid in plain sight.

Kenny may have had no home and no respect. Maybe even no hope. But he had rage. Rage that someone in a position to help thought him of no more importance than a scab on the civic rump.

He downshifted for a red light and watched a flock of seagulls wheel and soar overhead. He opened the side window and let the ocean in. He wasn't far from the Embarcadero. Not far from confronting the devil in the Italian loafers.

*He's there.*

The rage swelled. He tasted bile. He swallowed, but all the saliva in the world wouldn't take this burn away. Shops and parking signs and pointing slack-jawed people blurred past. The bus banged through intersections, careened around vehicles, frightened everyone in its path.

He was different now. He ignored stoplights and the screeching mayhem in his wake.

Relentlessly, the quivering compass needle of the too fast bus held to the path of truth. There would be a reckoning. Unless he missed his guess, it was now about two blocks over and two blocks down.

Kenny screamed the monster man's name.

Gordon, do you smell gas? Gordon?"

Oh, he smelled gas all right. *All the better to torch you with, my dear.* Too bad the last thing she would smell would be the burning of her own flesh.

It was the little that was left. Hadn't he tried, really tried, not to permanently damage anyone? Those warning shots across the bow were meant to discourage. Could he help it if the Dixons were foolhardy and incapable of recognizing the signs? They should have admitted defeat long before now.

What was left? To make a statement. Cassie Dixon was unexpected, yes, but maybe the fates had decreed she should be a part of that statement. She would know now, beyond any doubt, that he was behind the troubles, and that revelation would not do. This way, at least, he could spend the rest of his days in prison knowing that the Dixons had been stopped and Taste brought to the ground. It was their own fault; they just wouldn't back off.

"Gordon, are you in here?"

He tensed, set the Molotov cocktail on the floor, peeked around the corner of the spice cabinet. Cassie, back turned, stared at his array of modified wine bottles.

"Like them?" He rushed forward, knife raised. She turned, face contorted in shock. The heavy wooden meat mallet, held in both hands, swung for his wrist. It connected with surprising force and a shooting pain rocketed the length of his arm.

The knife flew across the room and clattered to the floor behind the salad prep table.

With a bellow, he bore down on her, then ducked aside and took a glancing blow to the temple. Blood streaming into one eye, he grabbed a large stock pot hanging from an overhead rack. Using it as a battering ram, he forced her back against the wall. Her swinging blows clanged harmlessly against the pot and he was finally able to wrench the mallet from her hands.

Gordon tossed the pot aside, grabbed her arm, twisted it behind her back, and wrenched her hand toward her shoulder blades. She yelped. With his free hand, he grabbed a white dish towel and pressed it to his head.

"Stop struggling!" he snarled in her ear.

"Ow! Gordon, stop!"

He yanked. She cried out again and went still.

He lowered her arm a little.

"Are you crazy, Gordon?" She panted and a single sob escaped her throat. "For the love of ... you're the chairman of the board!"

"You wouldn't understand, Cass. My father traded us for the streets—his wife, his children! Never looked back. And now here's all this gorgeous real estate being lavished on bums and dopeheads just like him. They don't deserve it. He doesn't deserve it. It's a sinful waste and I'll not have it!"

"Think, Gordon. If each of us got what we deserved, we'd all be doomed. We're not judge and jury. Let's redeem the ones we can. You can right your father's wrongs, Gordon. Don't throw everything away like this, *please*!"

She tried to squirm from his grip, but he tightened his hold.

"Stop, Gordon! Please!"

"Save the speeches, Cass. Do you think for one minute I don't know what you'd do the minute I set you free? No, it's over for me, but not before I make one last gesture that no one can possibly misinterpret. You've seen my incendiary devices. We're about to have a kitchen fire to end all kitchen fires. And you'll have an excellent view of it all through the window of the walk-in freezer. Now move!"

"No, Gordon, no! This is insane. Think what you're doing. So far, no one has died. You won't have to do as much time if it's not a homicide."

"Move!"

"Please, Gordon, don't leave Beth without a mother. I swear, as God is my witness, I will ask the courts for leniency. God can turn this around. We can get you the help you need!"

He marched her up to the freezer door, jerked it open, and shoved her inside. "Looks to me like the only one in need of help is you. I've disabled the fire alarms, but maybe you'll get lucky and help will arrive before you cook in there. Maybe not. You think you've got problems? Arson and homicide should keep me out of circulation for as long as I've got left."

"What about the guard? He's right outside the building."

"I'm sorry, Cassie, really. If I'd been more adept at this ..."

He slammed shut the freezer door and slipped a bolt through the handle to prevent it from being opened, so she couldn't escape by simply pressing the safety handle that opened the door from the inside. She rattled the handle but soon stopped. Through the window, he watched her sink to her haunches, hugging herself with her arms, head bowed. Probably praying. Not a bad idea if you put stock in that sort of thing.

Maybe she'd die of hypothermia before the explosives went off. That would be merciful.

He opened the door to the loading bay and whistled. "Sid, a hand, please."

The uniformed Sid, a balding man slight of frame, approached. "Yes, Mr. O'Neal, whatcha need?"

"Maybe you could help me move some boxes in the freezer? I messed up my back hauling bark dust, of all things."

"It don't take much to throw a back outta whack." Sid threw him a sympathetic smile and accompanied him to the freezer. O'Neal slipped the bolt. "There at the back, in the far corner." As soon as the guard stepped over the threshold, O'Neal threw a shoulder against the door and rammed the bolt home.

Muffled protestations and banging from inside the freezer were ignored.

The explosives were close to the floor, some in the kitchen, the rest in the dining room. He needed time to escape, but not so much time that the heat buildup activated the overhead sprinklers prematurely and doused the flames. A mere $100,000 in damages and Taste would be back in business in less than six months. No, he needed nothing less than total destruction.

He moved three of the bottles into the hallway leading to the dining room and left three where they were. He would do the kitchen last—no windows—and exit through the loading bay, recover his car, and drive off.

Drawing the curtains closed at the windows in the dining room, he ran back to the bottles. He lit the small hand torch used to caramelize the sugar on burnt cream desserts.

He took one last look around at the beautiful hardwood floors, the elegant treatments in greens and burgundies, the Tiffany lamps and elegant furnishings, and felt a moment's regret. Then he touched the flame to the rag in the neck of the wine bottle, took a deep breath, drew back his arm, and hurled the bottle at the wall.

# Chapter 27

Turn the car around!"

Police Special Detail Lane gave Nick a skeptical look. "What for?"

"We need to get back to the restaurant now!" Nick, taut as a bowstring, twisted in his shoulder harness to peer out the rear window of the patrol car.

"You're sweating, Mr. Dixon. Maybe you were released from the hospital a little too—"

Nick's jaw went rigid. He locked eyes with Lane. "I can't explain it. My gut tells me go back. I listen to my gut. My wife's in danger, do you hear me? *Turn this car around!*"

Lane studied him a moment, then reached for the radio handset.

Nick flinched, heart racing. "What are you—"

One-handed, the officer whipped the car into a tire-screeching U-turn and hit the siren. "Take it easy, Mr. Dixon. I'm calling for backup."

He allowed the acrid smell of burning wood, cloth, and decorative fixtures to fill his nostrils. Not exactly the smell of victory, but it would do.

The Italian leather loafers took a step closer to the black orange flames devouring curtains and wallpaper. The heat knocked him backward, but he basked in it a moment longer and tried to imagine his sodden father writhing at the center of the inferno. No good. Try as he might, he could not conjure his father's face. All that came was the apparitional facelessness of winos and crackheads by the thousands.

With a frustrated growl, he fled the dining room and ran down the hall past metal serving carts and empty coat racks into the kitchen. Tears blurred his vision, his effort to see his father's face.

He snatched up one wine bottle, lit it with the hand torch, dropped the torch, lit a second bottle from the first. He tilted back on his heels, raged at the ceiling through clenched teeth, and hurled one bottle against the far wall and one against the walk-in freezer door.

The two containers of gasoline exploded with a demonic roar, sucking up the air in the room with a whoosh, slamming him back against Carmina's sweet potato fry vat.

He roared in pain, face blistering in the intense heat, then turned and retreated into the loading bay. Banging into shelves, donated restaurant equipment, and the pristine BMW parked there, he groped for the double doors and rolled the closest one into the ceiling. Though the sudden sunlight blinded him more, he followed the polished contours of the car and groped his way to the driver's side door.

Behind the wheel, he started the car, put it in gear, and shot through the opening, down the alley, and for the first time in his life, bottomed out and didn't care. He spun the wheel, hit the street with a horrific bang, gave the wheel a vicious jerk to the right, and narrowly missed a bread delivery van.

He thought first of heading for Vegas, of hiring some plastic surgeon to make him a new identity. Hide in the desert.

Wait it out. God wouldn't be fooled, but God knew too much already.

He felt a resurgence of purpose. The fire was a cleansing. Some might call it evil, but was not every great movement in history preceded by a purge?

*Why not enjoy the fruit of my labors before I go? Watch that fire cleanse Pop's memory right out of my head forever.*

He cranked the wheel right, cutting off a Metro bus, and ignored the blare of a horn and the rude gesture of the irate driver.

The BMW screeched to a stop in the loading zone at the front entrance to Taste of Success. Smoke seeped from window and door seams. Orange spirits danced and peeked around and under blackening curtains.

A long-dormant sensation thrilled his innards and caressed his mind. Its name welled up from the bowels, expanded the chest, soothed the seeping blisters of the once-fair face. It produced a taste in his mouth stronger than fragrant wine or raw gasoline. No name was sweeter than . . .

. . . *satisfaction.*


Kenny ignored the aged flower child wannabes waving to the psychedelic Jesus bus from the street corner. Two blocks more—just two blocks.

The street sloped down to the industrial area along the water. Kenny feathered the brakes and gripped the wheel, knuckles white as bleached bones.

He could see the front of the restaurant from here. The street he was on ended in a "T" at the Embarcadero. Extend the street and it would pass right through the front door of Taste of Success and out the back loading and delivery area and into San Francisco Bay.

He thought he heard distant sirens.

Kenny jolted upright in the driver's seat.

A block away, dead ahead, a steel gray BMW.

*The* BMW.

A figure behind the wheel. Face turned away, staring at the restaurant.

*No matter. It's him. The ... monster.*

Kenny's stare was a tractor beam of death. All else fell away. He stomped on the gas.

Cassie, bare arms numb with cold, felt her core temperature dropping. The explosions, the orange light flooding the small window in the freezer door, Gordon's face distorted with bitter hate—she knew what it meant.

*Be joyful always.*

*Pray continually.*

*Give thanks in all circumstances ...*

Paul's words to the Thessalonians were what she could muster. That and an aching desire to tell Nicky how deeply she loved him, how bleak the thought of leaving him.

Like a zombie, Sid removed his jacket, drew his weapon, and, breath streaming from a rigid face, took two stiff steps toward her.

Still huddled on the freezer floor, Cassie cringed and squeezed her eyes shut. *No, not Sid, too ...*

The weight of the coat settled gently around her shoulders. She breathed in the smell of old leather, felt the momentary warmth from Sid's body enveloping hers.

"K-keep down, M-Mrs. D-Dixon. C-Cover your ears and k-keep this j-jacket over your head."

Two blasts from the gun were followed by the immediate roar of flames and the acrid smell of things not meant to burn.

She opened her eyes and pulled down the jacket. Smoke hung low in the air, weighted by frost. Shattered glass lay at the base of the door. The hole where the glass had been admitted a choking, bitter smoke.

"To l-let the heat in and the c-cold out." Nearing retirement, Sid, small and thin in a faded short-sleeved cotton shirt, looked to have aged ten years. His words were feeble apology for the small hole in their prison that gave equally small comfort.

"G-Good, Sid. C-Can you reach through and s-shoot the bolt off?" She'd seen more ludicrous things done in the name of television drama.

Sid hesitated, face creased in fear. Cassie felt sorry for him. He just wanted to finish out his rent-a-cop days and retire without ever really having to play the hero.

"I'll t-try."

He shuffled toward the door, grabbed his chest, and let loose a strangled cry. He clung momentarily to a five-foot wire rack of frozen dairy products before collapsing to the floor under cascading bricks of cheese and butter.

He moaned once and went stone still.

"Sid! Oh, d-dear Lord!" She watched his thin chest, willing it to rise and fall. It was motionless as death.

Cassie crawled to his side, coughing and choking on the smoke.

*Stay low, stay low ...*

She felt for the carotid. The artery through the rough, whiskery skin told her nothing.

Somehow she managed to straighten him out so that he lay flat against the frozen floor. Cassie stuffed the jacket between his bare arms and the frigid metal. Movements clumsy and drained of feeling, she tipped back Sid's head, cleared the airway, pinched the nose, and breathed two breaths into the old man.

Between each breath she pressed methodically down fifteen times on the sternum with her hands joined, just as she had learned from the CPR instructor. With each compression she spoke a single sluggish word.

"Give ... thanks ... in ... all ... circumstances ... Give ... thanks ... in ..."

Just before the intersection, Kenny hit the horn.

The bus barreled across Embarcadero, narrowly missing a boat and trailer.

As if in slow motion, Gordon O'Neal turned to stare out the driver's side window of the BMW, eyes wide with horror.

In a split second, as if awakening from a trance, Kenny thought of the words of the World's Tallest Priest and mashed down on the brakes.

*Ours is not to harm.*

The Jesus bus slammed into the BMW and drove it through the front wall of the Taste of Success into a dozen burning tables and halfway across the dining room floor.

Tons of bus ground to a stop, flames lighting its interior in a bright, undulating eeriness.

Intense heat.

Terrible vision of being broiled alive.

Pain worse than anything he'd ever felt on heroin. Like the steering wheel had driven his ribs against his backbone. *Got to get out. Now!*

Kenny grabbed the lever, wrenched open the doors, and as best he could, bent over in pain, exited the bus.

Welcome to hell.

Fire fell in strips of burning materials like volcanic fallout, and searing heat whipped about him in scorching gusts. Kenny's lungs filled with hot soot. He bolted for safety back along the path made by the bus, coughing and gasping.

He could smell his own hair singed by heat and burning embers.

*Restore his life.*

The words were from the priest's prayer back at the manse when everyone thought Kenny was still sleeping it off. The only thing he would add is, *Hurry up.*

Impossibly, he could not take another step. The man in the BMW, what about his life? Who would restore him? *Give me a stinkin' break. That guy didn't give a flying dirt clod about me.*

Kenny turned back. Couldn't help it. What kind of person left a man to burn to death? Even if he was already dead, the thought of his charred remains was too much. He was no monster after all. Kenny had finally looked into his eyes and seen the same frightened child Kenny knew he had inside him.

He shielded his face from the heat and ran around to the BMW's passenger door. The driver's side was welded to the bus's bumper and grill.

The door wouldn't open. *Power locks.*

He peered through the glass. O'Neal was slumped against the wheel, unconscious, mouth open, face spider-webbed with blood from the impact and the shattered glass. Kenny knew no way could he get in on that side, plugged as it was with bus.

Gunshots sounded from the kitchen. Kenny panicked. *Who else is in here?*

He stepped back and, despite the pain, lifted a foot and kicked the passenger window. Three more kicks and the glass shattered. Pulling down the sleeve of his shirt to cover his fist, he bashed the remaining glass from the window frame and climbed through.

He groped for the seat belt release, then backed out of the front seat pulling O'Neal with him. The guy was deadweight and stocky to begin with, but in several stabbing grunts and heaves, Kenny somehow got him outside the car.

His ribs throbbed. He had no energy to carry or drag two hundred pounds of man out of the building. It felt like ragged ends of sharp bone were already at work shredding the flesh along his back and sides.

"Oh, God, I can't." He slumped down beside O'Neal and wrapped thin arms around the man's head to protect it from the heat. He tried to shrink back from the heat, but the BMW radiated nothing but. His heart jumped. *Gas tanks! The car, the bus, they'll blow this place to kingdom come!* But he couldn't move and began to cough uncontrollably. The only prayer he could think of went something like, *Now I lay me down to sleep . . .*

It began to rain. A great drenching downpour from the ceiling. The sprinkler system burst forth in full soak. Instantly, the flames began to subside.

Sirens. Shouts. Pandemonium. Hoses and more sweet, blessed water. Strong hands beneath his arms lifted him carefully onto a backboard, up, up, and out. He coughed. "No pain meds, okay? I got a little problem with drugs."

Air, great smokeless waves of it, sweeter even than the water. And words, words he never expected to hear again. "It's okay, kid, we got you now. You're going to be fine."

"And that other guy?"

"He's in bad rough shape, but should survive. The Beamer's a total loss. What happened here anyway?"

Kenny Burstyn didn't know how he was ever going to answer that question.


Emergency vehicles converged at the front of the ruined building; the back end of a wildly painted bus projected onto the sidewalk.

Nick's heart dropped. *Dear Lord, what in the world . . .*

Officer Lane took a sharp left, then sharp right into the alley at the rear.

Before the patrol car came to a stop, Nick was out the door. He bolted through the open loading bay. *That was closed when I dropped Cassie off.* He reached for the handle of the door leading into the kitchen.

*Hot.*

Taking a deep breath, he put a handkerchief to his nose and opened the door. Flames leapt at him. He ran crouched over. "Cass! Answer me, babe, where are you? Cass!"

He heard a feeble scream above the din of fire and firefighters. "Inside the freezer! Hurry, Nick, Sid's had a heart attack!"

He grabbed the handle, jerked the bolt out, and threw wide the freezer door. Cassie, sparkling with frost like a winter fairy, knelt hunched over beside the security guard's inert body. Nick surrounded her in his arms, shocked at how cold she was.

"G-Gordon O'Neal l-locked us in and set f-fire to the building." Cassie's words came in labored gasps, her voice brittle and faint. "T-Take over these c-compressions, can you?"

Nick helped her up and swiftly knelt in her place and resumed the rhythmic breaths and compressions. "Are you hurt, Cass? Can you move?"

"I'm okay. H-Help Sid. I d-didn't have a breath left. And s-something awful happened out f-front. I heard this t-terrible crash—"

Truck engines, thuds, gushing water, and a hail of shouts sounded from down the hall. And without relief, the awful crackle and whoosh of fire.

Officer Lane burst through the door and threw a blanket around Cassie and one to Nick. Nick's face dripped with perspiration.

"Lane, a paramedic, please, and fast!"

"Roger that."

Nick threw the blanket over his arm, lifted Sid, and ran outside where he continued the compressions and shouted for Lane to wrap the guard in the blanket.

An ambulance raced into the alley, screeched to a stop, and disgorged two young males who immediately took over from Nick.

They bundled Sid into the back of the ambulance without once stopping CPR. Just before they drove away, one paramedic shouted, "We'll get him to Mercy General right away. More help's coming."

Just then a second ambulance pulled up and two more paramedics made Cassie as comfortable as possible with more blankets and what Nick called "fancy hot water bottles." He never left her side, even while the several burns he had sustained were being treated.

He held her hands, rubbed warmth back in them.

Cassie looked at him through tears. "Oh, Nick. Why would Gordon do this? What if he's still inside there somewhere, dead?"

"I don't know. And you probably don't know this, but that crazy hippie bus Father B sometimes drives plowed right into the front of the building. I saw the rear end sticking out."

"Oh, no! Father B?"

A paramedic turned to them. "I don't know about any Father B, but if you're talking about Gordon O'Neal, he was in there, all right. Weirdest thing I ever saw. The bus T-boned a Beamer and both vehicles crashed through the front wall. They're still in there. Next to the Beamer is this frail straggly looking kid holding your Gordon O'Neal. Just the two of them, that's it. Afraid we don't know if O'Neal's going to make it; he was pretty bashed up in the crash. So was the kid. Bunch of busted ribs, and yet he asked us not to give him anything for pain. Says he's got a problem with drugs. Heroin, from the looks of those arms."

Nick looked at Cassie, then at the paramedic. "Did you get a name on the kid?"

"Yeah." The paramedic took Cassie's pulse. "You folks help run this place, right?"

They nodded.

"Guess it's okay then. Says he's Kenny Burstyn. I probably shouldn't say anything, but the police ran it and he came back a missing person out of Sacramento. Parents worried sick. We see it all too often in this town. Now me, if I was going to run away? I'd run a heck of a lot farther than that, at least a couple states over. I wonder why Mom and Dad didn't pop down here and check out the shelters and stuff. If that'd been me, my parents woulda taken this city apart brick by brick until I turned up. Funny how some people are. I probably shouldn't say anything, but it makes you wonder why they have kids."

Nick put the side of his finger against Cassie's cheek and wiped away a tear. "Yeah, well, sometimes life just goes a direction nobody planned."

# Chapter 28

The day of the Great San Francisco Food Fight dawned sunny and clear. Thirty minutes before the noon start, thermometers surpassed sixty degrees. Several city blocks jammed with spectators, food vendors, street musicians, and souvenir hawkers were cordoned off to vehicular traffic. A show of force by the city's finest kept the lid on unauthorized food fights and other acts of uncivil ingenuity.

A city dump truck laden with vegetables past their prime, flanked by six motorcycle cops in all their flashing spit-polished glory, snorted to a halt, raised its bed, and disgorged a half ton of oozing produce into the street in a smelly heap.

Media trucks dumped camera crews and reporters to conduct instantaneous on-the-street interviews and take up their positions in specially lighted staging areas where pecking order became immediately apparent. The networks and cable giants were front and center, the local news affiliates and independents consigned to outlying real estate and creative use of zoom lenses. They took turns getting setup shots beside the pile of food fight ammunition.

Even the foreign press—London, Paris, Tokyo, Hong Kong, and Mexico City among them—scrapped for every inch of sidewalk or elevated vantage point.

Giant video screens at several strategic locations flashed the action at Market and Van Ness for the burgeoning crowd.

That morning's *Chronicle* carried a front page McTavish special report bristling with bombastic conviction and what for her was an excess of exclamatory punctuation:

"There is no sabotage—not poison or fire or fear—capable of stopping Taste of Success from succeeding in its holy mission to rid this city of its homeless blight.

"Blight, I say, the blight of drunkenness, drugs, and despair!

"Blight, I say, the blight of heedlessness, homelessness, and helplessness!

"Blight, I say, the blight of sons and brothers and fathers, daughters and sisters and mothers, for whom our fair city is their dead end, for whom our stairwells and door stoops are the scenes of their nightmare horrors, for whom our collective indifference shipwrecks their last shred of human dignity!

"It ends today! Today we fight back. No more finger-pointing. No more blame. No more 'I'm better than you.' Today our weapons are a salad of change, tomatoes and melons and onions by the sacks full. For it is by food, by full bellies and full hearts, that we will change attitudes on both sides. No more victimizer and no more victimhood. Here's how to catch fish, how to make a way, how to make a life. The Creator gave us the tools, and from this day forward we pick them up and put them to work as he intended.

"Today's Great Downtown Food Fight will provide millions of dollars to expand Taste of Success to all parts of the city and to every San Franciscan by birth or adoption who needs a new start. Those physically unable, age-restricted, or mentally incapable will receive proper shelter and care from a city of compassion. Those who are able will team up to provide for those who aren't, and in the process will find their own purpose and fulfillment.

"And so let him who is without sin cast the first tomato. On second thought, I'll do it or we'll never get this thing started. Mr. Mayor? Governor Mitch? Nothing personal, but you'd better prepare to duck. I'm coming after you and I never miss. Meet me at high noon and don't you dare be late!"

In the VIP seating area on an elevated riser, Cassie tucked the blanket tight around Mickey Durrell's shoulders. The bicycle messenger in a wheelchair, face stitched, arm in a cast, leg in a sling, and ribs bound with tape, smiled his thanks. Despite severe injuries, his eyes shone with the light of freedom from hospital confinement.

Next to him, Beth, Cody, and Mags played Go Fish on an upturned lettuce box.

"You got a three?" Mags leaned forward as if trying to read Cody's mind.

"Go fish." Cody's cards remained tight to his chest.

Mags scowled at him. "Once had a boyfriend as uncooperative as you. Millionaire's son."

Beth laughed. "And?"

Mags lifted an eyebrow. "And I got him a job parking cars in Mongolia. Good riddance!"

Trina, eyes closed, rested her head on Jorge's shoulder. Both of them wore similar dreamy smiles.

Nick squeezed Cassie's shoulders. "Is that McTavish getting ready to lob the first tomato?"

He brushed his lips against her neck and Cassie felt a thrill along her spine. "Sure is. She looks like a Maine lobsterman in that getup." He smoothed her ratty old jean jacket and straightened the collar.

"Where do you suppose she found a yellow tartan rain slicker?"

"What McTavish wants, McTavish gets. Look at the tam under the headgear. Do you think the mayor came here by his own volition or did she threaten to beat him up?"

"Cass, shame on you! You know Muira McTavish employs strictly verbal fisticuffs." Nick applied a gentle circular motion to her temples and was glad he wore a faded trench coat that was not only Scotch Guarded but buttoned all the way to below the knees.

"Mmm, that feels nice. Just don't you be too sure about her. Father B, can you join us for an early supper this evening? We're having breakfast."

The priest, in aviator goggles and rubber coveralls big enough for two people, grinned. "Those famous lemon soufflé pancakes I've heard so much about?"

"Fluffy and lemon zesty. And popovers with fresh cherry jam, plus fried ham and sausage scramble."

Father B smacked his lips, his goatee bobbing. "That should place me in an excellent frame of mind for the Sunday sermon titled 'Man Does Not Live by Bread Alone.' I accept. By the way, I was bowled over when the diocese appropriated $10,000 for the Taste Revival Fund. Here I couldn't get those skinflints to requisition so much as a new stapler for the cathedral office."

"Did you go through their wives?"

"Well, no ..."

"Did you use honey or vinegar?"

"I threatened the wrath of God."

"And the result?"

"I bought my own stapler."

"Men!"

Nick patted the priest on the back. "Our gender dooms us. I'm glad to report that our security man Sid is doing some better. The heart attack was a mild one, as heart attacks go. He's hanging up his holster, though. Going to Arizona to be near his daughter and grandkids. Tell me, Father, when is Kenny's court date?"

Father B moved his goggles to his forehead. "I have good news on that front too. Ken, due to diminished capacity, exploitation while under the influence of a mind-altering chemical, and the Taste board's kind refusal to press charges, will be released to my temporary custody. His parents are driving in from Sacramento tomorrow, and we're going to get him both drug counseling and community service to help him make amends. All of it will be at the Mission under the able guidance of Mother Josie's love and fine cooking and Leon's impressive biceps.

"I've spoken with Lieutenant Reynolds. Ken may have to spend a couple of weeks in jail and go on probation, but I'm confident, God willing, we'll have him ready to reenter the Taste program by the Fourth of July."

All around them was a growing anticipation. Thousands of conversations were punctuated by the occasional "whoop-whoop" of a first aid ambulance moving into place. The aroma of hot dogs, cotton candy, and popcorn lent a county fair excitement. Along the rooftops of the businesses and offices that lined the streets, building owners and the people who knew them found the best views for the combat to come.

An announcer introduced the combatants, each of whom had a turn at the microphone.

Governor Mitch von Bruegger called McTavish "the goddess of gourmet."

McTavish called the governor "the Zeus of zucchini." "It has been scientifically proven that women have more taste buds—and therefore more taste—than men. If I were you, I'd grab a stationary object and hang on for dear life."

The crowd roared and chose sides, chanting the names of their favorite champions.

Nick checked his watch and sighed. "Too bad Gordon O'Neal went so far wrong. There won't be any second chance for him. I'm praying he makes it right with God."

Von Bruegger's imposing figure in rubber waders towered above the bantam roundness that was McTavish in tartan. They squared off and took aim. The crowd, along with the broadcasters, began to shout the countdown to noon.

Father B lowered his goggles into place. "I'll see that he has that chance. It does remind one of the damage done when we abandon or are abandoned by those God gives us. Without probably even realizing the effect of his choices on his son, Gordon's father became his tormentor."

"And Gordon became ours."

"... 5, 4, 3 ..."

"Oh, Nicholas!"

"Yes, my love?"

Cassie turned, an enormous tomato in each hand. "Remember how the salsa flew at our wedding?"

Nick stepped back just as the crowd erupted in wild cheers. "Cass, you wouldn't."

"I would."

And she did.

## Cassie's Lemon Soufflé Pancakes for Three

*2 cups cottage cheese*
*6 large eggs, separated*
*2 lemons (zest and juice)*
*1 cup flour*
*1½ tablespoons baking powder*
*¾ teaspoon salt*
*2 tablespoons mild vegetable oil*

*Combine flour, baking powder, and salt. Set aside. In a blender, whip cottage cheese, egg yolks, lemon juice and zest until smooth. Stir into flour mixture. In a chilled glass bowl, beat egg whites until stiff and fold into batter.*

*Using an oiled cast-iron skillet or electric griddle, cook on medium heat for two to three minutes per side. Use a thin spatula for flipping these delicate pancakes. Makes nine five-inch cakes.*

*Serve with fresh blackberries or frozen blueberries (thawed, and thickened with a bit of cornstarch and sugar). Top with crème fraîche.*

### Crème Fraîche

*1 tablespoon sour cream or buttermilk*
*1 cup heavy cream*

*Combine sour cream or buttermilk and cream in a bowl. Let thicken in refrigerator for at least 8 hours. Whip the crème fraîche just before serving.*

## Share Your Thoughts

**With the Author:** Your comments will be forwarded to
the author when you send them to *zauthor@zondervan.com*.

**With Zondervan:** Submit your review of this book
by writing to *zreview@zondervan.com*.

## Free Online Resources at
## www.zondervan.com/hello

 **Zondervan AuthorTracker:** Be notified whenever your
favorite authors publish new books, go on tour, or post
an update about what's happening in their lives.

 **Daily Bible Verses and Devotions:** Enrich your life
with daily Bible verses or devotions that help you start
every morning focused on God.

 **Free Email Publications:** Sign up for newsletters on
fiction, Christian living, church ministry, parenting, and
more.

 **Zondervan Bible Search:** Find and compare
Bible passages in a variety of translations at
www.zondervanbiblesearch.com.

 **Other Benefits:** Register yourself to receive online
benefits like coupons and special offers, or to participate
in research.